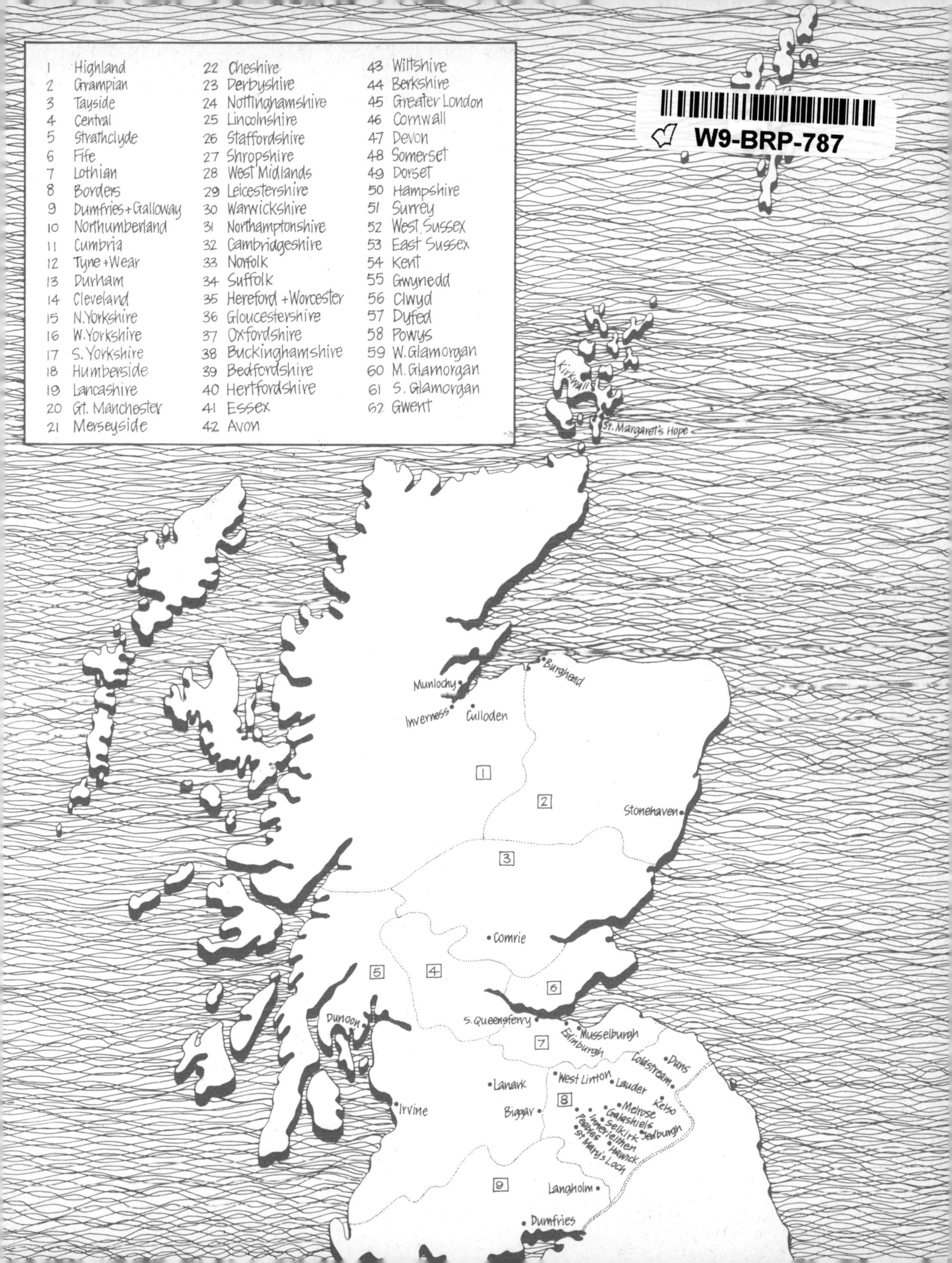
1 Highland
2 Grampian
3 Tayside
4 Central
5 Strathclyde
6 Fife
7 Lothian
8 Borders
9 Dumfries + Galloway
10 Northumberland
11 Cumbria
12 Tyne + Wear
13 Durham
14 Cleveland
15 N. Yorkshire
16 W. Yorkshire
17 S. Yorkshire
18 Humberside
19 Lancashire
20 Gt. Manchester
21 Merseyside
22 Cheshire
23 Derbyshire
24 Nottinghamshire
25 Lincolnshire
26 Staffordshire
27 Shropshire
28 West Midlands
29 Leicestershire
30 Warwickshire
31 Northamptonshire
32 Cambridgeshire
33 Norfolk
34 Suffolk
35 Hereford + Worcester
36 Gloucestershire
37 Oxfordshire
38 Buckinghamshire
39 Bedfordshire
40 Hertfordshire
41 Essex
42 Avon
43 Wiltshire
44 Berkshire
45 Greater London
46 Cornwall
47 Devon
48 Somerset
49 Dorset
50 Hampshire
51 Surrey
52 West Sussex
53 East Sussex
54 Kent
55 Gwynedd
56 Clwyd
57 Dyfed
58 Powys
59 W. Glamorgan
60 M. Glamorgan
61 S. Glamorgan
62 Gwent
Kirkwall
St. Margaret's Hope
Burghead
Munlochy
Inverness
Culloden
1
2
Stonehaven
3
Comrie
5
4
6
Dunoon
S. Queensferry
Musselburgh
Edinburgh
7
Coldstream
Duns
West Linton
Lauder
Lanark
8
Kelso
Melrose
Galashiels
Selkirk
Innerleithen
Peebles
Jedburgh
Hawick
St Mary's Loch
Biggar
Irvine
9
Langholm
Dumfries

The National Trust
GUIDE TO
TRADITIONAL CUSTOMS OF BRITAIN

Brian Shuel

The National Trust GUIDE TO TRADITIONAL CUSTOMS OF BRITAIN

Brian Shuel

Webb & Bower
MICHAEL JOSEPH

Illustration on title-page: *Abbots Bromley Horn Dancers*

First published in Great Britain in 1985 by
Webb & Bower (Publishers) Limited
9 Colleton Crescent, Exeter, Devon EX2 4BY
in association with
Michael Joseph Limited
27 Wright's Lane, London W8 5SL

Second impression 1986

Production by Nick Facer

British Library Cataloguing in Publication Data
Shuel, Brian
The National Trust Guide to Traditional
Customs of Britain
1. Folklore——England
I. Title II. National Trust
394.2′6942 GR141

ISBN 0-86350-051-X

Phototypeset in Great Britain by Tradespools, Frome, Somerset

Printed in Italy by New Interlitho S.p.A. - Milan

Contents

Dedication

With gratitude, respect, affection, amusement,
enjoyment, interest, fascination and, at times,
utter astonishment, this book is dedicated
to all the people in it.

...for over a hundred years

Despite what it says on the cover this book should really be called *A Selection of as Many Hundred-Year-Old British Calendar Customs as One Exhausted Writer-Photographer Thought You Needed to Know About and Could Manage to Get Around Within the Time Available*.

A book on this subject could contain a thousand entries, maybe even two thousand, depending on definitions as to what is and what is not a custom, but to do that properly would mean writing an encyclopaedia in several volumes. What you have here is my choice; rather more than an introduction, definitely less than a complete survey.

My interest began in 1963 when, almost by chance, I photographed the Bampton Morris Dancers. During the next ten years I covered about sixty customs, some of them several times. This book was first discussed in 1980. Though it was the end of 1983 before we definitely decided to go ahead, all the talk had got me going again and in the last five years I have revisited many of the customs I had seen earlier and added very many more.

It is easy enough to explain what *is* in the book; to justify myself regarding what is *not* included is a little harder. Calendar Customs are those which happen on one specific day of the year, and the particular examples which follow are also confined to their own location. First-Footing, Valentines, Easter Eggs, Harvest Festivals, Christmas Trees and the like are Calendar Customs too, but so well known and widespread that they need no further publicity. There is nothing either about intermittent ceremonies which crop up as the need arises, for example at weddings, funerals, birthdays, when an apprentice finishes his time, or when a building requires 'topping-out'. It is too difficult to find out about actual occurrences, and often an intrusion to take photographs.

Having established that the book is about Calendar Customs only, I still have to explain why so many are missing. Of the fully qualified categories only Fairs are completely omitted, purely for lack of space. For the rest there were three main qualifications for inclusion. First, where there are several similar events, I have chosen one or two to represent them all. This will inevitably provoke cries of 'why did you choose theirs when ours is so much better?' I understand this point of view very well and can only apologize for leaving them out; again space has been a great problem throughout.

Second, I wanted you to be able to see the customs. There are only two events included not open to the public, though I expect you could get in if you pleaded a special interest. They are the Baddeley Cake at Drury Lane Theatre, and the Pancake Greaze at Westminster School, included because they are both very well known and, frankly, too much fun to leave out. There are two others for which you would need a hard-to-come-by invitation. On Founder's Day at Chelsea Hospital a Pensioner relative would get you in; for the Royal Maundy Service, to get into the cathedral, unless you are a Recipient or otherwise involved, you would have to live in the diocese and be in favour with the Dean, though you could, of course, stand outside on the day and wave your little flag. Some of the legal customs are not really spectator events, but they would certainly let you in if you asked. With a tiny number of exceptions, which actually occur in full view of the public, the universities, public schools, army, City livery companies, professional and business institutions are left out completely. They are all hotbeds of tradition and ritual but they like to keep it to themselves. I need hardly mention that you cannot see the extinct customs either; I only put in very few for historical or comparative reasons, or because I happened to find particularly good quotations.

Third, all but a handful of these customs are over a

Founder's Day at Chelsea Hospital. You would need to be related to one of these fine old soldiers to get in to see the parade.

hundred years old, most of them very much more. The Ripon Hornblower, for example, will be a thousand years old in 1986; nobody knows how far back the real 'folk' customs go. I think there are only four events discussed which started since the Second World War: the Clowns' Service in London, the Coracle Races at Cilgerran, the Brighouse Pace Egg Play, and Saddleworth Whit Friday. This last is less than twenty years old in its present form, but its great success is due to its having been formed from two old-established customs. A few have lapsed and been revived by at least some of the same people; for me this counts as continuity. I know many 'revivals' of long-gone customs but I have not included them except in passing. You would not want to read about reproductions in a book on antiques, would you?

My ambition is simple: to give you some idea of what all these customs are actually like. If you take part in one, or there is one in your locality, you do not need me to tell you, though you may be interested to read about similar happenings elsewhere. The media have not served these customs well, apart from radio which is forced, by its very nature, to rely on the straightforward words of the people involved. Television finds the customs of Polynesian Islanders, Peruvian Indians and Masai Warriors of riveting interest, but treats our own as worthy of little more than 'colour' pieces. To be honest, even most of the books published so far give little idea. They tell you what happens, how, why, when, where, a few of them very well; but they all miss the lovely people, the feeling, the atmosphere. Is there an audience of thousands, or two men and a dog? Do they enjoy it, or is it a chore? Does the custom live and breathe, or has some over-protective committee choked it to death, stuffed it, and made it a museum piece? Above all, these books miss the *fun*, the sheer good-natured enjoyment, the pride in taking part in something absolutely unique.

I cannot communicate any of this to you in academic terms. You will have to come on this adventure with me, meet the people, the participants, the folklorists, the vicars and all.

Wherever I go I talk to the people I meet, though I am perfectly well aware that much they tell me may not be true. They *think* it is, and their story could well

Regretfully many interesting events had to be left out – this is Appleby Horse Fair.

be the one accepted locally; historians and folklorists can sometimes prove something completely different. And you can be surprised by how little people know or care about the history of their intriguing custom. Here is a cautionary tale from Gillian Bennett, a well-known researcher: she had recorded her mother's stories about her early life on a farm and thinking it might be a good idea to hear what her mother's three sisters had to say as well, was disconcerted to find that they all said different things! Her view is that people remember what they want to remember. Still, there are two hard and fast rules; *never* accept a morris dancer's testimony without checking it elsewhere – they tell you things just for the hell of it; if you ask a local how old his custom is he *always* says, 'Nobody knows – but it's definitely over a hundred years!'

Much of my information has come from folklorists, usually mentioned by name in the text, and they may recognize snippets from their published work. I do not accept there is a single thing in this book that they do not know already. On their chosen subjects all of them know far more than I do; whenever I have had the nerve to consult them they have invariably been helpful and generous.

I have divided the book into fourteen chapters. The first needs no explaining; it is really an introduction, but since nobody reads introductions, I called it Chapter 1. Chapter 2 does need explaining. I decided to sort the events into subjects, rather than presenting them in chronological order or by location. This seems perfectly straightforward and indeed is for most of them. But there are a number of awkward ones; some equally at home in two or even three chapters; others simply would not fit into any. I put the gregarious customs where they seemed most to enjoy the company; the others I made into this chapter on their own. These 'leftovers' are certainly not inferior. On the contrary, they are some of the most fascinating customs of all. There is nothing stranger than the Burry Man, nothing more extraordinary than the Boy Ploughmen, nothing more fun than Egremont Crab Fair, nothing madder than Cheese Rolling. These events are exceptional and they do prove the rule that Britain has some traditions as curious and absorbing as anything in the world.

Books convey so little of the sheer fun of most customs. This Marshfield Mummer and his audience are certainly enjoying themselves.

The other twelve chapters speak for themselves. They run from spring to winter, more or less, but with no intention to categorize them in this way. The vast majority of these customs are known as 'folk' customs. The word has several definitions in the *Oxford English Dictionary*; the one intended in this context is 'of the people'. One may infringe some law by suggesting that this means everybody except the ruling classes; but titled mummers and morris dancers are a decided rarity. It has always been the workers who performed the dances, plays, fire customs, street football, May customs, and for the most part it still is, though as their circumstances have improved, it is, curiously, academics who have come to take such an active interest. I know several graduate morris dancers and the like, and some who have obtained their degrees studying these very subjects.

Legal and Church Customs and Doles are less 'folkish'. Most of them have a definite historical reason for their existence and the ruling classes may take part. A few chapters, in this sense, are mixed. Fairs are in a class of their own, their charters legally granted, subject to heavy civic supervision; they are nonetheless run 'by the people for the people'.

My approach has been variable. Each group of customs has taken me along in a different way. Some have seemed more interesting in their history than in their practice, others exciting on the day and not at all thereafter. Some needed a certain amount of comparative study, others simply setting down individually. However, if my knowledge appears unusually sparse at times I plead in mitigation that my prime function was to take pictures and it is very difficult to gather information at the same time.

As for the photographs, some in the book may be surprising, not as you expect. I try to show events as they are, not as people hope or even think they are. I simply do not see the point of doing anything else. If the thing is visually dull it is not *my* business to liven it up; if I do, I turn it into a different event. Press photographers cannot take a picture without setting it up, and it is their pictures which are familiar. It is an odd phenomenon that photography has actually influenced many customs by causing the participants regularly to do things because they make the standard pictures. Television camera crews, on the other hand, are convinced that whatever is happening it is entirely for their benefit.

The origins of folk customs have given rise to a great deal of speculation, and folklorists can be divided into two distinct schools of thought. The traditional group has many persuasive members. Challenged, as we all are, by the lack of any real facts to explain how all these astonishing happenings originated, the early folklorists postulated elaborate theories, which they published in weighty books and papers. Thus all maypoles, indeed anything that stuck up, was a 'phallic symbol', all May Day ceremonies were 'pagan fertility rites', all plays symbolized 'death and resurrection, the triumph of good over evil', all street football stemmed from 'animal sacrifice', all fire customs were to 'burn out Evil to make way for Good', and so on. Traditionalists still do expound these and related theories, and, only now, with the passing of time, endless reiteration has given them the status of something close to established fact.

Modern folklorists, very much into painstaking research and against anything in the nature of wild surmise, demand hard evidence. They have failed to find it themselves; the references, they say, go back no further than the fifteenth century; all this 'pre-Christian fertility rite' stuff *could* be true but fails to account for the several hundred years between the references and the coming of Christianity to our shores. If I have understood their general feeling it is that most of these customs are not nearly so old as people used to think.

Personally, I do not want to get into deep waters on the subject. My experience has anyway been telling me for twenty years that the average morris dancer would think I was daft if I told him he was taking part in a pagan fertility rite. I have always been struck by the contrast between the simplicity and matter-of-factness of most of the participants compared to the erudition and extreme earnestness of those who study them. There is very little theorizing about origins in this book; if I know anything definite I will tell you.

Before I leave the subject it is worthwhile mentioning a paper given to a Calendar Custom Conference in London in September 1984, in which Dr E. C. Cawte, a researcher of thirty years' standing and author of several books on Ritual Drama, pointed out that the earliest references he could find to mumming plays was 1730, sword dances 1710, morris dancing 1582 and plough boys (a version of the folk play) 1413. These dates referred to descriptions of the events in a form we would recognize today. There were earlier references, but they were too vague to categorize. Dr Cawte insisted that these dates proved nothing except that it was exceedingly fanciful to assume that these traditions went back a further five or six hundred years. He did remark that, to be fair, the dearth of early references might not be wholly unconnected with the fact that printing had not been invented.

Customs evolve still. Most are very different from the way they were in the past and some I know myself have changed noticeably in the twenty years I have known them. Bits get added as they occur to somebody. Headington Quarry's Boxing Day is a good example. Morris dance sides start feuding and split into two or even, in one place, three sides. The Orkney Boy Ploughmen's 'horses' change sex. Padstow's Oss goes plastic. Nobody needs Farthing Bundles any more. Oddly enough, not one custom I have seen since 1963 has actually lapsed; a few are looking distinctly unhealthy, but several, on the other hand, are much more lively and popular than they were.

Practically every custom going now will survive the next decade at least because we are going through a period in which people care about 'worthwhile' things. Real ale has triumphed, you can buy a decent loaf of bread, wholefood prolongs active life, we want to rehabilitate even our most undistinguished houses rather than clear them away and build comfortable double-glazed new ones, we worry about ecology and wildlife, new is bad, old is good. Everywhere people say: 'It would be a shame to let these old customs die out.'

Well, I agree it is sad when a nice old tradition passes away, but depressing to come across one kept going as a sacred duty, on a life support machine, as it were. In this respect spring customs seem to bring out the worst in people. Events in Padstow are still exceedingly robust but everywhere on May Day there used to be outrageous goings-on. Modern permissiveness notwithstanding, most May gatherings have degenerated into olde worlde pageants of pretty little girls in pretty dresses, pretty garlands, pretty ribbons, with yokels, maypole dancing and coronation ceremonies for the May Queen. This is not what May Day was about; there is no joy in it, no fun, just a lot of anxious kids feeling stupid and cold, wondering if they are doing it right. And on the sidelines there will be a committee congratulating themselves on their organizational skill and their success in once again 'keeping an olde custom alive'.

I once met a local press photographer at one of these and he said, 'I've been here every year for over twenty-five years. I can tell you to the second when everything will happen, and to the blade of grass where it will happen. They have exactly the same characters in exactly the same costumes every year.

The fate of a thousand May Day customs – a lot of anxious kids feeling stupid and cold.

They tell me that the children are different each year but I can't tell if this is true from my photographs. If my paper asks me to do this again next year I may kill myself!'

Not all committees are like this, or course. Some are wonderful; they get everything together, then they let it happen. I accept that some customs are simply too big to control without some kind of organization but my favourite kind of committee is like the one they had at Stonehaven, where on New Year's Eve the fishermen and their friends gather in the High Street to swing huge fireballs around their heads like hammer throwers. Anyone is welcome, even you and me, but it is not to everybody's taste since it is extremely dangerous. When we were there about thirty whirling Scots were risking their lives. Some years before, someone had suggested a committee should be formed to control this potential disaster. At the inaugural meeting it was unanimously agreed that any attempt to control it would also ruin it. They voted not to form a committee and went home. So far no calamity has occurred, the event remains terrifying.

Still, benign committees can be an important factor in keeping customs alive and well. A selection of others would include the practical need to do them, the enjoyment, the fun, the freedom, the families, the fame, the financial gain, their place in the village year – 'Old Bert died about Well Dressing time' – and, I have to admit, a kind of primaeval motivation. One of the Minehead Hobby Horse party actually did say to me twenty years ago, that if he failed to turn out for sunrise on a cold May morning, with not a soul about to see him, 'the sun might not come up at all – I couldn't stay in bed anyway!'

Money and families should not be underestimated for their part in keeping a tradition going. Dancers and mummers always collected as they went, and indeed still do. Nowadays it is beer money, but in the past the activity made a big addition to meagre wages. Mummers often went off around the neighbourhood for several days at Christmas time, and morris dancers made extensive tours in the summer. These groups were often made up from one or two families and their approved friends; youngsters were born into the tradition and accepted it as part of everyday life. This

A custom joins the media, but with lovely girls like these the presence of Fleet Street is guaranteed. The trick is to assemble the talent in the first place.

kept many groups going for generations and some famous families are going strong still; the Fowells at Abbots Bromley, the Williamse's at Uttoxeter, for example. But I know of one mumming family who just decided they did not want to do it anymore, and were not prepared to let anyone else; another who have kept a play going for a century but are thinking of giving up because the money is not good enough.

Other customs flourished because they gave those involved licence for a day to behave how they pleased. The rest of the year they led a hard and often miserable life; just this once they were free, and by many accounts they took their opportunities with enthusiasm. Philip Stubbes wrote in the sixteenth century: 'On May Day eve the folk of every Parish take them from theyre homes and goe, some to ye woodes and groves, some to ye hilles, ther to spend ye night in wicked fornication and to return at dawn with birch boughs and branches of trees to deck theyre assemblies withal.' As I have said, May Day is not what it was, or if it is I have no sensational revelations. I am still looking into it. The street footballers still create havoc wherever they go; of all British customs this has probably changed least over many centuries, even if only a few games have survived the hostility of property owners and the police. Most of the fire customs are controlled now: Lewes, Hatherleigh and Stonehaven have their moments; only the madmen of Ottery St Mary are completely uninhibited. The Barrel Rolling here is fantastically exciting but at the same time really dangerous and frightening to participants and spectators alike. The men often burn themselves horribly; a man in Exeter once told me his secretary had to be taken home early she was so petrified.

So much for established folk customs. Not all of them are as spectacular as these. They crop up year after year, relaxed and matter of fact; you hardly notice they are happening at all. There have been several occasions when I have been the only spectator. They do not always make a big deal of these things, you know. *Real* customs do not, in any case, happen for the benefit of visitors, tourists or folklorists; they happen in spite of us.

Sometimes people invent customs in order to attract visitors, tourists and the more gullible folklorists. Cidermakers sponser Wassailing, brewers sponsor anything that encourages people to drink beer, everybody sponsors Pancake Races. These are not real customs and if people stop coming they simply disappear again into richly deserved oblivion. You can tell which they are by the smocks and the heartiness of all involved.

It is almost impossible to start a custom as such. They need to begin for some other reason, catch on, and then gradually establish custom status without trying. My own personal theory is that a custom can only be started in the clothes you stand up in. The moment you introduce 'period' or 'rustic' costumes, the second you start mouthing your 'archaic' speech, the whole affair is doomed to be nothing but a bad joke. The only really successful example of a deliberately started custom I can think of is Up-Helly-Aa, and that replaced another. The Shetland Islanders had a wild tradition of pulling flaming tar barrels through the streets during the midwinter festival. This 'Disgraceful and Barbarous practice' was prohibited in 1874. Nine years later the first Up-Helly-Aa procession took place and in 1889 the 'Viking' longship made its appearance. Lerwick may not have approved of 'tar barrelling' but it surely needed something to replace it. Their answer has grown into what is undoubtedly the most spectacular Calendar Custom in all Britain even if, in me at any rate, it still provokes a vague uneasy feeling that someone simply sat down and invented it.

As for why customs fade away, there can be many reasons: there is no longer a need, they are no more fun, malign authorities, lack of money, a changing village, the death of the person who kept it going, alternative attractions, a good old-fashioned row. Children are often unreliable, they have no feeling for tradition, naturally, so why should they care? Parents can make them do things when they are small, teenagers have to be very determined to put up with the derision of their mates, or resist the alternative charms of their girlfriends. Bampton and Headington Morris Dancers both have boys' teams but few of their members survive into the adult sides. Only street footballers are no problem; youngsters cannot wait to be allowed to join in. Acceptance is almost like an initiation ceremony.

The importance of many of these customs should not be underestimated. In very many places it is by far the biggest event of the year, not only to be enjoyed on the day, but prepared for and thought about for weeks, even months, in advance. Up-Helly-Aa is in a class of its own in this respect, with related activities going on most of the year. The costumes, fund-raising dances, the food, the drink, the halls, the hair-dos, the home-comings and all the other essentials keep most of the traders in Lerwick solvent. Lewes Bonfire Night, Bridgwater Carnival, Helston Flora Day, Padstow May Day, Warrington Walking Day, the Dunmow Flitch Trials and all the Scottish Common Ridings take over their towns absolutely. If you have not been to a mega-custom you can have no idea. And on an individual level to be Guizer Jarl, Braw Lad, Callant, the winner of Doggett's Coat and Badge, the Guides Race or the Kirkwall Ba', or to be a Royal Maundy Recipient, may be the pinnacle of a person's entire life.

These things mean a great deal to the British. They are deeply ingrained in people's lives, loved, enjoyed, but not taken too much for granted. They are not museum pieces; they are as much a part of our lives as summer holidays and Sunday lunch.

I hope you enjoy the adventure as much as I did.

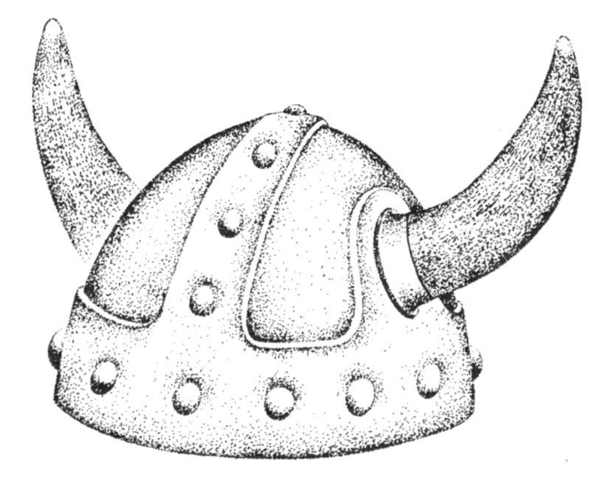

the exception proves the rule

Let us begin with a tour around Britain, as far north as Orkney, south-west to Devon, into Wales and over to the East End of London, to visit ten customs which have absolutely nothing in common except their uniqueness. It will take us all year, for each of these events has its proper date and it happens that together they cover every season. One takes over a whole town for fifteen hours, another lasts barely fifteen seconds. Most of them are extremely popular; a couple look as if they might vanish clean away. Some are for children, some for adults, one for foolhardy adolescents. Some are pretty, some robust, some well documented, some a mystery. They all arrived in this chapter because I could not find a home for them elsewhere; if I had been looking for a sample collection I could hardly have found ten better customs.

It is not just the events, it is the sum of the events that make Egremont Crab Fair special. It starts at seven in the morning when they raise the greasy pole, and finishes after ten at night when they give a cup to the man who makes the most horrible face to become Gurning Champion of the World. In between there are street races, the Applecart Parade, morris dancing, sports, a terrier show, wrestling, hound trailing, a sentimental-song contest, a pipe-smoking contest and, among certain non-participating elements, an entirely unofficial beer-drinking contest. The only thing which does not seem to happen on the day is a fair.

In 1984 all these events were presided over by the Queen of the Fair, not a butter-wouldn't-melt-in-her-mouth 12-year-old, but a full-size, very pretty girl with a mass of dark hair, an official sash and a mini-skirt. She enlivened everything with her presence, her attitude throughout one of good natured amusement, and she awarded prizes not with a queenly peck but a great big passionate hug.

Egremont is an ancient little town in that surprisingly industrialized no-man's land between the Lake District and the sea. There has always been plenty of farming in the area and this probably gave rise to the Crab Fair. To mark the end of the agricultural year, to give them an opportunity to do some trading and have a celebration, Egremont was granted a charter to hold a fair in 1267, and it is still held on the Saturday nearest to September 18. Exactly why it is called the 'Crab' Fair is not clear. The name obviously refers to crabapples but it is what the fruit has to do with it that causes puzzlement. One account says that the people were allowed the freedom to collect whatever wild crabapples they wanted, another that it was the custom of the Lord of the Manor to attend the Fair, distributing them liberally as he passed amongst the peasantry. Whatever, the day is known locally as 't'Crab' and an important ritual is the Applecart Parade. This is not as impressive as it sounds; an ordinary lorry drives slowly up and down Main Street while some men on the back hurl hundreds of apples to the youngsters clamouring in their wake. It is considered great good luck to get an apple; some of the more aggressive end up with pocketsful.

The Greasy Pole is for the young as well. It is tall, at least thirty feet, and well greased with a nasty mixture of fat and soft soap. In 1984 there was a nice leg of lamb firmly fixed on the top, wrapped in a plastic bag. Occasionally the boys fail altogether to get at the prize, in which case it is given to an old people's home, but this time they managed it in three hours, showing great ingenuity and determination. The plan was to form a kind of human ladder which it was possible to climb. At times there were eight or ten of them clinging desperately to the pole, each supported on the one below. As it happens they never did get to the top in this way, the bottom ones unable to hold up

Egremont Crab Fair. The most celebrated episode in a day-long event is the 'Gurning' contest. This is Gordon Blacklock, champion in 1984.

their friends on top, but so many clinging bodies made the pole much less greasy. In the end one daring lad was able to go up himself, a knife clasped dramatically in his teeth, in order to cut off the meat. The fact that he completely wrecked the leg of lamb while he was at it did not in any way interfere with his moment of triumph.

Egremont Crab Fair has become very much a sports meeting. In the morning there are street races, though the real runners prefer to preserve their energies for the proper athletics meeting in the afternoon. As well as this there are Hound Trails and Cumberland and Westmorland Wrestling, a sort of mini Grasmere Sports (see Chapter 11) and with many of the same contestants. The Terrier Show is a little out of the ordinary, though, with classes unknown to Crufts: Working Terrier, Any Pet Dog, and Lurchers. Jack Russells are the only real breed acceptable in this country company.

It is in the evening that Egremont makes its most persuasive claim to fame, when they gather in the Rugby Club car park to decide the Best Junior Joke Teller, the Best Sentimental Song Singer, the Fastest Clay Pipe Smoker and the Gurning Champion of the World. Though conducted on a splendid stage, constructed of corrugated iron on an old trailer and made nobody knows when, though disorganized, somewhat drunken, cold, uncomfortable and hopelessly difficult to photograph, it is actually one of the funniest occasions I have ever had the good fortune to attend. It is not just the performers, it is the audience as well, for everyone knows everyone, the heckling is often better than the show and partisanship is an essential ingredient.

Around 9 o'clock their most celebrated contest began. To 'gurn' according to Wright's *Dialect Dictionary* is to 'snarl as a dog; to look savage; to distort the countenance', and one can only say that this definition goes little way towards describing the hideous facial contortions achieved in Egremont. I hope the wind never changes in the middle of the contest. Evidently, this was once a common pastime in the area but this is now the only place officially to carry on the tradition and so famous have Egremont gurners become that they have even achieved the ultimate accolade of being asked to take part in a television commercial. For some reason gurning can only be done through a horse collar, 'gurnin' through a braffin', and a special one is kept here for the purpose.

The Junior Championship came first. I asked a lady how all the kids could possibly distort their angelic countenances so grotesquely. 'Oh, they work very hard at it,' she said. 'Mine's been practising for weeks. Every now and again he appears round the door and frightens the life out of us with a new variation he's thought up!' He came second in the end, my friend being of the opinion that the judging had been fixed. The kids did well considering they had all their teeth, a grave disadvantage overcome by astonishing inventiveness. The adults, on the other hand, tended to place too much reliance on their lack of them and therefore ended up with very similar results. Gordon Blacklock managed to put one over on his toothless rivals by putting his teeth back in, only the wrong way round, thus producing a countenance of truly repellent hideousness which earned him the title of World Gurning Champion 1984.

The Widow's Son pub in Devons Road, Bromley-by-Bow, in the East End of London is the scene of a touching ritual, surviving not only by long established custom but also by obligation as a condition of the lease.

Every Good Friday lunchtime a sailor adds a hot-cross bun to the large cluster of nasty looking specimens among the lanterns and hanging plants above the bar. There is mild controversy about the origin of this custom, but it seems that some time in the early nineteenth century a widow who lived on or near the site kept a hot-cross bun for her sailor son whom she was expecting home for Easter. He never did return and the widow never gave up hope that he would. Each year until she died she kept another bun for him. Some accounts say she lived in a house which was knocked down to make way for the pub; others that the pub was already there and that she was the landlady. Either way, it makes a moving story.

At an early stage of its evolution it became the duty of a serving sailor to hang up the bun. The pub is in the heart of dockland, and as sailors were numerous in the area the honour belonged to the first one to appear on the day. Things have changed; not only have the docks run down, sailors are no longer thick on the ground. The landlord therefore has to make involved arrangements to get an immaculately uniformed rating onto the premises. In 1982, when I was there, his difficulties had been compounded by the small problem that the entire Royal Navy was engaged on

The Widow's Bun. Each Good Friday a sailor must add a new hot-cross bun to the collection. In 1982, British sailors being elsewhere, an American was happy to oblige.

more pressing business in the South Atlantic. Undeterred, he had the good sense to ask the American Embassy for a replacement and they had been pleased to send along the amiable OS2 Douglas J. Carlin, who regarded it as a great privilege to help Britain in her hour of need, and have his photograph taken with the local Pearly King and Queen.

The actual ceremony only takes a moment, the occasion makes the pub so full that most people hardly notice. Regulars, of course, are familiar with the permanent collection of buns. In 1982 there were about 50 hanging there; the more ancient ones are kept safe in the cellar. In 1941 Christina Hole reported in *English Custom and Usage* that there were 171 altogether; by now there may well be over 200, all no doubt in a surprising state of preservation. On Good Fridays there is a free issue of spicy fresh hot-cross buns for everyone in the pub, and also for the kids hanging hopefully about outside.

The bell-ringers of Shebbear parish church turning 'The Devil's Stone'. (see page 19)

Cheese Rolling at Coopers Hill; few survive the headlong chase without mishap. (see page 24)

The Plough 'Horses' of St Margaret's Hope, complete with decorated harness. *(see page 22)*

The tiny village of Shebbear, on the west side of Devon, can offer one of the oddest, most fleeting customs in the country, observed by a cast of tens. There is a large boulder on the little green outside the church. It is said to weigh about a ton, and the church bellringers are unlikely to dispute this for every November 5 at 8 p.m. it is their duty to turn it over and thus ensure good fortune in the village for another year. In 1940, being short of numbers, they decided not to do it. Immediately the war news became so appalling that a week later they felt compelled to do it as their contribution to the war effort. The result is history.

It is generally agreed that this curious duty has nothing whatever to do with Guy Fawkes. Otherwise nobody has the slightest idea why they do it, or how long it has been going on. There are no ancient references, merely assurances from the elderly living that 'my grandfather and great-grandfather did it'. Naturally there are legends of a diverting nature. The crucial point is that this boulder is an erratic; geologically speaking it has no business to be in Shebbear; its nearest habitat is in Wales. Legend A says that the Devil left the boulder there on his way from Heaven to Hell. Legend B says it was brought to nearby Henscott, intended as the foundation stone for their parish church. It vanished during the night and turned up in Shebbear. The Henscott men laboriously rolled it back again but the next day it was back in Shebbear. This went on for some days until Henscott finally accepted that some force bigger than they were was telling them something. Legend C has it that the boulder was some kind of altar stone brought by an unknown sect, but this is not given credence by the locals.

All this mystery has earned it the popular name of 'the Devil's Stone'. Even the village pub has taken the name in spite of the fact that the locals know it simply as the Shebbear Stone, and to tell the truth, slightly resent its diabolical status. On Guy Fawkes Night the bellringers assemble in the church, ring a few changes and then, just before eight, toll an appallingly discordant peal. In 1983, when we were there, they did this twice, considering their first effort to be insufficiently cacophanous. Then they went out to the stone, the vicar said a prayer, the bellringers got their crowbars under the stone and heaved it over. And that was that.

While the purpose of turning the Shebbear Stone remains obscure the traditional reason for the clangorous bell-ringing is to frighten away evil spirits, even the Devil himself.

It is well known that evil spirits do not like noise. This is the reason for firing shotguns through the branches when they Wassail the Apple Trees in Carhampton in Somerset. The word 'wassail' comes from the Anglo-Saxon *wes hal*; 'to be of good health' and wassailing in general was a convivial drinking custom observed particularly on New Year's Eve and Twelfth Night. It was not unlike carol singing; a party would tour around soliciting householders to offer hospitality, or to fill their wassail bowl with drink or money. This sociable custom has all but died out now, though a friend reports seeing a party in Bodmin in 1984, and there are probably others around in the South and West. Their wonderful songs live on, though, and can often be heard in folk clubs.

Wassailing the Apple Trees is a closely related, but different custom. Once wassailers offered it as part of the service, as it were, to bring good crops as well as good fortune to the house; now it has a more organized character. At Carhampton, a small village on the main road three miles from Minehead, they still do this on the night of January 17, Old Twelfth Night. The event has had its ups and downs in the last thirty years and was barely hanging on in 1984 when I was there last.

Until the middle of the 1950s wassailing the trees in the orchard behind the Butchers Arms had been very much a tradition of the publican and his friends. In 1957 the apple growers of Yakima, in the State of Washington, about a hundred miles inland from Seattle, and, the way they tell it, 'the Apple growing Capital of the World', got news of this and decided to start their own wassailing ceremony. Naturally this involved tremendous ballyhoo and the annual election of a 'Wassail Girl'. In 1966 the chosen lady was Miss Carol Clark, an air stewardess, who came over for the Carhampton ceremony bearing the 'sterling silver Wassail Bowl' used in the 'Yakima rite'. Two regulars from the Butchers Arms were despatched to collect her from Heathrow; she must have been some pippin because they were still speaking of her in awed voices eighteen years later. She also provoked the attention of the press and television and suddenly the wassailing at Carhampton became a great media event. In 1967, when I first saw it, there were hundreds of people there, and a popular West Country group called Adge Cutler and the Wurzels to sing a wassail song. It continued in this way for a few years, enjoyed by the public at large, reviled by traditionalists for its commercialism. Then in the mid 1970s the orchard was sold and three houses were built on the land. The wassailing disappeared altogether for a couple of years. Tradition dies hard, though, and it crept back again. In 1984 there were forty or fifty people there.

To tell you the truth it is probably very much like it was thirty years ago; though the orchard has shrunk to two trees.

The new publican, Peter Robinson, was trying very hard, even if the freezing weather was not being very helpful. A great cauldron of cider was put to heat up on the stove in the skittle alley, and sugar and ginger were added in liberal quantities. Peter ceremonially dunked in it a little bag which, he claimed, inevitably, to be a secret concoction of rare spices from the mysterious orient but which everyone else swore was the clearings from the pub ashtrays. When the cider was judged, after much tasting, to be ready we all gathered near the larger tree, to drink its health and sing the wassail song:

Old apple tree, we wassail thee,
And hoping thou wilt bear
For the Lord doth know where we shall be
Till apples come another year.
For to bear well, and to bear well
So merry let us be.
Let every man take off his hat,
And shout to the old apple tree!
Old apple tree, we wassail thee,
And hoping thou wilt bear
Hatfuls, capfuls, three bushel bagfuls
And a little heap under the stairs
Hip! Hip! Hooray!

The last three lines of this splendid song were shouted out by everyone. Then two pieces of toast were dipped in the cider and carefully placed in a fork of the tree. These are to feed the tree and the good spirits who watch over it. Next, six sporting gentlemen fired their shotguns through the branches, to frighten off the evil spirits. In some places it used additionally to be the custom to bang trays and anything else that would make a loud noise. Finally, there was a half-hearted attempt at a sing-song. This was not a success as everyone was more interested in getting at the hot cider, being in danger of freezing to death.

One of the strangest characters in Britain is the Burry Man of Queensferry, that little town that nestles between the southern ends of the two mighty Forth Bridges. Before the road bridge was opened, in September 1964, the ferries which gave the town its name had been in business for 800 years. Since 1687 the burgh has had the right to hold its Ferry Fair, which now takes place on the second Saturday in August.

The day before belongs to the Burry Man, an extraordinary and sinister figure covered from head to foot with burrs from the burdock plant. Not a square inch of human flesh is exposed except his hands, in which he holds two poles topped with fine bunches of hydrangea. A brightly coloured hat of roses, chrysanthemums and carnations sits on his head, and a flag is fastened tightly round his waist like a cummerbund. He cannot move in this crucifying outfit. Bending his limbs would be not only painful; the burrs would stick to each other, leaving bare patches and rendering him mangy. He is obliged to spend the day with legs apart and arms outstretched like a gingerbread man, and thus he perambulates the town, visiting pubs, factories, shops, his family and the Ferry Fair.

Really he has nothing to do with the Fair, though for some reason the committee has acquired the right to choose the Burry Man from the men who apply. This is an unusual right, since folk characters like this invariably stay in the hands of families and their friends, the same person often turning out for decades. In fact, Homer Sykes reported in *Once a Year* that in 1971 the Burry Man was the local grave digger, John Hart, who had done it 'for many years'. In 1982, when I was there, it was Arne Fredriksen, who had also been Burry Man the previous year and in 1979. One of his two attendants, Alan Reid, had done it in 1980 and in the six years before Arne. The only condition of employment is the Burry Man must have been born in Queensferry; in case you are worrying about the eligibility of Mr Fredriksen, Arne's father was a Norwegian sailor who married a local girl and settled. However, it is my painful duty to reveal that his other attendant was a Liverpudlian named Brian Burns. It is the Burry Man's privilege to pick his own attendants; Arne could see no good reason why he should not choose an Englishman and make this little bit of history.

So at about 7.30 in the morning they were at the Town Hall, with attendants in their best suits, other helpers in their everyday scruff, photographers in their anoraks, Arne in a fetching ensemble consisting of thick longjohns and vest, old jeans and an old heavy sweater and another pair of longjohns on top. The burrs were already prepared in twelve-inch squares on newspaper ready to be pressed into place. It takes several days to collect them all; Arne complained that burdock was supposed to be common in the area but he could not find any. It did not take long to cover him all over. The flag was carefully fixed in place, on this occasion a Scottish Standard, yellow with a red lion rampant manoeuvered into position on his stomach. Then they put a thick black balaclava over his head and covered that with burrs as well up to and over the brim of his pretty hat. Before 9 o'clock he had ceased to be

The Burry Man on his rounds in South Queensferry.

Arne Fredriksen and had become the Burry Man.

Getting him down the steps of the Town Hall was the biggest problem of the day. His first call, by tradition, is at the Provost's house to have his first dram. It was impossible for him to drink properly, since all liquid has to be taken through a straw. Thereafter he tours the town, moving from place to place in stiff-legged step with his attendants, one on each side supporting his arms as he holds on to the decorated poles. When he stopped he stood silent and forbidding. Few people approached him, in pubs or outside, except to feed him more whisky. People were glad to see him nevertheless, regarding his annual visit as essential to good luck. Children seem to love him; a few follow him all day shouting 'Hip, hip, hooray! It's Burry Man's Day!' Arne's mother told me that 'we were always sent out with four jam pieces and a bottle of lemonade. It was the only time we were allowed to stay out all day.' Some of the young were detailed to collect money, for there are substantial sums to be made.

I recall during their tour a visit to Arne's mother where she fed him fingers of bread through the straw-sized hole in his face; a visit to a futuristic electronics factory; the Pakistani newsagent who rushed out and gave the Burry Man and his attendants half a bottle of whisky; a visit to the distillery where 'we get everything *but* whisky'; the horrified reaction of a lady who came upon them unexpectedly round a corner; the visit to the Forth Bridge service area surrounded by bewildered motorists; their obligatory appearance at the Fair – 'they *insist* we come, the Fair would be a disaster if we didn't' – and the bus driver who made an unscheduled stop and encouraged all his impatient passengers to contribute to the collection.

It has to be said that by the late afternoon the Burry Man's attendants were propping him up. Exhausted and full of whisky he was extremely relieved to get back to the Town Hall where they stripped him in moments and left him comatose in his underpants for ten minutes before his wife, Julia, managed to prod him back to life. Suddenly he revived and in no time was himself again.

In the evening it is the custom for the Burry Man, in civilian clothes, and his friends, relatives and attendants, to gather in the pub of the Burry Man's choice for an almighty booze-up during which he ceremonially presents his hat to the landlord to keep until the next year. In the past all the landlords used to gather on the Town Hall steps and bid for the hat; nowadays, Arne remarked cynically, 'though they say it's a great honour to have it, they canna be bothered to go and bid for it!'

The origins of this unique custom are unknown. The Burry Man is always referred to as ancient, though records of this one hardly go back as far as the last century. There are well-documented reports of Burry Men in two other places far away to the north, in Fraserburgh in 1864 and Buckie 'down to the middle of the nineteenth century'. Both were intended, for impenetrable reasons, to promote better herring catches and it is perhaps their failure to do so which caused them to fade away so long ago. There has never been any suggestion that the Queensferry Burry Man had anything to do with herrings though I think it is worth pointing out his strong resemblance to the English Green Man.

Now here is an unusual thing, a folk custom that we do know all about; perhaps not precisely how or why or when, but near enough. It is unusual in another way; because it is very little known outside its area it is not weighed down with heavy folklore theories.

The Boy Ploughmen of St Margaret's Hope, Orkney, can be seen on the third Saturday in August. Time was when there were similar contests, but now this is the only one. The event has been through several evolutionary stages, and my informants suggest that this is probably what happened.

The Orcadians have always been farmers; at some time, not too long ago, perhaps about a hundred years, a farmer who liked making things made a miniature plough for his son so that he could imitate his dad at ploughing time. The idea caught on until, eventually, a ploughing match was suggested; the farmers had them, so why not the boys? The early boys' contests took place in the fields; an elderly man told me, 'my Da used to do it on the tatty land', but long ago they moved to the beach, to the firm, flat, wet sand left after the tide goes out. Younger brothers were brought into play to act as horses and the 'horses' found themselves being dressed up like those in a real ploughing match. This gave rise to a second contest, for the best dressed horse. In time the ploughmen decided they were better off without their junior partners; at this stage the two things became quite separate. Freed of the need to work, the horses became more and more decorated until they could hardly move. About twenty years ago the boy-horses became girl-horses. Until recently the whole affair took place on the first Wednesday of the Easter holidays, approximately at ploughing time; now is is held in August 'because of the weather and the tourists'.

All this sounds simple enough, but gives little idea of this fantastic happening. Though the boys and girls have moved apart, either half of the event would have been worth the journey to Orkney. St Margaret's Hope is on South Ronaldsay. If you take the passenger ferry from John O'Groats, you will land at Burwick, a non-existent place with a wooden pier. St Margaret's Hope is on the left, a bit less than half-way on the bus journey to Kirkwall. It has that characteristic island look of a place where nothing ever happens, and on the appointed afternoon it was still wearing it half an hour after events were due to begin. I was not too anxious; hard-won experience has taught me to bide my time; the more casual a place is beforehand, the better the custom will turn out to be.

Sure enough, the Cromarty Hall was suddenly alive with mums dressing up their primary school-aged daughters in the most bizarre costumes we had ever seen. First they have to become 'horses'; second they have to be profusely decorated. To satisfy the first condition they wear dark suits, horse collars, bridles, reins, plumed hats, and 'feathers' on their wrists and ankles. All these items are profusely decorated, literally like the most overloaded Christmas tree, with bells, baubles, tinsel, beads, rosettes, ribbons, tassles, plastic flowers, cracker novelties and anything else which may have come to hand during the several generations it took to bring them to their present advanced state. You could hardly see the girls underneath it all.

During the afternoon they stood in a solemn line outside while the judges deliberated endlessly to decide, first, which had the most astounding decoration and, second, which had the most functional and efficient harness. They inspected the latter most thoroughly, making sure it was set up correctly and would work. This all took ages, provoking unrest among fond parents and the imminent collapse of several horses. The girls accepted it with dignified good grace, but the smallest, no more than 4 years old, endured it for an hour without a flicker of expression until finally she began, imperceptibly, to cry.

However, it transpired that there was method in the judicial tardiness; the tide was too high for the subsequent ploughing contest and they were stalling until it went out! While their sisters were on display out front, the boys were sitting in a sheepish row displaying their ploughs to a separate panel of judges, genuine ploughmen and farmers. These ploughs, or 'ploos', as they call them here, are fine working replicas of the real thing, the right size for a 7- to 14-year-old boy to use. There are two categories, wood and metal, with a prize for the best plough in each. The wooden ones tend to be the older (some are thought to be seventy or eighty years old), kept lovingly in families all those years, and polished and varnished for their annual appearance. The metal ones are newer; a couple were brand new in 1984, but they are no less beautiful and, the experts told me, no less efficient. The boys themselves do not dress up, but there was some evidence that they had been instructed to appear clean and tidy. The only time the ploughmen and their horses appeared together was at the end of the judging of the horses, just to have their photograph taken. They always have an equal number of boys and girls. In a small community like this available talent can vary wildly, but this was a good year with eighteen of each. There is an upper age limit of 16 but I was told that it is rare for anyone to go past 14. The 15- and 16-year-olds consider it exceedingly wet to be interested in such things.

We saw no more of the horses. The rest of the afternoon was for the 'plooing'. The contest was billed to take place on the Sands of Wright, but at the last minute the committee decided the sand was not good enough and transferred the fixture to another beach. This is normal; they just choose the one with the best sand; too soft and it blows away, too hard and it breaks up. Even after all the delays, the tide was only just far enough out, the men marking out the 'rigs' still dodging the waves.

The Boy Ploughmen. Colin Scott, champion in 1984, demonstrates his skills.

The contest is exactly like a real ploughing match in miniature. Each contestant is given a measured area to plough, called a 'rig', about four feet square. The rigs were in one long straight row, allocated according to expertise, the older and more skilled at one end, the young novices at the other. There were six prizes on offer: for the straightest furrows, the neatest ends, the best finish, the best 'feering' (the first furrow; difficult to cope with), the first finished and, the big one, for the Best Ploughed Rig. Each contestant was allowed an adult helper to advise on tactics but not to handle the plough. The whole affair was conducted with great intensity; spectators either rooting for their young or, if they were visitors, marvelling at the skill on show. Concentration among the ploughmen fell off along the line of rigs. The young ones waded in with reckless abandon; first finished was about the youngest. Roaring 'brrrm, brrrm,' throughout, he had completed the job in about five minutes, ignoring the entreaties of his father-assistant to pay just a tiny bit of attention to what he was doing. At the other end, Colin Scott took it slowly and deliberately, oblivious to all around him, taking the best part of an hour to plough a rig of the utmost perfection, each furrow as straight as a ruler and precisely the same width as the one next to it. He finished it all off like an artist framing his picture and in the end there was nothing else for the judges to do but declare his the Best Ploughed Rig.

The judges did not watch all this work and only appeared when everyone was done and the knowledgeable crowd had withdrawn. They had no idea who had ploughed each rig. They were the same farmers who had earlier inspected the ploughs and they set about this task with equal seriousness. Indeed, it was a characteristic of the entire afternoon that *everything* was important and not to be taken lightly. They deliberated for at least half an hour, measuring, comparing, arguing, before they were satisfied with their verdicts.

Egg Rolling at Avenham Park, Preston. A rare collection of traditionally decorated eggs. Most children use chocolate Easter eggs.

Hundreds of children gather in Preston, to roll eggs down the grassy slopes of Avenham Park on Easter Monday afternoon. I am sure they have no idea why; they do not compete, or even communicate with each other, it is simply the thing to do and whether they are Anglo-Saxons, Asians, West Indians, or Chinese, the sight of all these kids enthusiastically and earnestly trundling brightly coloured Easter eggs down the hill until they break is really quite extraordinary.

Eggs have always been associated with Easter and early spring. It is said that they symbolize birth and resurrection. Egg Rolling is only one of several games which used to be played at this season; some folklorists declare it to represent the rolling away of the stone from the entrance to Christ's tomb. Easter eggs have been around for centuries but the chocolate varieties we know today are a comparatively recent creation, appearing barely a hundred years ago. Traditional Easter eggs were hardboiled and brightly coloured. There were many ways of colouring them. Families had secret recipes; common dyes were cochineal, spinach leaves, logwood chips, gorse blossom and onion skins, and the more creative could achieve multicoloured decoration by binding bits of vegetation, cloth or waxpaper around the egg before putting it on to boil.

These were the eggs that were put in front of every child at breakfast on Easter Sunday, and they were also the eggs that they rolled down the hills, not only at Preston but all over the British Isles.

Avenham Park is in a bit of a mess on Easter Monday afternoon, covered with silver wrapping paper, since the custom now is to use chocolate eggs instead of real ones. Traditionalists may deplore this development; the Preston dogs love it. There are still a few old-fashioned eggs to be seen, but not many, and oranges are frequently used instead. The suggestion has been made that the oranges represent the sun which will shortly arrive with the spring; the truth is that oranges roll a great deal better than eggs whether chocolate or hardboiled.

On Dunstable Downs they use *only* oranges but in a different way. The local greengrocers club together to supply several crates which are hurled down Pascombe Pit to the excited kids waiting below.

Even the yellow cheeses they roll down Cooper's Hill, near Brockworth in Gloucestershire, have been offered as 'possible sun-symbols', an interpretation which would astonish the foolhardy youths who hurl themselves after them.

Should you belong to the school of thought which holds *all* British customs as at best bizarre, at worst completely mad, you have only to utter the words 'Cheese Rolling' to prove your thesis. Though powerfully challenged by the Barrel Rolling at Ottery St Mary, and the Broughton Tin Can Band, this is certainly my nomination as Britain's Maddest Custom.

Cooper's Hill is a high wooded ridge just off the road between Brockworth and Painswick. The wood is dense, except for an inexplicable gash from top to bottom about fifty yards wide with a tall maypole permanently at the top. There is a fine weathercock on top of the pole. It is here, at 6 o'clock in the evening of Spring Bank Holiday, that this famous event takes place. Hundreds of people come to watch, the St John Ambulance bring reinforcements, the local rugby players volunteer their services as defensive marshalls, a Master of Ceremonies, in a white coat and a top hat, decorated with red, white and blue ribbons, is on hand to supervise, and a number of local youths are assembled to risk their lives. The basic event is this: a seven-pound cheese is rolled down the appallingly steep hill (it has a gradient of 1 in 3), and the youths rush after it. They have no hope of catching it, but the first down wins it.

Tradition says that the annual event is to perpetuate grazing rights, though nobody is too clear about this. Pagan fertility rights have, naturally, been mentioned. The custom is certainly old, well established in the early nineteenth century; a notice has been preserved announcing 'two cheese to be run for' in 1836. The cheese is Double Gloucester; on all three occasions I have been there there have been four, though accounts say this fluctuates according to the number donated. Each is covered neatly with cheesecloth and decorated with red and blue ribbons. Evidently the cheeses were once encased in protective wood, but certainly not now. During the last war the wooden case was used with a token cheese ration inside, and thus the custom survived throughout.

The weather can have a surprising influence on the occasion. If the hill is dry and hard, the cheeses hurtle down with colossal speed and have been known to bounce clean over the protective nets at the bottom and even the houses behind them. The pursuing youths also career out of control and end up in the local hospital. On the other hand, if it is soft and wet and muddy the cheese goes more slowly, the lads are not far behind it, and the carnage is less serious.

All four races are exactly the same, except that the third is for girls. Anyone can enter; there are no territorial restrictions. They got ready, looking aghast down the horrifying precipice, wondering who got them into this fine mess. In 1983 most of them were full of a mixture of rum and cider, apparently the favoured courage-inducing cocktail at that moment in rural Gloucestershire. Special guests are invited to roll each cheese and one of them was ready with the first. The Master of Ceremonies shouted 'One to be ready, two to be steady, three to prepare, four to be off!'. On 'three' the cheese was sent on its way rolling and then bouncing down the hill. On 'four' the competitors hurled themselves after it. Their descent was not a pretty sight; they rushed headlong at first, soon lost control, tumbled, rolled, staggered, but eventually, as the gradient eased near the bottom, managed to get on their feet again for a final dash into the arms of the waiting rugy players. There are usually a few broken bones; sprains, bruises and deep shock are accepted as normal.

If you think this is a thing that people only do once in a moment of misguided bravado, there was one lad who had already won two cheeses in previous years, another, dressed in nothing but a tee-shirt and jock-strap, who was so determined to win that he went in all three races, and indeed finally did win the last one. The statistics of plucking up courage are plain; in the first race there were 12 runners, in the second 18 and in the last 28. In the girls' race there were only 4 starters, who all survived intact. It has always been my contention that, in most things, girls have a lot more sense than boys.

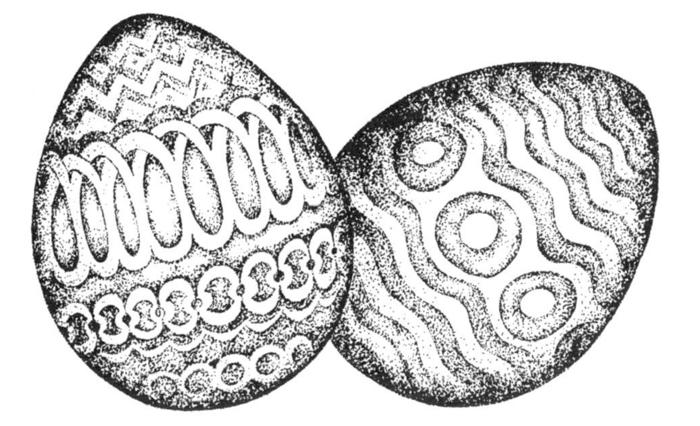

more matter for a May morning

May Day in 'Merrie England' has been much written about, usually in floridly romantic terms though in reality it was not so much pretty and graceful, as boisterous, drunken and licentious. Indeed it was considered so abanonded by the Puritans that they denounced it roundly. The Victorians finally turned it into the chaste and respectable celebration seen on a thousand village greens today. Personally, I blame Tennyson:

> Of all the glad New-year, mother, the maddest merriest day;
> For I'm to be Queen o' the May, mother, I'm to be Queen o' the May.

Happily, there are exceptions. Padstow's Oss is one, or rather two, of the great folk characters of Britain, and May Day in this pleasant Cornish town is an unforgettable experience. Here May Day has not run down; every year it gets more lively. It is alive enough to adapt to changing conditions and even in the twenty years I have known it it has become noticeably different. The only problem really is its success; Padstonians are inclined to feel overwhelmed by their visitors.

No one knows the origins of this remarkable custom. Fanciful stories and claims of pre-Christian antiquity abound but the first real reference to Padstow hobby horses appear in 1803, in a history of Cornwall. It seems to have arrived at something like its present form by 1824 when an account described it as 'being extended with hoops, and painted to resemble a horse'.

A Padstow Oss is not like any other hobby horse. It is black. A circular hoop, covered with canvas and almost six feet wide is supported on the carrier's shoulders. A skirt hangs down four feet all round. This, too, was once of canvas, blackened with tar or lamp-black, but it has gone through evolutionary processes and is now made of plastic sheeting. This is obviously much lighter; in the old days it weighed ten stone or more. Thus we have a sort of shiny black drum, with the bottom open. A small decorated horse's head, with snapping jaws, sticks out to the front, a short tail to the back. The carrier's head emerges from the top of the drum, covered by a tall conical hat and an alarmingly grotesque mask.

There are two Osses in Padstow, the Old Oss and the newer, Blue Ribbon Oss. They look very much the same except that the Blue Oss is slightly bigger, has a fine white beard, and a red, white and blue ribbon is fixed around the outside of the hoop. In any case, you would find no difficulty in telling which you were looking at because Padstonians decorate themselves with ribbons, hats, sashes and sweaters, over their predominately white clothes, according to whichever Oss they follow. The town is fairly evenly divided between red, for the Old Oss, and blue for the new.

Traditionalists still tend to dismiss the Blue Ribbon Oss as an upstart even though it has been out continuously since 1919. About the turn of the century the Maying got out of hand so a 'Temperance' Oss appeared, with blue followers. His appearances were intermittent up to the Great War but after that returning Padstonians decided to reincarnate him as the 'Peace' Oss, and to collect money for charity, which they still do. The temperance connection has long gone. There used to be aggravation between the two parties but nowadays, though partisanship is fanatical, there is no animosity and they always dance together towards the end of the day. It is remarkable how different the two parties look; the Red Oss party has a warm red glow, while the Blue party is much brighter. Each party is led by a Master of Ceremonies in top hat and morning suit.

Padstow Old Oss.

May Day in Padstow begins on the stroke of midnight. They do not want to waste a moment. Outside the Golden Lion they sing a 'Morning Song', which goes on for several verses. Then they visit many other houses in the town and sing appropriate verses outside.

In the very early morning the Old Oss team go out and gather greenery to decorate the centre of town and a boys' Oss, called the 'Colt', tours around. But it is the appearance of the two grown-up Osses that everyone waits for. The Blue Ribbon Oss bursts forth from the Institute at 10 o'clock. The effect is electrifying, especially for a first-time visitor. The band starts up the wonderful Padstow music on accordions, melodeons and drums. The beat of these drums goes on, hypnotically, all day while the Oss swoops and swirls wildly about, encouraged by his Teaser, scattering spectators as he goes.

The Teaser dances with him at all times in a characteristic strutting, stiff-armed style, brandishing his special club, a short pole with a large padded leather end, decorated appropriately. In the past the Teaser often wore a striking costume, even at one time a mask like the Oss. Nowadays all followers take a turn, including the women.

Originally the women were chased by the Oss, whose object was to get them under his skirt. A woman thus captured, and marked by the black, was sure to become pregnant within a year. The superstition was so strongly held that young unmarried girls would run a mile rather than be caught. However, the status of women has changed so radically that this part of the ritual has become much diminished. The Oss can have a lighter skirt, women take a much more active part in the celebrations and, in 1983, I even saw one carry the Blue Ribbon Oss for a short spell. I was told this was the first time a woman had ever done this, but I cannot be sure this is true.

Every so often the drums cease and the Oss 'dies' to the ground, and lies there while his followers sing a verse of mournful dirge:

Oh, where is St George,
Oh where is he oh?
He is out in his long-boat all on the salt sea oh.
Up flies the kite and down falls the lark oh,
Aunt Ursula Birdhood she had an old ewe
And she died in her own park oh!

This astonishing verse revives the Oss and, with one bound, he is himself again. It has, naturally enough, given rise to wild speculation. The most popular theory is that Aunt Ursula enlisted the help of the Oss to frighten off French invaders hundreds of years ago but historians dismiss this. I do myself, though I, in common with everyone else, have no suggestion to offer as to who Aunt Ursula Birdhood actually was.

The Old Oss emerges from the Golden Lion at 11 a.m. and behaves in much the same way. Both of them tour the town by arranged routes which do not cross until they meet in Broad Street in the early evening. The whole of Padstow is consumed by the occasion. The drums, the savage Osses, the strutting

Minehead Hobby Horse setting off on his early morning pilgrimage while the population sleeps.

dancers, all have an extraordinary primitive power.

A hundred miles up the coast in Minehead there lives another Hobby Horse. He is so closely related in form and construction that the two towns have been claiming for centuries that the other stole the idea.

The Minehead Hobby Horse is not circular, but boat-shaped, not black but multicoloured, not ferocious but cheerful and friendly. Nor does he bring out vast crowds to join in the celebration; Minehead stays at home and the Hobby Horse comes to them. He does not leap and whirl, he steps jauntily. The reason for his comparative lack of energy is quite simple; he is extremely heavy. The frame is made of wood, about eight feet long and a little more than a shoulder-width wide. The skirt is of hessian sacking and reaches to the ground. It is painted with many roundels, each in two colours, and in any combination of red, white and blue. Large letters proclaim him the Sailors' Horse. The top is completely covered with hundreds of cloth strips which flutter in the breeze and when he 'shakes' himself; on the other hand, they keep him indoors in wet weather because if they get sodden the whole thing is too heavy to carry. He has a conical head, also decorated profusely with ribbons, with feathers on the top. For a face he has a clownish tin mask. He has a long tail which trails along the ground and is occasionally whipped into play to chastise anyone who has caused displeasure.

Intermittently a rival appears in Minehead, the Town Horse, denounced as an upstart by the Sailors' crew. Attendants called 'Gullivers' come and go. These have the same tall hats and masks and dress in the same colours and materials as the Hobby Horse. Their function is to collect money. At one time they were notorious for their conscientiousness; one of their absences lasted half a century after they clubbed to death a man who refused to pay up.

The Sailors' Horse comes out several times. His first appearance from his home on the quay is on the last evening of April, known locally as Warning Eve. Until well after dark he dances through the streets accompanied by his musicians, on melodeon and drum. He chases children, bows politely to respected adults, and generally warns Minehead that he will be out and about in earnest in the next three days.

On May Day he makes two appearances. The first is before dawn when he makes a pilgrimage through the sleeping resort, up the hill past Higher Town to Whitecross where at 6 o'clock he must bow three times towards the rising sun. The crew are reticent about this ritual but it appears to have deep significance for them. They return to the quay more cheerfully and there are more people about, delighted to see them.

The crew all work during the day. The Hobby

Horse does not reappear until the evening. On May Day he always visits Dunster Castle and tours the lovely village. The following two evenings he is out in other parts of the district. He is very popular, always ready with a bit of horseplay, always ready to reward donations with a polite and courtly bow.

At 6 o'clock on May Morning the choristers of Magdalen College, Oxford, climb 144 feet to the top of Magdalen Tower and sing a Latin hymn. The cause of this custom is unknown but its effect is an assembly of thousands of undergraduates, visitors, tourists, morris dancers, photographers, hamburger sellers and academics in the High Street below.

It is said that a Requiem Mass for the soul of Henry VII was once sung at this hour. A bequest by Lord Berkeley in 1491 apparently pays some of the expenses, though the Tower was not completed until 1509. Another suggestion is that it celebrates the building of the Tower itself. By the eighteenth century the occasion had developed into a substantial concert until one day, the story goes, the choir arrived late and ill-prepared; panic stricken they sang the first thing that came to mind, *Te Deum Patrim Colinius*, part of the College grace. I cannot guarantee the veracity of this story, but the choristers still sing the seventeenth-century hymn to this day. I was told that, until recently, it was impossible to hear what they were singing anyway; these days three carols come over loud and clear through a public address system. The singing is followed by a pealing of the tower bells.

The great popularity of the occasion is probably accounted for not so much as a primitive desire to welcome in the May, on the part of the undergraduates at least, as a diverting way to round off their all-night parties, essential to university life at this time of year. In 1984 an astonishing sartorial range was on view from evening dress with white tie and full-length dresses, through lurid fancy dress, to advanced punk. For the next two or three hours several teams of morris dancers performed around Radcliffe Camera, Broad Street and St Giles. All the pubs and cafés were open and full. Everyone was having a great time, but by 9 o'clock it was back to business as usual in the streets of Oxford.

This is fortuitous for it leaves plenty of time to drive

May Morning in Oxford. Apart from the hymns on Magdalen Tower, there is morris dancing in the city centre.

six miles north to Charlton-on-Otmoor to witness another May Day custom, which is very different.

The *Buildings of England* considers the rood screen in St Mary's Church to be 'the finest and most complete in the county' without mentioning at all that the decorated cross which permanently surmounts it is unique in Britain, if not the entire world. This cross, about human size, is the survivor of two, or possibly three, which stood on the screen as recently as the middle of the last century. One represented Christ, the other the Virgin Mary and it is the latter which is there now.

Every year on the day before May Day, and again on September 19, it is taken down to be redecorated overall with fresh green leaves from the box wood tree, relieved with white artificial flowers. The cross is still referred to in the village as 'she'; a lady called Granny Smith who decorated her for many years early in this century would not have her referred to as anything other than 'My Lady'. She is not a regular cross; below her small head and arms she has a waspish waist and spreads out at the bottom like an old-fashioned skirt.

Long ago she used to be carried around the parish on May Day, accompanied by morris dancers. Now, apart from an outing in 1977, she stays in the church, and a procession comes to her in the form of the children from the local school, who walk to a special service carrying little wooden crosses, decorated all over with flowers. After the service they leave their crosses by the rood screen, below the garland cross. The service is a recent addition to the day, barely twenty years old, but the decorated crosses have been a feature of Charlton-on-Otmoor May Day for a very long time. Formerly the children took them around the village singing a special song in return for pennies.

Abbotsbury children are still allowed to benefit from taking their beautiful garlands around the village on 'Old' May Day, May 13. This delightful custom has been diminishing steadily over the years due to perfectly understandable, if regrettable, circumstances. It has come under unexpected attack a couple of times recently and thus flourishes with renewed vigour because of the fury of those who keep it going. Thirty years ago a new village policeman confiscated the garlands *and* all the money on the grounds of unlawful begging. This provoked a terrific row and earned him a rebuke from the Chief Constable of Dorset. The second attack was more sustained. This was to do with the schools and time off and the like and was greatly exacerbated by an influential villager who thinks it should be stamped out anyway because of its 'pagan origins'!

The outrageous heathen practice which gets everyone so worked up is this: the children of Abbotsbury, between say 5 and 15, carry two large garlands and show them to every house in the village. One garland is made of wild flowers, the other of garden flowers, and the two are taken separately. Garden enthusiasts compare blooms with their own, nature lovers test out the kids on the names of the wild flowers. Every villager expresses pleasure at seeing the garlands once again. Everyone is happy to contribute to both collections, knowing full well that the children keep the money. At the end of the morning the cultivated garland is placed on the War Memorial while the other is abandoned because wild flowers do not last. That is all there is to it. Disgraceful!

There was much more to it once, though. Abbotsbury, on the Dorset coast, one of the most attractive villages in all Britain, once had a small but thriving

Abbotsbury Garland Day – the garden flower garland on its rounds.

fishing fleet which worked off Chesil Beach. Garland Day marked the opening of the mackerel season which was much celebrated in the village. Each boat produced its own garland; the adults made it and the children showed it off around the houses. Afterwards the garlands were taken to a service in the church, then to the beach where there were picnics and games. In the evening the garlands were mounted on the bows of the fishing boats and taken out to sea. In the distant past they were thrown in; old people in the village say that they never remember this happening, they were simply brought back again. Nor were they ever thrown in from the beach; 'a photographer made us do it a few years ago but that's the only time!'

The custom dwindled with the fishing boats. The last one, which belonged to the Arnold family, gave up in 1983. They have been the mainstay of Garland Day for many years and it was Mrs Ellen Arnold who had the idea of one garland being of wild and the other of cultivated flowers. She made them herself and would not allow any of her extensive family near them. The children had to go out, collect the flowers and leave them in her porch, then she made them behind closed doors. Her daughter, Bette Dalley, told me in 1984, 'when she got too old to do it, we hadn't a clue. We had to figure it out for ourselves – and then we had to put up with her criticism when she thought they weren't right!' The Abbotsbury Garlands are about two feet high, bell-shaped and carried by two children holding a pole thrust through the middle.

The Castleton Garland is a similar shape but much bigger because a hefty man has to get inside and carry it on his shoulders. Fully decorated it weighs at least six stone. This garland is a robust but inelegant beehive-shaped construction of wood, string, wire and an old bicycle wheel to which is tied a profuse but random mixture of wild flowers and greenery. There is a slot in the top and into this fits the Garland 'Queen', a smaller but most elegant posy of the best flowers, attached to a foot-long peg, made by expert village ladies.

The Castleton Garland is prepared during the day on the premises of one of the six village pubs who take it in turn to host the ceremony, which begins at 6 o'clock on May 29, Oak Apple Day. It is by no means certain that the affair has anything whatever to do with Charles II, whose restoration to the throne is commemorated on that day. Nevertheless the Garland King and his Lady who ride at the head of the procession are both dressed in Stuart costume.

The King carries the Garland, completely covered by it from the waist upwards, so that his horse has to be led. He is surely an advanced variation of the once popular Green Man. His Lady follows at a respectful distance, riding side-saddle and looking very decorative. She has only been a real lady since 1955; before that she was a man, the time-honoured man/woman who still appears in dozens of customs around the country. By all accounts 'she' used to be a bit of a bawd. Her bonnet was always donated by the host pub.

These two are followed by the band and a procession of dancing girls in white dresses. The children dance to a tune very like the Helston Furry Dance. Until 1948 the whole affair was organized by the church bellringers who had been associated with Garland Day for the previous 199 years at least. This very first reference to the event was in the churchwarden's accounts for 1749: 'for an iron to hang ye ringers garland in, 8 pence'. It was their habit to perform a morris dance on the occasion until they refused in 1897 on the grounds that they were too embarrassed. This is thought to be the only example of shy morris dancers in recorded history.

The procession tours the village, dancing and taking refreshment at each pub. Eventually they arrive at the church. The 'Queen' is removed from the top of the Garland and the Garland is hoisted straight off the King's shoulders and hauled to the top of the church tower. It is placed on the centre pinnacle, above the clock. The other pinnacles are already decorated with oak branches. The garland stays there until every single flower is dead, usually about three weeks. The children give a display of maypole dancing on the village green. Then, finally, the 'Queen' is placed on the War Memorial while the band plays 'The Last Post'.

Maypole dancing is a controversial subject in folklore circles. Though accepted by the entire population, with the exception of a minute proportion of folklorists, as the quintessential May custom, the fact is it is not an ancient British tradition. It seems to have arrived from Europe to be taken up by theatrical performers in the first half of last century. By about 1850 it had filtered down to popular performance, via morris dancers to little girls, and from that time it has been at the centre of countless May Day happenings. Nowadays morris dancers would rather die than maypole dance. The pastime is particularly associated with schools, and some of the responsibility for this must go to the eminent art critic and man of letters, John Ruskin. In 1881 he became associated with Whitelands College in London, a teacher training college for women. He had the idea of creating a May

Ickwell May Day. It is quite unusual for adults to take part in maypole dancing. Here they have completed a complex dance.

Day custom for the girls, 'the likeablist and lovablist' to be their Queen for the year. The idea was that the girls would go out into their schools and spread the word about May Day and maypole dancing, and it is evident that the scheme was very successful. The custom continues to this very day.

There are far too many May customs of this type to discuss here; we will have to be content with a few of the better known. There is morris dancing around the maypole at Ickwell in Bedfordshire, early on May Morning itself, but this is unpublicized and intended for the village.

'Ickwell May Day', on the other hand, happens on the Bank Holiday which follows on the first Monday of the month. It is an old-established festival first referred to in parish documents in 1563 and it centres around the fine red and white maypole which stands permanently on the extensive village green.

This is a great gathering with stalls and side shows, visiting dance teams, a pageant, the crowning of the May Queen and much maypole dancing. The maypole dances are performed by three groups, juniors, teenagers and Old Scholars. It is unusual, in my experience, to see adult maypole dancers but they performed more intricate manoeuvres, called Spider's Web and Gypsies' Tent.

Apart from familiar May Day personnel Ickwell has characters called 'Moggies' – the Sweep and his Wife, and the Lord and Lady (all men, I need hardly mention), dressed appropriately, the first two with blackened faces. Their curious name may have something to do with the neighbouring village of Mogerhanger. Their primary functions are to clown about and collect money. Long ago they used to make house-to-house calls in a larger more organized party, carrying garland poles and May boughs, soliciting ale as well.

Wherever there is a permanent maypole there is also likely to be some kind of ceremony, even if not on May Day. The Puritans denounced maypoles as 'stinkyng ydols' and wanted them done away with, but a good number survive all over the country. That is not to say the same *pole* survives; naturally they have to be replaced from time to time, but many disappeared simply through decay.

Knutsford Royal May Day has one completely unique feature – 'sanding' – carried out in the early morning.

Wellow in Nottinghamshire does not have to worry about this possibility, since their latest pole, erected in 1977, is of stainless steel paid for by a grant from the EEC. They have the Wellow Maypole Celebration on the Spring Bank Holiday. The May Queen is voted into office in a public election – the electors are everyone in the village aged over 17, 'we used to have the kids as well but there was far too much bribery and corruption!'

There is controversy as to who has the *tallest* maypole. Ansty in Wiltshire, not far from Shaftesbury, replaced their 76-foot pole in 1982 with one 96 feet tall and at once registered their claim. That at Barwick-in-Elmet, just to the east of Leeds, has long been popularly accepted as the tallest, though it is, in fact, a couple of feet less. However, it is much more famous because of rituals concerning it.

Every third year the Barwick-in-Elmet maypole is lowered on Easter Monday, painted and, if necessary, repaired and then raised again, amid rejoicing, on the Spring Bank Holiday. The next time will be in 1987. In both directions the operation seems to be incredibly complex and nerve-wracking, achieved by traditional means, with dozens of ladders, ropes and about 200 strong men. Three Pole Men are elected by the villagers to supervise. When lowered the maypole is carried, on the shoulders of all the men, to a nearby field to be painted white with a spiral stripe of red and blue. There is a *tradition* that anyone who steals it can keep it, but so far this has not happened.

Four large garlands hang half-way up the maypole and these are replaced as well. They are beehive-shaped and though they all look the same, each is made by a different village group, and decorated with 1500 multicoloured cloth rosettes; forty-two red, white and blue ribbons with bells on the end hang below, and a little wicker basket full of artificial flowers.

Maypole raising day is attended by celebrations, sports, processions and music. At six in the evening the men carry back the pole and it takes them a good two hours to get it upright again. It used to be the custom for a man to complete the successful day's work by climbing up the pole to adjust the fox weather-vane on the top, but insurance men have put a stop to that.

Knutsford Royal May Day Festival is by far the biggest of the 'traditional' celebrations. This one is not on May Day either but on the first Saturday in the month. The afternoon is taken up with an enormous procession led by the Town Crier and consisting of at least 400 people: children in a multitude of costumes, bands, no less than five morris teams and the May Queen herself with numerous attendants. It takes the best part of an hour for them all to pass by on their way from the Old Town Hall to the Heath where an elaborate crowning ceremony takes place, followed by dancing and displays.

Knutsford May Day began in 1864 and had reached something very like its present form by 1875. It became 'Royal' in 1887 following a much-enjoyed visit by the Prince and Princess of Wales. Royalty attended again in 1929 in the shape of the Princess Royal. The May Queen is crowned every year with a replica of Queen Elizabeth's crown, made by a London jeweller, which she is privileged to keep.

Apart from the impressive spectacle three other things make the day interesting. First is the presence of so many North-West Morris dancers. This style of dancing is not seen much outside the area (see Chapter 4) and it is an unusual opportunity to compare several teams. The second thing is the Jack-in-the-Green,

Children bring garland crosses to Charlton-on-Otmoor church on May Morning. *(see page 31)*

Girls of Ickwell Green all dressed up to attend their May Queen. *(see page 33)*

The four garlands which hang halfway up Barwick-in-Elmet maypole. *(see page 34)*

A less familiar part of Great Wishford's Grovely Day is their fine house decoration.

who plays an important role near the front of the procession. This folk character, commemorated, with his close relation the Green Man, on so many pub signs, has almost become extinct, though he was once very familiar. He has always been present at Knutsford and this is one of very few places where he can be seen. The *Oxford English Dictionary* says a Jack-in-the-Green is 'A man or boy enclosed in a wooden or wicker pyramidical framework covered with leaves'; as far as I could tell, the example at Knutsford was a middle-aged man encased in a sort of wire-netting basket covered profusely with cedar.

The third phenomenon is the most interesting, completely unique to Knutsford. Early in the morning two men, Alf Gilbert and Ray Neal, go out and about in the town 'sanding'. There is an engaging legend to account for this curious custom. The town owes its name to King Canute who forded a river in the vicinity. He got sand in his shoes and a newly married couple happened to pass as he was pouring it on the ground. He wished them as many children as there were grains of sand. Be that as it may, the gentlemen go out with bags of dyed sand to create mottoes and flourishes on the ground outside important buildings in the town. The *most* important is that of the Royal May Queen, where they allow their creative powers full rein. In 1983 their efforts spread half-way across the street and spelled out the words, 'Long may she live. Happy may she be. Blessed with contentment and from misfortune free. Our Royal May Queen Paula Williamson.' Shops and other private houses can have sanding too but they have to pay for it. The day is notorious for rain, but this is beneficial to the sanding as the dye soaks into the pavement and lasts for months. If it is very dry and breezy it simply blows away.

Strictly speaking Oak Apple Day at Great Wishford, in Wiltshire, should be in Chapter 9 on Legal Customs, but it turns out like a May custom and, obviously, it happens in May, so it has earned its place here.

In 1603 a Court held in Grovely Wood settled a long-standing dispute between the inhabitants of Wishford and Barford St Martin and the Earl of Pembroke concerning grazing and wood-gathering rights. One valuable right established was that:

> . . .the olde custome is and time out of mind hath byn that the people and inhabitance of Wishford and Barford aforesaid may lawfully geather and bring away all kinde of deade snappinge wood Boughes and Stickes that be in the Woodes at Grovely at their pleasure without controlment and none other besides them may lawfully fetch any there at any time.

The rights still exist, in spite of various Acts of Parliament which have threatened them, and very early in the morning the villagers go out into Grovely Wood to celebrate and perpetuate them by collecting fine oak boughs.

To reaffirm their rights they were

> . . .to goe in a daunce to the Cathedrall Church of our blessed Ladie in the Cittie of new sarum. . .and theire make theire clayme to theire custome in the Forrest of Grovely in these words: Grovely Grovely and all Grovely.

At 10 o'clock in the morning they do indeed go to Salisbury Cathedral, six miles away, where four women of the village, dressed in old fashioned clothes with bonnets and sacking aprons and carrying small oak branches, dance in the nave. Then they and their friends from the village stand before the altar and cry 'Grovely! Grovely! Grovely! And all Grovely!' This part of the ceremony died out for some time but was revived in 1951.

They dance again outside for the benefit of tourists and visitors, before returning to Great Wishford for the rest of the day's festivities. First is a great procession through the village led by a band. Two men carry a banner proclaiming the immortal words plus 'Unity is Strength' and decorated with oak apples. The banner and procession are strongly reminiscent of a Friendly Society Walk. The day is organized by Wishford Oak Apple Society which has been responsible for Grovely affairs since 1892. The four dancing ladies accompany the banner, now carrying on their heads bundles of 'snappinge wood'. They are followed by the men with their oak boughs, gathered earlier. Then comes the rest of the village in assorted costumes, on foot or in hand-drawn carts. There is a Society lunch, fancy-dress contests, sports and games. The May Queen is crowned and there is maypole dancing. Wishford is decorated overall, some houses with inventive exuberance, and everybody wears oak apples.

A tree is at the centre of an intriguing custom which also takes place on May 29 at Ashton-on-Clun, near the Welsh border in Shropshire. The tree is a 250-year-old black poplar which stands in the middle of the village. It is unremarkable except for the fact that a number of large flags stick out from among its branches at all times, and this is the day on which three of the villagers take them down and put up new ones. They do this without ceremony, at any time convenient to them all.

So this is not a spectacular event. But *why* they do it is certainly not without interest. The custom possibly began in honour of Brigit, or St Bride, with tokens left in branches as offerings. Comparable customs exist such as 'clootie wells'. The tree was once known as The Bride's Tree, but this may equally have been because of an event said to have happened in 1789. On May 29 that year the Lord of the Manor, John Marston, brought his new bride, Mary Carter, home to the village. The tree was decorated with its new flags and the bride was delighted when she saw them. Some versions of the story suggest that she thought they were there in her honour, but it is more probable that the custom was already long established, and she did not know of it. She insisted that the Marston family should pay for new flags each year, and it came to pass that they did, until they finally left the Manor in 1951. Not only did they provide the flags but they also had their staff put them up.

Since the Marstons left, Arbor Day, as it is called, has been the responsiblity of the parish council. They soon discovered that fifteen or sixteen flags cost a lot of money. For a few years they bought some and made the rest; as well as a Union Jack, and St George's Cross, they had all kinds of national flags, plain colours, and creations from the WI and other local groups. In 1955 they decided to organize a fund-raising fête. One of the men putting up the flags told me, 'this was a good idea, but it ended in a hell of a village row – fights even!' Nobody dared risk another fête until Jubilee Year, 1977, when a special effort was called for. This time it passed without incident and it has survived as an annual event.

The fête is held on a Sunday near to Arbor Day and is rapidly becoming a more substantial event than the one it is indended to finance. A recent addition to the festivities is a re-enactment, by children in period costume, of the arrival in the village of the newly-wed John and Mary Marston.

Arbor Day at Aston-on-Clun is a very casual affair when these men simply take down the old flags and put up new ones.

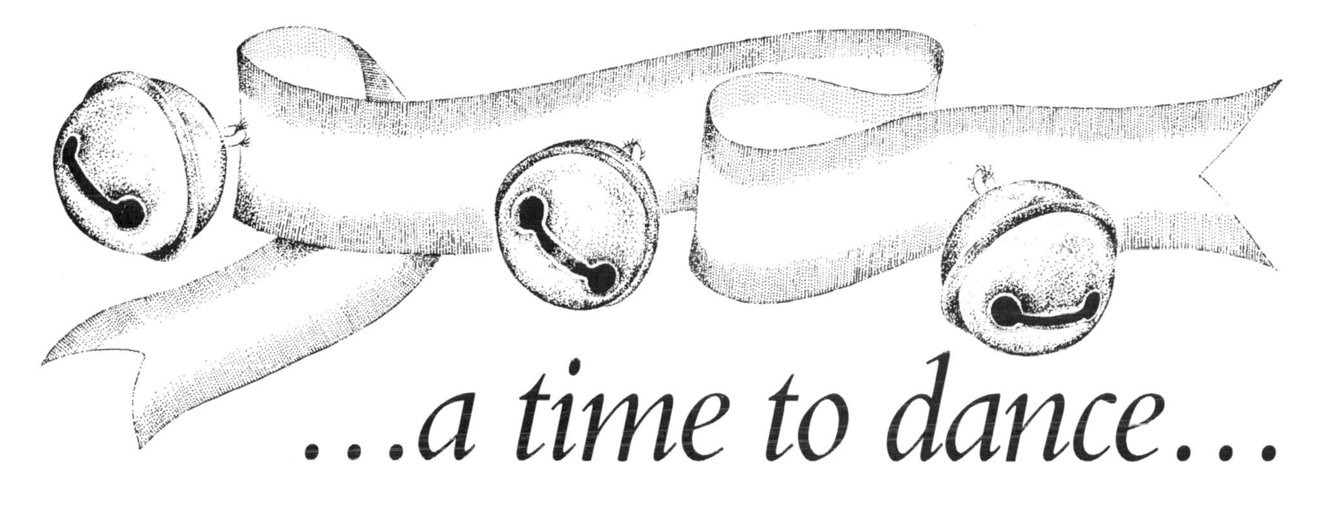

...a time to dance...

The dances in this chapter are 'ritual' dances and should not be confused with social dances, meaning country, square or even ballroom dances, involving men and women of variable expertise in an entirely informal way. Ritual dances, by contrast, are performed at particular times of the year, by organized, trained and uniformly costumed groups. Apart from the Helston Furry Dance, which is quite different from the rest, they are by tradition exclusively male, even if females have made untraditional appearances here and there.

England is particularly rich in ritual dances and they very conveniently sort themselves into distinct geographical and seasonal groups. Morris dancing is the most famous English folk dance of all. *Everybody* knows about morris dancers, in their whites with their handkerchiefs and bells and flowery hats. There are so many 'sides' – or groups of morris dancers – that people can be forgiven for thinking it is countrywide tradition. Not so; the dance is native to the south Midlands, particularly Oxfordshire and Gloucestershire, thereby giving it its accepted name of Cotswold Morris. The origin of 'morris' has caused endless speculation. One of the first references to a 'moreys daunce' was in 1458; it was once thought to derive from 'moorish' and consequently the dance itself to have arrived from North Africa. This theory is no longer in favour. Alternative theories appear in books and papers from time to time only to be denounced in reviews in the next issue of the *Folk Music Journal*.

There are only four genuinely old sides in existence: at Bampton, Headington Quarry, Abingdon and Chipping Campden; all the hundreds of others are comparatively recent sides dancing the enormous repertoire of Cotswold dances. Music is normally provided by fiddle, concertina or accordion, occasionally 'pipe and tabor', a whistle played with one hand, a small drum beaten with the other.

A side consists of six dancers plus a fool and/or another character such as a hobby horse. The dancers are distinguished by the variety of trappings they wear. The four traditional sides will demonstrate what I mean. Bampton wear black bowler hats with flowers in the front secured by a wide multicoloured band tied so that its streams out the back; they have ribbons of any bright colour tied around their upper arms and wrists; they wear smart white waistcoats. Abingdon wear profusely decorated top hats; green baldrics with a narrow yellow stripe. Headington Quarry wear blue cricket caps and blue and red baldrics. Chipping Campden do not wear hats at all, nor do they have baldrics; instead they wear green, yellow and red rosettes sewn onto their shirts front and back, and red chokers with white spots.

Virtually all morris sides wear white shirts, most wear white trousers, all wear bell pads on their legs. Early morris photographs show sides in more ordinary looking clothes; even earlier engravings have them in individual costumes. Still, there is a painting in Cheltenham Art Gallery, famous in folk circles, which shows a fine side celebrating the harvest, dressed in identical blouses, breeches and stockings, complete with baldricks and splendid hats. One of them is out of step.

There is a wide variety of styles, but fundamentally Cotswold Morris, in the view of a lay observer, is a colourful, lively, exuberant, jumping-about kind of thing. Handkerchief dances are by far the most common with their familiar flourishings. Stick dances are a large secondary group during which stout sticks are struck forcefully together. There are also a great number of dances with an individual character, as well as morris jigs, solo dances for star performers to show their skill. The Bampton men enjoy dancing jigs and

Headington Quarry Morris Men performing a stick dance twenty years ago. In 1984 all the same dancers were still there.

this would have been the type of dance used by William Kemp, a celebrated comic actor, on his extraordinary excursion in 1599 which created so great a sensation, that he was induced to print an account of it entitled *Kemp's Nine Daies Wonder*, 'performed in a daunce from London to Norwich'. Kemp did not dance non-stop, but had many adventures on the way which were very amusingly recounted in his pamphlet. At Sudbury a butcher offered to dance the fourteen miles to Bury St Edmunds with him but dropped out exhausted after barely half a mile:

> As he and I were parting, a lusty country lasse being among the people, cal'd him faint-hearted lout, saying, 'If I had begun to daunce, I would have held out one myle, though it had cost my life.' At which words many laughed. 'Nay,' said she, 'if the dauncer will lend me a leash of his belles, I'le venter to treade one myle with him myselfe.' I lookt upon her, saw mirth in her eies, heard boldness in her words, and beheld her ready to tucke up her russat petticoate; I fitted her with bels, which she merrily taking, garnisht her thicke short legs, and with a smooth brow bad the tabrer begin. The drum strucke; forward marcht I with my merry Mayde Marian, who shooke her fat sides, and footed it merrily to Melford, being a long myle. There parting with her (besides her skinfull of drinke), and English crowne to buy more drinke; for, good wench, she was in a pittious heate; my kindness she requited with dropping some dozen of short courtsies, and bidding God blesse the dauncer. I bade her adieu; and, to give her her due, she had a good eare, daunst truly, and wee parted friends.

Bampton is a very pleasant village about 15 miles west of Oxford. The most striking feature of the place is the number of large houses, built of Cotswold stone, set in their immaculate gardens, and it is these that give the Bank Holiday its very special character. By tradition the dancers visit all the 'big houses', and by tradition all the hundreds of spectators go with them. I was there once when the morris men led their army into a garden where the young master and his friends were playing croquet on the lawn. Without a word the dancers pulled up the hoops, kicked the balls out of the way and got on with the real business of the day.

Bampton Morris sides are accompanied by a Fool who carries a bladder with which to belabour dancers who make a mistake, or anyone who crosses his path. He needs to be an extrovert, up to all kinds of mischief, full of repartee, but also a good dancer since he had to join in some of the dances. Most Costwold Morris sides have a Fool.

Bampton has one tradition which is unique, their cake. A very nice spicy fruit cake is placed in a round silver container; the cake and container are impaled on a real sword; the sword tip is decorated with flowers and ribbons. One team carries its cake in a 'tin' handed down for generations, the other in one presented by the Morris Ring 'in memory of William Wells 1868–1953'. The whole is riddled with symbolism. The cake is said to represent the fruits of the earth; I am sure I do not have to tell you what the sword represents; the flowers represent spring and prosperity. It is considered good luck to have a morsel of cake, but you have to pay for it; the Cake Carrier also carries a collecting box.

The daytime belongs to Bampton Morris Men; there are three sides enjoying the privilege of dancing where they like, the visitors enjoying the atmosphere. Things change in the evening. Dancers are invited from outside, other morris sides, perhaps some from the North-West, possibly even sword dancers. The whole affair turns into a mini folk dance festival.

Headington is on the east side of Oxford and the Quarry was once the source of all the limestone which built the Oxford College. It was inhabited entirely by 'Quarry roughs' and their families. While the men hewed stone, their wives washed the clothes of the young gentlemen a couple of miles away. The last quarry closed in 1949.

Headington has had a morris side since at least 1800. The first written record was about 1850, referring to earlier times but it was not until Boxing Day 1899 that they made their unscheduled entry into 'folk' history. Times had been hard in the Quarry because of exceptionally bad weather so the morris men decided to go out to earn themselves a bit of money. Cecil Sharp, already a noted collector of folk songs, happened to see them from a window of the house he was visiting, and the incident led him into a lifelong involvement in morris dancing and eventually to his formation of the English Folk Dance Society in 1911. Sharp died in 1924 but his name lives on at the headquarters of the English Folk Dance and Song Society, just north of Regent's Park, known to its friends as C♯ House.

Apart from this claim to fame it so happens that the Headington Quarry side are the best Cotswold Morris dancers I have ever seen; if you have other views on the subject I do not want to hear them. Headington sides tend to work in generations; the present side was quite new when I first saw them twenty years ago and there were not many of the previous side left. *They* had been around for ages before that. There is evidence from a dancer named Joe Trafford that when he joined in 1897 the side had been together for forty years! When Cecil Sharp saw them in 1899 the leader was their musician, William Kimber, a legendary figure in morris lore. He and Sharp became lifelong friends. 'Merry' Kimber lived on until 1961 and died, aged 89, on Whit Monday just as the side were about to go out on their annual rounds. They decided to go anyway. In 1967 they introduced a new dance into their repertoire called 'Merry Kimber'. There is a street in the Quarry called William Kimber Crescent and they begin their tour with it here at 6 p.m. There has been a Kimber in the side since the middle of the nineteenth century, and there still is.

There are twenty-eight different dances belonging to Headington Quarry, an unusually large repertoire, of which nine are their dramatic stick dances. Instead of the familiar handkerchiefs, short sticks are knocked together in complicated and quite dangerous-looking movements. What distinguishes this side is their extraordinary togetherness; they dance closer, with more precision and bounciness than any other side I have seen. In 1984 they had their boys team out with them, miniature versions, who performed with exactly the same nonchalant verve.

In 1560 the churchwardens' accounts for St Helen's, Abingdon, have the entry 'For two dossin of Morres belles, ls', which would seem to indicate reasonably ancient origins for the Abingdon Morris Dancers. They come out each year on the Saturday nearest to June 19. Some accounts say this is the feast of St Edmund of Abingdon, though my Penguin *Dictionary of Saints*, which I believe, says his feast day is November 16. The town used to hold a midsummer Horse Fair and it is more likely to be connected with that. This occasion was enough of a revel to inspire the election of a Mock Mayor, a character in the tradition of the May Queen or the midwinter Lord of Misrule. Mock Mayors were not uncommon but few survive today; the Mayor of Ock Street, Abingdon, is easily the most celebrated.

Though the Mayor of Ock Street has no function,

The Mayor of Ock Street, Abingdon, Leslie Argyle, taking office in 1983 with his Sword, Sash and Drinking Cup.

he is officially the 'Squire' or leader of the morris men. He is properly elected each year; a ballot box is placed outside the Cross Keys and all inhabitants of Ock Street (the street is real enough) and all members of the morris side are entitled to vote. Any dancer who also lives in Ock Street gets *two* votes; there was only one such in 1983.

The mayor has ancient regalia – remember he is a *mock* mayor – consisting of sash, sword, collecting box, drinking cup and the Ock Street Horns. Legend says that in 1700 a black ox was presented by a farmer to be roasted at the fair. A fight broke out about who was going to have the horns. After a tremendous fracas the Ock Street men emerged victorious, led by a man called Hemmings, one of the morris dancers. Ever since then the horns have been carried before the mayor and members of the Hemmings family have been closely associated with the event. Leslie Argyle was elected in 1980 and has been Mayor of Ock Street ever since. I think it is worth mentioning at this point that at present there are *two* morris sides. The 'Abingdon Traditional Morris Dancers' elect the mayor; 'Mr Hemmings' Morris Dancers' don't. Feuding broke out a few years ago which *might* have had something to do with the election.

On their Saturday in June two sides are to be seen but only one mayor. Dancing starts in the morning; the sides are out all day in the streets, at the beautiful almshouses, at old people's homes, all over the place.

At 4 o'clock in the afternoon the new mayor is proclaimed with considerable ceremony and presented with his regalia. He is then 'danced in' with the Abingdon 'Squires Dance', before being carried in state to visit all the pubs in Ock Street during the rest of the evening. He is carried, shoulder high, in an aged bentwood and wicker chair which has been decorated with flowers.

Each year it is the pleasure of the Abingdon Morris Dancers to invite other dancers to join them in their celebrations. In 1983 they had some Swedish dancers, the Oxford Morris Men, and the North-West Morris team from Garstang who insisted, while taking their turn chairing the mayor, in performing their processional dance. They managed very well as it happened, but the mayor was unable to conceal his alarm.

Ten years earlier they had had the nice idea of inviting the other traditional Cotswold Morris sides. It must have been one of the very few occasions when all four have been seen together. I just happened to be there that year, 1973, and it is the only time I have ever seen the Chipping Campden men dancing.

So much for the Cotswolds. This is not the only kind of morris dancing; there are two distinctly different types in Derbyshire and the North-West. The Derbyshire Morris is a sort of buffer tradition between the other two and is now represented by only one side, in Winster. Their style leans towards the south, though their appearance and numbers towards the north-west. They have a formidable basic side of sixteen dancers plus four 'characters' and a musician who plays the concertina. They wear whites but have the unusual practice of decorating themselves with whatever baldrics, sashes, rosettes or flowers take their individual fancy. They come out on Wakes Saturday in Winster, towards the end of June.

North-West Morris is distinctly different and is not much seen outside Lancashire and Cheshire, which is a pity since it is exciting and spectacular. Teams invariably wear extravagant costumes, hats covered with flowers, broad, bright sashes and cummerbunds, knee breeches, stockings and clogs. The clogs are of the type once worn all over the North, with wooden soles and heels, and heavy black-leather uppers. There are usually eight or ten dancers in set pieces but their characteristic processional dances can include any number. I have seen a photograph showing thirty-four taking part in a parade. Performances are very vigorous, a little regimental, with much stepping and stamping of feet and twirling of slings or short batons. A peculiarity of North-West Morris is the habit of dancing figures rather than established dances; each team has an extensive repertoire of its own figures which the leader calls out, by number, during the actual performance, so neither spectators nor dancers know what is going to happen next. A friend assures me that 'it keeps us on our toes'. The whole effect is much more weighty than Cotswold Morris and they are usually accompanied by a small band (rather than a single musician), consisting of concertinas or accordions and a bass drum. At Bacup they turn out with a whole brass band, but without a drum.

The popularity of this style of dancing has had its fluctuations. It was at its height in the last twenty years or so of the nineteenth century, declined up to the First World War, came back briefly in the 1930s, and has suddenly become popular again in recent years. No team has survived throughout, except Bacup which is not like the rest anyway, as we shall see later. Four new teams started up during the late 1960s, one of which was Garstang, tormentors of the Mayor of Ock Street, and they are all flourishing now.

The Manley Morris Dancers were formed in 1934. Manley is a village six miles north-east of Chester. Recently the dancers have established an annual appearance on the pedestrianized streets of the city in May 'on a Saturday close to Rogationtide', but it was in October 1984 that I saw them there, in the midst of their Golden Jubilee celebrations. Fifty years of dancing will qualify them for inclusion here.

The team was started by Dorothea Haworth, who ran a country dance club in Manley. She was often asked to provide display dancers for local functions, but did not consider social dances suited to this purpose. She thought a fine team of morris dancers would be much better and was lucky to get hold of Bob McDermott from Royton to train one up for her. Bob remained trainer and 'conductor' until he died in 1962. He was succeeded by Dorothea's brother, Leslie, a significant change since Bob was tiny, not much more than five feet tall, and Leslie was a giant with a big white beard. The present leader is Arthur Webb who has been with the team for the whole fifty years, along with two others, Albert Fletcher and their concertina player, Caleb Walker.

The team made a fine sight with their red and blue sashes, yellow cummerbunds, clogs with bright red laces and tall narrow-brimmed hats covered with tin badges and plastic flowers, as they passed along the ancient streets of Chester, adding authentic atmosphere for delighted tourists and Saturday-morning shoppers. There were eight dancers in the team, plus the leader, two centre dancers, who are young boys, and a band of two or three concertinas, a side drum and a big bass drum. After lunch there were two more concertina players in civvies.

The Britannia Coconut Dancers, from Bacup, though definitely a North-West Morris team, are, in fact, the exception to most of the foregoing rules. We can forgive them for this since they provide on Easter Saturday the most astounding dance occasion in the entire Custom Calendar. They are the only genuinely old traditional team going, though there are a number of others approaching acceptable antiquity.

We first went to see the Britannia Coconut Dancers on Easter Saturday in 1964. Arriving in Bacup in the late morning I was not able to find them. It was raining heavily; depression was everywhere in the gloomy little mill town on the edge of the desolate Pennine moors; the mills were in trouble, rehabilitation had not yet reached that part of Lancashire, even the people were dressed in unrelieved dun. Bacup has perked up no end now, but then I was reduced to wandering disconsolately about wondering what disaster had caused the cancellation of this famous dance custom. Gradually, I became conscious of a band playing amid the roar of buses and lorries. At first it was hard to be sure, but suddenly I spotted them plodding down the centre of the road in single file, dressed funereally, seven of them, with a stout man on bass in the lead, tapering to thinner men with smaller instruments at the end. On either side of the road there were four strange-looking figures, and another anxiously controlling traffic with a long whip. As the band made its inexorable progress the dancers appeared to be performing a processional dance; one group ran along their side of the road, 1–2–3–skip, 1–2–3–skip, while the other observed a little ritual dance on theirs. Then the runners stopped to dance and the dancers set off to run, and so on until they were in the centre of town among the sodden shoppers. It was still raining, but the sun had come out; the Britannia Coconut Dancers had arrived.

Wherever I go, whatever I do I will never forget my first sight of this extraordinary group of dancers, with their blackened faces, black fishermen's sweaters, black breeches, black clogs decorated with gleaming brass studs, white stockings, white skirt with red hoops, shapeless white hats decorated with red, white

Britannia Coconut Dancers divide into two groups of four to perform their processional dance along the road.

and blue rosettes, pompoms and blue feathers. Each wore five wooden discs, one on each knee, one in each palm, one at the waist, which they knocked in complex rhythmic patterns as they danced. These discs are the 'coconuts', in reality bobbin tops from the cotton mills. The man with the whip is 'the Whiffler'. His original job was whipper-in, to keep the dancers up to the mark, but now his no less important role is to save his friends from being run over.

Apart from the processional dance, which is particularly impressive in a long street of mill workers' houses, they have several others, of two distinct types. 'Nut' dances include quite complicated figures with the added problem of their tattoo with the wooden discs. 'Garland' dances are performed with each dancer holding a flexible semi-circular hoop completely, and thickly, covered with red, white and blue tissue paper. The garland dances are cheerful and lively, and much less strange than the nut dances.

It is not known for sure how old the Bacup dance is. Romantics claim all kinds of origins for it, some suggesting that miners brought it with them from Cornwall when they came north looking for work. Current research points out that Cornwall has nothing remotely like this, puts Bacup firmly into the North-West Morris tradition, though in a sub-group of one. Apparently, there were similar teams in the area before the First World War. *British Calendar Customs* quotes a 1908 newspaper: 'Last Easter but one witnessed the jubilee of the cocoa-nutters Morris Dance which was founded at Bacup in 1857.'

They are based in Britannia, a village at the top of a long hill out of Bacup on the road to Rochdale. It is here that they start their day, at nine in the morning, gradually working their way towards town, calling at pubs, estates, the fire station, the old people's home, dancing in the street, in convenient open spaces. Everywhere faces appear at windows as they pass by, accompanied by their army of admiring, but sometimes tiresome, followers who come to see them from all over Britain. They arrive in the town centre about lunchtime, and then set off in the afternoon in the general direction of Stacksteads where they finish by about 7 o'clock. At one time it was a matter of honour to do *every* pub in Bacup, a formidable task, but the current team consider ten hours' worth is enough.

For all the eighteen years I have known the team, up

Handsworth Sword Dancers outside the parish church in 1965.

to 1982, when I last saw them, their leader was a courteous, kindly man called John Flynn, who died in December 1983. John was an excellent illustration of the effectiveness of folk disguise. He was known to thousands in his shiny black make-up; in his everyday clothes, with his horn-rimmed glasses and wavy white hair it was impossible to believe he was the same person. He would not let standards slip for a moment. Nor would any amount of gold have induced him to allow his beloved 'nutters', in the mid-1970s, to accept the offer of a starring part in a potato crisp commercial, with the company name emblazoned on their costumes.

One other important point about North-West Morris is that this is the only English ritual dance tradition of which women are a long established part. Records of female and mixed teams go back well before 1900 and there are several going today. The proliferation of women's Cotswold Morris sides is very recent.

If morris dancers bloom in the spring and summer, sword dancers come out in the winter. The English sword dances are absolutely different from the Highland variety in which crossed swords are placed on the ground and the dancer steps between the blades. The English carry their swords, each man holding on to that of the next to form a continuous chain. There is no need to be concerned; the swords are not sharp, indeed they are not swords at all, but strips of flat unsharpened metal. They dance their figures linked together, usually culminating in a sword 'lock' which is displayed to the astonished spectators by the leader. A lock is formed of the swords plaited together to make an arrangement which will not fall apart when held up by a single point. There are several complicated intertwining figures which result in different locks. Music is provided by a fiddle, concertina or accordion. These characteristics are common to all kinds of English sword dancing. However, there are two distinct types: 'Longsword' and 'Rapper'.

Longsword dancing is native to Yorkshire. The 'swords' are about three feet long, made of stiff, flat strip steel about an inch wide. There are usually six dancers plus one or two 'characters'. The dance is fairly deliberate, but requires considerable skill to execute the complicated figures with graceful aplomb.

There are two traditional teams near Sheffield, at Handsworth to the east, and Grenoside to the north, and a third at Goathland on the moors near Whitby. There are also several newer teams, of which Loftus is a noteworthy example. Dress is variable but usually of a vaguely military aspect, possibly because the dancers themselves thought that that was where the tradition originated. Folklorists reject this notion; in fact the longsword dance was part of the version of the folk play performed in this area, as described in Chapter 13. The actual play has vanished, though the ritual decapitation of one of the characters in the sword lock is still part of the dance in most places.

It is just possible to see two fine longsword dance teams on Boxing Day if you are a fast driver, and can find your way across Sheffield. The Grenoside team come out at 11 a.m., perform their dance once only, outside The Harrow, and then go on, for reasons best known to themselves, with a programme of Cotswold Morris dances. Grenoside is about three miles north of the city centre, Handsworth is the same distance to the east. They come out a little earlier, but perform three times, the last being outside the parish church at midday, so it is usually possible to pick them up there. It is worth the effort because the two traditions are surprisingly different.

Grenoside dress in smart red tunics, not plain but of good strong furniture fabric in a paisley pattern, white trousers with a broad red stripe, and black school caps trimmed with gold braid. They wear clogs on their feet, a carry-over from the quarries in which most early Grenoside men would have worked. Their Captain wears a fox fur hat with the head at the front. For those with a taste for minutiae, the fur is mounted on an army officer's pith helmet with 'Army and Navy Stores' still printed inside. When the group reformed after the Second World War, from the remnants of two others, the 'old' team and the scouts team, the old Captain, by now too old, refused to give up his hat, which was made of a hare skin mounted on a policeman's helmet.

The hat is important. The dance is a survival of the death and resurrection theme; during the dance when the dancers form their lock it is placed over the head of the Captain for him to be 'decapitated' by having his hat knocked off. This occurs towards the beginning of the performance, and the rest of the dance is in order to resurrect him.

A quite lengthy song survives, too, with which the Captain introduces the dance in true folk play tradition. The first and fifth verses are:

> Ladies and gentlemen, I'll have you make room
> Contented a while for to be
> It is I and myself that hath brought us along
> And my trade you will quickly see.
>
> Since that we have all come hither
> Fiddler draw thy strings, advance
> Play beside us, here to guide us
> And these lads will show you a dance.

The dance itself, performed to a fiddle, is livelier and faster than most longsword dances and includes 'stepping' throughout, as in 'rapper' performances. Towards the end the Captain bursts into song again for a single verse, before being joined by the whole group. There is another short spell of dancing before the end. The whole performance takes about ten minutes. Then into the car and off to Handsworth.

Here there are eight dancers who perform to the music of a melodeon, and sometimes a concertina and a tin whistle as well. The dress is an imposing military uniform, generally agreed to resemble most closely that worn by the Light Dragoons in 1825. They are entirely black and white except for maroon cuffs and hats. Their jackets are black velvet, with wide white braiding down the front. Their trousers are white and they wear black leather gaiters and heavy boots.

These boots make a characteristic stamping as they dance, keeping an even pace throughout in spite of the tune changes which accompany the various figures. Geoff Lester, in his informative booklet about the team, describes it as 'a rhythmical jog-trot with heavy emphasis on the right foot'. They are very impressive to watch, their smart uniforms appearing to inspire parade-ground precision in their dancing. In recent years, to reward the faithful for coming to see them, they have expanded their performance to include a mumming play and a few Christmas carols as well as their unique dance.

Away on the other side of the county, all of Yorkshire being one in sword dancing circles, there is another traditional team which comes out on the Saturday after Plough Monday, which, as everyone knows, is the Monday after January 6. It was once the custom to parade a plough around villages on that Monday to promote good crops in the future, and some money forthwith, for the party of Plough Bullocks, Plough Jags or Plough Stots involved ('Stot' is an old English word for bullock). This practice was common in the eastern counties of England, where a version of the folk play, known as the Plough Play, also flourished. Sword dancing was part of the play. Thus, it has come to pass that the sword dancers of a moorland village seven miles south of Whitby are known as the Goathland Plough Stots.

Though the Goathland men no longer take their

Grenoside Sword Dancers about to 'decapitate' their Captain by knocking off his fox fur hat with their sword 'lock'.

plough around with them, it is not too long since they did; now they take it to the parish church to have it blessed on the previous Sunday. When I first made enquiries in the 1960s, the Goathland custom had lapsed; their then leader, Mr Scarth, a waiter in one of the village hotels, told me he simply could not raise a team. However, he must have managed it soon afterwards for they were alive and well through the 1970s and by 1980, when I went back, they were able to field *three* teams on the day, even if one was for young boys, given blunt wooden swords for the occasion.

The boys were dressed in blue and white striped tunics. The youth team and the adults both wore a casual mixture of light blue and pink tunics, and the adult team wore red commissionaire-type caps. At 10.30 a.m. the whole lot of them gathered outside the Goathland Arms for the first performance of the day. They danced together, attended by an assortment of 'Bettys', fools, scarecrows and musicians. It was all very casual, indeed the whole day was very relaxed.

After some communal dancing in the centre of the village, the main team went off by themselves. They went all around the neighbourhood calling at houses and pubs, dancing in gardens. The villagers were delighted to see them but there were no crowds of visitors on the streets. The six dancers were accompanied by a 'Betty', dressed up in a shawl, a long skirt and a fetching hat but still every inch the jovial, local butcher. Their leader was a Butcher too, by name Ron, a builder. It was the Betty's lot to be decapitated in the lock, though joviality was a little strained at this time as he was anxious about the expertise of one or two of the dancers. The basic dance is similar to the other two places except that the style of doing it is quite different. The dancers wore their own everyday shoes so there could be no stamping or step dancing. It had a decorous quality, a kind of indoor feel, a holding back lest the floor should get damaged. This dance is catergorized as being one of the 'Cleveland family'.

Just ten miles away to the north-west the Loftus team dance in a very similar way. This is a very fine team, first prizewinners at Llangollen in 1953. They were formed in 1950, and their dance is based on published evidence of the former Loftus tradition.

The rapper dance belongs exclusively to the miners of Northumberland and Durham and differs greatly from the longsword dance though it must have derived from it originally, probably not much more than a hundred years ago. This dance is performed at breakneck speed by just five dancers wearing clogs or tap dancing shoes. In between the intricate figures they induge in a burst of frantic step dancing. Their swords are much shorter, of flexible steel with a handle at each end. There is a suggestion that these approximate to the real implements used for scraping coal dust and sweat from pit ponies. The word 'rapper' was used in coal mining for a special signal lever used to give a warning that a conveyor was ready for use. It has also been mooted that 'rapper' came from 'rapier'; certainly in one place in Yorkshire the longsword dance was known, in the last century, as the 'rapier dance'. Another mystery.

Whatever the derivation of the name, the fact is that the rapper dance is so spectacular and challenging that many morris sides take it up for the sheer pleasure of mastering it. In 1984 I saw a group of *American* morris dancers perform it. There is only one traditional rapper team that turns out regularly, the Royal Earsdon Sword Dancers. The High Spen team is intermittent; the Monkseaton team, though formed in the 1950s, is probably the best known.

The Helston Furry Dance is most celebrated for the music to which it is danced. Apart from its excellence, which is not in dispute, two renderings of it are inclined to drive Helstonians mad with rage. The real music is traditional, but in 1906 Katie Moss used it for her song 'the Cornish Floral Dance', later immortalized by Peter Dawson. What annoys them is that it has *never* been a 'Floral' dance, but a 'Flora', 'Furry' or 'Faddy' dance. While the day is often called Flora Day, the *dance* is invariably called the Furry Dance. 'Faddy' was once common, but is becoming obsolete. The other rendering which irritates Helstonians is the one which reached the top of the hit parade not so long ago, played not by their own Town Band, but by a lot

Helston Furry Dance winding its way through the narrow streets of the town.

of foreign opportunists from Yorkshire.

Flora Day is a tremendous occasion in Helston. The town is decorated overall with bunting, flowers and greenery, and all inhabitants wear their spray of lily of the valley. Nobody knows exactly how old the dance is or when it assumed its present structured form. It is thought to have been an ancient May ceremony which became mixed up with the feast of St Michael, patron saint of the parish, which is on that day, May 8. In 1790 the *Gentleman's Magazine* wrote:

> About noon they assemble and dance hand in hand round the streets, accompanied by a fiddler, and thus continue till it is dark; this is called a 'Faddy'. In the afternoon, the local gentry go to some farm house and have tea, sillabub and other refreshments, and then return in a Morris dance to the town and dance throughout the streets till it is dark, claiming a right to go through any person's house, in at one door and out at another. Here it used to end, but corruptions have crept in, by degrees, for the gentlemen now conduct their partners, elegantly dressed in white muslins to the ballroom, where they finish their dance and, after supper, faddy it to their respective homes.

Dancing is still the main occupation of the day but now it is highly organized, as it has to be with over 1000 taking part and fifty times that many in the town to watch. There are four dances during the day, at 7 a.m., 10 a.m., noon and 5 p.m. They are all very long processional dances led by the hardworking Helston Town Band, but each follows its own particular traditional route, not only through the streets but also through houses, shops, offices, gardens and round the bowling green. The dance is rudimentary; couples step forward for a couple of bars hand in hand at shoulder height, the lady to the right; then they grasp the other hand and gracefully dance for a couple of bars. That is all there is to it. The only problem is that it goes on for an hour and a half or more, exhausting on a warm day, a lifetime on a wet one.

For all its simplicity a certain amount of discipline is expected. Displays of spontaneous abandon are not frowned upon because they do not happen. The whole business is taken with the utmost seriousness, but it is also a joyous and spectacular event. Like all really good customs, it has evolved over centuries; this one has evolved in an untypical way.

The Early Morning Dance begins at 7 a.m. This was once, specifically, the Servants' Dance so that they could have their fun and still be on parade when the gentry came down to breakfast. Now it is danced by the young men and women of Helston, the men in white shirts, dark trousers, identical black and white ties, the girls in smart dresses of their own choice. They perform with decorum, of course, but with youthful liveliness. It is the best dance to see, if you can manage to get there at that hour of the morning.

Also, it is possible to see what is going on, which it manifestly is not during the other three dances.

By the time the Children's Dance begins at 10 a.m., Helston is full. This dance was introduced in 1922 and has grown to many times the size of the others with 700 or more kids taking part, all dressed in white, the girls with flowers in their hair. Of course they all want to take part, but frankly it gets a bit of a shambles because they cannot hear the music!

The Principal Dance sets off from the Guildhall as the clock strikes twelve. In another dramatic change of character, the Furry Dance becomes a splendidly imposing procession by guests from a Buckingham Palace garden party, the ladies in extravagant hats and colourful dresses, the men in immaculate morning suits and grey toppers. This last convention must be comparatively recent, but still it always seems to have been the thing to dress for the Furry Dance.

Edward Cunnack, Chairman of the Stewards for many years, said that in the past there was no argument that the Principal Dance was strictly for the gentry, 'but today it is by the invitation of the Stewards'.

The last dance is at 5 p.m. This one used to be for the town tradespeople; everyone had their turn. Now it is led by the Early Morning Dancers, but this time everyone is allowed to tag on at the end, spectators, Helstonians, 'grockles' (visitors), and all.

The Abbots Bromley Horn Dance has caused folklorists, local historians and scholars more anguish than any other custom in this book. In spite of exhaustive research they have no idea how, why or when this completely unique ritual arrived in a comparatively obscure village half-way between Burton upon Trent and Stafford.

At 8 a.m. on the Monday after the first Sunday after September 4, the horn dancers collect six ancient sets of reindeer horns from the parish church, then, accompanied by 'Maid Marian', a fool in jester's costume, a hobby horse, a boy with a crossbow, another boy with a triangle, and a musician who plays the accordion, they tour the parish, dancing outside houses and pubs and nearby Blithfield Hall, until well after dark. They dance countless times during the day and walk in single file between places, often not even pausing before or after a performance. It is an exhausting routine, said to be about twenty miles, though I do not believe it can be *that* far. Last century they used to cover over thirty miles but they took four days to do it.

The dance itself is extremely simple. There are no intricate steps to be mastered, which would be difficult in any case because of carrying the heavy horns. They come on in single file, form a circle, then a kind of figure of eight which culminates in two facing lines of three. These lines approach, retreat and pass through each other somewhat in the manner of a fight. Finally, they form the circle again and walk off. The horns are supported on the shoulders with the head just below the dancer's chin.

It is not just the origins of the dance, it is also the horns that cause such puzzlement. It is a long established but unwritten rule that the horns must never leave the parish but in 1976 it became urgently necessary to repair one of them. A friend of mine, Teresa Buckland, become involved in this and, with the permission of the leader of the dancers and the vicar, took the opportunity to get the antlers carbon dated. She set out her findings in *Lore and Language*, January 1980. 'This gave a mean date AD1065 plus or minus 80 years'. Scrupulously fair, as ever, she points out that this proves nothing except the age of this particular set of horns; the others may be different, the dance may be much younger, or for that matter, much older. Then there is the problem that they are *reindeer* horns of a species extinct in Britain centuries before that date. So where did they come from? Tess sets down the various existing theories, and sums up, 'Scandinavia appears the likeliest home for the antlers, although why they should be taken to a village which does not appear to have been of any great political or economic significance is a mystery'.

Each set of horns is set into a carved wooden deer's head and mounted on a short pole, which is for the dancer to hold. Experts have pronounced the woodwork to be sixteenth century. All the heads are painted brown, three of the horns are also brown, the other three off-white. The darker set have apparently seen several changes of colour and are known by the dancers as 'the blue horns'. The leader of the team, by tradition, carries the largest set, 39 inches from tip to tip, weighing $25\frac{1}{4}$ pounds. The lightest set weighs $16\frac{1}{4}$ pounds.

As for the dance, the favoured theory seems to be that it celebrated, or possibly encouraged, a successful hunt. There is a song in *As You Like It* (IV, iii), written in 1593:

> What shall he have that killeth the deer?
> His leather skin and horns to wear.
> Then sing him home.
> Take thou no scorn to wear the horn!
> It was a crest ere thou wast born:
> Thy father's father wore it
> And thy father bore it
> The horn, the horn, the lusty horn
> Is not a thing to laugh to scorn.

Abbots Bromley Horn Dancers on the lawn of Blithfield Hall.

The first reference to this specific dance is in 1686. The costumes they wear look authentically ancient but they were, in fact, invented by the daughters of the vicar in 1860. Before then they wore their everyday clothes. I must say the Misses Lowe did a remarkable job, for the washed-out browns and greens and the floppy brown berets add a wonderfully foresty flavour to the event. Obviously they have had to be replaced from time to time but they have always kept closely to those original designs. The current set were made in 1948 by theatrical costumiers in London.

The day has extraordinary atmosphere, even with a good number of twentieth-century followers in close attendance throughout. If you are lucky enough to get a glimpse of this group performing in their natural habitat, without surrounding jeans, cameras, videos, cars, even ordinary human beings, the effect is positively mediaeval.

Members of the Fowell family are said to have been involved for over four hundred years. The present leader is Tony Fowell, in his mid-30s, and a lorry driver from Uttoxeter, who succeeded his late lamented father, Dennis, in 1982, and who looks disconcertingly like him. Douglas Fowell has been their musician for years. In 1982 there were two others taking part, Gary and Neil, as well as assorted cousins and in-laws. They are all extremely proud of their connections with this unique tradition, all ready annually to take a day off work, unpaid, to take part. Family solidarity has been helpful now and then when they have had to fight off take-over attempts from the village, also intensely gratified to be the home of Europe's oldest dance.

In fact, the Fowells have an unexpectedly relaxed attitude towards the whole business. They never hesitate to put in Fowell girls if they are short of men, which causes purists to tut-tut like battery hens, and it is their amiable habit to invite the occupier of whichever establishment they are performing outside to join them in a dance. I have seen them dance with many a buxom barmaid, the local doctor and, on one memorable occasion, three policemen in uniform. The music is a surprise as well; it is not traditional at all, but modern standards which happen to take Doug's fancy.

You'll never walk alone

Processions are part of many of the events in this book; this is a chapter about customs in which the procession *is* the event.

The Lord Mayor's Show in London is probably the best known, and the most impressive. Although apparently little more than an annoying commercial extravaganza which causes traffic chaos on the second Saturday of November, it does have an interesting and very ancient history. Furthermore it is a statutory obligation.

In 1215 King John granted a charter to the City of London giving the right to elect a mayor each year on condition that he should present himself to the Sovereign, or to his representative, for approval, and to 'swear fealty'. This condition is still the primary reason for the Lord Mayor's Show, for he is making his formal visit to the Law Courts to make his declaration before the Judges of the Queen's Bench. It is the first official engagement of his year in office, following his election on Michaelmas Day, September 29, and his swearing-in at the Guildhall on the day before the procession.

Though the title *Lord* Mayor has never been specifically granted he has been addressed thus since the beginning and, while in office, signs documents like a real Lord, with his surname only followed by 'Mayor'. He is head of the oldest municipal corporation in the world and, in the City, ranks above everyone in the land except the Queen. Thus, the Lord Mayor of London is a very important person indeed and it is appropriate to make a spectacular show.

The whole occasion is a curious mixture of tradition, in the form of coaches, military bands, uniforms and dignitaries, and up-to-the-minute commercialism provided by well-known companies and organizations in the form of elaborate floats. It is true that these floats are, for the most part, of lighthearted design and manned by ordinary company staff on a day out, in funny costumes, but there is the inescapable impression of a mobile trade exhibition – which is, of course, intentional since tradition and commerce are two essential characteristics of the City of London.

The Lord Mayor himself rides in a magnificent coach designed by Sir Robert Taylor and built in 1757 by Berry and Barker of Holborn, at a cost of £1965. Manned by splendidly liveried coachmen, drawn by six fine shires belonging to Whitbreads, gleaming in the autumn sunshine, it is nevertheless said to be exceptionally uncomfortable. It can be seen throughout the rest of the year in the Museum of London.

In the procession the Lord Mayor is escorted by the Company of Pikemen and Musketeers of the Honourable Artillery Company (HAC), an impressive body of business and professional men dressed in the uniform of the original soldiers who formed the Company back in 1537. The HAC is part of the Territorial Army, with about 400 active members and 2000 veterans from whom the Pikemen are drawn. The HAC have always had City connections, though their participation in the Lord Mayor's Show is recent.

The first pageants were recorded in the sixteenth century. A feast was held in 1501, an addition to the procession which subsequently turned into the Lord Mayor's Banquet, now held on the Monday following the Lord Mayor's Show. It is an occasion of surpassing grandeur; it was not always so. In 1663 one S. Pepys attended:

> At noon I went forth, and by coach to Guild Hall and there was admitted. . .we went up and down to see the tables; where under every salt there was a bill of fare, and at the end of the table the persons proper for the table. Many were the tables, but none in the Hall but the Mayor's and the Lords of the Privy Council that

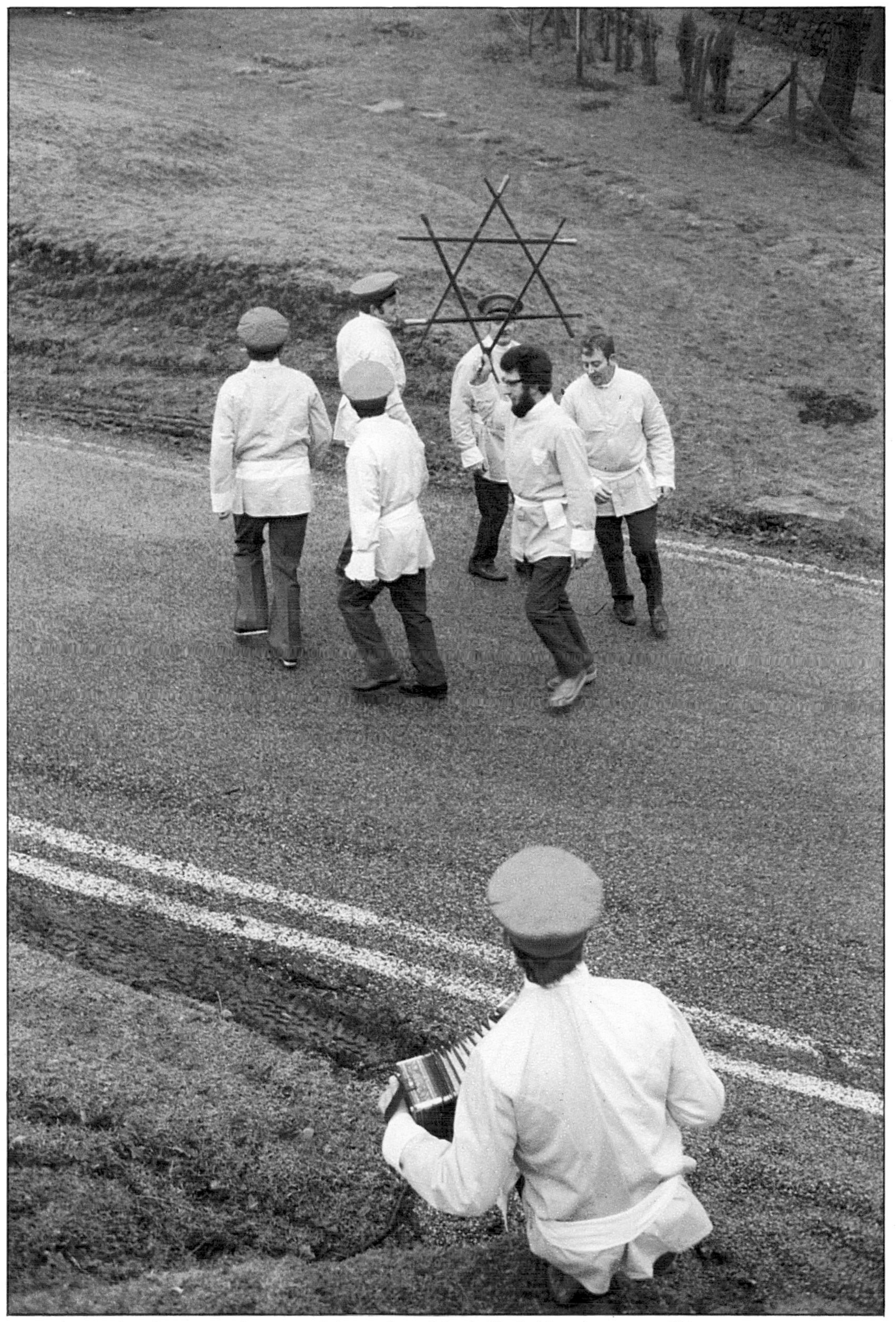

Goathland Plough Stots, a longsword dance from North Yorkshire. *(see page 48)*

The Manley Morris Dancers in the streets of Chester. *(see page 45)*

Warrington Walking Day is a vast 'Whit Walk' but in the middle of summer. *(see page 62)*

> had napkins or knives, which was very strange. . . Anon comes the Lord Mayor, who went up to the Lords, and then to the other tables to bid welcome; and so all to dinner. I sat. . .at the Merchant Strangers' Table; where ten good dishes to a messe, with plenty of wine of all sorts, of which I drunk none; but it was very unpleasing that we had no napkins nor change of trenchers and drunk out of earthen pitchers and wooden dishes. . .After I had dined, I and Creed rose and went up to the lady's room, and there stayed gazing upon them. But though there were many and fine, both young and old, yet I could not discern one handsome face there; which was very strange. . .I expected musique, but there was none only but trumpets and drums, which displeased me. . .Being wearied with looking upon a company of ugly women, Creed and I went away, and took coach and through Cheapside, and there saw the pageants, which were very silly. . .

We now take a taxi and to Upper Thames for an altogether more accessible little procession.

The Vintners are eleventh in the order of precedence of the ninety-four City livery companies but first in this book since two of their ceremonies are included. It would be absurd to suggest that the others had no ceremonial; it is simply that it goes on behind closed doors, for members and honoured guests.

The Vintners emerge, if briefly, at 11.50 a.m. on the second Wednesday in July (unless a more prestigious happening should occur to alter it) to cross Upper Thames Street from Vintners Hall to St James Garlickhythe for a service following the election of their new Master. The procession is led by the Bargemaster, Beadle, Stavesman and Clerk in ceremonial dress, followed by the new Master, three Wardens in caps and gowns, and his Court of Assistants. All carry nosegays and, to help them negotiate what was once a distasteful stretch of road, their way is swept clean with a broom by a Wine Porter in white smock and top hat.

Nosegays, which crop up in several customs, are posies made up of sweet- and strong-smelling flowers

The Vintners Procession. A Wine Porter sweeps the road with a broom for the Bargemaster, Beadle, Clerk, Chaplain, Master, Wardens and Court of Assistants.

and herbs. Long ago they were essential to those of delicate sensibilities to protect them from evil streets and the great unwashed; today we have less need for them, so they rarely appear, except on an occasion like this. They are an infallible sign of ancient origins.

The Wine Porter is of interest too. Vintners Hall which backs on to the river was once, but no longer, the actual warehouse into which wine was unloaded. The Wine Porters were appointed by the Vintners Company and had exclusive rights to handle wine in the Pool of London. As the Pool declined and new handling methods developed, numbers dwindled until they were finally disbanded in 1963.

Nineteen years later, Harry Draude, the last surviving Wine Porter, was wielding his broom for the twenty-fifth time while all the others present were wondering who would be doing it if he passed on. It was in this year, 1982, that Harry was much disconcerted to find his normal route barred by impenetrable roadworks, causing him to improvise a long diversion. Furthermore, it was pouring with rain, necessitating the addition of large black umbrellas to the usual regalia.

As for the age of this entertaining spectacle, it is certainly many hundreds of years old. Mr Taylor, the Beadle, claimed 'seven hundred years, easy', but I fear he was exaggerating since the first charter was granted to the Vintners Company on 15 July 1364.

A less ancient, but much more splendid spectacle can be seen at the Royal Hospital Chelsea, if not by everyone, at least by the relatives and friends of the famous Pensioners.

Strictly speaking, Founder's Day should be May 29, the anniversary of the day in 1660 when their 'Pious Founder', Charles II, was restored to the throne of England, but for many years it has been more convenient to hold it on a Friday morning in early June. The King, fleeing from the Roundheads after the battle of Worcester in September 1651, is said to have hidden in an oak tree at Boscobel House near Wolverhampton. Historians do not take this story too seriously, even if the incident is celebrated on a thousand 'Royal Oak' pub signs. Boscobel is doing very well out of it, and May 29 has for centuries been known as Oak Apple Day.

It is a busy day in the Custom Calendar, though few of the events have the remotest connection with the tree-climbing monarch. Most are spring customs, and some have to do with trees. Worcester remembers the King by covering the Guildhall gates with oak branches. This was once done with some ceremony and the people wore oak twigs and fixed them to their front doors. Today, a young lady in the Guildhall reports, 'Someone from the engineers' department does it early in the morning'. Northampton, too, used to show its gratitude to Charles II, who helped them recover from a disastrous fire in 1675, by a procession of the mayor and corporation and all the town's children carrying oak apples. Now they content themselves with placing a wreath of oak leaves around the neck of his statue at All Saints Church.

Easter is a busy weekend in London. Hampstead Fair is on throughout. On Sunday there is a parade in Battersea Park, with floats, clowns, and, frankly, not very exciting. Another parade can be witnessed on Monday morning in Regent's Park, altogether different and extremely entertaining.

The Harness Horse Parade, as such, is less than twenty years old but its pedigree is impeccable, the result of a union between the Cart Horse Society, founded in 1885, and the Van Horse Society, founded in 1904.

The original, and continuing, purpose of both was:

> . . .to improve the general condition, treatment and management of horses and ponies; to encourage those in charge of horses and ponies employed for transport purposes to take a humane and intelligent interest in their well-being, and to show a spirit of kindliness towards their animals; and to encourage and assist all those using horse-drawn transport to achieve a high standard of care and cleanliness.

There being little else but horse transport a hundred years ago, inevitably there were people who treated horses badly. To this day motorized commercial drivers are not noted for their finesse and there is no reason to suppose that their predecessors were, in general, any more considerate. Caring people were so outraged at the way horses were treated that, in the great tradition of Victorian Good Works, they formed the London Cart Horse Parade Society, with the formidable Baroness Burdett-Coutts as their first President. For their inaugural Parade in Regent's Park there were 150 entries. Soon they had to be limited to 1000 before declining, by the 1960s, to a disappointing 26. Their day was always Whit Monday.

When the London Van Horse Parade Society held their first show in the Park in 1904, it was on Easter Monday. From the beginning they attracted larger numbers, reaching an astounding 1259 in 1914. But they too fell victim to the internal combustion engine. In 1966 the two societies agreed to hold a single parade.

The Harness Horse Parade in Regent's Park is an engaging mixture of human 'characters' and equine specimens from tiny ponies to enormous shires.

The young may not realize what a long time it took to complete the change-over from horse to mechanized transport. Sainsbury's, for instance, bought their first two Foden Steam Wagons in 1907, but it was not until thirty years later that they finally said goodbye to their last horse and van. All through the inter-war period their then Chairman, 'Mr John', a passionate horse lover, regularly had comparative figures prepared to prove his point that horses were cheaper. It was only when his trade became enormous and his empire expanded beyond the limitations of horses that he gave in. The funny thing is, though, that for local light delivery or collection work horse-drawn transport is still the most economical, which is why there are regularly more than 300 entries for the present Harness Horse Parades.

Many of the rigs are in full-time work, though some are used more for publicity value, but an increasing number belong to private enthusiasts. The most engaging thing about the Parade is the astonishing variety of horses, vehicles and drivers. Mighty shires and Clydesdales tower loftily over tiny Shetlands, even the occasional donkey. London Trolleys, Pickering Floats, York Spinners, Norfolk Carts, Bradford Flats, English Victorias, Offord Spindle-Back Gigs, Well-Bottom Gigs, Spider Phaetons, French Waggonettes and Lincolnshire Hermaphrodites all gleam with loving care. Fresh-faced country girls drive happily alongside portentous bowler-hatted brewers' men and villainous looking totters.

Across the road from St Sepulchre's Church on the site now occupied by the Central Criminal Court, the Old Bailey, stood Newgate Prison. St Sepulchre's was connected to the prison by a tunnel through which, on the night before executions, a man walked tolling a bell and reciting a far from encouraging rhyme which ended:

> And when St Sepulchre's bell tomorrow tolls
> The Lord have mercy on your souls

The following morning, as prisoners were led out to

Tyburn Walk. Though they are invisible, there are at least 400 pilgrims stretching back down Oxford Street.

make their last journey, the Great Bell of Bailey in the Church Tower would toll solemnly and dramatically.

At 3 p.m. on the last Sunday in April, Roman Catholics gather on the pavement outside the church to make the walk to Marble Arch in remembrance of the 105 Catholic martyrs hanged at Tyburn during the Reformation. This is not a joyful procession, but solemn, devout and silent. At its head is carried a large wooden crucifix; a bishop is among the leaders. Rosaries are fingered, prayers whispered. Along the length of High Holborn and Oxford Street puzzled tourists stand aside and leave them to their devotions. There are two detours on the way, to churches in Ely Place and Soho Square. In 1984 about 400 made the two-and-a-half-mile pilgrimage, completed by a service in and outside Tyburn Convent at 5 o'clock. The convent is in Bayswater Road, only 200 yards from the site of the infamous gallows, now marked by a stone on the Marble Arch traffic island.

Public executions were held at Tyburn for 400 years until 1783. Some of the victims were notorious villains like Jack Sheppard or Jonathon Wild, most were petty criminals, but too many had committed no crime at all except that of being different, like the 105 Catholics.

Warrington Walking Day is a tremendous affair. In 1984 about 4500 children took part, plus adult clerics, choristers, bandspeople and parents making, perhaps, 6000 in all. The rest of the town, it seemed, turned out to watch. Most of the shops and offices were closed.

The Walk was started in 1832 by the rector, Mr Powys, as an alternative to Lachford and Newton races which annually, on the Friday nearest June 30, corrupted his parishioners. He sent the children on a 'procession of witness', no doubt reasoning craftily that their parents would be obliged to go too. His plan was so successful that the free churches joined in in 1857 and the Roman Catholics in 1920. The race meeting has long since disappeared from the calendar.

The Walk starts from the Town Hall at about 10 a.m. The place and time are central to the event. The Town Hall, a very fine house built by Gibbs in 1750, has a huge lawn in front, and wonderful golden gates. Before 10, parties are on their way in from all directions from their church or hall or headquarters.

Everything has been worked out carefully so that they will arrive on the lawn at the time which will put them in the right parade position. It is a miracle of organization. The mayor and mayoress are there too, to review the troops from a dais opposite the gates. Thousands of people line the streets, many very well set up with chairs and flasks of tea. There is a great party atmosphere.

After 10, the Walk begins. It takes an hour and a half to clear the lawn and the first walkers have toured the town and are on their way home before the last have even started. Most groups carry a banner and are led by a band. It is surprising how many kinds of bands there are – pipe bands, jazz bands, kazoo bands, whistle bands, American-style marching bands, even the odd brass or silver band, looking and sounding a little out of date among the razzmatazz. For this is a lively procession. Everyone is smart, most of the girls wear white, and lots of flowers are carried. Mr Powys would have been gratified.

Manchester has two Whit Walks, one for Protestants, one for Catholics, both of them even bigger than Warrington. At Cardiff there is a similar procession at Corpus Christi.

Religion was not the only motivation. In 1841 William Howitt wrote, in *Rural Life of England:*

> Clubs, or Friendly Societies, have substituted for the old church ceremonies, a strong motive to assemble in the early days of Whit Week as their anniversary; and the time of the year being so delightful, this holiday has, in fact, become more than any other, what May-day was to the people. Both men and women have their Friendly Societies, in which every member pays a certain weekly or monthly sum and on occasions of sickness or misfortune, claims a weekly stipend, or a sum of money to bury their dead. . .they were, and are often, the poor man's sole resource and refuge against the horror of falling on the parish, and have helped him through his time of afflication without burthening his mind with a sense of shame and dependance.
>
> Well then may they come together on one certain day. . .to hold a feast of fellowship and mutual congratulation in a common hope. . .Accordingly on Whit-Monday the sunshiny morning has broke over the villages of England with its most holiday smile. All work has ceased. . .Forth comes streaming the village procession of hardy men and comely women, all arranged in their best, gay with ribbons and scarfs, a band of music sounding before them; their broad banner of peace and union flapping over their heads, and their wands shouldered like spears of an ancient army, or used as walking staves. Forth they stream from their clubroom at the village alehouse.

This is almost exactly what happens, more than 140 years later, in Fownhope, near Hereford.

Their banner proclaims the Heart of Oak Friendly Society to have been founded in 1876 but one of their members, Lewis Haines, an expert on the subject, says that was the year the doctor's wife presented the banner and the club is much older. It was formed for male agricultural workers. Subscriptions have never been exorbitant; even today they stand at 7½p per week. Thus, lavish benefits are not to be expected and cases of extreme hardship are entitled to 75p. Friendly Societies survive mainly for social reasons but they have served their members well in the past. Employers liked them too, for they relieved them of some responsibilities.

Fownhope, naturally, chose May 29, Oak Apple Day. Sixty years ago they moved to the following Saturday, now it may sometimes be the one after that. At 4.30 a.m., Michael Andrews goes out into the woods to cut an oak sapling: 'I've done this for the last fifteen years or so. I know by now that I've got to go out in the days before to make sure I find one that's exactly right! But I can't cut it till the day or it would wilt.' He trims it and decorates it with ribbons, for later he will carry it at the head of the procession.

A little before 10 o'clock the members arrive at the New Inn, the village clubroom, arranged in their best, and carrying their club staves, each stave decorated with flowers and long enough to shoulder like a spear. Sixty or so of their 100 members usually turn out; in the past they were fined for not attending.

Led by Michael with his sapling, the banner and a fine silver band, the procession sets off for the church. During the service the same three hymns are always sung – 'Through the night of doubt and sorrow', 'Fight the good fight' and 'Onward Christian soldiers' – because long ago when few farm workers could read or write, one Reverend West insisted that they learn them. Afterwards the Club Walk continues around the village, calling on the vicar, the doctor and some other houses. At each place there is beer for all, the band plays, speeches of welcome are made and everyone has a very good time. Lunch is taken at The Green Man, eventually, after which club members are not expected to take too much interest in the fourteen Grand Stalls, the 'fantastic majorettes' on the school field, the Pole Fight to decide the strongest man or woman in the village, or the delicious meat from the pig which has been roasting since early morning.

The fishing industry, too, had its Friendly Societies and its Club Walks. There were several on the east coast of Scotland, though now only the one at Musselburgh survives.

'The Honest Town' is just to the east of Edinburgh, almost a suburb. The River Esk flows into the Firth of Forth here, dividing the ancient town from the part called Fisherrow, once a separate village. The harbour was built in 1700 and by the middle of the nineteenth century over sixty boats were working out of there. A very close community grew up; they were all fisher families, they married each other and cared for each other. Two Friendly Societies flourish here and their banners hang in the Scottish Coastal Mission Hall. Today only ten boats are based here, with work for fifty men but they bring their fish in elsewhere. The decline is general in Scotland, but is made worse in Fisherrow by the circumstance of only two hours of water on every tide. 'In the old days', one lady remarked, 'the women had to *carry* their men through the shallow water and mud so that they could go off all clean and dry. We could always go home and change.' But they are still 'fishers' here. Many of the men go off to work on other boats, and every family has connections with the industry.

So they can muster a good 400 for their Fishermen's Walk, first recorded 1768. There have been several stops and starts since then; in 1868 it was revived for its centenary, in 1968 it had to be revived again.

As the fishers always supported each other in bad times and in good times, when catches were big, they were happy to put money aside, in a box which is still in the Mission Hall. There are three locks on this box and three different people hold the keys. The most senior was the Boxmaster, who carried his on a sash. The money was used in the traditional way, to benefit the needy, but also to pay for this annual outing. Thus called Box Meeting Day.

The Walk is in two parts, divided by a tremendous party. It all begins at the Mission Hall, in New Street, soon after 1 o'clock. The outward walk is strictly segregated. The men and boys go first, even carrying boy babies. They look cheerful enough, but dignified, in their navy blue jerseys as they walk along behind a pipe band and their banner announcing 'Fisherrow Friendly Society – weel may the boatie row'. The ladies follow immediately. Led by another band, this

Club Day of the Heart of Oak Friendly Society at Fownhope is the biggest day of the year.

time brass, and their own banner – 'United Fishermen's Friendly Society 1868' – they look jollier, in their bright clothes and waving white handkerchiefs.

Musselburgh does not turn out in force, but is certainly glad to see them as they set off towards the harbour and walk right through the centre of town, along the mighty A1, to Pinkie House to have their party. It was here that I met Mrs Amy Orr, who told me:

> I used to sell fish from the creel – that's a big basket. I'd pick it up from the harbour and go off on the train to the place I used to sell it, walking round the houses. Did it for years and years until I gave up soon after the war. Started when I was 14.
>
> These are the traditional clothes. You don't get in here without them. The women wear a striped flannel petticoat and an apron called a 'brat'. They all wear them slightly different because there are different jobs we do – selling, net weaving or on the dock. All of us wear a 'Kirking Shawl'. The reason they are called this is that everyone used to get married on Friday, then they had to go to Kirk on Saturday and Sunday – and have the bridesmaids to supper on Sunday – and they wore this shawl, so it was a 'Kirkin' Shawl'. They were handed down from mother to daughter. This one belonged to my great grandmother and must be a 150 years old. The edging is made from the same stuff as the fish nets were at that time. Most of these clothes are old or parts of them are. Even the small children's are handed down.
>
> As for the men's jerseys, well, they're all different too. Fishwives always knitted, they had plenty of time. They're finer than the island jerseys but the patterns are similar. The designs mean things, you know, like trees and branches mean prosperity. All the new ones must have been knitted by the older women. The younger ones can't do it I'm afraid.
>
> We always have a wonderful time here, with dancing and talk. We see all our friends who come back each year. The best bit is the walk back to Fisherrow. There's often dancing and singing. We're all mixed up together then and the men wear the girls' shawls. It means a lot to a young girl if a man asks for her shawl, it's almost a proposal.
>
> Tomorrow's good too – all the post mortems! But tomorrow all the clothes are put away till next year.

The Fishermen's Walk in Musselburgh is a fine sight with the men in their navy blue jerseys and the women in their shawls and aprons. Some of the costumes are over 150 years old.

Music for a while

I first found out about the carol singing near Sheffield when I was enquiring about something else. 'Don't know anything about that,' people would say, 'but you must come and hear the carols before Christmas.' Intrigued, I investigated, only to find there were books and learned papers on the subject, and that the local newspaper had even produced a special supplement. In short, I was one of the few people in England not to have heard the news. The *most* learned paper, and, for that matter, the *Sheffield Star*'s Carols Supplement, were both written by Dr Ian Russell upon whom I have leaned heavily, and gratefully, for background information.

The *Star* lists thirty-four 'of the best places for carols' in an area mainly to the west of Sheffield, north as far as Penistone, south to Dronfield in Derbyshire. They take place in pubs, working men's clubs, convenient halls. They may be organized concerts with a pre-arranged programme, or spontaneous, though never *dis*organized, pub gatherings. They may involve choirs, silver bands, *ad hoc* collections of enthusiasts or the singing may be unaccompanied. A pub may have only one or two gatherings or several; two of the most famous, the Royal Hotel at Dungworth and the Blue Ball at Worrall, have carols every Sunday lunchtime between Remembrance Day and Christmas. On the other hand, a band may be particularly keen; in 1983 the Stannington Brass Band turned out *every day* from the 15th up to and including Christmas and Boxing Day but in different places.

I was told: 'Stannington once had a famous group of farmers. Sang in harmony. People used to walk miles to hear them. They would sing from twelve to one and then home to lunch. There were no women allowed then – they were at home where they belonged, cooking.' He shook his head nostalgically, 'By 'eck, that were t'real carol singing!'

These are not the carols of your local parish church, or King's College, Cambridge, nor the ones so often repeated on your doorstep. The giggling children who sing 'We wish you a merry Christmas' would be discomfited to be asked for verse two, and astonished to hear that in this part of Yorkshire it goes on, 'Now bring us some figgy pudding', then 'For we all like figgy pudding'.

Some familiar tunes have different words; likewise familiar words may have different tunes. An informant at Dungworth told me that here they have seven alternatives for 'While Shepherds Watched' and that once in a while they take it into their heads to sing them all. Ian Russell tells me that he has noted about twenty-five different tunes in South Yorkshire for this one carol, though no pub would be likely to use more than eight or ten. The most popular is 'Cranbrook', composed about 1800, requisitioned and handed down to you and me as 'On Ilkla Moor bar t'hat'.

Many of the carols are not holy – for that matter, many of the singers would deplore the suggestion that they were either – they are Christmas folk songs. 'The Christmas Tree' is a popular example. I heard this wonderful song at Dungworth sung by 77-year-old Wilf Daff, a fine and famous singer in the district. No one else would have the temerity to sing this at the Royal Hotel:

> Who comes this way so blythe and gay,
> Upon the merry Christmas Day,
> So merrily, so cheerily,
> With his peaked hat, and reindeer sleigh,
> With pretty toys for girls and boys,
> As pretty as you e'er did see,
> Oh this is Santa Claus's man,
> Kriss Kringle with his Christmas tree.
> Oh! Ho! Oh! Ho! Ho ho ho ho ho ho ho ho ho ho!
>
> The jingle, jingle, jing, jing, jing,

Carol singing in the Royal Hotel, Dungworth. There is not too much drinking for obvious reasons.

Right merry we shall be,
Yes jingle, jingle comes Kriss Kringle,
Come with your Christmas tree,
And welcome, welcome, welcome Kriss,
Right welcome you shall be,
Oh there he is, yes, yes, tis Kriss,
Tis Kriss with his Christmas tree,
The Christmas tree, the Christmas tree!

Being a folk tradition, rather than under the wing of the Church, these carols tended to be passed on orally resulting in many local variations. The *Star* gave the words of eighty-four carols, while books have been published recently with the repertoire from such places as Worrall, Bradfield, Stannington and Oughtibridge. This is a thriving tradition, expanding if anything, but changing as all good traditions must. Originally it was something which went on in homes and pubs, but now it is tending towards more formal concerts.

Mary Harper, of the Royal Hotel in Dungworth, has no misgivings about continuing the tradition in her bar. She is proud that her pub is one of the most famous; indeed, some experts name it the best, though others favour the Blue Ball at Worrall. Dungworth, though no more than five miles away from Sheffield city centre, continues to be unusually remote. It is not a place you pass through, but one you go to on purpose, if you know where it is. And the Royal Hotel is not impressive, as I am sure Mary would admit. Normally twenty or thirty would be a very good house; but on these Sunday lunchtimes maybe 200 find their way inside while the unlucky and those who suffer from claustrophobia have to stay in the street. The audience was a healthy mixture of local farmers, folk-song enthusiasts, choral singers, 'university types', even the local MP, on the day that I was there.

The resident musician that day was David Smith, who is also to be heard at the Three Merry Lads, Lodge Moor, on Saturday nights during the same period. Good musicians are in great demand. They are very important to a good session. Not only do they have to know the local repertoire and play well, they also have to have the personality to lead everybody, and the ability to extemporize the 'symphonies' which announce the carol and go between the verses. Even unaccompanied sessions need a strong, imaginative leader. Band accompaniments, on the other hand, need to be more organized.

There was no announcement of the carols; David simply played the introduction to the one he fancied, the initiated started singing, the uninitiated frantically searched through their books or supplements for the words. Everyone sang enthusiastically, and the beer, if you could get at it, was of secondary importance. It was a truly wonderful experience, worth a 150-mile drive any day.

In Dunster, near Minehead in Somerset, Jimmy Griffith told me he had sung their carols for years. His book of them contained eight. The most popular was curious:

> I hear along our street
> Past the minstrel throng
> Hark they play so sweet
> On their haut bois Christmas song.

A group of men used to go all around the village on Christmas Eve finishing at the Luttrell Arms at midnight with 'Good Christian Men Rejoice'. The hotel is the scene of another ancient Christmas custom, revived here in 1935, Burning the Ashen Faggot. Instead of the more conventional yule log, West Country people used a stout bundle of ash branches bound together with 'witheys', strips of ash like those used in thatching. As each withey burst in the flames another round of drinks was called and, at the Luttrell Arms, a carol was sung. But, Jimmy Griffith complained, 'They don't want to listen to carols these days. We manage to get in one or two but that's all. Anyway the old carol singers aren't around any more and we have trouble getting enough to go out. One of them died recently – he loved the carols so much he asked for his favourite to be sung over his grave.'

I heard the Reverend Geraint Vaughan-Jones, vicar of Mallwyd, near Machynlleth, talking about the *Plygain* on a radio programme, so I rang him up. He explained that the *Plygain* was held during a special evening service, usually in the first couple of weeks in January, and was very well attended. 'After the third collect I call *Plygain* and people come forward to sing – in Welsh, of course. The whole thing is impromptu. They sing in small groups, mostly trios and quartets, usually families, who tend to "own" carols and woe betide anyone else who tries to sing them. They always sing unaccompanied. Sometimes they're a bit bashful and there's a lull so I call for a regular hymn while they sort themselves out. On a really good night there can be up to thirty-five or forty carols. It can go on for a couple of hours.'

Originally this service was held long before dawn on Christmas Day; the word *plygain* is Welsh for 'cock crow'. People would walk through the night to be at church by the appointed time, perhaps 4 or 5 o'clock, to sing their carols by candlelight. Until the turn of the century the custom was observed all over Wales, in many places preceded by torchlight processions and lively Christmas Eve parties. Today it survives in a small area of Mid Wales, and at a less demanding time of day.

Further to our conversation Mr Vaughan-Jones sent me this letter:

> Dates for the *Plygain* are always set – either the day or the date – for example, at Llanymawddwy it is always on the 6th of January (the Epiphany), here at Mallwyd it is always the 13th – the octave, whereas Llanerfyl and Llanrhaeadr-ym-Mochnant both hold theirs on the first Sunday in the New Year and Llanfihangel-yng-Ngwynfa on the second Sunday. Most of them begin at 7 p.m. in these degenerate times! It used to be 5 a.m.
>
> *Plygainiau* are held now in the area bounded roughly by the valleys of Dyfi, the Banwy, the Vyrnwy and the Tanat. I think that nearly all the churches still hold *plygainiau*, and many of the chapels do so nowadays as well, although that is a fairly recent development, since in the last century the Dissenters regarded them as a relic of Popish superstition and preached against them.
>
> . . .It would be invidious of me to name any one church as the leading one, but the four or five mentioned are pretty representative, and usually manage to hold a successful *plygain* with a fair number present. . .

The Ripon Hornblower is not exactly musical but he deserves his place in this chapter because this is possibly the oldest civic custom in Britain. It is thought to be almost a thousand years old, and to have begun when King Alfred granted a Charter to Ripon in 886. Until 1604 it was the responsibility of the Wakeman to keep watch over Ripon during the night and he signalled the beginning of his duty by blowing the horn. In that year, the Wakeman, Hugh Ripley, became the first mayor under a new charter and the mayor officially took over this responsibility. He appointed subordinates to do the actual work, and a Hornblower to let him know that the watch was set. To this day, in addition to blowing a long blast at each of the four corners of the obelisk in the Market Square he has to go off and blow a fifth outside the mayor's house. The original charter horn is never blown; adorned with silver badges of former Wakemen, it is used only as regalia. It was replaced in 1690 by another horn which was itself retired in 1865 when the present horn was specially made. The sound it makes is a little disappointing; not a strident and deafening blast, but more a plaintive, mournful call. A certain amount of creativity is permitted, some Hornblowers favouring as long a blast as possible, others as loud, and others a medium length crecendo. Some blow with bravura, others with anxiety lest nothing should come out.

Derek Tyreman, Hornblower at Christmas 1982 when I was last there, told me that 'it's the very devil to blow when you're freezing cold. It's much easier in the summer. Tourists often ask if they can have a go. Not long ago a young lady asked. I handed it over thinking she'll never get a sound out of it but she played us a tune. She was a professional horn player!' Derek had held the office for four years then. His deputy, on duty on Boxing Day, had been doing it for two and a half years. He turned out to be an amiable American computer expert, grabbing a piece of old England and making it his own; and why not, since the job is advertised when vacant? Evidently this is fairly frequently. There are no ancient family traditions to keep up, the pay is just £1 per day plus 50p petrol allowance, while the inconvenience is in inverse proportion. Bainbridge, thirty miles north-west in Wensleydale, has a similar custom observed only during the winter months. They have no such problem since the Hornblower has been a member of the same family for over a century, but the newspapers were full of it in December 1983, when 11-year-old Alastair Metcalf was the latest member of the family to be appointed.

Dobcross, Delph, Diggle, Friezeland, Lydgate, Scouthead, Micklehurst, Grotton and Top Mossley are some of the exotically named places around Saddleworth which go mad on Whit Friday. This splendid day out is an amalgamation of two or more older customs. The churches in this part of the country have always liked their Whit Walks. The brass band movement is strong and they like their contests.

At Dobcross, where I happened to find myself, these events were losing their impetus but by some miracle Church, Chapel and Band managed to come together in 1967 to make The Dobcross United Whit Friday Effort. Other villages arrived at the same solution so that now Whit Friday is the big day of the year in all Saddleworth, that black stone-built area on the edge of the bleak and forbidding moor between Lancashire and Yorkshire. Indeed, Dobcross is so much on the border that the roses on the band uniform badge have alternate red and white petals, a declaration not lightly made.

The day is divided into two distinct parts; the morning is a classic Whit Walk, the evening a frantic, furious and quite unique band contest. At 9.45 a.m. the Dobcross Band appeared from their clubroom in Platt Lane, playing the first march of the day, 'Hail Smiling Morn', as they made for the congregational church to pick up the children and lead them into the Square. The vicar stood on the raised area outside the pub, the band below ready to play the hymns, everyone else in the street. After a short service a fine procession formed, led by the band, their four officials importantly in front, with the vicar, choirboys and girls, cubs and guides with posies, villagers and banners following off down the hill, along the bottom road, under Saddleworth Railway Arches and into Uppermill. Here a vast crowd was waiting in the High Street to see Dobcross and all the other processions arrive. It was essential to play well here, to put on an intimidatingly good show, to make it known who was going to win all the prizes later on.

On the playing field a huge congregation of children, bandspeople and others accumulated for an ecumenical service, conducted from a lorry trailer by an impressive array of clerics including a bishop, and a man having trouble with the public address system. After this, everyone took part in the same mighty procession as far as the Arches before dispersing in all directions back to their own villages. The Dobcross Band led their troops home by a much longer more exhausting route.

In the afternoon, there are games and sports and suchlike. Until a few years ago the bands were expected to give a concert during these events but they finally managed to convince everybody that it was too much to march all morning, do a concert all afternoon and win several contests all evening. Now they have a rest, a meal, a modest amount of beer, a little rehearsal perhaps, and gird their loins. They need to.

The contests start at 5 p.m. It is a little difficult for a non-playing outsider to understand exactly what is going on, so I asked Percy Woodhead, Chairman of the Dobcross Band, to sort it all out for me later.

In 1984 there were fifteen contests, one in each of the Saddleworth villages, the others nearby. These are not like big national contests, split into divisions and, taken deadly seriously, with money and prestige at stake. This is a completely unique occasion, but with enough fun and challenge to attract some of the world's finest bands.

Saddleworth Whit Friday. Dobcross Band.

Each contest is open to any brass or silver band. There are no entry forms; nobody knows who is going to turn up until they appear. They pay a 50p entrance fee then play strictly in the order they arrive. The bands march a short distance to the contest platform, led by an official bearing their name on a placard. The judge, lurking behind a curtain in some convenient spot, usually somebody's bedroom window, is not supposed to know who they are. They have ten minutes to play for him, and for the thousands of spectators enjoying the free show, any quick march of their choice. They then pack up and make off at high speed for the next village. Each contest has a first, second and third prize, one for the Best Local Band, one for Deportment; then there are special prizes here and there for things like Best Cornet, Best Youth Band, and so on.

The point is not just to win, but also to get around as many contests as possible before the 11 p.m. deadline. It takes skill and local knowledge to triumph. Each band rides around in a coach with a runner to organize things for them. Arriving at a contest, he rushes up to the contest secretary to sign in. If three or four bands are already waiting he has to decide whether to stay or dash off to the next contest. Some are more prestigious than others, and there may be a queue at the next one too. Very tricky. In 1984 the *British Mouthpiece* reported that one band only managed four contests, while one contest had no bands until nearly 7 p.m! Percy said that Dobcross got around nine villages, one down on the previous two years. He could not tell me what the record was, seeming to think that anyone claiming more than ten was surely lying. The local bands have the added problem that, traditionally, they play last in their own village contest – and this is not always easy to organize. The officials have their experts too, of course, for some can hear many more bands than others. In 1984 Dobcross heard 36, but one village managed a record 50. At the end of each contest the judge announces the results 'then everyone boos him, unless he awards first prize to the local band'.

Most of the bands are from the North, but one comes regularly from South Wales while the British Airways Band, based at Heathrow, has done very well on more than one occasion, to the chagrin of the locals. Currently as many as ninety bands can be

Saddleworth Whit Friday service at Uppermill.

expected, and in case you should think that these are just run-of-the-mill outfits you should know that in 1984 Brighouse and Rastrick won 4 Firsts and 3 Seconds; Wingates won 3 Firsts, 1 Second and 1 Third. Dobcross bagged 2 Seconds, 1 Third, 3 Deportments, 1 Best Local and 1 Best Basses.

Another kind of band assembles in Broughton, just south-west of Kettering, at midnight on the first Sunday after December 12. Nobody knows who will turn up or what instrument they will have chosen to play; everyone knows that for the next hour there is going to be a lot of noise.

For this is the annual appearance of the Broughton Tin Can Band, a body not entirely composed of the sort of youths one might expect, but including a couple of mums and some quite young children allowed out to join in the fun. I drove up through the rain from London to find about thirty people near the parish church clutching cans with stones inside to rattle, cans to beat with sticks, cans to beat against other cans, dustbin lids, anything potentially loud. At midnight they set off around the entire village.

Nobody knows why they do this, least of all the band. They only know that it has always been so. It is a strong tradition kept going even through the war by a token bandsman, and surviving legal attempts to suppress it. There is a definite feeling in the village that if they fail to do it once they must never do it again. It is said that the custom originated to scare away gypsies who persisted in camping nearby; the rector favours the quite different theory that it is connected to St Andrew's Day, November 30. The church is dedicated to St Andrew, thus the villagers are protesting at the interference with their feast day when the calendar was changed in 1752. Bang! Bang! Bang! 'Give us back our eleven days.' Bang! Bang! Bang! The band parades on the first Sunday after Old St Andrew's Day.

Whatever the explanation, this is a mad custom, if amusing and good natured. I suggested that their behaviour might possibly be considered bizarre but they pointed out that anybody who thought it a good idea to drive all the way from London on a foul Sunday night just to take a few snaps . . .

We are gathered together

The most striking characteristic these religious customs have in common, apart from religion, is their extraordinary charm. Aggression, fear, debauchery are hardly to be expected, it is true; but I simply did not expect to be so beguiled.

One of the most charming ceremonies takes place on the Sunday nearest to Candlemas, February 2, an important day in the Church calendar, the Feast of the Purification of the Virgin Mary and the Presentation of the Infant Christ at the Temple. The parish church at Blidworth in Nottinghamshire is dedicated to St Mary of the Purification and on that Sunday afternoon the parishioners symbolize these events with their Cradle Rocking service.

The parents of the most recently baptized boy baby in the parish bring him to the church. During the service they present him to the vicar. The vicar takes him to the altar and, holding him, recites the special 'Rocking Prayer'. He then places the baby in an ancient wooden cradle and, with the parents kneeling either side, and the other children present clustered nearby, he gently rocks the cradle while the general thanksgiving is said by the whole congregation. During the rest of the service the baby, all being well, sleeps quietly in the cradle. This enchanting little custom was revived in the church in 1922.

Since its revival it has continued annually without interruption, though apparently it is sometimes a problem to find an appropriate baby. The churchwarden told me in 1984 that they rely on the district nurse to keep them informed. Sometimes they have babies from other denominations though they still have to live in the parish. The chosen baby is always one that has been born around Christmas and often he is baptized during morning service on the day of the Cradle Rocking. That year the 'Rocking Baby' was Philip Simon Merry, born on Christmas Eve, a placid soul who slept throughout, unmoved by the occasion, unlike his parents who were bursting with pride. There is a board at the back of the church with the names of all the Rocking Babies since 1922. Several were present at the 1984 service, every one very proud to have been honoured.

The cradle is very old. It is made of wood which had been completely, and beautifully, covered with yellow and white flowers.

St Blaise's Day is at this time also, on February 3. This early Christian martyr died a horrible death around AD300 by having his flesh torn by iron combs such as are used to card wool. As a result of this unpleasant fate he became the patron saint of the wool industry, celebrated by impressive processions and events in towns where wool was very important. The wonderful diarist, Parson Woodforde, taking time off from detailing his gastronomic intake, described a fabulous procession in honour of St Blaise, on March 24, 1793: 'We were all highly delighted indeed with this Days Sight – it far exceeded every idea I could have of it. . . I never saw a Procession so grand and well constructed'. There were also annual celebrations at Colchester, Northampton, York, Bradford and elsewhere, but all these have now completely vanished.

On his way to prison St Blaise is reputed to have performed a few miracles, one of which was to remove a fishbone from the throat of a child who was choking to death. This made him also the patron saint of people with sore throats. This circumstance is celebrated in an unusual service at the Roman Catholic Church of St Etheldreda in Ely Place, Holborn, in London.

During the service two long candles are blessed and then tied together in the form of a cross. The priest calls the worshippers forward and places the candle cross under their chins, and bestows a blessing saying, 'May the Lord deliver you from the evil of the throat, and from every other evil'. The ceremony was originally intended for those suffering from genuine ailments, but now anyone who feels inclined can come forward.

John Stow was a remarkable man who died in 1605 and was buried at St Andrew Undershaft in Leadenhall Street, where there is a splendid monument to him. In his earlier days Stow was a tailor, and he later became an industrious historian best remembered for his *Survey of London*, the first substantial history of the City. He was a Freeman of the Merchant Taylors Company who erected the marble monument in 1905, replacing a terracotta one placed there by his widow. It shows Stow writing at his desk and is full of elaborate literary symbolism. Its most engaging peculiarity is that he is holding a real quill pen.

On, or near April 5, the anniversary of his death, there is an impressive ceremony to replace this quill with a new one. Until 1983 it was always the Lord Mayor in person who came to perform this task, but now it has been decided to alternate with the Alderman of Aldgate ward. A service sponsored by the Merchant Taylors and the Middlesex Archaelogical Society is held, and after the lesson the assembled dignitaries proceed to the memorial. The old quill pen is removed and handed to the verger, who in return supplies the new quill pen. The Alderman or Lord Mayor then places it carefully in the hand of John Stow, after which he himself is given a quill pen in a presentation box.

It used to be the custom to award the old quill pen to the pupil in a City school who wrote the best essay about London. All these winners are recorded in a book kept in the vestry of the church, but in 1974 it was not awarded 'there being no winning entry'. It has not been awarded since.

Incidentally, but relevant to this book, St Andrew Undershaft owes its peculiar name to a giant maypole which, until 1549, was erected annually beside the church. John Stow himself in his *Survey of London,* published in 1598, wrote:

> These great Mayings and May-games, made by the governors and masters of this city, with the triumphant setting up of the great shaft (a principal May-pole in Cornehill, before the parish church of St Andrew), therefore called Undershaft, by means of an insurrection of youths against aliens on May-day, 1517, the 9th of Henry VIII., have not been so freely used as afore. . .

Blessing the Throats at St Etheldreda's, Ely Place.

Two engaging thanksgiving services take place in London on the first Sunday in October. In the morning the Billingsgate Fish Harvest Festival begins at 11 a.m. in St Mary at Hill Church which is very close to the old market. Somewhat confusingly, the church is in Lovat Lane and not in the street called St Mary at Hill. Furthermore, the market moved east to West India Docks in January 1982 though this is still the market's 'parish church'.

Early in the morning a vanload of fish arrives to be laid out just inside the door of the church. In 1984 it took four men just over two hours to create an astonishing display. Three of these men were fishmongers, the other a Billingsgate porter. Fishmongers are favoured for this job since they do it every day, though never on this scale. One remarked, 'we counted fifty-four varieties of fish and shellfish – plus the four of us, of course, making fifty-eight'. Something like £500-worth of fish was donated by the Billingsgate Fish Merchants, which is one of the

John Stow with his new quill pen.

several organizations involved. The others in the trade are the London Fish and Poultry Retailers and the Billingsgate Porters. Two not in the trade are the officers of Billingsgate ward, including the Alderman himself, and the Church Army. The principal officers of all these attend the service. The Fishmongers Company, however, have nothing to do with it.

This unique Harvest Thanksgiving began in the 1930s. The Church Army approached the market and suggested it as a charitable exercise. Sam Sheppard, a former Superintendent of the market, told me they were delighted to agree. The occasion continues on the same basis; the Church Army still claims the fish and distributes it to the needy. I was grateful to accept a pair of dover sole myself, from the artistic fishmongers, who recognized my own unfortunate circumstances.

In the afternoon, at 3 o'clock, it is the turn of the Costermongers to hold their Harvest Festival at St Martin-in-the-Fields in Trafalgar Square, one of the best-known churches in London.

Costermongers are street vendors who sell fruit and vegetables. It is said their name derives from a variety of large cooking apples called a costard, once very common. They were regarded as the elite of the street vendors, a cut above the rest, and very snappy dressers. Everyone else was after their pitches, trying to steal their trade, and in time they evolved a system in which each borough had a leading costermonger family whose responsibility it was to protect the interests of the rest. These families became the Pearly Kings and Queens, their titles handed down from generation to generation to this very day. Their duties have changed, though, and now they devote themselves wholeheartedly to raising money for charity. They can be seen at many events in London, in their extraordinary suits encrusted with thousands of pearl buttons, the Queens and Princesses in extravagant feather hats, amiably posing for photographers, encouraging people to part with their money.

Harry Croft was 'The First of the Pearly Kings'. He died in 1930, and stands in effigy over his grave in St Pancras Cemetery in Finchley dressed in his pearly suit and a top hat. Though the Pearlies were recog-

The Ripon Hornblower has done his duty every night for almost a thousand years. *(see page 68)*

Broughton Tin Can Band; on a cold wet Sunday night who was madder, them or me? *(see page 71)*

Blidworth 'Rocking Baby' sleeping peacefully in his beautiful cradle. *(see page 72)*

The Costermongers' Harvest Festival.

nized as a powerful force before 1880 it was not until 1911 that they got together and formed an association.

The Costermongers' Harvest Festival was first held in 1923, appropriately down the Old Kent Road in a church which was destroyed in the war. Since then it has taken place in St Martin-in-the-Fields. It is the biggest gathering of Pearlies in the year. Well before 3 o'clock, some forty or fifty will be assembled outside the church, Kings, Queens, Princes, Princesses, Pearly Babies and the occasional Pearly Dog. They come bearing gifts, of fruit and vegetables, naturally, which will later be given to charity, and at the start of the service they enter the church in a splendid and colourful procession. Even the vicar has pearly vestments. The only problem on this occasion is the vast crowd of photographers and astonished tourists.

A similar difficulty is encountered at Holy Trinity, Dalston, at 4 p.m. on the first Sunday in February. There are no tourists, since none has heard of Dalston, but there are certainly photographers, for the congregation is, to say the least, out of the ordinary. This is the annual Clowns' Service, admittedly of more recent origin than almost anything else in this book, but still forty years old and too amusing to leave out.

The first Clowns' Service was held in 1946 in St James's, Pentonville Road, to commemorate the great Joseph Grimaldi who was buried there in 1837. This church was made redundant in the 1950s and since then the service has taken place in Dalston.

The number varies, but as many as fifty clowns have been known to attend, in full costume and make-up, a mixture of professionals and amateurs, the former a little patronizing to the latter, the latter subdued and humble in the presence of the masters. I hardly need to describe the service. Imagine for yourself pews filled with clowns praying, singing hymns, reading the lessons. In the middle there is a short ceremony at the memorial, at the end of which all the clowns say together,

> Dear Lord, I thank you for calling me to share with others your most precious gift of laughter. May I never forget that it is your gift, and my privilege. As your children are rebuked in their self-importance and cheered in their sadness, help me to remember that your foolishness is wiser than men's wisdom.

The service over, the congregation, and all the clowns, retire to the adjoining Church Hall for a wonderful free show.

During 1665 London was in the grip of the Great Plague. Official records state that 68,576 people died. Towards the end of that summer a consignment of cloth was sent from London to George Viccars, the village tailor in Eyam, Derbyshire. On September 7, Viccars had the misfortune to be the first victim of an outbreak which wiped out 267 in the village during the next thirteen months. It is generally accepted that fleas in the cloth carried the infection.

Though some fled at once the rector, William Mompesson, managed to persuade his parishioners that, though they themselves must accept the inevitable, they could at least save the rest of the district by completely isolating the village, agreeing not to leave and preventing outsiders coming in. Provisions were brought to the parish boundary; payment was left in a trough of vinegar. The scheme worked very well and the plague never did spread outside Eyam, but the result of their heroic sacrifice was that not one of the seventy-six village families survived intact. The rector's own wife, Catherine, died and her grave can be seen in the churchyard.

Enclosed gatherings of villagers being very unwise, the rector took to holding services in the open at a place which at once became known as Cucklet Church, a rocky, hilly, secluded spot just outsde the village. Every year on the last Sunday in August, a great procession leaves the parish church to wind through the lanes to this same place, now known as Cucklet Delph, to hold a Commemoration Service. It is a moving occasion with the rector, visiting clergy, a band, a choir and many hundreds of worshippers gathered in the afternoon sunshine.

Eyam Plague Service at Cucklet Delph, near the village.

The calculations to pinpoint the exact centre of such an eccentric shape as England must be more than complicated but someone in Meriden has done them and a cross on the village green proclaims his findings. At the other end of the green there stands an obelisk which is a memorial to the cyclists who died in two world wars. This was erected in 1921 and since that year an annual commemoration has been held on the

Sunday morning nearest to May 21.

Cyclists converge from all directions dressed in colourful gear. Bicycles litter the green as they take part in the service, during which wreaths are laid at the foot of the memorial. In 1984 I would guess there were two, maybe three, hundred of them there, but an older cyclist told me that between the wars thousands used to come, some from as far away as Scotland and the south coast. They would set off on their bicycles two or three days in advance, attend the service and then ride all the way home again. Cyclists are not so intrepid now, or perhaps they have less time, but clubs still use the occasion for a one-day long-distance ride.

Meriden does not *look* out of the ordinary but apart from being the centre of England it fosters not one but two unique traditions, the Cyclists' Memorial Service and the Woodmen of Arden.

William Hubbard 'departed this life the 4th October 1786 aged 63yr' and in his will he left a guinea to pay for the clergy and choir of St Mary in Arden, Market Harborough, to sing hymns over his grave on Easter Eve. Though this church has long since closed and now stands a well-preserved ruin in a pleasant park near the railway station, the vicar and choir of the parish church faithfully carry out his wishes. The guinea was part of the proceeds of some land which was recently sold for property development. The new buyers failed to see any good reason why they should hand over this huge sum each year and had to be legally advised of the errors of their ways. The guinea is now officially available in perpetuity.

In 1984 the singing took place on a beautiful late April evening. The vicar, curate and choir made a fine group around Hubbard's grave, which stands a little apart from the derelict church. There were about twenty other people there. The vicar said that in really nasty weather, such as the previous year when it was snowing, they have been known to do it by themselves.

It is worth getting there a little early, if only to read the other gravestones collected back to back around the church. One I liked particularly was for William Platt and his wife Sarah who died in 1811 and 1835 respectively:

> Stay reader stay, with pensive thought look round
> Behold these sculptured stones, this burial ground:
> Reflect! Prepare! Whilst this your fate you view
> Who next may die! Uncertain! Why not you?

In Oxford, on a Sunday morning near St John the Baptist's Day, June 24, a sermon is preached from the stone pulpit high in a corner of St John's Quad, in Magdalen College, the first quad inside the main gate of the College. The Dean of Divinity, the Reverend Brian Findlay, tells me that 'it is an official University Sermon, preached here because Magdalen has an endowment to pay the preacher, deriving from the mediaeval Hospital of St John the Baptist which stood here before the college was founded. The outdoor pulpit is one of the last surviving fragments of the Hospital buildings.'

The Cyclists' Memorial Service is attended by about 200 who cycle to Meriden from all over the country.

Seats are arranged on the lawn, functional for visitors, elaborately carved and magnificent for the President, Vice-Chancellor and Senior Proctors who arrive in a formal procession which also includes the preacher. A century ago, according to Chambers' *Book of Days*, 'the court was embowered with green boughs, that the preaching might resemble that of the Baptist in the Wilderness' but this is now left to the imagination. The service is short, not more than half an hour, with a hymn, one of those all-embracing University prayers, the sermon and a final hymn. The

A sermon is preached from the open-air pulpit in Magdalen College, Oxford, on a Sunday morning near St John the Baptist's Day.

preacher is normally a graduate who is up to attend the College Gaudy, or annual dinner for old students, held the evening before.

Between February 15 and September 14 the commercial salmon fishermen are out twice a day, at low water, on the tidal waters of the River Tweed. They use a method called 'net and cobble fishing'. A cobble is a flat-bottomed rowing boat and they use this to position a wide sweep of net which is then hauled in from the bank, with luck entrapping dozens of salmon. They do this by ancient right; the method has been in use for at least a thousand years.

At Norham, ten miles up-river from Berwick they waste no time starting their season. At 11.45 p.m. on St Valentine's Day they attend a short service at Pedwell Beach, down a lane behind Norham church, to bless the salmon nets, and thus be well prepared to start work on the stroke of midnight.

At any rate, that is how it used to be when there were plenty of fish, and plenty of fishermen, but stocks have gone down drastically in recent years. In 1984 there were four fishermen, three spectators and four photographers there to see the vicar of Norham carry out the Blessing, and recite the Pedwell Prayer:

> Good Lord, lead us. Good Lord speed us.
> From all perils protect us,
> In the darkness direct us.
> Give us, good Lord, finest nights to land our fish,
> Sound and big to fill our wish.
> Keep our nets from snag and break.
> For every man a goodly take, give us, good Lord.

It was an eerie scene under the fishermen's floodlights, the vicar in a cobble, the water glassy calm, with mysterious bird calls coming out of the freezing fog. When it was over the fishermen, muttering that the tide was wrong and that anyway there were no fish, disappeared into the night and went to bed.

Away at the other end of the country on a warm summer evening at the end of May the fishermen and inhabitants of Hastings come in large numbers to hear the vicar bless the sea. Earlier accounts describe a procession from the parish church but this no longer happens. Furthermore, the service has become interdenominational and the local Roman Catholic priest now takes part. The Salvation Army band plays the hymns and the clergy stand on the deck of the lifeboat, brought out of its shed for the occasion. In fact the lifeboat men take part too, looking after everyone and conjuring up chairs for the elderly.

The vicar's wife, perhaps relieved that I had behaved myself, told me that the previous year a photographer had intensely irritated everyone by setting up a ladder right in the middle of the congregation. Half-way through the proceedings the ladder, with excruciating slowness, toppled over leaving him in an undignified heap on the ground, and everyone else, including her husband, in hysterical laughter.

From blessings to encourage events, to thanksgiving to celebrate afterwards. In the middle of the thirteenth century the parish of Wicken in Northamptonshire was divided into two parts, Wickhamon and Wickdive. The parisioners were greatly displeased about this and set about bringing them together again. They finally succeeded two hundred years later, in 1587,

Blessing the Sea at Hastings.

and they celebated their success with a Love Feast which continues to this day. The Feast has always been held on Ascension Day on the lawn of the old rectory, which is now a hotel. Between the rectory and the church is the Manor House and the rector was always permitted to pass through the grounds on his way to and from his services. After a short service in the church at 10.30 a.m., the congregation follows the rector's same path which, as the rector puts it, 'passes through a field which is usually full of horses who either run off alarmed, or stand in a row watching us with astonishment'. The Feast was established in the parish records of 1587 to take place under the 'Gospel Elm' but this is no longer possible since the tree was struck down with Dutch elm disease and only the stump remains. They still sing the 'Old Hundredth' nearby before enjoying their Feast of cakes and ale. The cake is dark brown and highly spiced, especially with caraway seeds, baked by a local baker, inevitably 'to an ancient and secret recipe'. The ale is enjoyed by adults, children get lemonade, and the in-betweens have to make do with shandy. Average attendance at this celebration is about thirty; in the rector's words, 'a few interested locals plus a pressed group from the school with their music mistress who makes them perform. It's sometimes half-term though, and then we're lucky to get twenty!'

In the remote but beautiful border country between Hereford and Ross-on-Wye, Pax Cakes (*pax* is the Latin for 'peace') are distributed at four village churches on Palm Sunday. In 1982 I saw Pax Cakes given to the congregations of both Sellack and Hoarwithy, a feat made possible by the services ending at different times, and the churches being only two miles apart. There are also distributions at King's Caple and Hentland. There are no rules about times, simply that they should happen after services on Palm Sunday, the Sunday before Easter.

The ceremony is thought to be of ancient origin. In 1570 a Lady Scudamore left money to make sure it was kept up in the district. In her day, and right up to the end of the nineteenth century, the practice was to have a proper feast inside the church, to encourage peace and goodwill among the congregation. Now the Pax

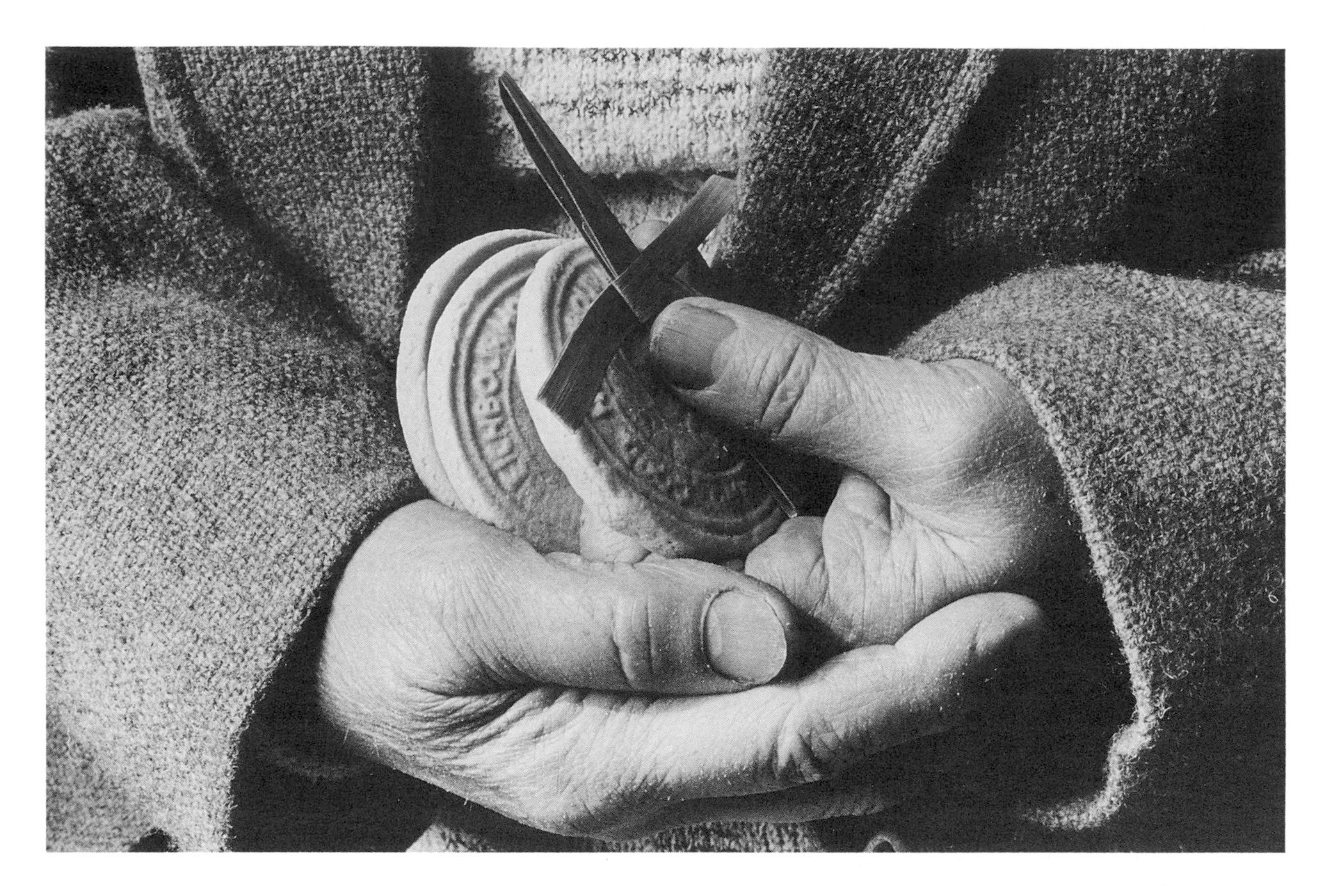

'Pax Cakes' are distributed on Palm Sunday at four village churches in Herefordshire. This was a member of the congregation at Sellack.

Cakes have become round flat biscuits, about two inches in diameter, bearing an impression of the Paschal Lamb and the words 'Peace and Good Neighbourhood' which the vicar utters to each person as he hands them over. The biscuits are made for all four churches by a baker in Ross-on-Wye; since Lady Scudamore's bequest has petered out, they are paid for out of parish funds.

At the church of St Michael-on-the-Mount Without, on the hill amongst the buildings of Bristol University, there is a short children's service on the morning of Easter Tuesday. It is well attended, for afterwards the children are given 'Tuppenny Starvers', huge spicy buns a foot across.

The first record of this cheerful custom occurs in 1739 when Peter and Mary Davis became involved. When they died they left a bequest to carry it on. There is a memorial to them in the church:

> Underneath lie interred the remains of Peter Davis Esq and Mary his wife both natives of Cardiganshire in the Principality of Wales but had long been inhabitants of this City and had resided upwards of 40 years in this parish. After having lived with the greatest harmony and conjugal affection for fifty two years unable to bear a separation soon followed each other she dying 16 Jan 1748 aged 78, he the 17 June following, aged 86.

There has been some discussion about the name of this custom. When it began there was great poverty in this part of the city and the idea was to give the children a treat, to give them tuppenny buns instead of the penny ones they were used to. For a long time the buns were intended for the choirboys, now they are for everyone, even adults are welcome if there are any left over. The vicar, the Reverend Michael Lane, says 'we usually order eighty or ninety but there's always a certain amount of panic in case they don't turn up. After all it is the day after Bank Holiday!'

There is a bun, too, for the children of Painswick, and a brand new 5p piece as well, after 'Clipping' the

Church Clipping at Painswick in 1969.

Church. On the Sunday afternoon of September 19 (or the first one after that date), the Feast of the Nativity of the Blessed Virgin Mary, according to the old calendar, 200 or 300 children of the parish join hands and encircle their church. While a special hymn is sung, they move forwards and backwards in the manner of a country dance making a lovely spectacle in their best clothes, the boys each wearing a button-hole, the girls a garland of flowers in their hair.

The origins of this charming custom are not definitely known. Theories range from the inevitable pagan rite to the more simple, and plausible, symbolic act of embracing the church as one would a beloved friend. The word 'clipping' may derive from the mediaeval *yclept*; the current *Oxford English Dictionary* in any case gives one definition of 'clip' as 'surround closely, grip tightly'.

It is certainly an old custom in Painswick even if, at times, intermittent. The Reverend W.H. Seddon, vicar twice between 1885 and 1897, wrote: 'When I came to Painswick some thirty years ago the Feast was still kept as a popular and especially as a children's festival, but the "clipping" of the church had been intermittent for some years. Many old people of the village, however, well remembered taking part in it in the days of their youth, and both name and custom were revived from their lips.'

I have seen it twice, if a good time ago. I am sure it continues as I describe. The first time I saw it, it had been raining furiously so the ceremony took place inside the church, the children forming as big a chain as space permitted. It was *still* delightful.

In the days before heating, or floorboards or even stone-flagged floors in churches, hay or rushes were often used as a means of combating cold and damp. It is not necessary now, of course, but in the way of things the business became a Hallowed Ritual which outlasted its original purpose.

Well, strictly speaking, it is not the strewing which survives as a ceremony. That tends to happen casually, even surreptitiously, organized by the verger and anyone else he can persuade to help. It is getting the rushes there which has evolved into spectacular happenings.

Rushbearing at Grasmere. These are just three of many 'bearings' carried in procession around the village, on the Saturday nearest to St Oswald's Day..

Chambers' *Book of Days* (quoting an article written in 1857) says:

> Though few are ignorant of this ancient custom it may not perhaps be so generally known that the strewing of churches grew into a religious festival, dressed up in all that picturesque circumstance wherewith the old church well knew how to array its ritual. In Westmoreland, Lancashire, and districts of Yorkshire, there is still celebrated between haymaking and harvest a village fête called the Rushbearing. Young women dressed in white, and carrying garlands of flowers and rushes, walk in procession to the parish church, accompanied by a crowd of rustics, with flags flying and music playing. There they suspend their floral chaplets on the chancel rails, and the day is concluded with a simple feast. The neighbourhood of Ambleside was, until lately, and may be still, one of the chief strongholds of this popular practice.

I am glad to report that the Ambleside Rushbearing is indeed alive and well and held on the first Saturday in July, but sorry to say that I have not seen it. Traditionally this Rushbearing was held on the Saturday nearest to St Anne's Day, July 26. Presumably it was connected with St Anne's Church which is now de-consecrated. The parish church, on the other hand, is dedicated to St Mary whose visit to her cousin Elizabeth (Luke 1: 39–41) is officially celebrated on July 1.

Ambleside is a very popular Lake District resort, overrun any day during the summer. By all accounts their Rushbearing is attended by a crowd of Royal Wedding proportions. Grasmere, four miles up the road, is popular as well. Their Rushbearing is very similar and perhaps even better known, but surprisingly, when I was there, there were not that many spectators and it was a very pleasant family affair.

Grasmere church is dedicated to St Oswald, whose Day is August 5 so their Rushbearing is held at 4 o'clock on the Saturday closest to that date. Preparations, supervised by Miss Rachel McAlpine, take several days. Apart from sorting out the children who will take part, the 'bearings' have to be made. These are devices which look as if they were made entirely of rushes but are in fact created by winding the rushes around strong and practical materials like wood, wire netting and string. They symbolize various biblical and historical themes, as well as things to do with St Oswald. There are nine big bearings each about five feet high, and several smaller ones, all of traditional design and used year after year. Many of them have been carried in the procession by generations of the same family; the frames are kept in their houses and the women carry out the decoration. Miss McAlpine claims the right to make the beautiful cross of golden Helenium which is carried at the head of the procession. The work takes the best part of two days as the ladies diligently and lovingly shape the rushes into intricate forms.

Most of their preparations are complete by Saturday lunchtime. Meanwhile the church floor has, mysteriously, acquired a layer of rushes. Long before 4 o'clock, children in their Sunday best begin to arrive in the vicarage garden to be instructed in their duties and to be given a new 5p piece for their trouble. Families appear in the streets at the same time, the children carrying home-made bearings, even the tiny ones come in pushchairs decorated with rushes and flowers. The bearings are handed over to their bearers, the larger ones for the choirboys, the smaller ones for the girls.

The most important people in the whole procession are the Rush Maidens. Originally, when the whole business really was to take rushes to the church, in Grasmere they used to carry them on cloth, or sacking, holding the corners. These girls do the same thing, only there are six of them, their load is symbolic, and they use a fine sheet woven very many years ago in the village. To be selected as a Rush Maiden is a great honour, requiring full marks for good behaviour. The girls, who are about 12 years old, also have to be of a reasonably standard size since their green dresses are provided for them. Evidently, a new set was made within the last few years because the previous lot which had been going 'for centuries' had finally fallen to pieces.

By the time everyone was organized the procession consisted of about 200 people. The choirboys led with their special rushbearings, the golden cross in front. Then came the band, then the adult choir and the clergy all carrying sprays of rushes. Next came the Rush Maidens, followed by the bigger girls and finally the little ones with their mums. There were few dads to be seen. They started from the church, marched right round the village and returned for a special service. The official bearings were placed round the altar, except 'the serpent' which is traditionally cast out to a special place outside the Sanctuary. All the other bearings, baskets, posies and rush crosses were left on the window ledges where they remained over the weekend.

On Monday they all return, collect their bearings and go off on a shorter tour of the village after which they have sports and tea. On this Saturday, after the service they simply repaired to the sports pavilion to collect a piece of ginger cake embossed with the words 'Saint Oswald'.

Fifty or so miles away, on the other side of the M6 near Appleby, there are two villages which hold Rushbearing ceremonies. Both have dispensed with the formality of putting rushes on the church floor and are content with processions of little girls wearing garland crowns. However, both villages make a festival of the day to the extent that exiles try to make an annual return. Since they are no more than a couple of miles apart there is some rivalry to put on the better show.

Warcop hold theirs on St Peter's Day, June 29. This tends to be the bigger procession, led by an army band since there is a camp nearby. In 1984 the Bishop of Penrith was in attendance. Great Musgrave turns out on the first Saturday in July. They allow the boys to take part, carrying rush crosses. Here they place their garlands and crosses around the font in the church and leave them there until the next year.

One practical way of getting the rushes to the church was by means of a Rushcart. Ritual grew up around these, though it was more robust, even liable to suppression because it became drunken and riotous. The Rushcart had completely disappeared by the first decade of this century but, about ten years ago, the Saddleworth Morris Men revived one with help from local breweries. It can be seen annually on a Saturday towards the end of August.

To quote Chambers, once more:

> the town clerk of Norwich was accustomed to pay to the subsacrist of the Cathedral an annual guinea for strewing the floor. . . with rushes on the Mayor's Day, from the western door to the entrance into the choir; this is the most recent instance of the ancient usage which has come to my knowledge.

He was ill-informed; the church of St Mary Redcliffe in Bristol has held just such a service since 1493 and it is still very much alive, while the Norwich one is no more. William Canynges was five times mayor of Bristol before he was ordained in 1468. He celebrated his first Holy Eucharist on Whit Sunday of that year. Another mayor, William Spencer, wished to commemorate this occasion. When he died, in 1493, he left a bequest to pay for three sermons to be preached on the Monday, Tuesday and Wednesday of Whit week before the mayor and corporation in the church. He left no guinea for the rushes or the nosegays which are such a feature of the event, but presumably they were standard then and have simply survived until today. Two of the sermons have lapsed; since the Reformation there has been just the one, preached on 'Rush Sunday'.

The nave is liberally strewn with rushes, a duty carried out by the verger and his son, with a small amount of help, in 1984, from myself. All the officials' pews are lined with nosegays, seventy in all, beautifully made in recent years by the two ladies who do the church flowers.

Before the service the Lord Mayor drives from City Hall in a splendid carriage, with a mounted police escort. On arrival at the north door of the church he takes his place in a procession. In front of him are an Inspector and eight stalwart police constables carrying maces, the Chief Constable, City Clerk, City Treasurer, Chief Executive, the St Mary's churchwardens dressed in morning suits and the Sword Bearer in a fine cossack hat. Behind him are the Deputy Lord Mayor, Honorary Freemen, ex-Lord Mayors, Honorary Aldermen, councillors and officers of the Corporation, a formidable array as they process slowly right around the church to meet an only

'Rush Sunday' at St Mary Redcliffe in Bristol. The nave is strewn with rushes and the nosegays are for the Lord Mayor, the Corporation and City Officials who are all obliged to attend.

marginally less impressive clerical procession near the west door.

The church was completely full in 1984, for this is a great social occasion. The sermon was preached by the vicar, Canon David Frayne. Afterwards there were photographs and gossip on the steps before the Lord Mayor drove off again, in state.

Ripon is surprisingly well provided with customs. Their wonderful 'Sword Dance Play' is discussed in Chapter 13. The mayor appears five times in a traditional procession to the cathedral. The famous Hornblower sounds his curfew every night of the year at 9 o'clock. For good measure the Royal Maundy Service came their way in 1985.

The Hornblower makes one other appearance in the city, in the pageant which is the centrepiece of the Feast of St Wilfred, held at the beginning of August.

Wilfred was a monk at Lindisfarne when he was made Bishop of York. Obviously a man of decided opinions, he was twice banished for them by the Archbishop of Canterbury. In 672 he returned from exile and came to Ripon, where he became Abbot of the monastery. The cathedral is dedicated to him and the crypt is said to have been built under his direction.

The pageant celebrates his arrival in Ripon. A man with a long beard, dressed in cream and white bishop's robes, wearing a mitre, carrying a crozier, rides a fine white horse around the city at the head of an impressive procession of floats depicting scenes from the city's history. St Wilfred is welcomed by the Dean at the west door of the cathedral.

The custom is old, though it has grown and altered over the years. The pageant was added about 1960. Before that St Wilfred carried out his tour with a handful of attendants and the city band. In the last century the returning saint was not a man at all but a wooden effigy, and it was the tradition to stop at all the public houses on the way.

On St Nicholas's Day, December 6, several parishes elect a 'Boy Bishop'. He is always one of the choirboys and, traditionally, he should carry out his duties until Holy Innocents Day, December 28, though modern

St Wilfred returns to the city of Ripon.

versions tend to stay in office for the whole year. The vicar's wife in Edwinstow, Nottinghamshire, told me that 'we call them "Child Bishops" because more often than not it's a girl these days. He or she acts as a kind of team captain for the year and wears a special red cloak. The only real duty is to read choir prayers.' There are, no doubt, a good number of Boy Bishops all with similar responsibilities. On January 7, 1985 *The Times* reported a revival at St Nicholas's Church, Bournemouth, curiously enough on the day that 10-year-old Ryan Williams returned to school and normal life. They showed a picture of him in cope and mitre.

For all there may be an increasing number, they are pale shadows of the original Boy Bishops elected annually all over Europe in most cathedrals and many churches during the Middle Ages. After the Reformation the custom was supressed in most Protestant countries. In England it was finally forbidden by Queen Elizabeth.

It is interesting to compare the present with the past: this description from *Picturesque Memorials of Salisbury* (1834), will give some idea of the pomp and splendour associated with this custom:

> No English Cathedral was more famous than that of Salisbury for its celebration of the boy-bishop custom. The fellow choristers of the boy-bishop assumed the titles of canons or prebendaries. Wearing copes and carrying lighted tapers, they went in procession to the Altar of the HolyTrinity and took precedence of the dean and canons residentiary. . .He wore the episcopal dress and a mitre, often surpassing in splendour that of the Bishop himself, and he carried a pastoral staff. Except the celebration of the Mass, the boy bishop might perform all other services usually performed by the Bishop. If the boy bishop died within his term of tenure, he was interred with the honours due to a diocesan bishop. It is popularly believed that a famous monument in Salisbury Cathedral is of a boy bishop in episcopal dress.

The Buildings of England noncommittally describes this monument as a 'miniature stone effigy of a bishop'. It seems obvious that Boy Bishops played a serious part in religious life, though modern versions have more in common with May Queens.

On Christmas Eve in Dewsbury the bellringers of All Saints Toll the Devil's Knell. This event really is faintly sinister, especially on a cold, wet night, but it is uncomplicated for they simply have to ring the tenor bell once for every year that has passed since the Nativity. Their only problem is to regulate their tolling so they will reach the right number by midnight. 'Sometimes towards the end it's like a funeral bell, other times we have to go like the clappers!'

This strange custom is said to have originated in the thirteenth century when a member of the influential Saville family killed a servant who had come to Midnight Mass against his orders. To atone, he inaugurated the bellringing. Be that as it may, it has gone on for a very long time, lapsing only twice in living memory, during the Second World War and when the vicar and the bellringers had such a row that the vicar forbade them to come into the church.

While the tolling may sound melancholy outside, inside the church tower it is quite a jolly occasion with several ringers to take their turn and help with keeping the score. While the ringer concentrated the others told us that until the Second World War there had been a gun fired every night in Dewsbury for 150 years because a local mill owner had made his foreman do it during the Luddite Riots to let the big house know that all was well, 'and we always had to get t'girlfriend home before ten o'clock gun!' Here endeth the lesson.

Tolling the Devil's Knell at Dewsbury. The bell must be tolled once for every year since the birth of Christ.

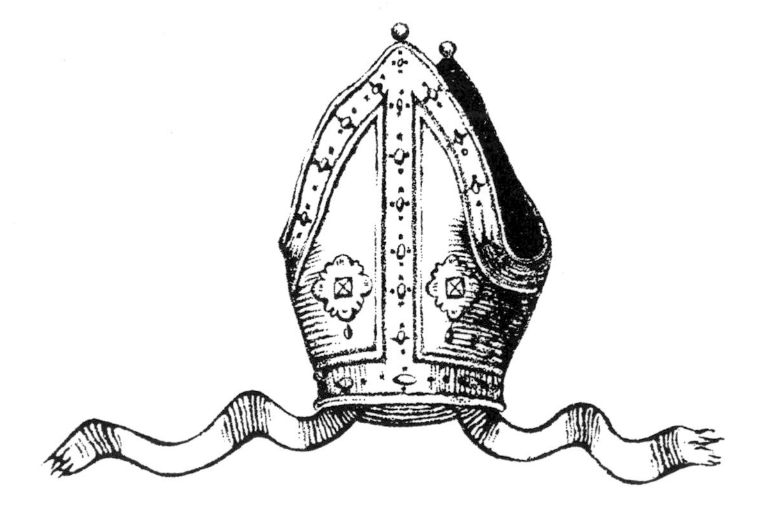

O ye Wells...

Wells have always been venerated. After all they supply free water, so it is natural to give thanks, or offerings, to encourage their everlasting flow. When Christianity arrived the Church first forbade pagan well worship, but then, recognizing a good thing when it saw it, took it over, to the glory of God. Many wells acquired the names of saints and to this day virtually all well customs have a strong religious aspect.

Holy wells are common, and their waters are considered to have miraculous properties. There are others into which people throw offerings, usually money, which can have a beneficial effect when passed on to a charitable organization, or miscellaneous objects such as pins, needles, buttons and shells, whose efficacy is less apparent.

There are a few 'clootie' wells, especially in Scotland. Clooties are little pieces of rag, the name having the same derivation as 'clout' in 'ne'er cast your clout'. St Mary's Well, near Culloden battlefield, just east of Inverness, is one of these. I had seen it many years ago and remembered seeing clooties on the trees round about. I rang up Eileen MacAskill of the Inverness Field Club to find out if they were still there. She said they were, and sent me all kinds of information, including a couple of pages from the Club Transactions for 1878:

> The proper season to pay a visit was the first Sunday in May, and in order that any benefit the water could bestow might be fully and completely reaped, it was absolutely necessary for the devotee to be on the ground immediately before sunrise. Consequently, on the previous Saturday night, crowds might be seen wending their way from all quarters to the sacred fount. When we call to mind that there was a public house, at a distance conveniently near on the line of the march, that the throng, consisting of male and female, was a very miscellaneous one indeed. . .we can more easily imagine than describe the wild scenes of riot and dissipation that were invariably enacted. Latterly the custom of visiting this well has fallen very much into disuse, being denounced from the pulpit.

In return I sent her a long and amusing piece from Chambers' *Book of Days*, published a little earlier in 1862, about another clootie well to the north of Inverness:

> Craigie Well is situated in a nook of the parish of Avoch, which juts out to the south, and runs along the north shore of Munlochy Bay. . .within a few yards of high water mark. . .Crowds were eagerly pressing forward to get a tasting of the well before the sun should come in sight; for, once he made his appearance there was no good to be derived from drinking of it.

The article is full of anecdote, and it was sufficient to send Eileen dashing off to Munlochy Bay to find out if the custom still went on. Sure enough it did, even if the few who attended regularly could hardly be described as 'crowds of lads and lasses from all quarters'. Eileen reported:

> It is still visited on the first Sunday of May before sunrise, indeed some of the rags had clearly been placed there very recently. I spoke to a farmer who owns the land today. He explained. . .that he clears the track to it every May because people do go. He marks the route to the well from the main road with blue twine tied to trees and fences. Between Munlochy and Tore villages there is another clootie well, dedicated to St. Boniface. It is right beside the main road and is covered with rags, so appears to be visited by large

A 'Clootie' well near Munlochy Bay, north of Inverness. Though May Day, or the following Sunday, is the traditional day for it, motorists can stop at this one throughout the year to tie up a clootie.

> numbers. . .many of the rags are very old because anyone removing a clootie is likely to inherit whatever problem was left behind at the well attached to the rag!

Naturally, I had to go and look for myself; in August 1984. St Mary's Well still had its clooties, in spite of clerical disapproval, though I would say there were less than there were twenty years ago. We were taken to see Craigie Well by the farmer's wife, who told us that the event was known locally as Wishing Well Sunday. The well would certainly not be easy to find without the helpful blue string, but it would be a pleasure looking for it since it is in an incredibly beautiful place. St Boniface Well was indeed surrounded by thousands of clooties; a family left several while we were there and passing locals told us that such is the enthusiasm of tourists that they rip their handkerchiefs to pieces and have been known to tear off items of clothing.

A more straightforward ceremony is to decorate wells with flowers and greenery, often in the form of garlands, usually during the spring or early summer. At Bisley, near Stroud in Gloucestershire, the children still do this on Ascension Day.

The well is impressive, restored in 1863. 'With five gabled waterchutes, and one more each side. Rural and pretty, and useful for providing drinking water' is Pevsner's judgement, though a notice strongly discourages this practice.

The garlands used are in the unusual form of letters, numbers and stars of David. The flowers, depending on what is available, are tied to metal frames which are used year after year. 1984 was lilac time.

After a simple service a procession formed in the schoolyard. Led by a band, the vicar and a cross-bearer, the children then walked down to the well. The first two pairs carried large stars of David, the next six individuals, the numerals and letters 1, 9, 8, 4, A and D, the following twelve the letters of ASCENSION DAY. Behind them another forty or fifty carried posies.

At the well they were organized, with some difficulty, into stepping forward in turn to hang their garlands on the hooks permanently fixed for that

Bisley Well, dressed with garlands on Ascension Day.

purpose. The stars went at each side, the date at the top, the day right across the well above the 'water chutes', and the posies on the ledge beneath. Even if a little subdued, they made a fine display, predominantly mauve and white, only the letter 'I' striking a subversive note, its maker preferring marigolds.

Everything in place, the vicar said a prayer, three children read from the Bible, a small boy played the recorder, the Ascension Day hymn was sung and, finally, the vicar blessed the well.

The whole ceremony was reverential and dignified, perhaps even solemn, by no means taken lightly, the odour of sanctity enhanced by the wild garlic which grows in profusion round about.

But really the custom of decorating wells belongs, without argument, to Derbyshire. Wells are particularly numerous in the county and the people are ready to give thanks for their good fortune. Indeed, they are so keen on Well Dressing in some villages, that they do it though they have no well.

It has not always been so popular, enthusiasm waxing and waning through the centuries. It is not known how far back the tradition goes. The village of Tissington has often being suggested as the original, even if there, as Christina Hole remarks, 'it is only supposed to run back as far as 1350'.

In Derbyshire a few garlands, bunches of flowers and greenery, will not do. This was their original way, but at some time, around 1800 it is thought, their present, much more elaborate, method began to evolve. In this county they frame their wells with substantial boards which are covered with clay into which have been pressed thousands of petals, flowers, leaves, greenery and other natural flora to create beautiful and uplifting pictures, patterns and words.

In 1984 the Peak National Park Office listed twenty-eight towns and villages where Well Dressings were held, but the total number of Well Dressings is likely to be over a hundred. Fortunately, they do not all happen at the same time. The first is blessed in early May (the exact date dependent on Easter), and the last in the middle of September. During this span it is possible to see at least one Well Dressing at almost any time, and several in June and July. On Sunday, June 26, 1983, I was able to see twenty-one wells in seven villages, though it has to be admitted that the first was

Dressing the well

Dressing the Well at Tissington. The boards are spread with a layer of clay about half an inch thick, which is soft enough to spread and take petals and other materials, but hard enough to stay put.

Strong outlines are made with coffee beans pressed into the clay. Other materials are often used such as alder cones, bark and maize. The picture is made up with petals, flowers, leaves and other natural things, but never manufactured objects.

After the boards have been completed they are erected in position around the well, with the support covered with foliage. This is Hands Well at Tissington.

The 'picture board' of a Tissington well with the original design pinned up for reference.

Hands Well, Tissington, has a commanding position at the top of the village.

HOW BEAUTIFUL ARE THY DWELLINGS
YOUNG MEN AND MAYDENS

The Scout's well at Tideswell in 1973 – a natural for the pages of this book!

before breakfast and the last after dark!

For very many years Tissington had the honour of opening the season on Ascension Day, others following at Whitsun. But the new Spring Bank Holiday is sometimes earlier than Ascension Day. Furthermore, the village of Etwall has recently started up on the second Saturday in May. Cynics declared this a simple ploy to be the first, though it is still possible for Ascension Day to be as early as May 1.

Villages dress their wells on regular days each year, such as the saint's day of their church, a bank holiday, or a commemoration such as that at Eyam to coincide with 'Plague Sunday'.

Though there are variations, the basic principles remain the same everywhere. In 1973 I spent a week at Tissington, and our guide, instructor and friend, the late Rennie Hayhurst, revealed some of the mysteries to us.

Tissington is an estate village. Its Jacobean Hall has been, for over four hundred years, the home of the Fitzherberts, and many of the villagers work on the estate. There are five wells. Hands Well has a commanding position at the top of the village. Hall Well, opposite the great house, is by far the most impressive in its undressed state. Town and Yew Tree Wells face each other at the bottom of the road. The latter appears to be dry, though this is deceptive since it is, in fact, the most copious, its production pumped to surrounding houses and farms. Only Coffin Well stands a little apart in a private garden. Its curious name is derived, disappointingly, from its shape.

Legend, notoriously unreliable, says that the custom started here in 1615. It is recorded, in Youlgreave parish register, that in that year 'there was no rayne fell upon the earth from the 25th day of March till the 2nd day of May, and then there was but one shower; two more fell betweene then and the 4th day of August, so that the greatest part of this land were burnt upp, bothe corn and hay'. A drought like this, bad enough now, must have been catastrophic in the days before reservoirs and mains water supplies. The Tissington wells, in common with many in the area, kept going.

Alternative legend suggests the custom started in 1350, the pure well water having protected the neighbourhood from the Black Death, particularly virulent at that time.

Whenever it began, a version of the custom certainly existed in 1758 when a visitor 'saw the springs adorned with garlands'. By 1818 another description shows the custom to have arrived at, more or less, its present form, which was attained completely by 1864 according to a long entry in Chambers, which is illustrated by a picture of Hall Well exactly as it is dressed today.

It can, therefore, be agreed that the Tissington Well Dressing tradition is very old, though there have been lapses. The present run, now very strong, only began in 1950.

Virtually the entire population of about 160 takes some part in the preparations, divided informally, by family, friendship, location, into five teams. There is no competition, but hard work and friendly rivalry keep each away from the other's workplace. Themes are usually biblical, though this is not obligatory. The choice is up to the designer of each well, with some consulting their colleagues, while others are more autocratic.

Choosing the subject is not easy, but once agreed, the picture, whether original, or from a book or photograph, has to be scaled up, by squares, onto large sheets of paper, the size of the actual boards. All this goes on far in advance.

About a week before Ascension Day the real work begins. The boards have to be repaired if necessary, clay has to be dug, and materials gathered. The boards have to be sturdy, to stand up to the elements and the weight of clay. Each village has its own configuration, some preferring a straightforward flat screen, others, like Tissington, having something quite complex. In Tissington, though the shapes vary in detail, each well is surrounded by an impressive 'outer arch' made of two substantial uprights supporting the 'letter board'. Inside this is the smaller 'inner arch' framing the central 'picture board', which is sometimes called the 'summer board'. All this woodwork is liberally studded with nails, their heads standing up to help keep the clay in place.

The year I visited, the boards were put into the village pond on the Saturday to give them a thorough soaking. Dry boards tend to draw moisture from the clay which would not only shorten the life of the dressing but would also cause it to crack up and fall to pieces. During the weekend the flower collectors were busy.

Here, as everywhere, materials are available according to the season, and spring wells are therefore likely to be different in character from autumn wells. 'If Ascension Day is early and the weather has been bad, we really suffer.' Designers try to avoid colours which are difficult to reproduce and include those which are available in abundance. If all else fails, the local florists are a last resort. Artificial flowers or other manufactured materials are utterly forbidden, even coloured pebbles, glass and shaped wood give rise to indignation. There have been reports of attempts to dye petals, which turned out to be a dead giveaway when the rest wilted and turned brown!

A characteristic of Tissington Well Dressings is

Yew Tree well, Tissington, in 1966. This was taken in the early morning of Ascension Day, by far the best time to see the five village wells.

their use of letters and patterns, on the outside panels, against the plain cream, or light greenish background provided by the mineral, fluorspar. It is found in quantities in Derbyshire, 'Blue John' being the most famous version. The cream version, which has a gritty consistency, is used on the wells. It is the most common, and is also used in steel making and, more mundanely, for gritting the roads in winter. The fluorspar is simply pressed into the clay to form a plain light area. I was told that rice was once the favoured material for this purpose, with the birds as well. It was used up to the Second World War but was then rendered illegal, and in any case unobtainable, by food regulations. Fluorspar was introduced as a substitute and found to be much better.

On the Sunday morning the boards were retrieved from the pond and the clay prepared. The clay was simply dug up from a local field, but it had to be properly prepared. By adding salty water to it, stamping on it, turning it with shovels, stamping on it some more, kicking it and cursing it, a process known as 'puddling', it gradually attained the consistency of butter. When judged perfect by Rennie, it was spread carefully, half an inch thick, over the boards.

Preparations were now more or less complete and it was time to start creating the pictures. Rennie laid his scaled-up drawings over the panels and 'pricked through' all the outlines. Then he removed the drawings and pinned them up around the shed to act as reference. Helpers began at once to make the outlines more substantial by sticking coffee beans or alder cones along them. The beans, hard and clean, cadged from the local Nestlé factory, were used for the lettering and the more intricate sections; the alder cones, bigger but less consistent, on the picture board and the more flamboyant lines. (In other villages alternatives may be employed, such as sweet corn to give a light-coloured line, or bark a more irregular, artistic one.)

This took the rest of Sunday. By then a strong line picture had appeared. All of Monday, Tuesday and most of Wednesday was taken up with 'flowering' and 'petalling', filling in the flat area with colour. All kinds of wild or garden flowers were used, as well as mosses, grasses, leaves, twigs, lichen – anything that grows. Some parts, especially the side panels, for the most part of lively abstract design, tended to attract the brightest and most striking colours, while others were more subdued and subtle. The 'picture board', regarded as the real examination of the well dressers' craft, was worked on by the most expert and experienced, using shades, colours, textures and shapes with extraordinary cunning. They built their pictures by pressing individual petals, with infinite care, into the clay. Whole flowers were not used, except tiny ones, like bluebells. (There is, though, an exception even to this rule – Barlow uses nothing but whole flowers.) 'Fields' were blocked in with handfuls of moss or something of that nature. Form and shadow, drapery, cloud effects, faces – anything seemed possible, and all with the added difficulty of having to lay petals overlapping like tiles so that rain would run off them.

During the days it was mostly the women petalling, after school joined by the young, later by the men. At all times there was a sociable, industrious but relaxed atmosphere, each team getting on with its own work. Doors were by no means closed, occasional visitors, even the odd bus-load of school children, being made welcome, so long as they kept out of the way and 'didn't ask too many daft questions'.

The insensitive sometimes complain that Well Dressings are boring, that they just sit there looking pretty, doing nothing. But it is at the creative stage that the real 'folk' activity takes place, this custom providing more genuine enthusiasm, communal involvement and sheer fun than almost any other.

Slowly, but steadily, the pictures grew so that by Wednesday tea-time they were all finished and ready to be put up. This is the only part acknowledged to be exclusively man's work. The boards are very heavy and to drop one is certain disaster, a crime for which there is no punishment severe enough. They were taken, with infinite care, by cart, trailer or hand to their respective wells and, over the next couple of hours, with patient deliberation, erected. The dressers watched anxiously, from time to time darting in to repair imperceptible mishaps.

As dusk was beginning to fall they were all complete. It was only then that the villagers permitted themselves to wander around, view the other wells and pass judgement. There is no contest at Tissington as there is at other places, only friendly rivalry, each person enjoying the untroubled conviction that his or her well is the best.

The very best time to see the Tissington wells is between 6 and 7 on the morning of Ascension Day, with the colours at their freshest, the light clear, the place deserted. Later the village will be overrun. After a couple of days the petals will show wear and tear.

The weather has a great effect. If it is very hot, sunny and dry, the clay dries up and cracks and the petals quickly expire; if it is very wet the whole lot rots. The ideal is cool temperatures with occasional gentle showers, and no wind. If the weather is kind, the dressings stay up until the following Wednesday; if it is unfortunate, they may be dismantled earlier. Most villages keep theirs up for about a week, some run for ten days, a few for only three or four.

The blessing was an imposing affair, attended by a bishop, several other churchmen and hundreds of visitors. After morning service a splendid procession emerged from the church to make its way to Hall Well, the first to be blessed and invariably by the senior visiting prelate. Hands Well, Coffin Well and Town Well followed, each blessed by a different priest. The remaining Yew Tree Well was, as always, blessed by the vicar of Tissington.

So that is how it was, in 1973, at Tissington. At other places techniques and ceremonies would be much the same, though few would claim equal status.

There is a vogue for Well Dressing these days. New villages start up each year, and many of them, frankly, are not very good at it. However, three with impeccable credentials are Wirksworth, Tideswell and Youlgreave. The first occasionally gets in ahead of Tissington, if Easter is very late. Wirksworth dressings, claimed to be pre-Roman in origin, began their recorded history on the arrival of piped water in 1827. They were displayed around the public taps and, at first, were called 'Tap Dressings'. Now that everyone has their own water supply, the taps have disappeared, but they still have their dressings, the boards simply being displayed in advantageous positions around the town. There are sometimes as many as a dozen substantial prizes being awarded for the best, in senior and junior categories.

Competitiveness encourages secretiveness. No one wants his rivals to get wind of his ideas, so preparations take place behind closed doors and visitors are discouraged. But the contest also encourages originality and daring, making the Wirksworth dressings among the best. It further encourages furious argument and a low opinion of the judges.

Tideswell, since taking up the habit after the Second World War, has a fine reputation for staggeringly detailed and accurate architectural screens. Each year reproduces a different cathedral or church. In 1984 we were treated to St Paul's, complete with red buses on Ludgate Hill, and Chesterfield Church.

Youlgreave wells are decidedly different from most of the others. This one is for the pensioners.

Another interesting feature about Tideswell is that their main screen, which is traditionally displayed on the green in the centre of the town, has several times been taken on fund-raising missions elsewhere, even as far as London. On behalf of Westminster Abbey, it stood for a week in Dean's Yard; on another occasion, on behalf of St Paul's, it stood at the head of the famous steps. Each time it bore an image of the nearby building, and caused wonderment among Londoners and tourists.

Youlgreave holds its Well Dressing on the Saturday nearest St John the Baptist's Day, June 24, to whom their church is dedicated. Though their tradition goes back to 1829, for the same reason as Wirksworth, they have a reputation for dangerously advanced work. Some hold Youlgreave well dressers to be the best, others dismiss them as untraditional, cads and bounders.

The truth is that their dressings *are* different, employing designs and techniques not seen elsewhere. They still use the approved natural materials, but at some stage it occurred to someone that, since they had to use a clay base, why should this not be built up into three-dimensional form? Thus, faces and bodies became modelled. Soon colouring was applied – provoking outrage among traditionalists, who included almost everyone, paint being regarded as far out of bounds.

Themes remain biblical on the whole, though surrounding decoration and lettering is likely to be much more complex and elegant than in other villages. In 1983, Coldwell End Well, at the top of the street, depicted 'Joseph' in a design of truly awesome sophistication, light years away from the accepted tradition. The inspiration was reported by a passer-by, somewhat disparagingly, to come from a lady 'with art school training' who was more than able to back up her ideas with an instinctive grasp of the possibilities of her materials. Her work encouraged idle speculation on the possible outcome of a collaboration between Youlgreave well dressers and abstract expressionists.

It's a lovely tradition and, with twenty-four other villages also taking part, the only one in this book which you stand a good chance of seeing on a random summer outing – provided you happen to be in the Peak District.

Oyez! Oyez! Oyez!

This chapter is about legal customs but the word 'legal' should not be taken too literally. Most are kept up with mock solemnity and obsessive attention to procedure, but with the greatest pleasure and enjoyment. They have little effect on present-day law even if they once did.

Thus, nobody is arguing about parish, or town boundaries to the extent that they *have* to be beaten at regular intervals; tithes of sufficient amount can be paid by cheque through the post, those of purely nominal value can be forgotten. The police and the magistrates' courts have rendered Courts Leet redundant; the Weights and Measures Inspectors have made Ale Tasting no more than convivial fun. There still are dozens of Bounds Beatings, many Courts Leet, countless rent or tithe paying ceremonies; this can be no more than a sample.

The real legal year runs from the beginning of October until the end of July. On October 1, or within a couple of days afterwards, the most senior members of the Judiciary assemble in the House of Lords to enjoy the Lord Chancellor's Breakfast. This is attended by most judges, from the Lord Chief Justice to Circuit Judges, and a number of Queen's Counsel and leading solicitors.

At 11.30 in the morning there is a service in Westminster Abbey where the Lord Chancellor reads the lesson. Roman Catholics have a simultaneous service in Westminster Cathedral. At noon they all file out through Poets Corner, to make an imposing procession in their wigs and robes, across the road to the House of Lords, led by the Tipstaff, the Permanent Secretary, the Assistant Sergeant-at-Arms carrying an enormous mace, the Purse Bearer and the Lord Chancellor himself.

The Lord Chancellor in procession from Westminster Abbey to the House of Lords for 'Breakfast'. Lord Hailsham is preceded by the Purse Bearer and the Assistant Sergeant-at-Arms carrying the mace. This was in 1972.

Weighing the Mayor at High Wycombe.

Inside the House of Lords, where the public are not admitted, the Lord Chancellor greets everyone personally at the door to the Royal Gallery. 'Breakfast' is not bacon and eggs, but more in the tradition of a wedding breakfast. My highly placed informant on legal matters described it as 'beer, sandwiches, cakes and buns and things' but his wife insisted it was 'the kind of things you get at cocktail parties'. Hot punch used to be a greatly enjoyed part of the occasion; to the annoyance of learned breakfasters this failed to appear in recent years.

A strange ceremony marks the beginning of the civic year in High Wycombe. The town has had mayors since 1285; owing to the Local Government Act of 1972 it is no longer a borough, but a 'Charter Trustee' town and part of Wycombe District. They elect a mayor and trustees.

Thus their engaging custom of Weighing the Mayor survives. At 6.30 on a Thursday evening towards the end of May a procession of civil dignitaries emerges from the council offices and proceeds along the High Street to the ancient Guildhall where the new mayor formally takes office. Immediately afterwards they assemble right outside.

The mayor is weighed first, followed by the mayoress, the ex-mayor and so on down the order of precedence to 'any other officials who desire to be weighed'. A beautiful old scale is used, a comfortable-looking chair suspended from a fine brass tripod, which has apparently been in operation for centuries. The weights are checked and recorded by the Chief Weights and Measures Inspector and announced in a stentorian voice by the Beadle, followed by the words 'and no more' or 'and some more', depending on whether the official has lost or gained weight. A loss is deemed to signify diligence over the past year, a gain sloth. Consequently he or she is cheered or booed as appropriate. I regret to have to report that in 1984 the retiring mayor had gained fifteen pounds; wild horses would not induce me to mention her name.

The Latin verb *rogare* means 'to ask or beseech' and Rogantiontide, five weeks after Easter, was a time

given particularly to prayers and religious processions around parishes to encourage the coming crops. Ascension Day, which immediately follows, became the day upon which the parish bounds were beaten. It is clear that in the past the two things were often combined. In 1625 George Herbert in *The Country Parson* pronounced that the procession should bring 'a blessing of God for the fruits of the field; Justice in the preservation of bounds' as well as 'Charity' provided by the goodwill of parishoners enjoying their day out together and 'Mercy' in the form of largesse given to the poor on the way.

He decreed that all parishoners were expected to turn out. On May 3, 1780 Parson Woodforde was still able to report that 'most of the Parish were assembled to go the Bounds' though he makes no mention of prayers or blessings. As usual, food and drink are uppermost in his mind. 'The Squire behaved most generously on the occasion. He asked me to go home and dine with him but I begged to be excused being tired, as I walked most of the way. Our Bounds are supposed to be about 12 miles round.' He must have been *very* tired.

Beating the Bounds of the parish of St Mary-the-Virgin, Oxford. The choirboys carry wands to assault the boundary marks, one of which can be seen behind the choirmaster. The boys also chalk the mark to show they have been there.

A further century on, another parson, Francis Kilvert, was in Oxford on Holy Thursday 1876, 'loitering along the celebrated Terrace Walk' when he came upon 'a company of people' Beating the Bounds.

At the present time two adjoining parishes in Oxford still beat their bounds on Ascension Day, St Mary-the-Virgin and St Michael-in-the-Northgate. In 1984 their parties actually met, the first time the vicars could remember it happening in many years of making their annual perambulations through the nether regions of the otherwise familiar colleges.

St Mary's set off after Holy Communion at about 9.15 with the vicar, nine choristers, the choirmaster and twenty or so others. Anyone is welcome, but to get into certain places they should have a wand for beating the boundary marks – a three foot garden cane. These are provided by the church, but the verger complains that 'people always pinch them'. The marks vary but most are rectangular, about ten inches across, either of metal or carved into the stone of the college walls. Each has a large diagonal cross, in the four corners of which are the letters S.M.V.P. The boys beat the marks, and in addition chalked in the letters and added the date. The whole affair was extremely good humoured, took us through all kinds of corridors, back alleys and kitchens as well as public roads. The boys seemed to remember the way better than the vicar. At All Souls, Fellows in their academic finery threw pennies for them onto the hallowed lawn, then entertained them in their dining room to cakes, sandwiches and squash. The Master of University College then threw pennies and toffees to scramble for in his garden. In Oriel they all had ice cream.

It was in a seedy passage near Oriel that we came across St Michael's. This caused delight on the part of the vicars and grown-ups and considerable badinage among the rival choirs. St Mary's were disgusted to find choir girls among the St Michael's boys.

St Michael's start later in the morning and conduct themselves a little more formally, and include in their party several undergraduates in gowns and mortarboards. At each of their marks the vicar cries 'Mark!' and the choirboys shout 'Mark! Mark! Mark!' as they beat it, until told to stop. Their tour is of a similar nature to St Mary's but includes one or two chain stores and the Roebuck Inn, before ending in Lincoln College at about 1.30 p.m. with a traditional lunch of bread, cheese, green salad and a dubious sounding but delicious drink called 'ivy beer'.

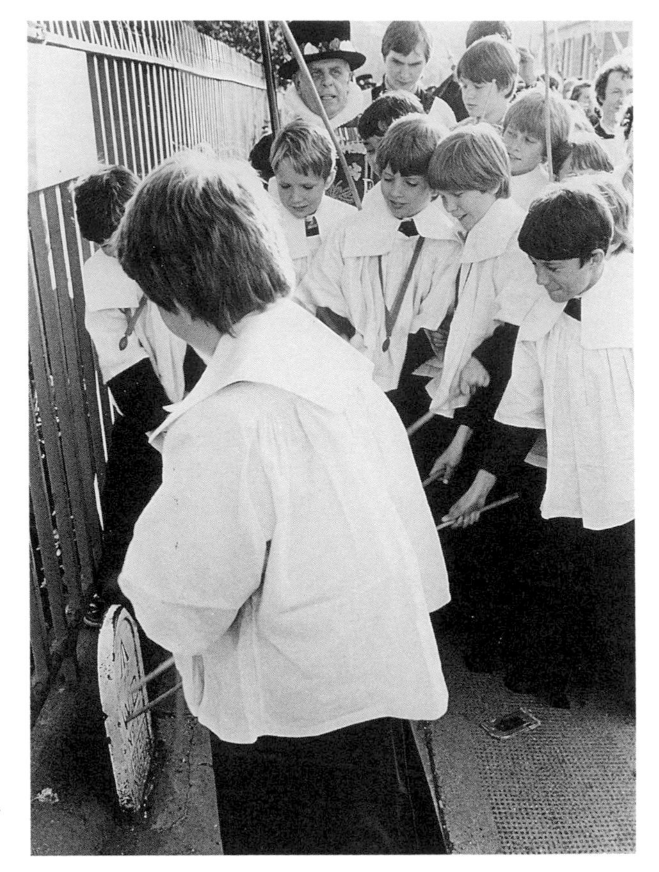

Beating the Bounds of the Tower of London.

There must be no end of parish boundary beatings around the country. Some are not carried out every year but every three or five years or at some quirkish interval. The Tower of London beat the bounds of their 'Liberty' every three years. The last time was in 1984. Though this is not a parish or a town, but the boundary of their jurisdiction, extending across Tower Hill to the Walls of Trinity House and the old Royal Mint, they still do it on Ascension Day.

There are thirty-one marks, each perfectly visible to passers-by, most of cast iron painted white with black lettering, a few flat in the footpath or even the middle of the busy road, all inscribed 'WD' and with its own individual number. WD is for War Department; the Tower is a military establishment. The numbers start near Tower Pier and go right round to the gate below the Tower Bridge.

Beating the Bounds takes place in the evening after the 6 p.m. Evensong in the Chapel Royal of St Peter ad Vincula, which is inside the Tower but open to the public. A substantial procession forms outside on the ground between the White Tower and the Jewel House, organized and led by the Chief Yeoman Warder carrying his mace, and including the chaplain, the choirboys with long willow wands, the Resident Governor, the Yeoman Warders and the families who live in the Tower, altogether at least 100 people.

Within the Tower they formed a procession magnificent to behold; once they emerged through the main gate they were immediately besieged by hundreds of tourists, interested Londoners and most of the world's photographers. The Chief Yeoman Warder put up with us all with good humoured tolerance, not in the least put out, chatting away to anyone asking questions. It was his duty at each marker to cry out 'Cursed is he who moves his neighbour's land mark. Whack it, boys. Whack it!' Whereupon the choirboys set about it with manic enthusiasm.

The vicar, churchwardens and official church surveyor of St Mary Redcliffe in Bristol do not beat their bounds but an ancient water pipe. In 1190 Lord Robert de Berkeley gave his 'Rugewell' in Knowle to the parish and for centuries it provided their only supply. Since the Second World War this supply has been cut off but these parish luminaries still have to turn out, on a Saturday afternoon in October, in order to retain their claim to certain related endowments.

In really nasty weather it has been known for none but the obligated to go; in 1984, thirty-six of us, and two Labradors, set off on the mile and a half inspection, down Redcliffe Hill, over the river, under the railway to Victoria Park. It was once ritual to hold up trains while they crossed *over* the railway, but this, perforce, died out years ago. In any case it is here that the flow of water peters out. To this point it flows very well, and in 1984 it was connected to, and supplies most of the water for, an unusual new fountain. In St Mary Redcliffe there is an intriguing roof boss in the form of a maze; the fountain is built to the same pattern. The water wells up in the centre, flows gently through the maze channels and is away a quarter of an hour later. Before this could be constructed, the City Engineer's Department thoroughly surveyed the Redcliffe Pipe and found it in good order, marvelling at some of the work carried out hundreds of years ago.

Near the fountain is the first marker stone, incised 'SMP', St Mary's Pipe. It is customary to bump newcomers on this and several were until the vicar and churchwardens became exhausted. Other stones are in streets, gardens, allotments. Landowners are obliged to admit access, and if necessary provide ladders to descend through manholes. No one is permitted to build above the pipe; even council terraces have gaps in them, and a path is kept open for the annual walk.

The spring is in the allotments behind Daventry Road, Lower Knowle, in a deep cavern big enough for several large men to stand up in. The whole affair was casual and relaxed, much enhanced by the engineer who had surveyed the pipe as part of his duties that summer but had become fascinated and was full of historical information. The afternoon ended, as always, with tea at nearby St Barnabas' Church.

The Redcliffe Pipe Walk takes the vicar, churchwardens, church surveyor, and anyone else who wants to come, along the one-and-a-half-mile course of the pipe to its source in an allotment in Knowle.

On August 15, 1983 the Town Clerk of Richmond gave notice 'that pursuant to the Charters of Queen Elizabeth (1576) and King Charles II (1668) and following custom faithfully observed since those times the Boundary of the Borough of Richmond in the County of York will be ridden and perambulated by the Council of the said Borough, the Lords of the Manor of Richmond aforesaid its Agents, Tenants and others on Wednesday 31 August 1983 at 9 o'clock in the forenoon beginning at the centre of the Bridge over the River Swale leading from Richmond aforesaid to Sleegill, when and where the Lords of the adjoining Manors and all persons interested may attend if they think proper. No dogs will be allowed

'Riding the Bounds' of Richmond in Yorkshire actually means walking the sixteen miles around the town.

on the perambulation.'

He did not give notice that this only occurs every seventh year, so be warned that there is ample time to get in trim for the sixteen-mile trek in 1990. A procession formed up outside the Town Hall in full regalia, and thus proceeded to Richmond Bridge to make the first 'Proclamation and Claim against Hipswell and Hudswell'. This was conducted with civic formality, speeches and official photographs.

But thereafter, divested of robes, ceremonial hats, and almost all formality, the official party set off at a cracking pace around the other eighteen boundary stones. The mayor was in command, now casually dressed but still wearing her chain of office. The Pindar was on hand to hack a way through with his axe if necessary. The Halberdiers were there to protect the mayor. The Bellman and Crier was along to ring his bell and cry the Proclamation each time. The Water Wader was there to wade into the waters of the River Swale, carrying the mayor, to inspect one of the boundary stones. The Aldermen, Councillors, Officials and Burgesses were attending because it was expected of them, I was there to record the occasion for posterity, and the other 500 people were out for a very pleasant if exhausting, walk.

A similar event takes place at Laugharne, near Carmarthen, even more exhausting, over twenty miles, every third Spring Bank Holiday. The last time was in 1984.

Laugharne, pronounced 'Larn', apart from being beautiful, is famous as the resting place of Dylan Thomas. It is equally interesting as one of the very few towns still administered by a Corporation, the head of which is the Portreeve who presides over a fortnightly Court Leet and Court Baron, under a charter granted by Sir Gwydo de Brione in 1307. They honour all the conditions of this charter, including perambulating the bounds on their 'Common Walk'.

On the day, the Court sits in the very early morning, as the dawn inches up. The Walk is an item on the agenda. When the subject of the bounds comes up they set off to inspect them; having done so, about eight hours later, they reconvene to declare everything in order, or decide what to do if it is not. The Portreeve, accompanied by his Halberdiers, Mattock Men, Flag Bearers and Guides, followed by several hundred energetic walkers, sets off at 6.30 a.m. Only children under 12 are banned. There are twenty-six places on the route, named in the original Charter, where the Mattock Men must leave a mark to denote their passing. These points are called 'hoisting places' because officials have the right to challenge anyone in the crowd to name the place correctly – Mackeral Lake, Chief Hill, Beggars Bush, Moildin Green – and if they fail, hoist them upside down by their legs and beat them three times with the Constable's staff. This is still done, with enthusiasm but without grievous bodily harm.

The Guides are responsible for seeing everyone goes the right way. There is only one map, drawn in 1858 but, by tradition, never copied or brought on the Walk. At one point they should pass right through a farmhouse; on one occasion the door was locked so the Chief Guide kicked the door down. This caused acrimony resulting in the Court having to pay for a new one. All is forgiven, but to be on the safe side they now go by the yard.

The Border Scots are fond of their Common Ridings; indeed, they are addicted to them. From the beginning of June to the middle of August they can satisfy their craving in turn at West Linton, Hawick, Selkirk, Melrose, Peebles, Galashiels, Jedburgh, Duns, Kelso, Langholm, Lauder and Coldstream. No doubt there are lesser Ridings as well. Further afield there are similar events at Dumfries, Linlithgow and Lanark. Genuine connoisseurs should not forget to 'Ride the Marches' at Musselburgh in 1995; they do it every twenty-one years.

These are all tremendous festivals, dressed up with proclamations, processions, elections, 'rideouts', gatherings, sports and re-enactments. Some go on for a week or more. Most of them are not old, several are even post-war, but Langholm and Hawick, are well over two hundred years old and Selkirk is more than twice that. Selkirk is also the biggest, mustering a field of 545 horses in 1984.

Langholm is only seven miles over the border on the road from Carlisle to Edinburgh. Roadside boards proclaim it to be The Muckle Toon; proximity to England does not make it less Scots. Their Common Riding takes place on the last Friday in July. In 1759 the Court of Session in Edinburgh decreed that certain lands around the town 'belonged inalienably to the community'. Cairns and troughs marked the boundaries and for the first fifty years or more they were perambulated annually, on foot, by one 'Bauldy' Beattie, the town drummer. The first organized Common Riding was in 1816. The following year the first 'Cornet' was elected to act as Master of Ceremonies.

All Border Common Ridings have a figurehead, who carries the Town Standard at the head of his mounted cavalcade. He is not called the Cornet everywhere; in other towns he is the Braw Lad, Standard Bearer, Callant, Reiver or Whipman but his function is very much the same. He is almost invariably a bachelor, chosen by public election or appointed by the committee or, uniquely in Coldstream, simply invited by his predecessor. I call him 'he' because he is *never* a woman. Women are not plentiful on these occasions, though in half the Ridings they are allowed in as chief attendants, invariably named 'Lass', as in Braw Lass or Reiver's Lass. The two attendants are sometimes imaginatively named Attendants but more often Right Hand Man and Left Hand Man, who can be the principals from the previous two years.

The Langholm Cornet is publicly elected earlier in the year. I am assured that three times as many people turn out to vote for him as do in district or parliamentary elections. However, *anyone* over 15 who happens to be passing through town on election day can vote.

As everywhere, the Cornet and his Right and Left Hand Man wear traditional dress, which in Langholm consists of a black bowler hat, black coat, and black-and-white check riding breeches. Everybody wears rosettes with long ribbons which Common Riding enthusiasts collect. Normally these are in the town's own colours, but at Langholm they have had, for at least a hundred years, the odd custom of using the colours of the year's Derby winner. Nobody knows why this is. The committee have taken to watching the race on television in the factory that makes the rosettes so that they can approve the colours and set to work at once, as there are not many weeks before the big day.

On the day itself proceedings begin at 5 a.m. when the Langholm Flute Band marches round the town. Presumably this is to wake everyone up, but the young make it a matter of principle to have been up all night. At 6.30, high on the hills above the town, the Hound Trail begins. This sounds a bizarre time for such a thing, but it has been so since 1845 and the Langholm Classic is the most important trail in the Borders. Hundreds of people are up to see it, the bookies are there in force and between thirty and forty of the best hounds for fifty miles around can be expected.

The official Common Riding ceremonies begin at 8.30 when the Cornet arrives to take custody of the Town Standard. He carries it on parades in town as well as on the rideout to Witta Yet and Castle Craigs. And he carries it, streaming out above him, as he leads his troops up Kirkwynd at the beginning. This is one of the most dramatic happenings I have come across, and a huge crowd assembles to watch first the Cornet, then his two attendants, then 200 riders gallop up the steep narrow hill at full speed, the hooves clattering among the houses, and even small girls on manic Thelwell ponies charging along at an astonishing pace, the crowd cheering them on.

Langholm Common Riding begins with a fantastic charge up Kirkwynd at full speed.

At various points there are elaborate ceremonies, Fair Cryings, proclamations, and the cutting and turning of sods. About lunchtime they all arrive at Castleholm for the races. The Cornet leads his army on a ritual circuit of the racetrack. Later there are proper races for horses and riders who have taken part in the morning rideout. Inside the track there are athletics and Highland dancing. Finally at 9.15 p.m. there is a fine closing ceremony at the Town Hall.

The whole day passes with a characteristic Scottish combination of meticulous regard for form and procedure and overwhelmingly good humoured enjoyment. If all Common Ridings are like this it is not surprising there are so many of them.

Hawick has one unusual feature. Women are not allowed to take part in the ceremonial or the rideouts, in spite of annual protests and inevitably detected attempts to get in in disguise.

Lanark's 'Lanimers' is a substantial festival lasting the whole of the first week in June. Lanimer Day, on the Thursday, is full of ceremonial. Their Lord Cornet is not a young bachelor but a respected public figure, chosen because of his contribution to Lanark affairs. If, by unhappy chance, he is unable to ride he is sent off to the police riding school at Glasgow Green to learn.

England has nothing to compare with these massive events. The Boundary Ridings at Berwick-upon-Tweed and Morpeth, though they attract up to 200 riders, are little more than that. Lichfield has its Sheriff's Ride on a Saturday near September 8. It is a curiously exclusive affair. In spite of 100 riders and a triumphal return to the city in the early evening, led by the Sword and Mace Bearers, it is ignored by the population. It is a legal obligation, though, by the terms of a charter granted in 1552 by Queen Mary and confirmed by another charter, granted by Charles II in 1664, and still in force.

In the same city St George's Court sits with much solemnity and attention to legal ritual but with no powers whatsoever, on St George's Day, April 23. Everyone attends wearing a fine red rose. The mayor presides, the Sheriff is at hand, the Steward, High Constables, Pinners, Ale Tasters, Bailiff, Dozeners, and Pinlock Keepers are in attendance to make their reports. Most of these reports are in humorous form,

The Sheriff's Ride at Lichfield taking sherry with the Dean in the Cathedral Close.

though swipes at unwelcome developments in the city are seldom resisted. In 1984 the two High Constables went so far as to write, and perform together, an extremely funny Gilbert and Sullivan parody.

Under ancient regulations instituted by Edward VI, Lichfield's mayor was Lord of the Manor and, as such, entitled to summon a Court Baron and View of Frank Pledge. Frank Pledge was a system whereby small groups of people were bound to, and mutually responsible for, one another. If disputes arose within a group they could be settled at the Court by a process called View of Frank Pledge. All these laws are now obsolete but Lichfield still keeps the Court going for old time's sake.

Officials are appointed, with great formality, to carry out no duties; only the Ale Tester is reported to take his work at all seriously. A jury is selected, by the time-honoured army volunteer system, and properly sworn in. A roll-call of citizens supposed to attend is read out and absentees are automatically fined – in groats. One man wrote in, in 1984, apologizing for his absence on honeymoon. He was still fined 1000 groats, this being found an utterly inadequate excuse. The public are made very welcome.

There are a number of courts like this which have lost their power to local politicians, the weights and measures inspectors and the police, but which still sit, literally for the fun of it. There are also a number which sit in earnest, not to throw recalcitrants in jail, but to administer land, and to fix rents, grazing fees, fishing rights and the like, and make decisions about the upkeep of the area within their jurisdiction. Occasionally they impose nominal fines on transgressors.

Stockbridge, in Hampshire, hold just such a court in the middle of March. Twelve jurors are appointed for the Court Leet, which covers the whole area of Stockbridge, and six for the Court Baron which is the Manor's Court. The history of the Manor of Stockbridge goes back almost to the Norman Conquest but since 1947 it has been the property of the National Trust. It now consists of two tracts of land; one, of 90 acres, is marshy grazing land on the south side of the village, the other, of 136 acres, is downland around Woolbury Ring, a mile to the east. The previous owner, now 'Quondam Lady of the Manor', is Professor Rosalind Hill, who has written a learned paper on the subject. Though the Trust is the true Lord of the Manor, Miss Hill still presides over the Court, whose main functions, she writes, 'at present are the annual election of officers, the settling of the "stint" in accordance with the state of the pasture, and the discussion of such matters of common interest as can then either be determined on the spot by mutual agreement, or referred to appropiate bodies. Many of these are, in fact, settled in Court.' It has become customary to review events in the past year, with special reference to those who have died, and to announce happenings planned for the coming year. Three principal officers are appointed: the Bailiff, the Constable or Sergeant-at-Mace, and the Hayward. The third of these looks after the grazing and collects fees, which in 1984 were £15 for a horse, and £8–£10 for a cow depending on its size. All people owning land are known as Burgesses and have the right to shoot on the Manor on payment of a small fee, also collected by the Hayward. Fishing rights were also included once, but were sold a long time ago in a transaction that is still regarded as, at best discreditable, at worst illegal.

Miss Hill concludes: 'It cannot be emphasized too strongly that the holding of these courts is not simply a matter of antiquarian interest. . .they have proved themselves to be extremely useful as a place for the discussion of local problems and for the taking of decisions based on local agreement.'

Tradition says that John of Gaunt granted certain rights to Hungerford in the fourteenth century; historians and lawyers have been unable to prove this conclusively, though for well over two hundred years the town was in dispute with the Duchy of Lancaster whose vast estates surrounded it during that time. James I finally agreed, in 1617, that the Manor, with 'rents, pleas, perquisites of court of burgh, with fishery and fishing of all rivers and waters in the manor aforesaid' did indeed belong to the people of Hungerford. There were ninety-nine houses at that time; estate agents to this day consider it worthwhile to put on their boards the words 'For Sale. With Valuable Fishing and Commoners' Rights.'

Every year on the second Tuesday after Easter the Hocktide Court is held to appoint officers and discuss Commoners' business. The Constable presides, supported by the Portreeve, Bailiff and others, thirty-one officials in all. At 8 o'clock in the morning the Town Crier, Robin Tubb, sounds a 250-year-old horn from the balcony of the Town Hall and exhorts all Commoners to attend the Court one hour later on pain of being fined. The Court sits promptly at 9. A jury of twelve is sworn in; absentees are indeed fined.

Though this Court is the main business of the day, all the other activities are far better known. As the session begins, the Tithing men set off on their rounds. They are called the Tutti-men and they carry their Tuttipoles. Tutty, according to The *Oxford English Dictionary*, is 'a nosegay, a posy; a tuft or bunch of flowers' and this is exactly what they are: six poles with a fine bunch of daffodils, polyanthus and anemone at the top. Impaled on a spike in the middle of the posy is an orange which is handed over to each Commoner as a sort of receipt for their tithe. The tithes, unlikely to exercise the rent tribunal, are a penny from each man and a kiss from each woman. The kisses give rise to a fair amount of horseplay. It is also customary for the Tutti-men to accept liquid hospitality wherever they go; since it is their duty to visit every one of the Common Rights houses, of

Hocktide at Hungerford. The Tuttimen claim tithes from over a hundred houses in the town, a penny from the men, a kiss from the women. The business of climbing up ladders began as a joke but persists because photographers like it!

which there are over a hundred, during the day, you can imagine that it is quite testing. They are accompanied by the Orange Scrambler, Bob Lewington, whose official job is to keep them supplied with oranges and whose unofficial job, in the afternoon, is to keep them upright and pointing in approximately the right direction.

There is a traditional Hocktide Luncheon in the Town Hall, attended by Commoners and their friends and several important guests. After toasts to the Queen Duke of Lancaster and John O'Gaunt, newcomers are required to go through an initiation ceremony called Shoeing the Colt, carried out with an excess of zeal by the Official Blacksmith and his burly friends. The newcomer, who is anyone they do not happen to recognize, including VIPs and photographers, is captured after a ritual, and sometimes fierce, struggle. The Blacksmith then hammers a farrier's nail into the victim's heel until he, or she, yells 'Punch'!

A painful initiation must also be endured by new Freeholders of Newbiggin-by-the-Sea. Since 1235 the Freeholders have owned a tract of land on the seaward side of Newbiggin about a mile and a half long by a third of a mile wide. It is divided into seventy-seven 'stints' – not actual plots of land, but shares of the whole. There are sixty Freeholders.

Many Freeholders acquire their share through inheritance, some by moving into a house which 'owns' one. It is possible simply to buy a share; in the mid-1980s a stint cost £1500, and I met a lady whose husband had given her one as a wedding present. There is no residential qualification; most Freeholders live elsewhere. Each owns a different proportion. At the present time the biggest is twelve stints, the smallest one-sixteenth. The land is all let off, to householders, a caravan site and, most substantially, to Newbiggin Golf Club. Rents therefore produce a dividend of about £150 per stint. The entitlement calculations must be formidable.

Each year on the third Wednesday in May the Freeholders hold their annual meeting and have a convivial lunch. They also perambulate the bounds, distributing peanuts as they go. They used to give out nuts and raisins but the health inspectors insisted that raisins were unhygienic. On the way they collect rents from a few householders who have not bought their gardens. The bounds take them along the foreshore on a pleasant walk around the golf course. On the eighth fairway there is a stone – in fact now a concrete replica since someone stole the stone – and it is here that new Freeholders are 'dunted'.

This does not happen every year, naturally, but in 1984 there was a new Freeholder, Julia Green, nervously awaiting her fate. Her father, already a Freeholder, had told her a harrowing tale of his own dunting. Many other Freeholders and a fair number of interested spectators gathered round to see Julia gently lifted and lowered – she was an extremely pretty lady – three times onto the Dunting Stone. At the same time a fourball jumped up and down on the tee yelling 'Fore!'

The dunting ritual observed, the Secretary announced 'Oyez, Oyez, Oyez! Be it known unto you here present that Mrs Julia Green is this day admitted a member of the ancient Body of Freeholders of Newbiggin-by-the-Sea in the County of Northumberland. God Save the Queen!'

Of all the events in this book none could be more accurately described as living history than Laxton Jury Day and Court Leet. The field system of farming was used in England for centuries. It was based on three large open fields, divided into strips. Each year one field was used for the 'bread crop', one for the 'drink crop' and the other lay fallow. The crops were rotated. The system died out with the decline of feudalism, and the coming of more efficient farming methods, but Laxton, in Nottinghamshire, still keeps it going; it is now the only place in Britain which does. Even though the farmers who work the system complain that it is hopelessly uneconomical and inefficient in this day and age, they appear to be interested in it and proud to be associated with it.

Such is the importance of Laxton that when Lord Manvers' estate came up for sale in 1951 it was bought by the Ministry of Agriculture, who passed it on thirty years later to the Crown Estates. The whole estate is about 1800 acres, of which two-thirds are farmed normally. It is a condition of tenancy that farmers must take part in the working of the other third.

The three fields are large: Westfield and Southfield are approximately 170 acres each, while Millfield has almost 220. A certain amount of each is in 'sykes', marshy and unfarmable. Each field is divided into strips a furlong in length and a chain wide (220 yards by 22 yards).

The farmers themselves administer the system by means of a Court Leet, held in early December in the Dovecote Inn. About a fortnight earlier they hold their Jury Day on which the twelve farmers picked the previous year, led by their Foreman and the Court Baliff, go out to inspect whichever of the three fields is about to lie fallow. They check the markers which

Boundary Riding at Richmond; the Bellman and Crier make a 'Proclamation and Claim'. *(see page 108)*

Sod-cutting and Turning' at Langholm Common Riding. *(see page 110)*

Whitby Penny Hedge is carefully constructed of 'stout stowers' and 'yedders'. (see page 124)

Laxton Jury Day. The Foreman of Southfield, Bill Haig, checks the position of a boundary post with other Jurymen.

divide the strips and replace them if necessary, make sure no one has strayed over his border, look at paths, fences and drains, and note any bad farming practice. Back at the Dovecote they discuss their findings and suggest fines for transgressors which are usually in the order of 50p or £1. This is an informal meeting of the jury only.

The Court Leet is a little more formal than Jury Day – though no special robes are worn for the occasion – properly opened and closed and presided over by the Steward, a solicitor who comes from Newark. All the farmers attend, or are fined if they are absent. The jury for the following year is sworn in and the Foreman for next year's field officially takes over. Foremen, once appointed, remain in charge of their field until retirement. Though only one field is inspected each year, there is always a certain amount of work to be done. All problems which arose on Jury Day are settled at the Court. There is full and frank discussion, a certain amount of needling, and attempts are made to impose fines. It is to the jury's advantage to levy at least some money for it goes towards Jury Day lunch the following year.

In 1732 Daniel Defoe on his *Tour through the Whole Island of Great Britain*, found the inhabitants of Wirksworth in Derbyshire to be,

> . . .a rude boorish kind of people, but they are a bold, daring, and even desperate kind of fellows in their search into the bowels of the earth. . .This town of Wirksworth is a kind of market for lead; the like not known anywhere else that I know of. . .The Barmoot Court, kept here to judge controversies among the miners, that is to say, to adjust subterranean quarrels and disputes, is very remarkable: Here they summon a master and twenty four jurors and they have power to set out the works underground. . .This court also prescribes rules to the mines. . .Also they are judges of all their little quarrels and disputes, in the mines, as well as out, and, in a word, keep the peace among them; which, by the way, may be called the greatest of all the wonders of the Peak, for they are of a strange, turbulent, quarrelsome temper, and very hard to be reconciled to one another in their subterraneous affairs.

I have alway found Wirksworth people reasonably agreeable. They still have their Barmoot Court, in April and October, but now the lead mining has all but ceased. Prospectors and miners still have their rights and if they find lead anywhere in what is known as 'the King's Field', so long as they are not in a churchyard, an orchard or on the highway, they are entitled to stake a claim. They must do this at the Court, which is presided over by the Steward, a real lawyer in wig and gown, and by the Barmaster, a qualified mining engineer. These two are appointed by the Queen, who as Duke of Lancaster owns all the land.

Should the claim be accepted and the miner produces lead, he has to divide it into three portions. It is measured in a Court measure made in 1512; twelve parts to the miner, one to the Duke of Lancaster, and every fortieth part to the vicar. The Barmoot Court is now a fairly lighthearted affair, though it still carries legal power. It is preceded by ale and cheese, known as 'Miners' Refreshments', followed by a traditional lunch of tomato soup, roast beef, Yorkshire pudding, cauliflower cheese, peas, baked potatoes, college pudding with rum sauce, and a special punch.

There were a number of these trade and agricultural courts. The Ancient Order of Purbeck Marblers and Stonecutters, for instance, has an Annual Meeting, not called a court but very much the same thing, every Shrove Tuesday at midday, in the Town Hall at Corfe Castle.

Articles of Agreement drawn up in 1651 were already referring to this Order as 'Ancient'. It was probably founded in the Middle Ages; present members insist that they were forerunners of the Freemasons though they have no connection with them now. Article Ten makes it clear 'that if any of our company shall at any time revele or make known the secrets of his company. . .he shall pay for his default. . .ffive pound', so I cannot vouch absolutely for any of this information. Their meeting is not open to the public; in any case there would be no room for them in the miniscule Town Hall.

Purbeck Stone is a shelly limestone, which is converted to marble when polished. Most English cathedrals have some Purbeck Marble, some a great deal, and it was used in the repair of the Temple Church in London, which was badly damaged in the Blitz. Nowadays the quarrymen do little marbling and most of their work is in providing untreated stone for building and fancy landscaping. There are still about twenty quarries, worked, for the most part, by fathers and sons, as they always have been. The heyday of Purbeck quarries was six or seven hundred years ago; when the Articles were agreed in 1651 there were 160 signatories; today the Order has 'about fifty' members, not all of whom work in the trade. A few outsiders are accepted if they have family connections. Article Six states 'that upon any acceptance of any apprentice into the company he shall pay unto the wardens, for the use of the company, six shillings and eightpence, and one penny lofe and two poots of beare.' This condition is maintained. 'Apprentices' have to be over 21.

On Shrove Tuesday the church bell is tolled for five minutes to summon the quarrymen to the meeting at noon. A short service opens the proceedings. In 1985 the Company business was lengthy; an anonymous informant divulged that this was because members were anxious about their standing with their new landlord. The apprentices, therefore, had to wait two hours across the road in the Fox before they were called over to present themselves to the Wardens. Each brought with him four bottles of ale, a small 'marblers' loaf', and 33p. This ritual is not what it was; in the past the unfortunate apprentices had to carry brimming mugs of beer across the road without spilling any, between two lines of quarrymen intent on making sure that they did.

Article Seven says that each member should pay twelve pence on the Shrove Tuesday after his marriage and, surprisingly, 'the last married man to bring a ffoot ball, according to the custom of the company'. This is required for the best known, but least important part of the day. An ancient right of way exists for quarrymen to transport their stone from Corfe to Owre Quay, over three miles away to the north-east. When this road was actually used for the purpose it was necessary, once a year, for the quarrymen to kick the football along the whole length of it to keep it open for them. Near the quarry the road passes through Owre Farm and a peppercorn rent was paid – a pound of peppercorns. This is still paid, though the football marathon has become no more than a ritual, and rather dangerous, kickabout along the streets of Corfe, to the dismay of lorry drivers and the fury of righteous motorists who roll down their windows and shout things about hooligans and the police. The football is not a fine new one each year but a battered looking specimen used for as long as it survives. The Warden admitted 'the ball sometimes gets squashed, but so far we haven't lost any of our members!'

The Dunmow Flitch Trials are among the most celebrated customs in Britain, for they have been in

The Annual Meeting of the Ancient Order of Purbeck Marblers and Stonecutters in the Town Hall at Corfe.

existence for nine hundred years or more. Though they have changed in the way they are conducted, the underlying principle has remained the same for all these years; a married couple have to

> . . .swear by Custom of Confession
> That you ne'er made Nuptial Transgression
> Nor since you were married man and wife,
> By household brawls or contentious strife,
> Or otherwise in bed or at board,
> Offended each other in deed or in word
> Or in a Twelvemonth and a day
> Repented not in thought in any way
> Or since the Church Clerk said Amen
> Wished yourselves unmarried again
> But continue true and in desire
> As when you joined hands in Holy Quire.

They are put on trial, before judge and jury, with 'Counsel' for and against them. If their claim is upheld they are awarded the Flitch. A flitch is a whole side of bacon. In the distant past this was an extremely valuable prize, and it is still worth winning today. In those days the trial was taken very seriously, but now there is a great deal of levity – though it is by means always a foregone conclusion that the happy couples will win.

The precise origin of the trial is unknown. Some historians credit Robert Fitzwalter, Lord of the Manor in the thirteenth century, others the monks of Little Dunmow Priory. Since one is known to have been a benefactor of the other, maybe both are correct. The first account of an actual trial was in 1445 when one Richard Wright won it; it seems that in the earliest trials the man applied and spoke up for himself while his wife was not consulted. The custom must have been well known long before this, because it crops up in two classic texts written towards the end of the fourteenth century, in terms assuming readers know all about it. William Langland's *Piers Plowman* mentions it, and so does Chaucer in *The Prologue of the Wyve's Tale of Bathe*, when he says:

> The bacoun was nat feet for hem, I trowe,
> That som men han in Essex at Dunmowe.

Though the Flitch was so well known it was not an annual event. Indeed sometimes fifty years elapsed between trials, and applicants had first to pursuade the Lord of the Manor of his obligation. In 1854 Harrison Ainsworth published his novel *The Flitch of Bacon* which aroused great interest locally, for there had been no trial for a century. They decided to revive the trials but as the Lord of the Manor of Little Dunmow refused to have anything to do with the scheme, the trials were held in Great Dunmow in 1855, Mr Ainsworth presiding. They have been held at irregular, but frequent intervals since then. I have a press cutting for June 2, 1925 when, for some reason, the trial was held in Ilford. G. K. Chesterton was the judge and the winning couple were represented by Sir Harry Slesser, the Solicitor General! Since the Second World War the trials have taken place every leap year, like the Olympic Games. A committee member remarked, 'more often and everyone would get fed up with them, less often and they might disappear altogether'. They are held in mid-June 'after Wimbledon and before the Essex Show', in a marquee on Talberts Lea.

The jury consists of 'six maidens and six bachelors of Dunmow', the girls in pretty hats and white dresses, carrying posies, the boys in immaculate suits. 'Leading Counsel' are celebrities, known for their gift of the gab; the 'agony aunt' and writer Claire Rayner has taken part in the last three trials. The trials are conducted according to ancient procedure; the tenor of events suggested by the fine quill pens provided for learned counsel – actually, biros with feathers sellotaped to them. The whole affair is enjoyable and lighthearted; nevertheless the jury make up their own minds, and if they are unconvinced they find 'for the bacon'.

There is no shortage of claimants. Hopefuls fill in a detailed form, the committee interviews ten couples selected from these, and finally chooses four to go on trial, with one in reserve. They do not have to come from Dunmow and they can be of any age. Their names are not revealed until they appear in the dock. In 1984 Chris and Kate Metson were on trial; Kate's grandparents had won the flitch in 1948, Chris's parents in 1954. They live right in Dunmow, and, predictably they won. Another couple from the West Country were not so fortunate; the jury found 'for the bacon' and they had to go home empty-handed.

The Dunmow Flitch Trials. The Claimants are in the dock on the left, the Flitch is on the right.

The payment of dues and tithes is largely a matter of handing over a cheque these days. Sometimes however there is a certain amount of attendant ceremony, although it may be quite informal. A friend told me that she lived in an estate cottage and that every Lady Day she was expected to go to the local pub, along with all the other tenants, pay the whole year's rent to 'Sir John' in person, who then bought them all a drink. Feudalism lives.

Some dues are more bizarre. The annual ceremony of rendering the Quit Rents by the Corporation of London to the Queen's Remembrancer takes place at the Royal Courts of Justice every October, normally in Court 4, the Lord Chief Justice of England's Court. If they can find out which day it is, one of the nation's best-kept secrets, a limited number of members of the public are welcome to attend.

The Queen's Remembrancer is the Supreme Court Official responsible for collecting debts due to the Sovereign. An officer of the Court proclaims: 'Tenants and occupiers of a piece of waste ground called "The Moors" in the County of Salop, come forth and do your service.' The City Solicitor then takes up a blunt billhook, a sharp hatchet and a hazel rod. With the utmost bravura he makes futile attempts to break the rod with the billhook, and then successfully cleaves it into two pieces with the hatchet. He gives one half to the Court as his rent and retains the other as his receipt. The Queen's Remembrancer declares 'Good Service'.

Then the official proclaims: 'Tenants and Occupiers of a certain Tenement called "The Forge" in the Parish of St Clement Danes, in Greater London, come forth and do your service.' The City Solicitor then counts out six large horseshoes and sixty-one nails with suitable ceremony. The nails are in bundles of ten with one over. The Queen's Remembrancer acknowledges, 'Good number'. The point is that neither of these properties really exists. The tenants have been released from their obligations to the Sovereign and the rents are a token in kind, hence the name 'Quit' Rents.

The Salop rent has been paid since 1211 at least, and the Forge since 1235. This actually was a forge originally granted by Henry II to Walter Le Brun. There was once a tilting ground nearby and the King may have considered the horseshoes and nails would be useful. It is thought to have been where Australia House now stands. The horseshoes and nails themselves are over 550 years old; they are kept by the Queen's Remembrancer and loaned every year for the ceremony.

An equally strange tithe-paying ceremony takes place in a field between Rugby and Coventry in the cold of a November dawn. Three weeks before the event, the local paper announces, 'Notice is hereby given that the Annual Audit for receiving the Wroth Silver due and payable to His Grace the Duke of Buccleugh and Queensberry on Martinmas Eve Before Sunrising will be held on 11 November at 6.45 a.m. at the Knightlow Cross, Ryton-on-Dunsmore, when all from whom payments are due are required to attend.'

At 6 o'clock in the morning a surprisingly large and cheerful crowd gathers in the Dun Cow near Knightlow Cross. The pub is all lit up, the car park is full and the lorry drivers on the busy A45 must wonder what on earth is going on. Inside everyone is drinking hot rum and milk. Just before 6.45, nicely centrally heated on a cold and frosty morning, the crowd moves a few hundred yards up the road to Knightlow Hill, to gather around the Cross. There is not actually a cross there but a large square stone with a hollow in the top in which the cross once stood.

Many of the crowd are there to pay Wroth Silver on behalf of their parish. There are twenty-five parishes represented, all part of the Hundred of Knightlow, of which the Duke is Lord of the Manor. Oddly enough no one knows exactly what the fee is for, though they pay it happily enough, since over many centuries this has been one of the very few transactions in the world of finance to remain unaffected by inflation. Also, they obviously like coming; most of them are there year after year.

Just as it becomes light enough to read, the Duke's agent, Mr Royston, produces his list and prepares to collect the Wroth Silver. He warns that 'non payment thereof forfeiture of 100 pence for every penny, or a White Bull with red ears and red nose'. This unusual forfeit in fact refers to the wild white cattle once common in England but now only to be seen in Chillingham Park, Northumberland. The last time one was demanded was in the middle of the last century but the proffered beast was rejected on the grounds that 'he did not fully answer the description'.

The agent then reads out the parishes and the amounts due, 'Arley, ½p; Astley, ½p. . .' and so on. All except three of the parishes pay between ½ and 1½ pence. Leamington Hastings pays 5p, Long Itchington pays 11p, and Harbury has to cough up 11½p. The reason these three have to pay so much is thought to be connected with the number of cattle in the parish when the fees were set. With each change in currency the Wroth Silver has simply converted to the nearest equivalent. The total payable is 46p, though contributions usually add up to a little more. As each parish is called, its representative steps forward and throws the money into the stone saying 'Wroth Silver'. If anyone fails to show up, someone else just pays for them. It is a curiously moving, almost religious ritual.

Afterwards everyone returns to the Dun Cow for a formal breakfast. Traditionally the Duke paid for this but inflation *has* had an effect on this part of the occasion. Since the Wroth Silver accounts for about one-tenth of one breakfast, the 150 people attending have to buy tickets in advance. There are speeches, toasts in hot rum and milk, and all are expected to smoke churchwarden pipes.

It seems a bit hard that an amiable farmer from Hawkser, near Whitby, should still be paying for the crimes of the man who owned his land in 1159. John Hutton used to feel that if he did not go on paying, someone – he was not sure who – might come along and take his land away; now, as we shall see, he need no longer worry.

Some commentators see the Whitby Penny Hedge as a simple tenure service but a well-known legend makes much better reading. 'In the fifth year of the reign of King Henry II' three noblemen were out hunting near Whitby when a wounded boar took refuge in a chapel where a monk from Whitby Abbey was at prayer. The monk shut the door to keep hounds and hunters out. The hunters were displeased and set about the monk. When the Abbot heard of this he ordered the noblemen to be put to death but the dying monk pleaded for them on condition they carried out the following penance 'for the safeguard of their souls'.

> you. . .shall come to the Wood of the Trayhead. . .and there shall the Officer of the Abbot blow his horn, to the intent that you may know how to find him, and he shall deliver unto you, William de Bruce, ten Stakes, ten Stout-Stowers and ten Yedders, to be cut by you. . .with a knife of a Penny Price; and you Ralphe de Piercie, shall take one and twenty of each sort, to be cut in the same manner; and you, Allatson, shall take nine of each sort, to be cut as aforesaid; and to be taken on your backs, and carried to the town of Whitby; and so to be there before nine of the Clock (if it be full Sea, to cease Service), as long as it is low water, at nine of the Clock, the same hour each of you shall set your Stakes at the Brim of the Water, each Stake a yard from another, and so Yedder them, as with Yedders, and so Stake on each side with your Stout-Stowers that they stand three Tides without removing by the Force of the Water. . .And if you and your successors do refuse this Service, so long as it not be full sea at that Hour aforesaid, you and yours shall forfeit all your lands to the Abbot, or his successors. . .

The 'Service' has persisted to this day. John Hutton has carried it out for nearly thirty years; before him his brother did it for eight and before that his father for no less than fifty-two years. His land is part of the Manor of Whitby. The Abbot has long since departed and the Abbey is an impressive ruin.

At 9 o'clock on Ascension Eve Mr Hutton and his son and the Bailiff of the Manor assemble on the foreshore, below Church Street, to erect the Penny Hedge. A considerable crowd assembles to watch them. The hedge is constructed from Stout Stowers, hedge poles banged into the mud and bound together by 'Yedders', pliant strips of wood. The final hedge is about 4 feet 6 inches high and twice as wide. The Huttons are great experts: their hedges have never failed to withstand three tides. When it is complete the Baliff blows an ancient horn and cries, 'Out on ye! Out on ye!' which the legend claims to be the words of the monk to the over-enthusiastic hunters.

However, in 1981, the family failed to make the hedge at all. The monk obviously knew a thing or two about the moon and Easter, and the tides. Though it had been 'up to the tops of our boots once or twice' this was the first time ever that the tide had been too high. The story made the BBC Radio 4 'World at One' News, where a gloomy sounding John Hutton insisted, 'The legend is firmly established. If the tide is wrong we are relieved of the duty. If the tide was right and we didn't do it I'd have to forfeit my lands – such as they are. It would be wrong to do it now. I expect the horn and mallet will end up in a museum.'

He was out again in 1982 and 1983 and 1984. . .

Most people are happy to bequeath all to their beloved relations. Some, having no relations, or disliking those they do have, prefer to help their favourite charity, a hospital, a school, a cats' home. A few feel it necessary to perpetuate their names by leaving money to pay for annual happenings such as literary prizes, feasts, sermons, hymn singing or rowing races.

A surprising number are magnanimous enough to leave at least part of their estates to the 'deserving' of one kind or another, poor, children, widows, or whoever. Almost every parish in Britain seems to have one or more bequests to administer, most of which will be handed over, or used as instructed, without any fuss or fanfare. But occasionally people have to make conditions, some verging on the bizarre, before they will allow even the most deserving to have a tiny share of their wealth, and it is these conditions which transform simple charity into Hallowed Custom. To tell you the truth, if you wanted to start a really genuine tradition this would be much the best way to do it. Other events appear and disappear; a bequest lives on because your executors are obliged by law to carry out your wishes. You would have to die first, which is a small difficulty, but otherwise it should do well.

George Carlow of Woodbridge in Suffolk made his claim to fame just in time, the day before he died. A book about the town, published in 1811, says:

> A Rent Charge of Twenty Shillings a Year, charged on a House in the New Street. . .This Sum is yearly distributed in Bread to the Poor. . .George Carlow was by Trade a Salesman; a strict Sabbatarian. . .He lies buried in the Garden belonging to the above mentioned House, under a large Monument, upon which the Bread is usually placed, previous to its being given away. His Epitaph, (alluding to the Donation, and being singularly remarkable in its Composition) is here preserved:
>
> Here lieth ye Body of George Carlow who departed
> this life the 24th Day of March 1738 aged 76 years.
> Wep for me Dear Friends no more
> Because I am Gone a little Before
> But by a life of Piety Prepare Your Selves to follow me
> Good friends for Jesus Sake Forbear
> To move the Dust Intombed Here
> Blesed be the man that spares thes stones
> Cursed be he that Removes my bones.
>
> Twenty Shillings Worth of Bread is to Be Given On this stone to the Poor of this Town On the 2. Day of February For Ever.

His actual will instructs that there should be distributed, 'Twenty Shillings worth of good wheaten bread. . .amongst the poor people of the parish. . .in two penny loaves, and penny loaves. . .the said Bread shall be always bought of the two poorest Bakers in the said Town'. The tomb is still there, reasonably maintained, and fairly legible, but its surroundings have become an inaccessible corner reached through the garage of the Bull Hotel. The original heirs and assigns of the will have, at some stage, turned into the vicar, and the poor of the parish into children from the local primary school. There was only one person present, an old lady, there for old times' sake, at pains to assure us she was comfortably off, unwilling to divulge her name lest she should acquire a reputation as one who accepted charity. The loaves had reduced in size and become excellent wheaten buns.

Biddenden Dole consists, these days, of a loaf, 2lb tea and ½lb cheese. The special biscuit has to be paid for. These gentlemen are the Trustees.

In Biddenden in Kent the pensioners have no such scruples. On Easter Monday 1983 eighty-five of them, or their accredited representatives, were ready, willing and eager to collect a large loaf of white bread, half a pound of cheese, two pounds of tea and a very special biscuit from a window of the old Workhouse. All pensioners and widows in the parish are entitled and most of them come along. This is a straightforward and good-humoured occasion presided over by four gentlemen whose job it is to compile the list of eligible parishioners, order the supplies and distribute them according to the current rules. There is nothing remarkable to be seen except the biscuits. These are an inedible mixture of flour and water and are obviously intended to be purely symbolic.

They show Eliza and Mary Chulkhurst. Biddenden's main claim to fame is because of these sisters. The village sign, hotels and restaurants exploit them and the Biddenden Dole is popularly supposed to have been initiated by them. According to legend they were Siamese twins, joined at the hips and shoulders, born in 1100, who died thirty-four years later within a few hours of one another. They are said to have left their property to the poor of Biddenden, the proceeds of twenty acres of land which became known as 'The Bread and Cheese Lands' and upon which the old Workhouse now stands. The most interesting things about the whole affair are, first, that nobody is sure that the girls existed and, second, that if they did, whether they actually set up the charity.

The historian, Edward Hastead, writing in 1790, insisted that the figures, already represented on the biscuits, were simply 'two maidens of the name Preston', to whom the land really belonged. Twice in the middle of the seventeenth century the rector, William Horner, attempted to prove that the proceeds belonged to him. Up to 1682 the distribution was made inside the church. Until then it included ale, which led to riotous behaviour and caused it to be moved into the church porch, and subsequently, at the end of the century, into its present position. To this day uncertainty about the history and origin of the event persists as alternate names imply – Biddenden Dole, Biddenden Maids Charity, Chulkhurst Charity. In practice it is unremarkable, but historically it is unique because its origins are unknown.

The Hospital of St Cross on the southern edge of the City of Winchester, was founded by Henry de Blois in 1136 as a home for thirteen poor men. It has expanded since, but it is still one of Britain's most ancient almshouses. From the beginning, in common with most such establishments, it had a Wayfarers Dole, whereby needy travellers had only to ask to be given food and drink.

The Dole continues to this day, though primarily in symbolic form. Because it is available every day, no questions asked, I have never actually managed to find the time to see it, but I understand that the first thirty-two people to turn up at the Porter's Lodge are entitled to a slice of bread, on an ancient wooden platter, and a drink of ale from a special horn mug.

The Butterworth Charity is distributed on Good Friday morning in the churchyard of St Bartholomew the Great, in London's Smithfield, 100 yards away from that other, much more familiar building dedicated to St Bartholomew, Barts Hospital.

Circumstances have changed this Charity as well. It is thought to have begun with a bequest in 1686 whereby twenty-one widows of the parish were to receive sixpence. This is not a huge sum of money but towards the end of the nineteenth century it looked as if funds were going to run out. A parishioner, Joshua Butterworth, therefore made the necessary arrangements in 1887 and the Charity has borne his name ever since. The sixpences were placed on his tombstone and the widows stepped forward in turn, knelt and picked one up. At the end of this ceremony each was additionally given half-a-crown and a hot-cross bun.

In 1982 the vicar conducted a short service standing on the tomb, with the choir assembled behind him by the church. He assured us that he had some sixpences but, alas, no widows, since none lived in the miniscule parish which consisted almost entirely of hospital, meat market and office premises. The money, such as it was, would be put to a good use, and meanwhile we were all welcome to a hot-cross bun.

Chambers, writing in the late nineteenth century, says, 'We have a Twelfth-Night celebration recorded in theatrical history. Baddeley, the comedian. . .left, by will, money to provide cake and wine, for the performers, in the green-room at Drury Lane Theatre on Twelfth-Night; but the bequest is not now observed in this manner.' Which is very odd because that is precisely the manner in which they do observe it to this day.

Robert Baddeley had the good natured idea of perpetuating his name, not by giving largesse to the poor, but a cake to his friends in the theatre that he loved. He was once a chef so the notion of centuries of Baddeley Cakes must have appealed to him. He was a successful actor, ancestor of actresses Hermione and Angela and the well-known and novelist V.C. Clinton-Baddeley.

When Baddeley died, in 1794, he left £100 to pay for the wine and cake, to be enjoyed by the cast of the show current on the day, in full costume and make-up, after the evening performance. The investment has long since failed to provide enough interest to pay for everything and many years ago the theatre took over the provision of punch. Baddeley still pays for the cake, though, and in a nice reverse of role it has been made for some years by an actor who became an expert cook whilst 'resting'. The only times they have missed the party have been when the theatre was dark between shows. It is not open to the public, for obvious reasons, but they allowed me in during 1972 during the run of *Gone With the Wind.*

Though Baddeley Cake is a justly celebrated tradition, it is less well known that the actor left a considerable sum of money to the Drury Lane Theatrical Fund, founded by David Garrick in 1766, for the relief of distressed members of the Company.

The Tichborne family has had its troubles over the centuries and has become well known on two counts, the second possibly as a result of the first. The Tichborne Dole has existed since the twelfth century, when its instigator forecast inevitable disaster should it ever be allowed to lapse. All went well until 1796 when it was suppressed because 'Dole Day was attended by scenes of confusion and disorder'. One of the results may well have been 'The Tichborne Claimant', one of the most celebrated cases in legal history, which occupied the courts for 291 days in all, and almost ruined the family.

Briefly, in 1853 Roger Tichborne, heir to the estate, near Alresford in Hampshire, sailed away in the direction of Valparaiso and disappeared. When his father, Sir James, died in 1862, it became necessary to find him. His mother refused to believe he was dead, so she advertised. At the end of 1866 a man appeared to claim his inheritance. Though he looked nothing like the young man everyone remembered, he said he was indeed Sir Roger. His mother, the dowager Lady Tichborne, believed in him and continued to do so

Cutting the Baddeley Cake at the Theatre Royal, Drury Lane, by the cast of 'Gone With the Wind' in 1972.

until she died in 1868, but none of the rest of the family did. It became an event of national interest. In May 1871 a civil trial began, to prove his claim. Ten months later 'Sir Roger' found himself, instead, committed to Newgate Prison on a charge of wilful and corrupt perjury. The consequent criminal trial lasted another ten months until in February 1874 he was sentenced to fourteen years' penal servitude. It was generally agreed that he was, in fact, a man called Arthur Orton, who had come across Roger Tichborne in Australia.

The case aroused such interest that *The Graphic* thought it worthwhile to print a special 'Literary and Pictorial Record, containing a complete History of this Cause Célèbre'. Included in the 32,000 words about the case were about 1000 on the Dole. Here are some of them, a little editing having been necessary in view of the Victorian habit of never using one word when ten would do:

> In the reign of Henry I, Sir Roger de Tichborne married Mabella. . .famed for her piety and charity, and it was commonly believed among the superstitious peasantry of those days that she had the power even of working miracles. When worn out with age and infirmities she petitioned her husband for the means of instituting a distribution of bread. . .on every Lady Day for ever. To this request her husband not only acceded, but promised her for the purpose as much land as she could walk around. . .while a billet of wood, which was to be lighted, should continue to burn. It would seem to have been a somewhat unkind condition to require a wife weighed down with age to perform pedestrian exercises of this kind; and the concession is unfortunately open to the suspicion of being dictated by the belief that the result would not deprive the Lord of Tichborne of any very large portion of his ancestral estates. . .Old Lady Tichborne was not to be daunted by the trifling difficulty that she happened to be bedridden. . .she succeeded in completing the entire circuit of the meadow before the last little tongue of blue flame hovering on the wreathes of smoke had finally dropped out, and the faggot was reduced to ashes. The spot. . .has ever since been known as 'The Crawls'. Lady Tichborne

> was said to have threatened the downfall of the house and the extinction of the name of Tichborne if any of her successors should be wicked enough to abolish the annual work of charity. Towards the close of the last century it began to be felt. . .that the Dole did but little good for the honest and deserving, while it attracted in great numbers the idle and dissolute. . .and was therefore at last abolished. Before long the old prophecy must have its fulfilment. Sir Henry Tichborne who succeeded to the baronetcy in 1821, was popular in the county. . .but the curse of Lady Mabella was upon him and his house. . .He had seven children of whom six lived and were celebrated for their good looks and their tall and handsome proportions; but all seven were daughters.

Other accounts vary a little in detail, but I am sure you have got the gist. Sir Henry's brother Edward had changed his name to Doughty on inheriting another estate. His other brother James eventually did succeed, and his son was the disappearing Roger. The Dole was hastily re-introduced and has continued until the present day. Christina Hole in her *Dictionary of British Folk Customs* relates an amusing story about how the rationing after the Second World War nearly stopped the Dole. For many years the Dole has been given in the form of flour, and the family has actually had to buy it. In 1948 the Ministry of Food refused the coupons. Fleet Street were not going to miss a good story like that and in no time more than 5000 coupons had arrived at the house. The Ministry relented.

I have not been there since 1966 when Sir Anthony Doughty-Tichborne was in residence. Sadly, he died two years later and the baronetcy became extinct since he had no male heir. His daughters still keep the Tichborne Dole going, though, no doubt nervous of the consequences should it lapse again. All the inhabitants of Tichborne and Cheriton parishes are eligible, a gallon of flour for adults, half a gallon for children, 'measured out using things we've had in the family for ever'. The self-raising flour is not produced on 'The Crawls', a field still part of the estate, but bought from a local mill.

It is a nice English occasion; a touch of ritual, a suggestion of feudalism, a whiff of eccentricity, and plenty of time for gossip.

I have not seen 'The Knillian', or the John Knill Ceremony, in St Ives, Cornwall, but I do intend to on July 25, 1986, when it is next due to be held. It must certainly be included, though, since the terms of this bequest are so extremely idiosyncratic.

John Knill was a public figure in the district, mayor of St Ives in 1767. He wished to be remembered after his death and he made sure of this by having a huge mausoleum built for himself at the top of Worvas Hill, fifty feet high and visible for miles. Unfortunately, he happened to be in London when he died and he is buried there. By 1797 he had arranged his bequest in the form of a trust and he lived to see the first distribution in 1801.

The whole amount to be given out comes to about £100, quite a fair sum in 1801, less so now and not so impressive when divided by the five years between each ceremony. The terms were as follows: £5 each to ten little girls under the age of 10, who were to wear white dresses and dance at 'Knills Steeple' for not less than fifteen minutes, before singing 'The Old Hundredth' psalm. They were to be accompanied by a fiddler who was to receive £1. Two widows, over the age of 64 had to attend to 'certify to the trustees that the ceremonies have been duly performed', for which they would get a fee of £2 each. Conditions for the other recipients are more long-term: £5 to the married couple over 60 who had raised the largest family without any help from the parish; £5 to the best knitter of fishing nets; £5 to the best packer of pilchards; £5 each to the two 'follower-boys' – apprentices – who had worked hardest during the previous fishing season; £10 for a girl who had been married since the previous December 31 'who was most worthy, etc, etc. . .' There were gifts to do with the tin mining as well, and finally £10 for a dinner for the trustees.

All this is still carried out as faithfully as possible, though some adjustments have had to be made because of changes in the fishing and mining industries. The mayor and all the town officials climb up to Knill's Steeple in their ceremonial dress and the day is treated as a great festival. John Knill achieved his ambition and is very well remembered in St Ives.

The Reverend Thomas Mayrick was more modest, but he was an idealist with a sense of humour. In 1841 he left a small sum to be invested in government stock, the interest of £2 10s 0d to be paid annually 'to the young single woman resident in Holsworthy under 30 years of age who is generally esteemed by the young as the most deserving, the most handsome, and the most noted for her quietness and attendance at church. . .may this well-meant example lead rulers to see and know that subjects are better directed and led by harmless amusement and by judicious reward, than by the fear of punishment'.

His well-meant bequest has become known, charmingly, as the Pretty Maid's Charity. The chosen beneficiary is presented to the town with great ceremony when she emerges from the church door as the clock strikes 12 on the first morning of St Peter's Fair. Until that moment her identity is secret and she has been lurking in the vestry since early morning lest anyone should see her. She is selected by the trustees, a sub-committee of those who administer Speccott's Charity – a much more useful and substantial, but less entertaining, endowment. The only other person that knows who she is is the photographer from the local paper, who divulged, rather roguishly, I thought, but in the strictest confidence, that because of press days it was his tedious chore each year to accompany her to a secluded spot in the countryside some days earlier and take her picture. This is a little-known facet of the custom.

Holsworthy is a pleasant little market town on the west side of Devon, near Bude. During the second week in July three customs have become amalgamated into one. The Fair is proclaimed by the Town Crier at 8 o'clock on Wednesday morning from a special, but unremarkable, point near the Market Square. It runs until Saturday. The Court Leet, which no longer has jurisdiction, is held on the previous evening. The officers, Portreeve, Constable, Weights and Measures Inspector, Ale Taster and so on, deliver their weighty reports, then they all go off to make sure that the Ale Taster carries out his duties with conscientious dedication in the town pubs.

So, after the Pretty Maid has been revealed, her first duty is to cross the road arm-in-arm with the Portreeve to pay an official visit to the Fair. The two of them sample the rides and games and the Pretty Maid gets an armful of teddy bears. Afterwards they have an official lunch. During the year she will find herself called upon for other tasks.

The Charity has increased, with inflation, to £5. Even so some of the girls doubt if it is worth it; in 1984 the Pretty Maid was an extremely shy 21-year-old pastry cook called Christine Bolt who emerged from the church like a condemned prisoner about to face a firing squad. She confirmed later that that was exactly how she felt. An official pointed out that most of the girls were convinced that the crowd would find them exceedingly ugly. 'Christine's great', he said, 'but some years I think it should be re-named "The Prettiest-Maid-We-Can-Find Charity"!'

The 'Pretty Maid' of Holdsworthy carries out her first official duty, a visit to St Peter's Fair with the Portreeve.

Next we have two charities in which beneficiaries are decided by the unexpected method of throwing dice. John How died in 1674, leaving £400 to be invested, the interest to be given to a maidservant who had been in service in the same house for more than two years. His unusual condition was that the mayor or magistrate of Guildford should choose two qualified candidates and they should settle the matter by throwing dice. In 1702, another Guildford man, John Parsons, left £600, the interest to be paid to a 'poor young man, who hath served an apprenticeship of seven years' yet was prepared, oddly, to swear before a magistrate that he was not worth twenty pounds. Should no claimant present himself the money was to be paid to a maidservant who had been in the same house for three years. As Parsons probably foresaw, male vanity did cause claimants to dwindle and the two charities have become permanently connected.

Properly qualified ladies are becoming increasingly difficult to find, but the ceremony is still carried out in the Guildhall, in the presence of the mayor, near January 29, the day on which John How died. It has become known as 'Dicing for the Maids' Money'. Everything is carried out with official attention to detail, and the results are recorded in the ledgers. The maid who throws the highest number claims How's Charity and the lower Parsons', with the diverting result that the winner gets less than the loser. However, the amounts involved are not large so the difference is not enough to cause trouble.

At St Ives in Cambridgeshire twelve children dice for Bibles each year. In 1675, Dr Robert Wilde died and this is an extract from his will on display in the church:

> £50 to be laid out on a piece of land as would so produce a rental of £3 p.a. to be expended in bibles and paid into the hands of the Vicar and Churchwardens. An annual sermon is for ever to be preached in the parish church on 'the Excellency, Perfection and Divine Authority of the Scriptures'. The Minister shall give notice when the sermon shall be preached and twelve children, six male and six female shall cast dice for six bibles. The Minister shall kneel and pray God 'to direct the lots of His glory' and receive 10 shillings, the clerk 12 pence. Such money remaining shall be expended by the vicar and churchwardens on a comfortable dinner for themselves, with as much claret and sack as the remaining money will provide.

Though the spirit of the bequest is observed faithfully, the practice has changed a little over the years. The sermon has gone, and so, the vicar complains, has the dinner, the claret and the sack. On the other hand six more Bibles have arrived. At one time the dice were thrown on the church altar, but this was too much for a nineteenth-century bishop who made the vicar move it to a table by the chancel steps. Later it was moved out of the church altogether and into the church school, but for the last twenty years it has been back on the table, as before. The original £50 was spent on land which became known as Bible Orchard and the rent from this paid for the Bibles. It was sold recently for a new library to be built on it, and the proceeds have been invested. As there is nothing in the will to say the children have to be Anglican, each of the other three churches in St Ives, Catholic, United Reformed and Methodist, provides three boys and three girls as well.

The vicar, Mr Moore, tries to hold the ceremony on real Whit Monday, the proper day under the terms of the will, but this is not always possible. The mayor usually attends. After a short address follow the Lord's Prayer, another prayer and a hymn, and the dicing. There is no interdenominational rivalry; the groups from each church compete among themselves, two boys, two girls and then the remaining boy and girl. Each throws three times and the highest total wins the Bible. Draws are settled by another throw. The churchwardens keep the score; the vicar says he is on hand to arbitrate 'and the Mayor and Mayoress are there to keep an eye on me'.

It is a charming little custom, but strange if you pause to consider the scene. Mr Moore describes it as 'our annual emergence from obscurity!'

Another unusual custom exists for children in the East End of London. It is not an annual event, though the way things are going it may well be one day, if it survives at all. The Fern Street Settlement was established in 1907 in Bromley-by-Bow, one of the hundreds of charitable organizations formed around that time to help the poor. This one is still going, dependent on contributions and donations for its own existence, yet providing meals-on-wheels, club facilities, outings and the like, for the elderly, and Farthing Bundles for children. The Settlement was founded by Clara Grant, and it was her kindly and imaginative idea to provide little surprise parcels, full of toys, puzzles, pencils, beads and bits of nonsense, absolutely nothing valuable, but special in the early days to kids who had nothing. She was not going to *give* them away, though. She felt they should pay for them, so she charged the smallest coin of the realm. For fifty years the children would turn up in their hundreds every Saturday morning, boys one week, girls the

Farthing Bundles. The arch has been raised a few times as children have benefited from the Welfare State.

next, to hand over their farthings and collect their bundles. Also they had to be small enough to walk under a wooden arch across which are painted the words, 'Enter all ye children small, none can come who are too tall'. Four feet was their limit.

Times have changed now and the young have pockets full of money – which is, of course, a good thing. They simply do not *need* their little presents any more, though there are still a few around who enjoy the surprise. By the 1960s it had become a fortnightly affair, boys and girls together; these days it is on the first Saturday of the month.

The bundles remain much the same, full of gifts donated by well-wishers, or bought out of meagre funds. The children who do come have to pay one pence, currently the smallest coin, even if it is worth ten times the original farthing. Inflation has struck in another way too. The Welfare State has made children bigger and the arch has had to be raised from time to time. It is now four inches higher than it was.

Henry Travice made provision for a graveside dole, the feature of which is that his grave is inside the parish church of Leigh, Greater Manchester, and recipients must pass through his pew to get it. On the end of the pew is a beautifully lettered brass plate bearing the inscription:

> Heere neere adjoyneth the buriall place belonging to the House of Mr. Henrie Travice late of Light Oakes, who departed this Lyfe the 7th of August Ano Doi 1626 aged 64 and give by his last will unto forty poor people of this parish five shillings apeece yearly to be delivered them neer his gravestone heerunder placed, on Thursday in the Passion Weeke forever.

The £10 is still paid out on Maundy Thursday during Evening Service. The money comes from a 'Rent-charge issuing out of Parts, Grounds or Lands at Cronton in the County of Lancaster'. Cronton is just north of Widnes, about fifteen miles away. It is not considered that forty poor people are likely to want to come for 25p so the spoils are now divided into three parts only, £4 to St Mary's parish and £3 each to Atherston and Tyldesley, one representative from each.

The affable vicar of Leigh, the Reverend Jack Finney, was the subject of a radio programme in 1984 on the life of a parish priest. Preparations for Maundy Thursday were discussed and I well remember his remark, 'I shall feel like the Queen on that day. . . '

The Queen herself, of course, distributes the Royal Maundy on that day during a service of the utmost splendour, far removed from the simple ceremony at Leigh. But the two do have something in common; the recipients at Leigh could well find themselves invited should the Maundy Service come to Manchester Cathedral.

The 'Recipients', as they are officially known, are the reason for including the Royal Maundy in this book, other royal occasions being, on the whole, inaccessible to ordinary mortals. In the distant past they were people in genuine need of money and clothes; today they are less needy but still modest souls who have been chosen from all over the diocese, and by all denominations, for the often unrecognized service they have given to the community. They are all pensioners and may include much loved lollipop ladies as well as worthy committee persons. There are an equal number of men and women, as many of each as the Sovereign's years of age.

This stupendous event has a long, involved and

interesting history. There is only room for the briefest summary here. All the details can be found in *The Royal Maundy* by Peter Wright, Secretary to the Royal Almonry since 1964.

The occasion derives from the episode in which Christ washed the feet of His disciples after the Last Supper on the evening before the Crucifixion:

> If I then your Lord and Master, have washed your feet,
> ye also ought to wash one another's feet.
> For I have given you an example, that ye should
> do as I have done to you. (John 13:14)

The symbolic act of washing the feet is still performed in the Catholic and Orthodox churches and in some Anglican parishes on Maundy Thursday. It has long appealed to monarchs, bishops and noblemen to perform this act of humility, and in time it became customary, in addition, to give alms. The first English monarch known to have been involved was King John, in 1210. The washing of feet seems to have persisted into the eighteenth century though the last king to do it himself was possibly James II, about 1685. During the last years of this ceremony it was carried out by the Lord High Almoner, who, to this day, as well as the other Almonry officials, attends the service girded with a large white linen towel, though only the almsgiving now survives.

In the early days the ceremony was held where the Court was in residence. For 200 years until 1890 it took place in the Chapel Royal in Whitehall, then for sixty years in Westminster Abbey, but this does not mean that the Sovereign took part. From the end of the seventeenth century until 1932, the kings and queens were content to leave the duty to the Lord High Almoner. George V took it up again in 1932 and his sons and granddaughter have continued. Indeed the present Queen has missed only four times, twice when on Commonwealth tours, twice after the birth of her younger sons. From 1952 to 1970 the service was held in alternate years in the Abbey and other cathedrals around the country. Since then the Abbey has been becoming a less frequent venue. It was last there in 1981, since when it has been to St Davids, Exeter, Southwell and Ripon. In late 1984 the Royal Almonry Office said 'there are no immediate plans for the Service to return to Westminster Abbey in the near future'. An official confided, unofficially, 'we were running out of recipients anyway'.

The service is spectacular. At the beginning, after the Queen has been greeted by the Bishop and the Dean, an awesome and splendid procession of something over a hundred people in ceremonial finery moves up the nave of the cathedral. It is divided into four groups. The first, led by the Crucifer and the Taperers, is mainly choristers and musicians including the Gentlemen and Children of Her Majesty's Chapel Royal. The second consists of cathedral clergy. Then comes the smallest group of the Head Verger, the Dean or Provost, Her Majesty the Queen, Prince Philip, Her Majesty's Suite and the Lord Lieutenant of the County.

The fourth group, extremely impressive, is the Royal Almonry Procession, the people who arrange and carry out, with the Queen, the Royal Maundy ceremonial. It includes, among others, the Yeoman of the Guard, the Children of the Royal Almonry, the Wandsmen, the Secretary and Assistant Secretary of the Royal Almonry, the Sub Almoner and finally the Lord High Almoner, in the toweringly impressive person of the Bishop of Rochester.

The Yeomen of the Guard were created by Henry VII in 1485 and are thought to be the oldest military corps in the world. They are not serving soldiers, however, but ex-warrant officers from the Army, Royal Air Force and Royal Marines. There are eighty of them in all and varying sized groups attend all state occasions. Twenty-four take part in the Maundy Service in their familiar scarlet uniforms. Two of them carry the Maundy money aloft on great silver gilt dishes with the leather thongs of the purses draped theatrically over the edges.

The Children of the Royal Almonry are the only part of this group to come from the diocese. Today they are chosen from local schools and they are rewarded for their services with a set of Maundy coins. They do not do anything, however, except attend as part of the entourage. Apparently until 1808 they were not children at all, but old men, who were paid the surprisingly large sum of £21 for their part in the proceedings, but my reference sources are all silent on the matter of what this part actually was.

There are two distributions of the Royal Maundy during the service separated by the second lesson which has, by recent tradition, been read by Prince Philip. There is no question of the Recipients queueing up; the Queen comes to them accompanied by the Almonry officials. She presents each Recipient with two small purses, one white with red thongs, the other red with white thongs. These are specially made of fine leather and quite expensive in themselves. The two are fixed together by twisting the thongs.

The red purse contains £5.50 in ordinary money in lieu of clothing and provisions given in former times. In 1906, the well-known photographer and Member of Parliament, Sir Benjamin Stone wrote, 'Much scandal was occasioned by the gifts in kind, particularly the clothing. The female recipients, with the

The Royal Maundy Service in Southwell Minster in 1984.

weakness of their sex for "trying-on", donned their garments. . .and loudly expressed their pleasure or dissatisfaction, according to their view of the fit. Money was therefore substituted.'

The white purse contains the famous Maundy Money. There are four silver coins, one, two, three and four pence, specially made each year by the Royal Mint. One of each makes up a set of 10p and each purse contains enough sets, plus the odd coins, to add up to the Sovereign's age. Maundy Money is legal tender, though not often used as such. Few Recipients would wish to part with it, unless it was to a dealer, a species regarded as a menace by Buckingham Palace, who refuse to divulge the names and addresses of Recipients to protect them from their unscrupulous habits.

It is a wonderfully colourful, interesting, moving occasion. Unfortunately, getting to see it is largely a matter of luck, unless you happen to belong to one of the groups directly involved. The Royal Maundy Service will come to your cathedral no more than once in a lifetime – and if it does you still have to get invited!

The Queen distributing the Royal Maundy in Southwell Minster in 1984. (see page 132)

The Woodmen of Arden shooting for the 'Silver Arrow' at their Grand Wardmote. *(see page 141)*

Cumberland and Westmorland wrestling at Grasmere Sports.

See the conquering hero comes

Everyone knows about the Derby, few know about Kiplingcotes Derby; everyone has heard of the Boat Race, few of Doggett's Coat and Badge. Not many are familiar with the Woodmen of Arden or the Knights of the Old Green, or the British Marbles Champion who triumphs on Good Friday less than a mile from Gatwick Airport. This chapter is about some of Britain's sports and games, unusual enough and particular enough to be considered Calendar Customs. Old as they may be, events like Ascot, Henley, Wimbledon and Cowes are too well known. Sports like curling, skittles, quoits and whippet racing are interesting enough for a different book. Highland Gatherings are wonderful but there are too many of them – though it is a pity to leave out the mighty 'heavies', and their cabers, big as telegraph poles, which you and I could not move, let alone toss.

'The World-famed Old English Games' at Grasmere are not entirely unique. There are others but Grasmere Sports is the big one, the one at which every fell racer, hound trailer, or wrestler wants to win, and to which 20,000 people go to watch them do it.

Nobody knows how old the meeting is, only that they have kept records of it since 1852. It is thought to be much older. The Sports are held on the third Thursday after the first Monday in August. Locals insist that it never rains, though it has been known to. Events begin on the stroke of noon, with the Long Leap followed by the High Leap, and the Under 15 Wrestling. By 6 o'clock 38 separate events will have taken place, including numerous track races, cycle races, 4 fell races, 3 hound trails, countless wrestling bouts and the Judging of the Wrestlers' Costumes. The whole afternoon is a miracle of organization.

There is money to be won, for, although old and traditional, Grasmere Sports are entirely professional. There is an extensive athletics circuit in Scotland and the North of England, and at the Highland Games too 'heavies' compete for money, while wrestlers, hound trailers and fell racers can win substantial prizes. Mind you, none of them is going to live on the proceeds but they are worth having. The principal events at Grasmere are worth between £50 and £100, donated by local companies.

So the athletes and cyclists take their business very seriously. However, it is the other events that the crowd has come to see. The Cumberland and Westmorland Wrestling begins at noon and finishes with the 'All Weights' contest in the afternoon. Wrestlers can enter any weight category for which they are qualified, and most will, so there are innumerable bouts.

This is an ancient and gentlemanly sport thought to have arrived in Britain with the Vikings. Icelanders have a similar style called Glima Wrestling. Cumberland and Westmorland Wrestling is nothing like the entertaining nonsense seen on television every Saturday. No quarter is expected or given but it is absolutely clean and fair. An association was formed in 1906 to organize and regulate the sport and they have laid down rules. Part of Rule 3 says 'that any wrestler attempting sham wrestling, personation, buying or selling a fall, getting into any weight to which he is not entitled, or otherwise misconducting himself, or in any way attempting a "barney", tending to bring discredit on fair and manly wrestling, shall upon detection be at once expelled.'

There are only a hundred or so regular wrestlers, who are all friends, knowing each other well; brothers, cousins, fathers and sons can compete

The start of Grasmere Sports Hound Trail.

without splitting families asunder. In the 1980s brothers Tom, Jim and Joe Harrington and their cousins George and Alf met almost weekly. In 1973 the first three won a title each at Grasmere. Tom is a great champion, though you would never guess it from his slightly ungainly appearance, mop of fair hair and horn-rimmed glasses.

All Weights Champion at Grasmere in 1984 was Joe Trelfall, one of another extensive clan. A legendary wrestler who was over 50 before he could be prevailed upon to retire was George Steadman who won fourteen times between 1872 and 1900. Steadman's trophies, history and photographs are on display in the Lake District Heritage Centre in Ambleside. There are plenty of cups to be won now, but the belts which used to be awarded have disappeared. The All Weights Champion at Grasmere wins the Kennedy Cup and £100.

The most striking thing about Cumberland and Westmorland Wrestling, to those seeing it for the first time, is the costumes. Rule 2 says 'that no wrestler be allowed to wrestle except in becoming costume'. The traditional becoming costume is white vest and long johns, a good pair of socks and velvet trunks of any colour, 'a plush seat-piece', which may be, and usually are, embroidered with exotic motifs such as flowers, birds or butterflies. The vests are often embroidered as well, and occasionally the long johns. The women do this, some achieving fame in their own right as there is always a formal Judging of the Wrestlers' Costumes.

The actual wrestling is fairly simple. The contestants hold each other, each with his hands clasped behind his opponent's back, with his left arm over the other's right and his head on his right shoulder. Rule 9: 'When both men have got hold and are fairly on their guard, play commences on the word of the referee, and, with the exception of kicking, the wrestlers are allowed to use every legitimate means to throw each other. To strike with the side of the foot shall not be deemed kicking.' The essential thing is that they have to retain their hold until one can throw the other to the ground, by superior skill, strength and timing. First down is the loser but if they are judged to have landed together this is a 'dog fall' and they start again. Major competitions are decided by the best of three falls. There are some strategems with entertaining names: the Hype, Swinging Hype, Buttock, Cross Buttock, Hank, Back Heel, Outside Stroke, Inside Click.

The wrestling goes on all day; the other two great events start and finish in the meantime. There are three Hound Trails at Grasmere Sports – well, strictly speaking there is *one* Hound Trail, a Puppy Trail and an Open Non-Winners Trail. This, too, is a popular sport in these parts with meetings almost every day except Sundays between April 1 and October 31. As betting is involved, skulduggery is not entirely unknown. The Hound Trailing Association (HTA), founded in 1910, has stringent rules to control the hounds, their owners and events.

Puppy Trails are of five miles, Hound Trails of ten which the winner must complete between lower and upper time limits for the result to stand. Not more than three people are allowed to lay the trail, which they do by dragging a 'trail rag', of specified size and material, around the course. The trail rag is soaked in a revolting concoction, which has to be mixed by an HTA chemist, consisting of 2 fl. oz. aniseed, ½ fl. oz. turpentine and 74 fl. oz. best paraffin. The hounds seem to like it. Not less than six scouts must guard the trail, to see that nobody tampers with it or the hounds. All the hounds have to be clearly marked just before the start to foil substitution. 'Hound catchers' are appointed to round up the winners at the end.

At Grasmere, according to Rex Woods, writing in 1977, it takes no less than 31 people to run their Hound Trail – 2 trailers, 19 scouts, 1 time-keeper, 8 catchers and Lord Lonsdale, by tradition of several generations, starter and judge. The course is always the same. The hounds set off enthusiastically and soon disappear while their owners, with a show of indifference, disappear too, to amble around the stalls for a while, watch a bit of wrestling, chat to their friends. Twenty minutes later, though, they are no longer indifferent. They reassemble at the finishing line, first to scan the hill tops anxiously through their binoculars, then, when the leaders are spotted, to set up a tremendous hullabaloo of whistles, yells, bangs, shrieks and other noises considered essential to encourage the hounds home with redoubled speed.

Occasionally this cacophony, plus the cheers of the vast crowd and 'John Peel' blasting over the public address system, puts a hound off. At the end of the Puppy Trail, when I was there, one of the leading group, realizing he had a good audience, stopped dead, looked amiably around and sat down to enjoy the delighted laughter. His owner, leaping about in a frenzy on the finishing line, was not amused.

Soon after the last hounds return in disgrace, excitement mounts again for the start of the Guides Race. This is a fell race; why it is called the Guides Race nobody seems to know. There are two suggestions: first, that it was for the mountain guides, of whom there were many in the last century when walking in the Lake District was fashionable; second, that the name derives from the guide flags on the route.

The course runs up a large field, over a wall, up through bracken and crags to the first flag, left along the ridge up to Butter Crag, 966 feet above the arena and almost too far away from it to be clearly seen. Then they hurl themselves down again by whichever route they choose. It took me twenty minutes to toil up to the first wall; it takes the winner about twelve and a half minutes to do the whole distance. It is, in turn, an arduous and horrifying race, taking tremendous stamina to reach the top in around ten minutes, reckless courage and sure-footedness to descend in less than three.

As the Guides Race victor hurtles towards the arena he is encouraged by the strains of 'See the Conquering Hero Comes'. I had heard this stirring tune less than three weeks earlier in very different circumstances, for the Woodmen of Arden also use it to acclaim winners at their Grand Wardmote.

During the first week in August, on Wednesday and Friday, I saw two events, both unique to their sport, very different, yet at the same time oddly similar. They are both the most important events in the year of their particular club, decided by the winning of 'ends'. Contestants have two attempts and each end is won by the man closest to the target. There are eighty members in each club and a great deal of formality in the way of ritual and dress. There are knights present in large numbers; the winner of one contest is dubbed 'knight' and called 'Sir' for evermore; the winner of the other contest is quite likely to be a real one. There is another difference: one contest is bowls, the other archery.

The Woodmen of Arden is a very exclusive archery society indeed. Membership is virtually hereditary, the election of non-family Woodmen an extreme rarity. Even the office of Warden is handed down from father to son. The 11th Earl of Aylesford is the seventh member of his family to be Warden since 1786. Though records have been kept since 1785, exactly 200 years ago, the Society is thought to be older. Something must have been going on at this time, though, for not only did they start keeping records, and persuade the Earl to be Warden, they also established their headquarters in Meriden by building the Forest Hall in 1788 to designs by Joseph Bonomi.

Other officers of the Society attain their rank by winning various honours in the Grand Wardmote. A wardmote, according to the dictionary, is a meeting of city wards. In the present context it refers to the wards of the Forest of Arden, when the foresters met to settle their differences in archery contests. The Woodmen have monthly wardmotes throughout the summer and their Grand Wardmote is in the week including August 1. All wardmotes are accompanied by a great deal of wining and dining and society business is, traditionally, settled after lunch over a glass of port. When formal business is being discussed Woodmen are expected to keep to the point; irrelevant remarks, jokes and the like are punished by a small fine, unless the joke has been funny enough to make the Warden laugh, in which case *he* has to pay the fine. Fines are payable to the Society Servant, the Marker, who officiates during archery contests, and also happens to be their very expert bowmaker. During discussions all contributions must be prefaced by honorifics such as 'My Lord Warden, Mr Adams, Brother Woodmen. . . .' For very many years the most senior member, after the Warden, was one of the Adams family.

At all times on the premises Woodmen wear distinctive dress. In cut it is not unlike conventional morning wear, familiar at Ascot and the better class of wedding, though in colour it is dramatically different. The coat is green, the waistcoat buff, the trousers white, the tie green. In place of a top hat they wear a wide-brimmed green shooting hat. Though the uniform is obligatory a certain amount of eccentricity is acceptable, even encouraged.

The Woodmen of Arden shoot only with the traditional longbow and wooden arrows, many of which have been made at Meriden by their own bowmakers. Until 1973 the appointment of Head Marker and Bowmaker had been held by members of the Thompson family for 141 years, and the present incumbent is Charlie Warlingham. The bows are made of yew, spliced in clever traditional ways to give great strength and spring. A full-sized bow is about six feet long with a 'pull' of about sixty pounds, but archers need several bows to shoot a variety of distances. Arrows, too, need to be made in several sizes. Made of cedar or pine, they are 25 to 29 inches long and matched in sets. A diverting quirk of the craft is that they are weighed against 'old' money; thus arrows weigh between 3s 6d and 5s 0d. Charlie keeps a stock of coins for the purpose. All modern archery contrivances, such as steel or fibreglass bows, sights or balances are regarded with contempt and utterly forbidden. However, the twentieth century has managed to intrude in the matter of bowstrings. They are no longer made of hemp, but of Dacron.

Woodmen practise two forms of shooting:, target shooting of 100 yards at 'Butts', and long distance shooting, of 180 to 240 yards, at 'Clouts'. Butts are large and flat with a target in the middle. Clouts are small and round, only 31 inches in diameter, and it is astonishing that they can get near them, let alone hit them at so great a range.

The Grand Wardmote lasts four days. On the first day they shoot at butts for medals, while on the other days at clouts for respectively the bowl, the Silver Arrow and the Bugle. On the Friday morning I saw them shoot for the Silver Arrow. Forty-two woodmen had 'warned in' to take part, evidently one of the best musters for years. This particular contest is decided by ends, the winner of each end being the archer whose arrow is closest to the centre of the clout, and the winner of the whole contest the archer who wins the most ends.

The pattern is exactly like bowls; the clouts are 180 yards apart; first they shoot from one clout at the other, they then retrieve their arrows and shoot back again. The result of each shot was signalled by the Marker, posted close by each clout. He has an extensive repertoire of signals to tell the distant archer exactly where his arrow has fallen. If it has actually hit the clout he is supposed to indulge in an extravagant pantomime of joy and jubilation. I noticed that Charlie Warlingham, an undemonstrative soul, confined himself to a moderately enthusiastic wave of his flag on the one direct hit I happened to see.

The Woodmen have two arrows at each end. They shoot in pairs, taking alternate shots. They normally shoot ten ends for the Silver Arrow but this time they decided on eight as there were so many contestants. Nobody managed to win more than one end, so the eight winners had to shoot a decider. The final victor turned out to be Simon Williams-Thomas. His brother Woodmen gathered about him and, with bows crossed above his head, they marched him off the field in triumph, singing 'See the Conquering Hero Comes'. Immediately, with impressive and time honoured ceremony, he was presented with his trophy, and everyone retired to the Forest Hall for a sumptuous feast.

Though these goings-on are on private property belonging to the Woodmen of Arden they do not mind the odd spectator so long as he keeps out of the way. Archery is, after all, quite dangerous; children and dogs are likely to be shot.

Away down in Southampton, hard by God's House Tower and across the road from the dock gates, it comes as a mild surprise to find the world's oldest bowling green. There has been a lawn here since 1187 but it is not thought to have been regularly used for

The 'Knights' of the Old Green wear formal dress to supervise the annual contest to elevate one of the ordinary club members to their ranks.

bowls until as recently as 1299 when the first Master of the Green was appointed. In the sixteenth century it was against the law for 'inferior people' to play the game at all, oddly enough because it was thought to divert their interest and energy from the practice of archery, at that time of vital military importance (Woodmen please note). However, the game persisted and fines were frequent. In 1705 the Southampton Old Bowling Green Club was formed. In 1894 their right to use the green was challenged by the Town Council and the Town Clerk was asked to prepare a report. He concluded that 'although the ground itself no doubt belongs to the town the present club who occupy and manage the Green would appear to have obtained prescriptive rights thereon from length of usure for the purpose of playing the game of bowls'. No rent has ever been paid by the club, though they do have to pay rates.

By the time the Town Council had got around to making trouble for them the club's unique Knighthood Competition was already 118 years old and it has continued annually ever since, including the World War years. The competition is open to all members of the club 'in good standing' who have not previously won it. Former winners cannot take part because they officiate. They are Knights of the Green; and all the hopefuls are Gentlemen Commoners. The Knights officiate dressed in immaculate morning suits and top hats, while the Commoners play in gleaming whites and club ties.

The competition begins, with considerable ceremony and in the presence of the mayor, at 3 p.m. on the first Wednesday in August. It is played in ends and usually continues for several days. The Knights have absolute control over the game. First they select the position of the jack. Ends are bowled from the last jack position but not necessarily to the opposite side of the green. The Knights might choose to go diagonally to a far corner making an unusually long end or to a point disconcertingly close. There can be any number of contestants – indeed this can vary from session to session; members are free to enter and leave as they please, though obviously the more ends they manage the more chance they stand of winning. Each contestant bowls two woods, the distance from the jack is carefully measured and recorded, and the wood is

The British Marbles Championship at Tinsley Green inspires intense passion.

removed, thus each wood is aimed at the jack only. The jack is a special one with a flat area so that it can rest on a penny. This enables the Knights to replace the jack in exactly the same position if it is hit. A wood which finishes against the jack is a 'toucher', one which moves the jack and itself comes to rest on the penny is called a 'lodger' and is unbeatable. Contestants may not go near the jack while the end is being played. Racing the wood is absolutely forbidden, and, in fact, they are not allowed to know the results of their efforts until everyone has bowled and the Knights formally announce the winner of the end.

The first man to win seven ends is acclaimed Knight of the Green. This may sound easy but with up to fifty good players taking part it can take more than a week to complete. In 1984 it took 74 ends, 10 days, 39 members took part and the eventual winner was 'Sir' Harry Hampton.

A few days later a splendid ceremony takes place to instal the new Knight. He will be known for evermore in the club as 'Sir' Arthur, 'Sir' Ernie, 'Sir' Bert, 'Sir' Harry and his wife will be 'Lady'.

All members want to win the Knighthood Competition. One told me, 'I even kept off the beer for the duration of the competition last year I was so determined to win. Didn't do me any good though, so this year I decided I might do better with extra!' Another struck a more cautious note; 'Well, part of me desperately wants to win and part of me hopes I won't – it doesn't half cost you know. You have to buy all the clothes *and* buy drinks for everyone afterwards!'

The Knights and the Woodmen, though they try very hard to win, compete with relaxed good humour enjoying the social occasion. You might think the game of marbles would be even more relaxed, a bit of casual play between small boys. You would be wrong. The British Marbles Championship is deadly serious, grown men break down with the tension of it all, appeals to the referee are delivered with a passion which would be the envy of any First Division Football player.

In 1879 W.D. Parish wrote in *Notes and Queries*: 'From time immemorial marble playing has been very popular. . .in Sussex; in some parts of the county Ash Wednesday, as well as Good Friday, has been known as 'Marble Day'. Referring to the game in Sussex it is said that the marble-playing season is strictly defined between Ash Wednesday and Good Friday.'

In 1934 the *Daily Mail* reported:

> Visitors to the Greyhound Inn, Tinsley Green, Crawley, on the Surrey–Sussex border, witnessed yesterday their third annual marbles match between the two counties. . .A large crowd watched the elimination of the players until Mr. Jack Arnold of Three Bridges remained as the champion marbles player of the year. In the old days, when marbles was a favourite game in Sussex, all marbles in use after 12 o'clock on Good Friday, then recognised as the last day for playing the game, could be confiscated.

Though this championship is only fifty years old there seems little doubt that marbles has been played at Tinsley Green for several centuries. The early history of the game is distinctly speculative, but the story I like best is the one which should be taken least seriously. During the reign of Good Queen Bess (as these stories always put it), a Surrey man and a Sussex man were competing for the hand of a girl from Tinsley Green. They agreed on a series of contests – archery, falconry, wrestling and other manly sports – but, after strenuous efforts, had arrived at no clear result. They decided to settle the matter with a game of marbles. History does not go so far as to record who won, nor, for that matter, whether the damsel was given the opportunity to choose for herself.

Today marbles is very popular around the pubs of Surrey, Sussex and Kent and the season has expanded far beyond Lent. There are leagues, knock-out contests and challenge matches. Competition among teams is no less fierce when it comes to choosing daft names; in past years the Toucan Terribles swept aside all before them; in the 1940s the Copthorne Sharpshooters were doing well; in the 1980s the Black Dog Boozers and the Bow Street Fudgers are the teams to beat.

This game, like any other, has its legendary characters. Len Smith won the championship a record twelve times up to 1973, Barry Ray having won several times recently is still going well. Wee Willie Wright was famous for his 'secret weapon', the hot water bottle he used to keep his thumb in tip-top working order while he won five times in the 1950s. Pop Maynard who led his team to victory in 1941 and 1948 and played right up to his death in 1963 at the age of 90, was even better known as a fine singer of traditional folk songs. Jim Longhurst, never an individual champion, was renowned for the great power and accuracy of his tolley work which could shatter a thick beer mug at four feet. This dangerous, and wasteful, accomplishment earned him the nickname 'Atomic Thumb'.

In 1983 there were twenty teams taking part outside The Greyhound. Several had dressed themselves up in fancy outfits but most of these were eliminated in the early rounds suggesting once again that, as in life itself, sartorial extravagance tends to be in inverse proportion to practical ability. Still, however outrageous some of them looked, there was no doubt that everyone was trying like mad to win. Any hint of fudging was immediately pounced upon. One captain, stonefaced, complained to the referee that one of the opposing team was using a tolley that was too big, then, having failed in this ploy, that the referee called time before the fifteen minutes were up. Defeated, he went off muttering darkly about an appeal to the Board of Control. Later, I noticed that this same man was doing well in the Individual Championship until he was 'killed' by his enemy with the tolley.

After many tense games the team contest was eventually won, for the second year in succession, by the Bow Street Fudgers, six policemen from Coulsdon. Most of the best players were on show for the Individual Contest, but it surprised nobody when Barry Ray emerged again as the British Marbles Champion of 1983.

It is surprising how many people want to go swimming on Christmas Day. Still, television pictures of people rushing into the English Channel are almost as much part of the festive season as the Queen. In London, there is a race in the Serpentine at 9 a.m., and another at Tooting Bec at 11.

The Serpentine Swimming Club was formed in 1864. Straightaway they held their very first Christmas Day race for the Peter Pan Cup, presented by Sir James Barrie himself, for he was a founder member. When I went to watch them, in 1983, dressed in my warmest clothes, they were having their 120th consecutive race. The weather, they insisted, was mild and warm; sometimes the lake was frozen and they had to make a hole in the ice to take a token plunge. In those infrequent years when the ice is frozen, they hold the actual race as soon as conditions permit. The coldest year any of them could remember, indeed none of them could forget, was 1969 when the water was at 32°F but failed to freeze over because the fierce east wind was making it too rough.

Most of the entrants were regulars who swim throughout the year, though a few just turn up annually for this race. At 9 o'clock they march in single file from the clubhouse led, usually, by a piper. Unfortunately the poor fellow broke his leg in 1983; he was there but regretted he had not mastered the art of playing on crutches. There were about twenty-five swimmers. This is a handicap race so they started according to their allotted times shouted out by the starter. They all swam furiously, determined to win the cup, though it has to be said that they fell some way short of Olympic standard. The delighted winner was an Ulsterman, Mario McClarnon.

Thomas Doggett was an Irish actor and comedian, manager in turn of the Haymarket Theatre and Drury Lane, well known and successful in London. In 1714 he was commanded to appear before King George I and it was his enthusiasm for the first Hanoverian monarch as well as his affection for the Thames Watermen that inspired him to inaugurate his race.

On the first of August 1715 he gave notice 'This being the day of His Majesty's happy accession to the throne there will be given by Mr. Doggett an Orange Colour Livery with a Badge representing Liberty to be rowed for by Six Watermen that are out of their time within the year past. They are to row from London Bridge to Chelsea. It will be continued annually on the same day for ever.' When he died in 1721, Doggett left an appropriate 'sum of money to continue the custom' to his executors who at once approached the Fishmongers Company desiring them

'to take the execution of the said Trust upon them in consideration of the sum of £300'. Nobody is sure why the Fishmongers became involved; Doggett does not appear to have been a Freeman of the Company. Still, they have looked after the annual race ever since in co-operation with the Company of Watermen and Lightermen who provide the contestants.

At the beginning of the eighteenth century there were 40,000 watermen working on the Thames between Windsor and Gravesend. The river was the main highway in London, and, since there were hardly any bridges, they provided the only means of getting across. There were many theatres on the south bank so the actors and the wherrymen would be well acquainted with one another. The watermen were all licensed, just like modern taxi drivers, and before

The Serpentine Swimming Club race on Christmas morning for the Peter Pan Cup, providing the water is not frozen!

these could be granted they had to serve a seven-year apprenticeship.

It was for newly licensed wherrymen that Doggett offered his Coat and Badge. They were to race from The Old Swan at London Bridge to The White Swan in Chelsea, a distance not far short of five miles, *against* the tide, rowing their regular wherries. As you can imagine, this was a monstrously hard task, taking four or five hours to complete. There was no shortage of entrants, though. For the first few years there were unlimited numbers. The Fishmongers soon realized that only six contestants would fit across the river so lots were drawn. This led to the buying and selling of places. There was betting on the outcome, nobbling of competitors. The Company persisted in their efforts to control the race. They introduced qualifying heats and policed the river during the race. In 1860 special racing boats were allowed. Soon after this they made the race much easier by rowing it with the tide. In 1906 they introduced racing skiffs much like those in use today. Since the 1950s the boats have been provided by the Fishmongers. In spite of all these changes the contestants still have to have the same qualifications, the only snag is that for some years there have not been enough of them. A century ago there must have been many hundreds of apprentices; even thirty years ago the average was around 250. Today there would be about twenty and not all of them will find a regular job on the river. So the Fishmongers decided to bend the rules, and if there is a shortage of proper contenders the previous year's losers can have a second attempt.

The race itself is longer and harder than any regular sculling race. Even with the tide it is something of an endurance test, taking about twenty-five minutes. The course remains the same, though both the pubs have long since disappeared. Instead of going on the tide at whatever time it happens to be right on August 1, the race is now always held on the day towards the end of July when the tide happens to be right at 11 o'clock in the morning. You can lean over London Bridge and watch the Fishmongers Company Bargemaster start the race alongside Fishmongers Hall. The race is followed by an impressive flotilla of pleasure boats full of Fishmongers, Watermen and Lightermen, for this is a traditional day out on the river for all Freemen and staff.

The race is not the end of the matter. Doggett's Coat and Badge consists of scarlet coat, breeches and cap, white stockings, black buckle shoes, and an enormous silver badge, as big as a dinner plate, worn on the left arm. This badge has on it the White Horse of Hanover, the word 'Liberty', and the name of its winner. Former winners of the race officiate each year, wearing their splendid uniforms. The Fishmongers' Bargemaster, who umpires the race, is also, by tradition, a former winner.

The latest victor, wearing his new Coat and Badge,

is presented to the Prime Warden of the Company of Fishmongers at their annual dinner at Fishmongers Hall in November. His win is described in extravagant terms, the Prime Warden drinks his health and he is escorted out to the tune of the Trumpet Voluntary.

For the rest of his life he is expected to be available to act as an escort for the Prime Warden on formal occasions, to accompany the Queen on the Royal Barge, to march in the Lord Mayor's Show and to make sure everything goes smoothly at succeeding Coat and Badge races. There are usually about forty former winners around so their duties are not too frequent.

As Chambers' *Book of Days* puts it: 'A more stalwart set of fellows, in more quaintly antique costume, could scarcely be found in any country, to serve as an honorary guard.'

Towards the end of August very different boat races take place away over in West Wales, near Cardigan. The Cilgerran Coracle Races and Aquatic Sports are not old, only thirty-five years or so, but the boats are of a design in use a thousand years ago.

Coracles are still used in the Teifi, the Taf and the Tywi. Not so long ago there were thousands of men earning their living fishing for salmon in these rivers. They worked in pairs, with a special net slung between the two coracles. Today declining fish stocks, the economy and the angling lobby have conspired to reduce professional coracle fishing to about twenty pairs divided between the three rivers.

The craft are ideally suited to this task. Extremely light, they drift on the tide, and when a salmon is taken they are infinitely manoeuvrable with one expert hand. Their appearance is invariably described as 'like half an Easter Egg'. Though there are traditional variations from river to river, basically a coracle is a hazel or ash frame covered with pitched canvas, about 3½ feet wide and 5½ feet long, with a sharp end and a blunt end which are, respectively, the back and the front. There is a seat across the middle upon which the fisherman sits, facing forward, paddling from the front.

There are modern fibreglass models but these are utterly forbidden at the Cilgerran Races. The course is

Coracle Racing at Cilgerran in West Wales. These craft are used for salmon fishing and, curiously, are propelled from the front, blunt end forward.

100 yards long, which takes an expert about two minutes to complete. This is a cheerful village affair, on a beautiful stretch of the Teifi beneath Cilgerran Castle. Events are contested with manic enthusiasm, but not regarded as a matter of life and death.

Kiplingcotes Derby is a nice mixture of formality and informality, as you might expect from Britain's oldest flat race. The formality comes through the observance of ancient Articles and sensible modern safety precautions, the informality through the casual way entrants and spectators show up according to weather and rival attractions.

The riders are not professional jockeys though there is money to be won in the race. This race transgresses Jockey Club Rules but 'the Stewards. . .have granted an exemption under Rule 204, II of the Rules of Racing. . .and therefore neither the horses or owners will incur a disqualification for taking part'.

'Kibling Coates' Race was founded in 1519, though the course, authenticated by its appearance on the Ordnance Survey map, is thought to have been in existence much earlier. The Founders included the Earl of Burlington, 4 Peers and 18 Knights and 26 Gentlemen who put up between them £365. At present there are three Trustees, Lord Manton, Mr A.R. Bethell, descendant of one of the Founders, and Mr Bill Pinkney, who very kindly sent me a copy of the 'Articles to be Observed and Kept', of which there are fourteen.

> *Firstly*: Every man that is a Founder he is to put in Twenty Shillings in Gold for his Stake when he hath a Horse, Gelding or Mare that Runs for the Prize; and every other person Four Pounds in Gold. . .
> *Secondly*: Every Horse, Gelding or Mare that runneth for the Prize shall be led out between Twelve and One of the Clock and shall run the Course before Two of the Clock in the Afternoon.
> *Thirdly*: Every Horse that Runneth for this Prize shall start Bridled and Saddled and shall Run with the Rider weighing Ten Stone weight, Fourteen pounds to the Stone, according to the Ancient custom.
> *Fourthly*: Every (rider) shall put their stake into the Clerk's hand at or before Eleven of the Clock. . .
> *Fifthly*: Whosoever doth stop or stay any of the Running Horses that Rideth for this Prize if he be either Owner of a horse that Runs or his Servant and be adjudged to hinder the Horse, his Horse shall win no Prize.
> *Sixthly*: Every Rider that layeth hold of any of the other Riders, or striketh any of them shall win no Prize. [And so on. . .]

The clerk, in 1984, was an amiable young lady called Susan Hillaby. She was not sure how long the job had been in her family; certainly her father and grandfather did it, probably her great grandfather. She assured us that she did it by inheritance and not because she knew anything about horses – 'I've only been on one once, and I didn't like it much!' And she was not doing it for the money either. She was entitled to 25p per stake, standing to earn £2.50 on the day as there were ten entrants. She admitted she fell down on some of her duties, failing to maintain the course as, ninthly, she was enjoined to do.

On the third Thursday in March, though, she was extremely efficient, as she weighed in entrants, making sure they were over ten stone, 'setting down the names of the Owner and every Horse, his Horse's Name and Colour and his Rider's Name', and collecting their £4 stake money. The previous year she turned away a would-be entrant who arrived two minutes after 11 o'clock. She conducted all this business by her scales at the winning post. When all the riders were ready they had to gather round to hear her read out such of the Articles as affect the running of the race, before they went off down to the start almost four miles away.

The course is not immaculate and custom-built like Epsom or Aintree, with fine white railings, but it is a definite and identifiable track. About half is along roads with exceptionally wide grass verges providing plenty of room for the horses. The other half is muddy, along the edges of fields, and quite hilly in places, though this is a flat race. The start is near Dalton Hall, about four miles to the east of Market Weighton and the course runs in a fairly straight line north-west across the A163, to the winning post near Kipling House Farm.

The race takes about eleven minutes. In 1984 the winner, for the second time, was Ken Holmes. The first prize, the proceeds of the Trust, was £36, which he returned to the fund as he had the year before. The young lady who came second won £37.50. It has always been a quirk of this event that the second prize was more than the first and in the past this has been known to encourage jockeying for second position.

Events like this are very difficult to photograph – at the beginning they look like any horse race, at the end they might be only one horse galloping past, in the middle you are cut off from more likely action at either end. I was with two friends, one another photographer, the other a frustrated grand prix driver. We did a thorough recce. The driver insisted we could easily photograph the start, then she would get us back in time to see the finish. The journey by road is exactly twice as long as the course, narrow

The winner of Kiplingcotes Derby in 1984, Ken Holmes.

country lanes for two-thirds of the way, a main road for the rest. I said she couldn't do it, opted to stay at the finish, and sent the other two down to cover the start. She announced her plan to the starter, Susan Hillaby's husband, Richard. *He* said she couldn't do it. He had tried himself. Bet her a fiver. Well, they got their pictures and she did make it with a full two minutes to spare. She arrived looking smug, the photographer looking ashen. Her dog, trembling on the back seat, was sick.

Shrove Tuesday is one of the busiest days in the whole Custom Calendar. It would take a conscientious folklorist twenty years to get around a representative collection of events. The best known have to do with pancakes. It is a day for generally letting off steam before the rigours of Lent. In many places a 'Pancake Bell' is rung to call people to church to be shriven, to confess their sins.

In Olney they still ring the bell and they still have the service; in between they have their celebrated Pancake Race. Several accounts say that the race was first run in 1445, without mentioning how they know this. Frankly, I do not believe them, though I accept that something of the sort has been going on in the town for a very long time.

Mrs Ivy Perkins, in *Olney Album* (1978), says that she took part in a revival in 1925. It seems that the sexton, Mr Barratt, had heard that Olney ladies, when they heard the Pancake Bell, were supposed to make a pancake, then rush along to the church and give it to him in return for a kiss. He spread the news, in the hope of getting his entitlement and, on the day, was delighted by several ladies turning up. Mrs Perkins complained that the vicar did not approve, 'especially the kissing. . .the first person allowed to kiss the sexton was his daughter, Kathleen!'

The race, in its present form, began in 1947 when it was revived by the then vicar, Mr Collins, evidently more fun-loving than his predecessor. Now the Olney Pancake Race is an organized event, measured, timed and controlled by certain conditions. The course is 425 yards long, from near the Old Bull in the centre of the village to the church gate. Only women can enter. In 1980 there were eight of them, and there are never likely to be more than a dozen. They have to be over 16 years old, a native of the village or have been resident at least three months. They must wear 'housewifely clothes', a skirt, an apron and a headscarf. And, of course, they must have their pancake in a proper frying pan.

It is not considered good tactics to have a pancake paper thin and light as a feather. It should be 'thick and 'orrible' as one entrant remarked, for it has to be tossed before the start and after the finish to demonstrate that it is indeed a loose pancake and not glued into the pan for easier carrying. If anyone drops her pancake she is permitted to pick it up again, though this loses valuable time. The contestants compete with great good humour, but they really want to win. The winning time is quite likely to be less than a minute.

The time is important for another reason. Since 1950 this has been an International Event. In 1949 one R.J. Leete, a citizen of Liberal, Kansas, read a magazine article about the Olney race and, being a man of action, at once cabled a challenge. Each Shrove Tuesday, the women of Liberal run over a course of identical length. Times are compared and an international winner declared. Liberal has won more of the exchanges to date, but there is not usually much difference in the times, sometimes as little as a tenth of a second. By the look of their official programme, Liberal has advantages in an organizing committee of around thirty, and well-controlled, extremely wide streets. Needless to say, the Olney approach is more casual. Still, the girls, and the spectators, were extremely angry in 1980 when a BBC television crew got in the way and impeded the very event they had come to film.

The Pancake Greaze at Westminster School in 1973. The chef throws a great thick 'pancake' over the bar and the boys fight for the largest piece. One year he confounded everybody by accidentally throwing it on the bar.

There are countless other pancake races around the country on Shrove Tuesday. Many have an honourable pedigree, but most are figments of PR men's imaginations. I have records of races organized by flour companies, kitchen equipment suppliers, egg producers, a crêperie, and a lemon juice company. I was once commissioned myself to cover a race in which the contestants were the beauty queens of all the leading grocery chains!

The Westminster School Pancake Greaze is non-commercial. It is a lively affair, combining both pancakes and very unruly Shrove Tuesday behaviour. The event is not open to the general public; apart from the school, only the parents of boys taking part are admitted and they may well be there to be on hand if their offspring should get seriously injured.

Jeremy Bentham mentions that this was going on when he was at the school in the mid-eighteenth century. This is an account which appeared in *Notes and Queries* a hundred years later, in 1860.

> At 11 a.m. on Shrove Tuesday a verger of the Abbey, in his gown and carrying a silver baton, emerged from the Kitchen followed by a school cook, in white apron, jacket and cap. The cook carried on a dish that, on close inspection, looked like a crumpet of substantial make. He advanced towards the school-room, the door of which was opened by the verger, who announced in majestic style, 'The Cook!' Thus ushered in, the cook, after glancing at the bar separating the Upper and Lower Schools, and twirling the pancake round once or twice in an artistic manner, tossed it over the bar into a mob of boys all eager to make what, we believe, is called 'a grab at it'. After a vigorous struggle. . .there came out from the mêlée, with disordered dress, a determined look, and an unbroken pancake, a big boy named Hawkshaw, who proceeded to the Deanery to claim a guinea. . .for his feat; the cook's fee was two guineas.

The procedure is little changed. I was there in 1973 and a mole in the shape of my young cousin has brought my information up to date. The venue is the same, the bar is still there. The procession has expanded to consist of the School Beadle with his mace, the verger, the Dean in person, the headmaster and the cook. The cook still has the difficult task of throwing the pancake over the bar. I like to think of him practising at dead of night. In 1934 he confounded the waiting boys by throwing *onto* the bar. The boys still struggle vigorously. The golden guinea is still given but now returned to be replaced by more legal tender. At the end the Dean now calls for, and has granted, a half-holiday for the school.

Though originally the whole school took part, since about the turn of the century numbers have been considerably reduced. Currently there is one boy from each class in the first three years and one from each house in the top two years, adding up to about thirty in all. Representatives – or, as my cousin puts it, victims – are elected by their peers. It has become fashionable lately to wear fancy dress. In the mid-1980s punk outfits, American football gear and drag are the most popular.

At Scarborough Museum they ring their Pancake Bell at noon. Actually it is a newly acquired bell, because their old one which came to the museum in 1861 from the Hospital of St Thomas the Martyr had become dangerously fragile. Museum staff had carried out this duty until 1979; since then the mayor has been happy to oblige.

Shortly afterwards, on the Southsands Promenade, the inhabitants of Scarborough arrive in their hundreds in order to skip. Shrovetide skipping is unique to this Yorkshire resort, though there used to be a very similar custom in Brighton on Good Friday. Until recently – ten to fifteen years ago – the Scarborough Skipping was a charming communal occasion. The fishermen used to bring long heavy ropes which they would stretch across the road and turn while everyone else skipped over them. There would be ten, a dozen, even fifteen people skipping on one rope. A favourite trick was to skip right along the road, running from one rope to the next.

Two things have happened to alter this happy scene. First, the fishing fleet has all but vanished, and second, the powers that be have made the road into a dual carriageway with a traffic island down the middle. It is impossible to swing a long rope even if the fishermen were there to do it.

Nevertheless they still skip. Now it is more of a family affair, with real skipping ropes, perhaps with mum and dad at either end, and not more than five or six skipping. The trouble is few of them are any good at it. They cannot manage more than half a dozen turns. Only a group from a health class with 'Keep fit with Julie' emblazoned on their chests, seemed in any way expert.

Perhaps this is the reason for quite a new development, absolutely in the unruly Shrove Tuesday tradition, which the young seem greatly to enjoy. The boys chase the girls and bear them off, screaming and struggling, to dump them in the sea. Feminist considerations apart, this is much more good humoured than it sounds. The girls express a ritual dismay at their uncavalier treatment; to be left unmolested and dry is much, much worse.

The skipping went on for three or four hours. Families came and went. There must have been thousands there during the afternoon. Only Julie's girls kept going throughout. When I left, at about four o'clock, they were still demonstrating their superhuman fitness, bouncing away outside the lifeboat station.

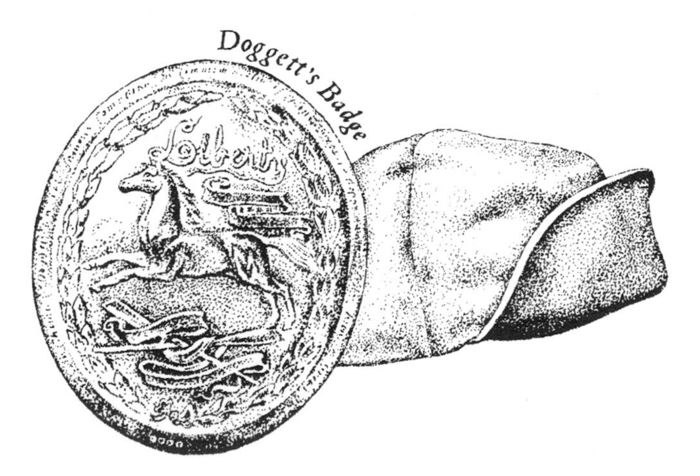

Doggett's Badge

...*knock a man down but don't 'urt 'im*

One of the problems with the games in this chapter is what to call them. The villagers who indulge in them – 'play' is hardly an appropriate word – have no difficulty, for each place has its own name; Hurling, the Hood Game, Hand Ba', Bottle Kicking, Royal Shrovetide Football even.

'Shrovetide Football' is quite a good name; the outbreak is most virulent at that time. But then, what are we to call the ones at Christmas, New Year, Old New Year, Candlemas, Easter Monday, the first Saturday after Easter? 'Mass Football' is undeniably accurate, but dull. 'Street Football' is much better, even if a few survivals are confined to the fields. It strikes a genuinely anarchic note, conveys the impression of things which violate respectability and traffic regulations, and could even cause some damage. 'Football' may, in itself, be a misnomer since in most of the games the ball is not kicked, but carried or thrown, while in a couple they do not actually use a ball! Still, 'Street Football' it shall be. (Though various police forces, called in to sort things out, have their own names for it. . .)

There must once have been a great number of these games. It is the only explanation possible for the uniformity of the ten or a dozen which still survive in Britain, in spite of efforts to suppress them. Early references to street football are numerous; the earliest I have come across is at Sedgefield. They claim theirs started in 1027, making the 1985 game the 958th in succession. It was suppressed in Chester in 1539. A history of Cornwall mentions 'hurling' in 1584. Most of the information seems to deal with the desirability of putting a stop to this uncouth practice. Derby's game evidently ended in 1846 following a reading of the Riot Act. Near Lampeter it survived a little longer. At Kingston-upon-Thames it ended in 1867 after police, drafted in specially to stop the 'riot', caused a real one. Dorking held out until 1897.

Matthew Alexander, in a paper given to a folklore conference in London in 1984, argued, most convincingly, that continuity was largely in the hands of tradesmen and the emerging middle class. Social status has always worried Britons. Until the late nineteenth century tradesmen were firmly among the lower orders. Thus they took part in, enjoyed and encouraged street football. As their status improved, they worried about their shops, their property, whether they should be seen taking part. They became local councillors, even MPs. Their attitude changed and they no longer wanted to be involved. On the contrary, they wanted to stop it; most of the street football games disappeared then. Even so, self interest can be a more potent force. In 1857 the mayor and council of Kingston had one of their periodic debates about whether the game should be allowed to continue. The mayor unexpectedly proclaimed, 'This is a free England and people should be allowed to do as they like'. He omitted to mention that he was the landlord of the pub holding the post-game supper.

The last really well-known game to succumb to repression was held at Chester-le-Street in 1932. Surviving games are probably too famous by now, in the category of untouchable Ancient Traditions. The Hand Ba' of Jedburgh has been to the High Court in Edinburgh, but survived on the grounds of 'immemorial' status. There used to be two days of 'Jethart Ba'', but then the people themselves agreed to confine it to one because it simply cost too much in terms of protecting their property and lost trade. At Alnwick the game actually *was* suppressed but then reappeared almost immediately, in 1837, in a much modified and more refined form, of the streets and into the Duke's demesne. If any of the extant games were to lapse, apathy would be a more likely cause. Disasters *may* succeed, however, where killjoys fail; foot-and-mouth disease stopped Ashbourne one year, though the death of Queen Victoria left Kirkwall unmoved.

Street football is a wild, unruly game, the uncivilized ancestor of our modern rugby and soccer. Strong men have been killed playing it; broken limbs, near suffocation, cuts and bruises are commonplace. In case you think I exaggerate, a man was drowned at Workington in 1983, another having fought valiantly at Arnhem died at Jedburgh soon after the Second World War. This certainly does not deter the dedicated; indeed, I was told that a coachload of Jedburgh enthusiasts often went off to take part in the Workington games.

Most games are between two teams, usually from different sides of town, 'Uppies and Doonies', or neighbouring parishes, or townsmen versus countrymen. Haxey and Atherstone are exceptions. At the former there used to be three teams struggling to propel 'the Hood' to their own pub; now, perhaps temporarily, there are two. At the latter it is every man for himself, the playing time is fixed and the winner is the man who has the ball at the end. Teams are of unlimited number. Though allegiances are fierce, visitors are normally tolerated so long as they conform to the manners of the game. Team colours are not worn but everyone knows very well which side he is on. Women are expected, and advised, to spectate.

Rules are practically non-existent though methods of scoring may be quite complicated. Goals can be several miles apart, though the average is probably about a mile. Streams are popular, or special posts or walls or buildings. Both Kirkwall and Workington harbours act as goals. In most games the object is to get the ball back to your own ground to 'hail' a goal.

Two kinds of ball feature. If a small hard ball is used, about the size of a cricket ball, the game is likely to be fast and furious with the ball 'hurled' or thrown about. Kicking is, in any case, decidedly unwise. If the ball is football-sized, or even larger, then a vast impenetrable scrum, punctuated by occasional bursts of frenzied activity, will probably be the outcome. At Haxey and Hallaton they do not use a ball at all, as will be explained later.

All street football occurs in winter, between Christmas and soon after Easter. Thus most, but not all, games go on long after dark. How the players know what is going on remains a mystery; the spectators have no idea. Most of the games take place right in the middle of town, with windows boarded up against the onslaught. Property is very much at risk, hedges and allotments can disappear without trace, and cars should be left in the next county. I talked to a local police constable at Haxey many years ago about the game and he told me how, in his first year there, he had left his car in the way: 'They damaged it something terrible. I had awful trouble explaining what happened to my insurance company. They said it sounded very much like riot and civil commotion to them and if it wasn't then it must be an act of God!'

On the day the law is quite literally suspended. Personal animosities are often settled openly. The police simply do not interfere, confining their activities to directing bewildered and anxious motorists on detours.

As for the origin of these ferocious mêlées, as usual, nobody really knows. Some folklorists, inevitably, go on about fertility rites, ignoring the point that infertility is a much more likely consequence. The Shrovetide games are popularly explained as another way to let off steam before the rigours of Lent, though this is not helpful regarding the others. Maybe it was simply a lively festival to help survive the bleak midwinter. Haxey has a story about the start of their Hood Game which must have been written by a Hollywood scriptwriter. Both Kirkwall and Jedburgh offer a macabre idea, which may say something about the Scottish mentality, even if, to be fair, neither town takes it too seriously. They say that the ba' was, in the beginning, the head of the leader of a defeated invading force, in one case Viking, in the other English, kicked around in triumphant jubilation. Jedburgh even has ribbons tied to their ball, said to represent hair. To this day these ribbons are greatly prized as trophies.

As you would expect, there are differences around the country in the way the game has evolved. Ashbourne, in Derbyshire, has what is probably the best known and the most archetypal example of street football. It is held on two days, Shrove Tuesday and Ash Wednesday. Both days are equally popular and the same preliminaries are observed. A formal lunch is held at The Green Man and Blacks Head in the centre of town attended by everyone who is anyone in Ashbourne. A guest of honour is entertained, from football or show business, or perhaps a well-known local, who will later start the game by 'turning up' the ball, that is to say, throwing it to the crowd. Here the game is called Royal Shrovetide Football because the Prince of Wales turned up the ball in 1928.

A little before 2 p.m. the celebrity appeared from The Green Man to be cheered through the streets on his way to Shaw Croft, the traditional spot to start the

Haxey Hood Game; the Fool is 'smoked' as he delivers his traditional speech. *(see page 166)*

Two of the Marshfield Mummers in 1966. *(see page 171)*

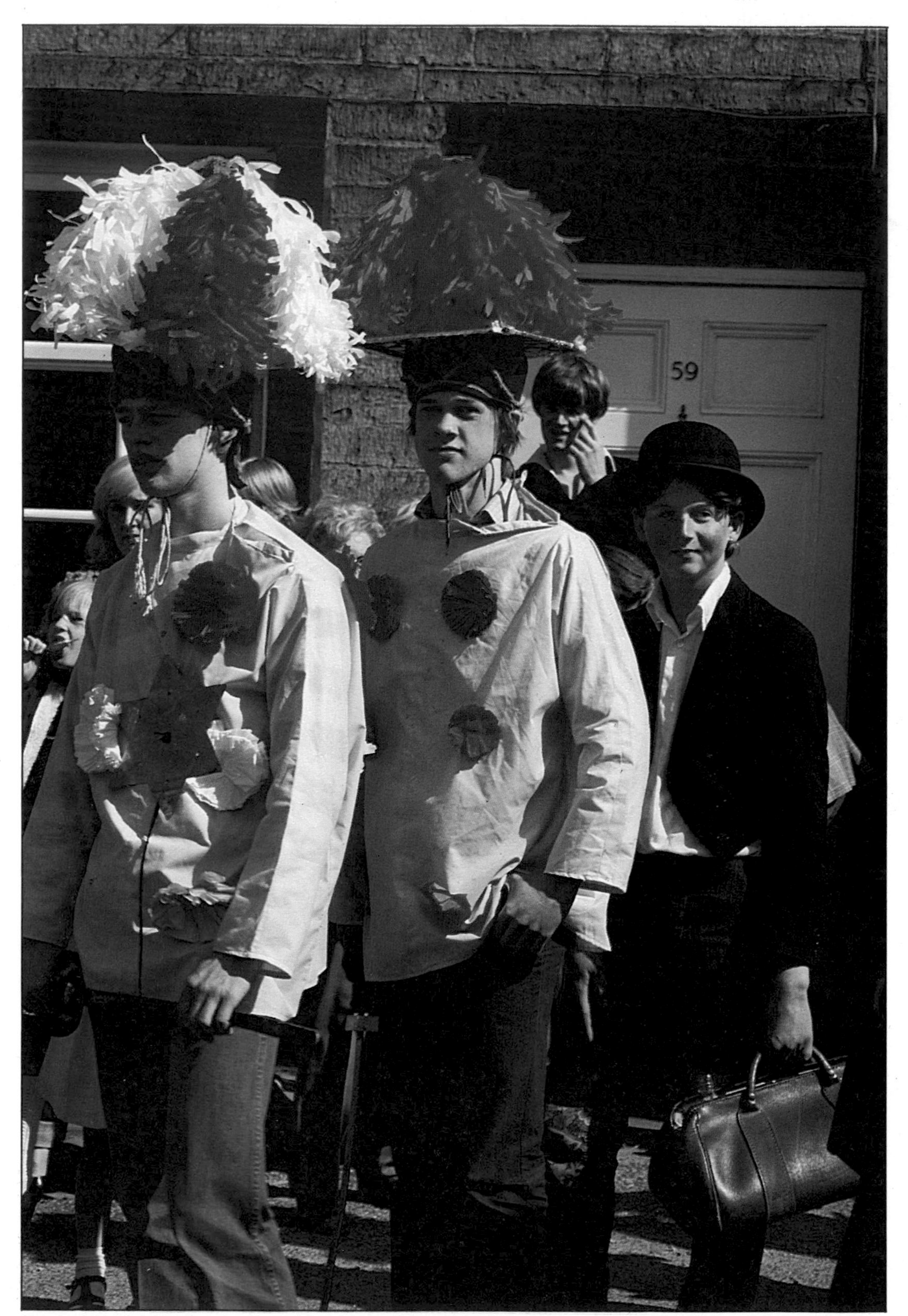

Boys of Calder High School perform the Midgley Pace Egg Play every Good Friday. *(see page 180)*

Royal Shrovetide Football at Ashbourne. Triumphant scorer for the Down'ards in 1984, Stephen Bott.

game, which is now a concrete platform in the middle of the large car park behind International Stores. He displayed the ball for everyone to see, a little bigger than a football, made of leather and filled with cork, painted with his name and appropriate motifs. Admonishments, including the instruction to keep out of the churchyard and the cemetery, were delivered. We all sang 'Auld Lang Syne' and the National Anthem, then the ball was turned up, and that was the last we saw of it for the next ninety minutes or so. Immediately a large scrum formed around it – known here, endearingly, as a 'hug'.

The game is between the Up'ards and the Down 'ards, between those born on the north or the south side of Henmore Brook, which flows through the town. The goals are three miles apart – two mills which are a mile and a half away on either side. As neither is working any longer the central spindles of the mill wheels have been erected as permanent goals, against which the ball must be touched three times to score. This is not as easy as it sounds. If 200 strong men surround the goal it takes a determined body to fight a way through. If neither side scores by 10 p.m. the game is abandoned and the ball handed to the police. On the other hand, if a goal is scored before 5 p.m. another ball is turned up. They have some left over from abandoned games.

This actually came to pass on the day that I was there. The impenetrable hug seethed about the car park for half an hour at least until, in a manoeuvre considered by watching experts to be extremely cunning, the Down'ards suddenly broke free and made off at speed across the fields for Sturton Mill. Puffing along in their wake I felt I had little hope of seeing what everyone regarded as the inevitable goal but I had failed to appreciate that getting there was one thing, goaling was quite another. It took forty minutes of heaving and cursing. Finally, amid cheers, Stephen Bott emerged triumphantly with the ball, his to keep as scorer. I have seldom seen a man more delighted. 'Bloody fantastic!' he gasped. 'Best thing that's ever happened to me. I always wanted one of these. Now I can go home, have a shower, change and watch the other game in comfort.'

The second ball was turned up at about 4.30. This time the hug moved at once into the middle of town where it raged for an hour or so before finding its way into Henmore Brook. Stephen Bott, by now showered and immaculately dressed, was on the bank to watch and encourage. We all saw more of the ball now, nobody wanting to be drowned at the bottom of a hug. There was furious rushing up and down the brook, everybody, especially the young, seeming to want to get as wet as possible. But it was dark now, hard to photograph and I felt I had seen enough. As I left I noticed Stephen, up to his waist in the river, struggling as hard as ever.

The Orkney Islands like street football. According to *The Ba' 1945–59*, a riveting book of reports from the two local papers, the islanders long ago would use any festive occasion as an excuse for a game, especially weddings. Now the Ba' thrives only in Kirkwall, on Christmas Day and New Year's Day.

The game probably came into the town about 1800. The sides are the same as they were then, more or less. First it was Farmers versus Fishermen, then Up-the-Gates and Down-the-Gates, now simply Uppies and Doonies. Visitors are welcome to play, their allegiance already decided by their method of arrival in Kirkwall. If they arrive by air they are Uppies, by ferry Doonies. This is nothing to do with the air or the sea, however, but the roads they will have had to take into town. Natives from above the Mercat Cross are Uppies, below Doonies.

The game was suspended during the Second World War. Kirkwall, and the islands which surround Scapa Flow, had more serious preoccupations. But they lost no time in reviving it; in November 1945 the Town Council debated the matter. There was obviously some argument, a few councillors regarding the war as a heaven sent excuse to stamp out this unruly behaviour. Three voted against, three abstained, but six voted to revive the Ba'.

On each day there are two games. At Christmas 1945 a third, for women, briefly appeared. *The Orcadian* reported that 'there was an element of male opposition. . .and soon after the game started they stole the ball, which was smuggled away in the crowd and was afterwards found in the Cathedral burial ground.' At New Year the paper simply mentioned tersely that the Uppies had won. The manager of the hotel I stayed in in the summer of 1984 recalled that the game never caught on because 'we were all afraid the girls were going to kill each other'.

The Boys' Ba' is thrown up at 10 o'clock and the Men's Ba' at 1. Boys become Men on their fifteenth birthday. The ball is like the one at Ashbourne, of leather filled with cork. The boys' ball is a bit smaller than the men's. Both games start at the Mercat Cross, right outside the massive, pinkish brown, unassumingly romanesque Cathedral of St Magnus. As the cathedral clock strikes the hour the ball is thrown up by a local personality. Sometimes it is impossible to hear the clock, if the wind is particularly violent. The Men's game usually takes between two and four hours, though it may go on well after dark, while at Christmas 1952 it lasted for only 4 minutes! The Boys' game usually lasts only for an hour or two.

The games are taken extremely seriously, and followed with informed interest by spectators. The local papers chronicle every move, many of which are more subtle than one might suppose from the appearance of the heaving scrum. There are all kinds of 'smuggles' and dummy moves, and each time lively incidents. At Christmas 1948 *The Orcadian* reported under the headline 'They didn't stop for lunch!' that 'the game moved partly through the lane at the back of the Albert Hotel. Here a bedroom window was pushed in and a number of players, with an Uppie in possession, passed through the room, the hall, kitchen and out through the yard, doing remarkably little damage beyond making things look a bit untidy.'

The goals are the harbour for the Doonies and Scapa Road, once the old Castle Wall, for the Uppies. The ball has to be submerged in the harbour, so the struggle often winds up in the freezing water. At the end of the game the ball is awarded, not necessarily to the man who scores, but to the man voted by the players themselves to be the most deserving. Occasionally this gives rise to heated argument; it is considered a great honour to be given the coveted ba'.

At Workington the game is known as Uppies and Downies too. There are three games each year, on Good Friday, Easter Tuesday and the following Saturday, known locally as the Friday Ball, the Tuesday Ball and the Saturday Ball. All games take place in the evening, 'about half six, seven, when the lads have had a few beers. They start on that little bridge over the beck that runs between the car park and the greyhound stadium.'

There is a new ball for each game, made of leather and stuffed with horsehair, a little smaller than a football. Apparently the privilege of throwing up, and providing, the balls rests with families. Bob Daglish and his forebears have been looking after the Tuesday Ball for generations. He claims this to be the true ball, the other two to be upstarts no older than the Great War. So, in 1984, I saw him stroll casually onto the bridge, without preamble and throw the ball to the assembled hordes and make his escape as best he could.

'Uppies and Doonies' at Workington.

Immediately the usual heaving scrum developed. Over the next few hours the battle raged through the beck, the car park, the allotments – to the alarm of the gardeners assembled to defend their vegetables – over the old railway, onto the sports field and off inexorably towards an Uppie victory. Scoring here is 'hailing'. Uppies hail at the Castle about a mile and a half inland from the harbour where Downies hail. Originally the contest was between miners and dockers, an alarming thought to contemplate.

Sometimes the game goes on far into the night, even two or three in the morning, not ending until the ball is hailed. On this Tuesday in 1984 the game stayed in gardens and fields; often it finds its way into town. The players have a reputation for mischievousness. On one occasion they burst into the Ritz Cinema, on another the Chinese takeaway.

The Atherstone game long ago was a similar kind of contest between men from Warwickshire and Leicestershire. But it has changed and evolution has made it every man for himself; the game lasts two hours, starting at 3 o'clock on Shrove Tuesday, and the winner is the man in possession of the ball on the stroke of 5 o'clock. A large ball is used, decorated with red, white and blue ribbons and filled with water to make it uncomfortably heavy to kick or throw about. The game is confined to the main street, part of the busy A5, heavily barricaded for the afternoon.

Alnwick Shrovetide Football has also changed drastically. This account is from George Tate's *History of Alnwick* (1866):

> Some forty years ago, Shrove Tuesday was a holiday in Alnwick. Crowds in the afternoon congregated before the castle gates; and at 2 o'clock, forth came the tall and stately porter dressed in the Percy livery, blue and yellow, plentifully decorated with silver lace, and gave the ball its first kick, sending it bounding out of the barbican of the castle into Bailiffgate; and then the young and vigorous kicked it through the principal streets of the town, and afterwards into the Pasture, which has been used since time immemorial for such enjoyments. Here it was kicked about, until the great struggle came, for the honour of making capture of the

> ball itself; the more vigorous combatants kicked it away from the multitude, and at last some one, stronger and fleeter than the rest, seized upon it and fled away pursued by others; to escape with the ball, the river was waded through or swam over, and walls were scaled and hedges broken down. The successful victor was the hero of the day, and proud of his trophy.

It must have been immediately after this, but long before Tate was writing, that the street element of the game was abandoned. Since 1837 the game has been confined to the pasture called the North Demesne. It is now an organized contest between the parishes of St Michael and St Paul with goals 440 yards apart. Both the scoring of, and actual, goals are called 'hales'. When I tell you that in 1984 there were 55 members on the Committee of Management and 40 players on the field you can see just how organized it is.

In the past there have been up to 1000 spectators. In 1984 there were only about 200. The Committee (who each pay £2 for the pleasure) assemble at the Castle where the ball is tossed from the Barbican to the Chairman by the Duke's representative. Everyone then proceeds down the hill sucking a local delicacy called 'black bulletts'. They assure me this is a tradition and they are purchased specially. They are led by Richard Butler, Piper to the Duke of Northumberland, playing 'Chevy Chase' and 'Lads of Alnwick' on the Northumbrian pipes. The £25 blue and white leather Dunlop football and the goal posts, in the shape of arches decorated with laurel leaves, are provided by the Duke. In 1983 St Paul's Church was sold to the Roman Catholics so this was the first year of confrontation between Protestants and Catholics! After the match was over, the Chairman tossed the ball in the air for the final part of the game. The first person to get the ball out of the Demesne can keep it. This usually means everyone ending up in the river. Finally the committee go off for high tea at a local pub. The piper plays for them and they drink the health of the Duke of Northumberland.

The games at Jedburgh, St Columb and Sedgefield are played with a much smaller ball, about the size of a cricket ball and just as hard. Kicking is not recom-

Shrovetide Football at Alnwick is unusually well organized in the Castle Demesne, with real though exotic goals.

mended, though at Sedgefield the inhabitants consider that the possibility of good luck which accrues from an annual kick far outweighs the probability of a broken toe.

These are essentially throwing, carrying and 'smuggling' games, called at Jedburgh 'Hand ba' ', at St Columb 'hurling' and Sedgefield simply 'the ball game'. They are if anything even wilder than the others and spectators are as likely to get hurt as the players. My wife, Sal, is still complaining about the blow she received at Sedgefield in 1968.

The Sedgefield game has altered quite a lot since those days though it is still a lively and popular affair. Until about 1970 it was a straightforward contest between tradesmen and farmers, their object to get the ball into one of the two streams and back again to the village green. Today there are three distinct phases in the game, instead of one continuous mêlée.

The ball is made of leather and painted with the words:

When with pancakes you are sated
Come to this ring where you'll be mated
There this ball will be uncast
May this game be better than the last.

Once the responsibility of the local publicans, taking turns, to supply the ball, it is now paid for by former winners of the game. This change occurred as a consequence of the Highways Act of 1980 which made street games illegal. Sedgefield, as you would expect, played on regardless, but the breweries told the publicans not to aid and abet. The ball is made in secret, behind locked doors, by a saddler somewhere in Darlington.

The publicans used to start the game as well. Now the honour is bestowed on someone deemed worthy. In 1984 it was 86-year-old Ralph Keton who had won the ball by scoring the winning goal in 1919. At 1 o'clock the starter passes the ball three times through the bullring on the village green, cries 'Alley off!' and throws it to the waiting crowd. The symbolism of this, and the rhyme, excites believers in fertility rite theories.

For the first hour or so the ball is kicked wildly about the village, all men, women and children anxious to get a touch to ensure good luck for the year. After that is is, officially, driven around to visit all the pubs in the neighbourhood, at each of which the man carrying the ball is entitled to a free pint.

This ritual is new to Sedgefield, but not unprecedented; something similar occurs at Haxey. At about 4 p.m. the game proper begins. Each hopeful struggles to get the ball to either of the two goals. One is in Aldersons yard, near the fire station, the other behind Spring House. Having submerged the ball that is not the end of it, for it has then to be conveyed back to the bullring and passed through it before a goal is declared. The convention is to work in groups; individuals declare their intention to score and get their mates to help them. Evidently, even in the team games, it has always been played in this way.

Until a few years ago the citizens of Jedburgh played Hand Ba' on two days of the year. The first was Candlemas, February 2, and the second Fastern's E'en. The *Oxford English Dictionary* says that 'Fastens Eve' is synonymous with Shrove Tuesday but in Jedburgh they have a little poem, 'First comes Candlemas, / then the new moon, / the first Tuesday after, / is aye Fastern's E'en', according to which they fix their game. This is usually Shrove Tuesday, but not always. However, they decided to give up the Candlemas Ba' some years ago because it was too expensive to board up the town twice in one month.

This must have been a blow to two local joiners, whose business it is to board up all the shops. Each shop and house has permanent fittings, even new buildings are built with them, and each has its own shutters which are stored by the joiners and erected the night before the Ba'. After the game they take them all down again, put them away, and send a bill to each of the owners.

The Candlemas games were, traditionally, for the younger men and boys and they are now held at midday on Fastern's E'en. A token ball is thrown up at the Mercat Cross on the original day. Well, it is not really Fastern's E'en anymore either; commerce has influenced this too and moved the Ba' on to Thursday, early closing day.

Most street football is confined to one game per day, at most three. Jedburgh managed no less than 15 in 1984, 6 for lads, 9 for the men. The balls, donated by local shops and organizations, are all made of leather in seven panels stitched together and filled with wet, compressed straw. They are a little larger than cricket balls and have long ribbons attached to them. These are said to represent hair, as mentioned above, and the first part of every game is devoted to trying to get hold of the ribbons to wear for good luck.

Once again, the contest is between Uppies and Doonies who were born, or entered the town, above or below a line which runs east and west through the Mercat Cross. South is Up and north is Doon. Uppies hail by throwing the ball over the Castle Wall, Doonies by rolling the ball across the course of the Skiprunning Burn. There is another, unique way of scoring as explained in a very informative duplicated handout about the game: 'A "cut" is achieved by cutting the stitching of the ball while it is held under water in specific parts of the River Jed. The Uppies can gain a cut in the stretch of water above the Abbey Cauld while the Doonies can gain a cut in the stretch of water above the Anna Cauld. A cut is of less value than a hail, but two cuts are better than one hail.' Cuts are comparatively rare.

Uppies tend to win through superior reserves and the fact that the roads from Bonchester and Denholm provide them with regular supplies of hefty rugby players. The contest is decided by the total number of hails achieved by each side. In 1984 the Uppies won both, the young 5–1 and the men 8–1, provoking a certain amount of aggrieved comment about incomers spoiling the game for the natives.

Each game starts with the ball being thrown to the waiting crowd from the Mercat Cross. The first ball of each game is thrown by a local dignitary, but the others are thrown by someone nominated by the donor, if not the donor himself. The first ball is thrown in the direction according to whether the thrower is an Uppie or Doonie but every other in the direction the previous ball was hailed – except that if the ball is lost or missing through being 'smuggled' a new game is started by throwing it straight up in the air.

Smuggling is a recognized part of the game though too much of it spoils the fun. The smuggler must submit to being searched by members of the opposite side who will usually ensure that he is held while the search takes place. I was told the story of a young lady who managed to hail by 'shoving it up her breeks'.

If the ball is detected it is brought back into play by being 'put up in the air', a ritual also observed if the ball goes on private property, is deadlocked in a scrum, or is kicked. The rules are unwritten, but upheld as rigorously as at an exclusive club. Though as violent as any street football, a fair amount of sportsmanship prevails. One of their endearing habits is to hand the ball over to a waiting friend to hail, often a girlfriend or some other lady, though it is just as likely to be a worthy man, too old or infirm to play himself. In 1959 John Cairncross, unable to throw the ball over the Castle Wall from his wheelchair, was allowed to push it through the gate. In 1984, 67-year-old Eckie Fairburn told the local paper that, 'some friends of mine in the Uppie ranks passed the ba' to me, and I stuck it in my pocket. I stood speaking to my Doonie friends with it still there, and eventually found an excuse to leave them and hail it at the Castle.'

Other Border towns have Hand Ba' as well, such as Duns, Hawick, Bonchester Bridge, Denholm. Some are of recent origin, and none is nearly as well known as Jedburgh. However, one or two of these do have an ancient and honourable division of players into married and unmarried.

I have not seen the hurling at St Columb in Cornwall but I feel I know all about it after reading Ivan Raby's book, *The Silver Ball*. He wishes me to make it clear that this is not football, but a throwing, catching, 'dealing' and carrying game. But I am sure he would agree that it falls well within our scope. Indeed, it sounds very much like Jedburgh Handba'.

Hurling has an ancient pedigree in Cornwall, having been recorded over four hundred years ago. It is very popular. In 1654 100 Cornishmen travelled up to London to give an exhibition of hurling in Hyde Park in front of 'His Highness the Lord Protector and many of the Privy Council and divers eminent gentlemen'. In 1725 Daniel Defoe, in his wonderful *A Tour through the Whole Island of Great Britain* observed that 'The game called the Hurlers, is a thing the Cornish men value themselves much upon; I confess, I see nothing in it, but that it is a rude violent play among the boors, or country people; brutish and furious, and a sort of evidence, that they were once a kind of barbarians. . . ' The game has gradually declined in popularity until today there are only two places where it lives on, St Columb and St Ives, and at St Ives, I am assured, it is but a shadow of the real thing, controlled and confined.

In St Columb the game is played, very much as always, on its two traditional days, Shrove Tuesday and the second Saturday in Lent. It is between the Townsmen and the Countrymen. Outsiders are not really supposed to play, though they do take part in the early stages. Towards the end of the game, by instinctive consent they withdraw and leave it to the parishioners. Allegiance is decided by where the players live, so it is possible to change sides by moving.

There are two ways of scoring, both of equal merit. The goals are stone troughs. The Town Goal is at Cross Putty, a mile south-west of the Market Square. The Country Goal is on the Wadebridge road, a mile to the north. Both sides make for a goal if possible, but, if foiled, they may opt for the other way of scoring which is to carry the ball out of the parish in any direction they fancy, or the opposition will allow. The only snag about this method used to be that the boundaries were so much further away than the goals. Recently another snag has appeared in the form of the St Columb by-pass which takes the A39 to the east of the town. Hurlers and speeding motorists do not need each other.

The ball is very interesting and unusual; it is cricket-ball sized, made of applewood and covered with sterling silver. This gives the game its popular name of 'Hurling the Silver Ball', though in St Columb they merely call it Hurling. Whoever scores can keep the ball until the next game. It is used until a new one is donated. When I spoke to Mr Raby in 1984 he thought the current ball had been going for four years. Anyone who has a mind to, and can afford it, can donate a ball. At that time they cost about £120. The donor is then given the old ball to keep. You might imagine that someone would feel the need to steal such a valuable item, but it has only happened once, in 1963, and then the conscience-stricken villain returned it a few days later. The ball does, very occasionally, get lost.

At the end of the game the winner is carried, on the shoulders of his mates, back to the Market Square where he 'calls-up' the ball again at the traditional hour of 8 p.m., providing the game is over by then. The Hurling Song is sung and then the ball is taken round all the pubs, in each of which it is ceremonially immersed in a large jug of beer, which then becomes 'silver beer' to be enjoyed by everyone.

The Bottle Kicking at Hallaton is a classic street football game, except for a few small details. The participants play in the fields, they do not use a ball, or even, for that matter, a bottle. They use three small wooden barrels, and they certainly do not kick them.

Easter Monday is a big day in Hallaton, a small village twelve miles east of Leicester. In the morning there is a children's parade, the last vestige of former Friendly Society Walks. But it is the afternoon which is important now, the annual 'Hare Pie Scramble and Bottle Kicking'. In 1892 the *Leicester Journal* gave 'particulars from the pen of an eye witness':

> At about 3 p.m. a selected deputation called at the rectory for pies and ale. . .which were taken to the Fox Inn, and a procession was formed in the following order: two men abreast carrying two sacks with the pies cut up; three men abreast carrying aloft a bottle each; a band of music; finally the procession of villagers increasing in size as it approached Hare Pie Bank.
>
> Two of the bottles were made of wood, iron hooped all over, without a neck, but having a drinking hole; these two bottles contained ale. The third bottle was a wooden dummy. When it could be obtained, a hare was mounted, in sitting posture, on top of a pole and was carried in the procession. Until this year a man followed the band with a basket containing penny loaves, which were broken up and scattered about as he walked.

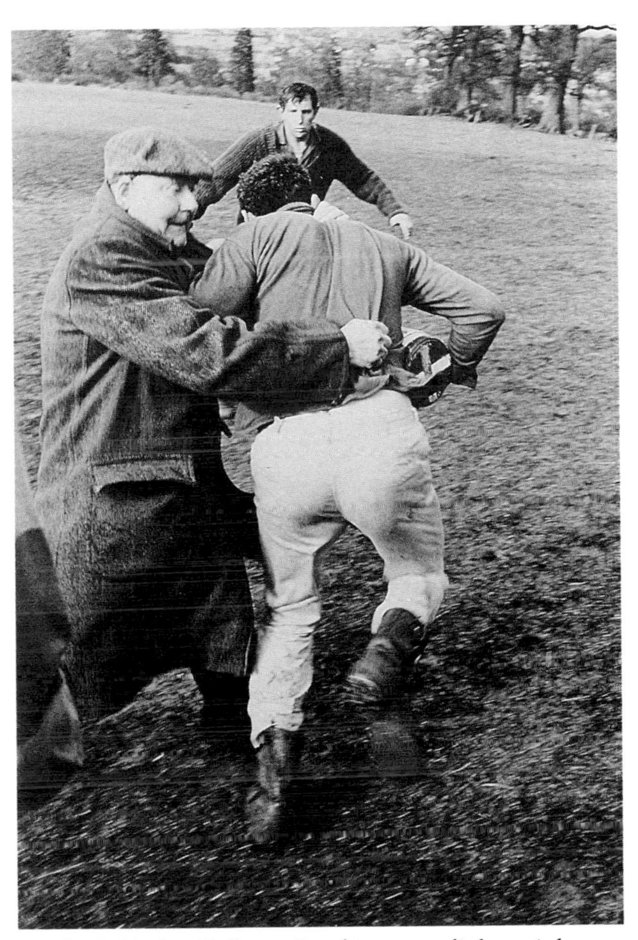

'Bottle Kicking' at Hallaton. People can get a little carried away!

> On arrival at Hare Pie Bank the essential conditions of the ancient observance were fulfilled. The pies were thrown from the sacks and scrambled for; no attempt was made to eat them. Then one of the ale bottles was thrown into the circular hollow in the mound, and the Medbourne or other villagers tried to wrest the bottle from the Hallatonians, whose task was to get the bottle, by any means, to their boundary line over the brook adjoining the village.' [The goals are two streams a mile apart.]

Little has changed ninety years later. The pie is not of hare but of beefsteak. The dummy bottle has acquired bright red, white and blue hoops. There was no sign of the hare on a pole. At the church gate the rector was waiting to cut up and distribute the pie. The Scramble was a token affair for the young, not taken very seriously. The pie was delicious, far from inedible like many early reports complain.

Everyone returned to The Fox at the top of the

village from whence, a little later, a much more business-like procession set off again for Hare Pie Bank, a field a little outside the village on the south side. Hefty rugby players had appeared to carry the bottles and there was an air of anticipation as everyone looked forward to the main event, the Bottle Kicking, a contest between the neighbouring parishes of Hallaton and Medbourne. The home team have to be inhabitants, outsiders must play for Medbourne. A native grumbled, 'Medbourne usually win because they bring along half the county rugby team.'

The contest is the best of three bottles. The first two are fought out using the two full barrels, the dummy is only used if a decider is necessary. There is no need to describe it as it was much as other games elsewhere. The only noticeable difference was that it was more open than some; more like a real game of rugby, though more fierce.

The Haxey Hood Game is one of Britain's best known annual events. It is not too difficult to understand why this is; it has men in decorative costumes, with odd titles; it has strange artefacts and ancient rituals; it has singing; it has a popular but improbable legend to explain its origin, and enough symbolic possibilities to keep folklorists speculating for a lifetime; and it has an authentic touch of madness which makes everyone love it.

The legend, believed by all at Haxey, is as follows. A Lady de Mowbray was out riding one Epiphany, some time between the twelth and sixteenth centuries; no one is sure of the year but they know which day. Records show that the family did indeed own most of the parish during this period. Her scarlet hood was blown off by a gust of wind and thirteen men who were working in a field nearby struggled for the privilege of returning it to her. She was touched and delighted by this show of gallantry but when the man who won the hood was too shy to return it to her she called him 'Fool' while a bolder one who did was dubbed 'Lord'. She said they should repeat the game on the same day every year and gave them a piece of land on which to play.

This certainly makes a good story, which can be used to explain some of the traditional happenings of the day, but the present game is little different from the others in this chapter. There are still thirteen officials, who represent the original group, called 'Boggins'. The 'King Boggin', Stan Boor, thinks that this entertaining name may derive, simply, from the boggy ground prevalent in the district, especially in midwinter. In an article in *English Dance and Song* (Spring 1966), Tom Randall has no doubts: 'the term seems to present little difficulty in interpreting, since it is a common one in the dialect of the region. "To boggin" intimates the thwarting of some scheme or plot. Indeed this is the specific task of the Boggins in the game.' Believers in the legend state that her ladyship just invented it.

All the Boggins wear red, like her hood. Folklorists tend to claim that the red symbolizes a sacrificial element. Three of them are senior to the rest. In charge is the 'King Boggin', otherwise 'The Lord of the Hood' or familiarly, 'The Lord'. Stan Boor has been the incumbent since the mid-1960s. His second in command is the 'Chief Boggin'. Both these important people wear coats of hunting pink and top hats profusely decorated with flowers, feathers and jewellery. The Lord also carries his Wand of Office, an impressive piece of regalia about five feet long, made from 13 thin willow sticks, bound together by 13 'serves', slivers of willow, each of which is wound round the wand 13 times. A new wand is made each year and older villagers insist on checking carefully that it is correct, otherwise the game cannot be played.

The Fool wears foolish things in addition to his red jersey. Traditionally his face is smeared with soot and red ochre in a ceremony carried out in public at The Kings Head at the beginning of the day's events.

The current Hood itself bears no resemblance to any garment. It is a cylindrical object about 18 inches long and 3 inches in diameter, substantially solid but slightly flexible, covered with fine brown leather. The inside is a piece of heavy rope. Sealed at one end is a Jubilee Crown and at the other a disc engraved with the names of all the Boggins in 1981, the year it was first used. It is a little thinner than its predecessor, which was considered too stiff and hard and which broke up in 1980. Mended, it is now in Lincoln Museum. The one before that had been used since far beyond living memory so had become part of the legend and definitely contained her ladyship's hood rolled up inside. When it finally broke open the villagers were disappointed to find it was filled with straw.

Inevitably theorists have been to work on the Hood as well. I am a little worried about the fertility-rite enthusiasts who suggest in their book that the game followed the sacrifice of a bull and that the Hood 'may have represented the bull's most vital organ, the penis'.

The Hood lives, for all but one week in the year, in one of two pubs, either The Kings Head in Haxey, or The Carpenters Arms in Westwoodside. Until 1981 another pub in Haxey, The Duke William, was also involved, but that year they put up the shutters and banned the Hood because they had a new carpet. The

Boggins took this setback in good part at first, even composed an amusing song about it, but the shutters are still up and their tolerance is said to have worn thin.

On New Year's Eve the Hood is claimed by the Lord and they all take it round the neighbourhood pubs where they sing their songs and invite everyone to attend the forthcoming game. They also collect money to defray expenses. In the early 1980s the singing had become quite organized. The Boggins were kitted out in smart red jerseys and had even started taking bookings. Traditionally they have three songs, which they call their own, but which are in fact extremely well known everywhere. They are 'John Barleycorn', 'The Farmer's Boy' and 'Drink Old England Dry'. They told me that they had learned several other songs for their various outings.

On January 6 events begin at noon. The Boggins, in their smart dress, visit the two pubs to sing their three songs. Just before 2 o'clock they all troupe up the village to the church gate. This phase belongs to the Fool. First he tries to run away, but he is captured by the other Boggins, by now changed into older red jerseys, who carry him struggling to the mounting stone to be 'smoked'. This was once a more significant part of the ritual which came on the morning after the game. Then the Fool was suspended on a rope and swung back and forth through smoke from a substantial fire until his 'friends' were prepared to let him down. An unfortunate incident put a stop to this long ago. As the Fool stands on the mounting stone to deliver his traditional speech, damp straw is burned behind him and he is enveloped in smoke. His speech is partly impromptu, but mostly words handed down. He exhorts everyone to 'play upright and downstraight', delivers any message applicable to that particular year and finishes 'so it's hoose agin hoose, toon agin toon, if a man meets a man knock a man doon – but don't 'urt 'im!'

Everyone then moves off to the hallowed field, half-way between Haxey and Westwoodside. It is just an ordinary field, one year ploughed, another fallow; in 1981 it was full of cabbages. The farmer who owns it is said to campaign ceaselessly to have the game banned but nobody takes any notice. It is here that the real action begins. Before the main Hood Game, twelve lesser hoods are individually thrown. These are simple rolls of sacking. The Boggins form a circle round the field and the players, mostly youngsters, struggle to get hold of the hoods and carry them through this cordon. This is not as easy as it sounds, and it takes an hour or more to get them all away.

As evening falls, the main Hood is thrown up. Instantly it disappears into a giant scrum never to be seen again until it emerges at the end of the game. There is no open running in the Haxey Hood Game. The object is to work the Hood to one of the two pubs, by means of the forces generated within the 'sway'. As there may be a hundred or more strong men in the sway, most of whom do not know what is going on outside, these forces can be said to be mysterious. The sway moves inexorably, like a giant beast, flattening all before it, steaming gently in the cold night air. Every now and again, someone is dragged out to be resuscitated. Only occasionally does anyone need to be taken away in the waiting ambulance.

It may take several hours to reach the pub, but when it does the landlord must touch the Hood to end the game. Then there are free, and much needed, drinks for all. Actually these are paid for out of the collections made previously by the Boggins. The Hood stays in the pub until next New Year's Eve. Since the Duke William closed its doors the Hood has been a couple of times to The Carpenters Arms in Westwoodside. Formerly this was a rarity, the honours being evenly divided between the two Haxey pubs.

All these games are authentic 'folk' customs, played to very simple rules. The rules of the Eton Wall Game are multitudinous and impenetrable. The odd thing is that it turns out very much the same.

It is played throughout the winter terms. There are special traditional games at 6 a.m. on Founder's Day, December 6, and Ascension Day but the famous Wall Game is on the Saturday nearest to St Andrew's Day, November 30. My young Etonian friend, Caspar Rock, attempted to explain what it was all about, though it is by no means certain he understood the rules himself, not being a player. The game is between Collegers and Oppidans. There are 70 Collegers at Eton, who have all won scholarships, and 1100 Oppidans who pay fees in the normal way. 'Though there are so few Collegers,' claims Caspar, 'they usually win because they're much brainier than the Oppidans. It's as subtle as a game of chess in there, you know.'

Watching, it is not apparent that superior intelligence is a significant factor. There are ten men in each team – three 'walls' who do the heavy work, two 'seconds' who back them up, three 'outsiders' roughly equivalent to the back row of a rugby scrum, and two 'behinds' who lurk outside the 'bully' ready to rush off with the ball on the rare occasions it appears. The bully is a heaving mass of bodies locked against the Wall, which runs along the west side of College Field and separates it from Windsor Road. Somewhere

The Eton Wall Game. An Etonian friend insists 'it's as subtle as a game of chess in there'.

inside the bully is the ball, naturally of unique design, a little smaller than a football, leather, with two flattened sides, an oblate spheroid.

There is a bold, vertical, white line towards each end of the Wall and the first objective is to work the ball along the Wall past the opposition white line. This is 'getting into calx', 'Good Calx' is at the College end of the Wall, 'Bad Calx' at the other. There is some business of pressing the ball at a certain height from the ground when in calx and crying 'got it'. If the referee says 'given', a 'shy' is awarded. After a shy the team can go for a goal. The goals are at Good Calx, an unimpressive black door, and Bad Calx, the stump of a tree. The ball has to be pressed against the goal to score, but if the defending team gain possession the opportunity to score is lost. Caspar was vague about this phase of the game, understandably since he had never seen a goal scored. The last one on St Andrew's Day was in 1909, when Harold Macmillan was one of the players, though one was scored in a lesser game as recently as 1973.

Fouls can be committed, such as 'sneaking', 'knuckling' or 'furking', for which distance penalties are awarded. Really it is only the presence of a referee which makes this game any different from the others.

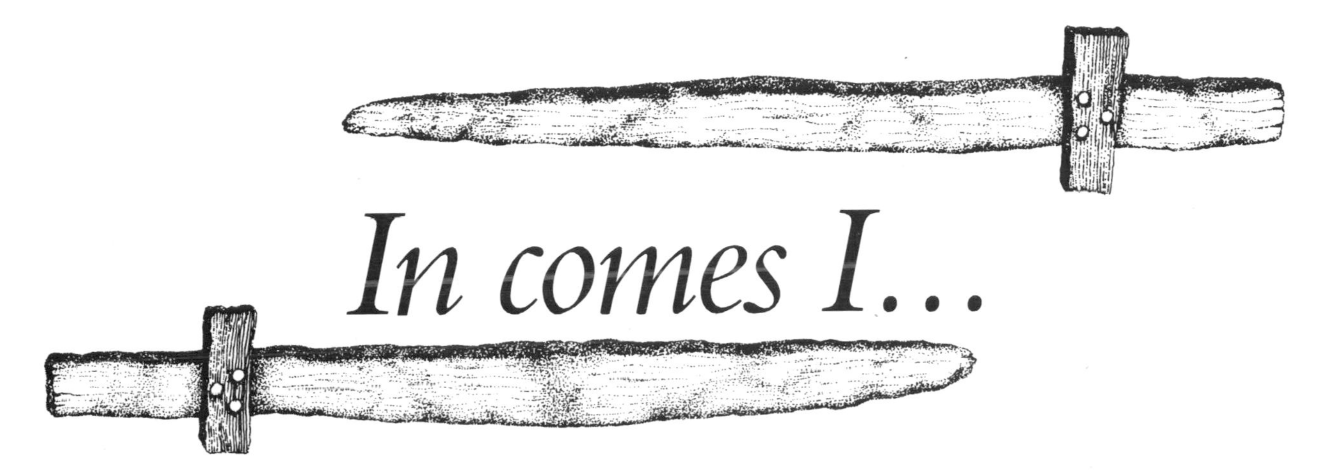

In comes I...

In 1967 the Folklore Society published an Index, through reliable sources, of all known examples of folk plays ever to have existed in the British Isles. There were 1105 in all: 926 in England, 5 in Wales, 32 in Scotland, 3 in the Isle of Man and 139 in Ireland; but there must have been very many more, unrecorded.

By 1950 all the Scottish and Welsh plays had vanished, but 33 English and no less than 35 Irish plays were still going. Today about a dozen survive in England, having, by now, achieved the status of Important Traditions. In Ireland the play also lives on strongly but in a more casual and unpredictable way.

Almost all English folk plays are of the 'Hero-Combat' type in which a hero challenges all-comers. The challenge is accepted. One of the combatants is slain. A doctor is called for and he revives the fallen man. This is the basic framework common to all the plays but, naturally, there are infinite variations. In some places there are two fights, nor is it always the hero who wins. But this simple death and resurrection theme is the crux of the matter. It is said to be symbolic, but of what is not clear.

There can be as few as three people involved, or as many as ten. It is not uncommon for men (women rarely take part), to play more than one part. In the past, arrangements depended on numbers available. Nowadays, the text having become Holy Writ, there is little change from year to year.

Similarly, the names of the characters have settled. St George or King George is the likeliest hero; but King William is not unknown and, predictably, the Irish favour St Patrick. Challengers include Bold Slasher, Turkish Knight (or occasionally 'Turkey Snipe'), Little Man John, the Black Prince of Paradine, Bold Soldier – something military, or belligerent. Only the Doctor keeps his title unadorned, with rare additions of a surname like Dr Good or Dr Phoenix. Father Christmas is normally in attendance during the Christmas plays to act as introducer or 'letter-in'.

The remaining players, not essential to the main business, are there to add colour and encourage a bigger take. Thus they are knockabout characters with fantastic names like Tenpenny Nit, Toss Pot, Saucy Jack, Trim Tram, Old Father Beelzebub, Old Tom the Tinker, Little Derry Doubt.

Costume is a disguise, often impenetrable. Alex Helm in *The English Mummers Play* has pointed out 'it was a fundamental necessity to preserve anonymity, for to be recognized broke the "luck".' However, in most cases it is perfectly easy to recognize the performers, though evidently bad form to say so.

There are three main categories of costume. The most simple, favoured in the more spontaneous atmosphere of the Irish plays, may involve no more than turning coats inside out and putting on anything that comes to hand. The English plays, being organized annual events, need something more elaborate.

In some places players dress in character – not very seriously, it is true, but recognizably as doctor, soldier, old woman, Robin Hood, or whatever. In others the much older disguise is preferred, with identical, or similar, costumes for all. Only the Doctor, in his top hat and frock coat, is a frequent exception. The commonest of these uniforms is a covering, plus hat, of paper or cloth streamers at once colourful and mysterious. In the North, smocks with rosettes or embroidered motifs are more popular. Everywhere headdresses tend to be spectacular.

The English folk play is entirely a winter custom, performed between All Souls and Easter, particularly at Christmas. Some plays are performed out of doors, others only in pubs, clubs or houses. Only at Ripon can the play be seen indoors and out.

Fine speeches, elegant phrasing, perceptive insights are not to be expected. Indeed, attempts at characterization are likely to be disastrous. The plays are often belted out in loud voices, at great speed. Usually the words make little sense. But the overall effect is marvellous.

Oddly, though the surviving examples in England are strong, varied and interesting, the tradition lives most easily in the border areas of Ireland. The reason for the presence of the play there at all is quite simple – it was brought by settlers. (Intriguingly, and irrelevantly, examples were reported in Canada, the USA and St Kitts in the last century, but they have not survived.)

Jenny Hicks, who lives in Maguire's Bridge, Co. Fermanagh, reports that the mummers are active but unpredictable. They tend to appear for a couple of years, vanish again, only to reappear in another village. Most of them are young men, in it for the beer. Older men are not usually interested, or are not allowed to be by their wives.

They tend to be shy – happy to perform for their mates but suspicious of outsiders, especially with cameras and tape recorders. It is hopeless trying to pin down times or locations.

Their costumes are mainly jackets turned inside out, and blackened faces. The traditional headdress, a kind of conical mask made of straw, gave rise to their name 'Straw Boys', but it is now seldom seen.

Texts are much the same as in England; there are no Gaelic versions. For all their casual attitude, the tradition in Ireland appears more lively and spontaneous than it does in England, for to ebb and flow in this way it needs to be deep in their way of life.

The English plays are accessible and reasonably regular in their places and times. A certain amount of variation is to be expected though, as will be seen in the examples that follow.

Marshfield is a small Cotswold village, twelve miles east of Bristol. In 1930, according to legend, the vicar, the Reverend Alford, overheard his gardener reciting part of a folk play. Knowing that his sister was interested in such things, he mentioned it to her. Violet Alford, an eminent folklorist, was more than interested. By Boxing Day 1931, the mummers had been reassembled, after many years of silence, and back on the streets.

Apart from the Town Crier, who leads the mummers between performances, ringing a bell, there are seven characters: Father Christmas, King William, Little Man John, Dr Phoenix, Saucy Jack, Tenpenny Nit and Old Father Beelzebub.

They all wear similar costumes covered from top to bottom with streamers of crêpe and newspaper. Because of this they are known locally as 'The Paper Boys'. They do not make these outfits new each year but simply repair them. Thus, some of the older costumes make quite interesting reading.

Most carry wooden swords, and some have special hats or implements appropriate to character. King William wears a paper crown, Father Christmas is predominantly dressed in red. Dr Phoenix carries his phial, Old Father Beelzebub his club. Saucy Jack has 'me wife and family at me back'.

The Marshfield play is performed in the street, though the text indicates that this was not always so. It is repeated five times; at the east end of the street, twice along the way to the Almshouses at the other end and, finally, in the doctor's garden. The whole lot only takes the hour between 11 and midday.

The presentation is dignified and somewhat formal. It is an unusually straightforward version of the English folk play. For the most part each man steps forward, does his piece, and calls on the next man. There are few histrionics and improvisations. Only the song at the end could be described as odd.

This is the full text of the Marshfield play, recorded on Boxing Day 1972.

The Paper Boys *appear in procession led by the* Town Crier. *They form a circle.*

THE TOWN CRIER Oyez, Oyez, Oyez!
I have much pleasure in introducing
The Celebrated Marshfield Mummers,
The Old Time Paper Boys.
God save the Queen!

Father Christmas *steps forward.*

FATHER CHRISTMAS In comes I, Old Father Christmas!
Christmas or Christmas not
I hope Old Father Christmas
Will never be forgot.
Christmas comes but once a year
Then we generally get good cheer.
Roast beef, plum pudding and mince pies
Who likes that better
Than King William and I.

KING WILLIAM Aye!

FATHER CHRISTMAS Room, room, a gallant room I say!
If Little Man John is in this room
Let him step this way!

LITTLE MAN JOHN In comes I, Little Man John.
If anyone defy me let him come on.
Cut me and slay me, as small as the dust
And send me to Jamaica
To be made into mince pie crust.
Room, room, a gallant room I say
If King William is in the room
Let him step this way!

Marshfield Mummers. One of them recently repaired his costume with Page Three of a well-known popular tabloid, to the great annoyance of respectable villagers!

KING WILLIAM In walks I, King William,
A man of courage and bold
With my sword and spear all in my hand
I gained three crowns of gold
I fought the fiery dragon
And bring him to a slaughter
And by the means of that I gained
The hand of the Queen of Europe's daughter.
Me and four men slew seven score
And gained the victory of a British Man of War
But thy mind's high, my mind's bold
Thy blood's hot. I'll quickly make it cold!

King William *and* Little Man John *have a fairly vigorous sword fight until* Little Man John *is slain and collapses*.

KING WILLIAM Room, room, a gallant room I say
If Jack Phoenix is in this room
Let him step this way!

DOCTOR PHOENIX My name is not Jack Phoenix
My name is Doctor Phoenix, a noble doctor.
I can cure more than any man can
I can cure the itch, the stitch, the palsy and the gout,
All pains within and none without.
Bring me an old woman of seven years dead
Seven years lying in her grave.
One pill from me
And this gallant boy will rise again.

SAUCY JACK What's thy fee, doctor?

DOCOTOR PHOENIX Ten pounds is my fee –
And fifteen I'll take of thee
To set this lad free.

SAUCY JACK Work thy will.

Here the Doctor *makes much of his expertise*

DOCTOR PHOENIX I have a little bottle by my side
Filled with the old English turpentine.
I place a drop on his lips
A drop on his thigh.
Arise, arise, Little Man John!

I long to see thee stand.
Open thine eyes and look around
I'll take thee by the hand.

Little Man John *rises, none the worse for wear, and resumes his place in the circle.*

THE DOCTOR Room, room, a gallant room I say
If Saucy Jack is in this room
Let him step this way!

SAUCY JACK In walks I, Saucy Jack,
My wife and family at me back.
Out of eight I have but five
And half of they be starved alive.
Some on the parish and some at home
Where I go and rest must come.
Make room, make room, I say!
We come to show you some activity today.
Activity of mind, activity of age,
Did you ever see the like
On any common stage?
Room, room, a gallant room I say
If Tenpenny Nit is in this room
Let him step this way!

TENPENNY NIT In walks I, Tenpenny Nit
With my big head and my little wit.
My head is big, my body small
I'm the biggest rough amongst them all.
My head is hard as iron,
My body hard as steel,
My trousers touch my ankle bones
Pray Doctor come and feel.

The Doctor *makes much of prodding and feeling.*

DOCTOR PHOENIX Ha! Ha! I certainly feel something hard.
You're a proper blackguard!

TENPENNY NIT Room, room, a gallant room I say!
If Father Beelzebub is in this room
Let him step this way!

FATHER BEELZEBUB In comes I, old Father Beelzebub,
On my shoulder I carry my club
And in my hand my money pan
What d'you think of me for a jolly old man?
A little of your Christmas ale
Would make us boys dance and sing.
A little of your money in our pocket
Would be a jolly fine thing.
Ladies and gentlemen sit down at your ease
And give us what you please.

He resumes his place in the circle and they all walk around singing.

ALL It's of a noble Welshman
I heard the people say
As I rode up to London
All on St David's Day

(CHORUS) Fal-la-la, fal-la-la, fal-la-la
Deed I do.
Hi, hi, hi, the people cry
We'll concern a king
Seated on a nanny goat
Just like a Christmas King.

Chorus

There is a house on yonder hill
So high I do declare
'Twas on a cold wild winter's night
My grandmother left me there.

Chorus

After this puzzling song they move off at once to the next location.

This song is unique to this play, though elsewhere groups end with songs of their own, or dances, or other business. These endings have no particular significance; they exist to encourage largesse.

Another group who also come out on Boxing Day are the Crookham Mummers who appear at 12 o'clock outside The Chequers in Crookham Village, which is in Hampshire, a mile or so south-west of Fleet. They look very much like the Marshfield Paper Boys, except that their costumes are made from wallpaper and two of them dress in character. The Doctor wears a top hat and Harley Street clothes, Father Christmas a Santa Claus outfit and the other five are dressed in paper streamers.

Basically, the text is similar, though it sounds as if an editor has straightened out the unsatisfactory bits to make it sound more logical. The mummers come on in single file, led by a concertina player. Bold Roamer introduces Father Christmas who proclaims him a great champion. King George accepts the challenge and slays Bold Roamer. Father Christmas bemoans the death of his son, calls on his other son, Bold Slasher, to avenge him. He gets killed too. Both sons lie side by side, dead. (It is, incidentally, extremely uncommon to have two corpses together.) Father Christmas calls for a doctor. With much business, involving saws, rubber tubes and bottles, the Doctor brings them back to life. The Turkish Knight then challenges, but is driven off. Finally Trim Tram comes on, does his nonsense bit, and asks for money.

Where it differs so much from Marshfield is in its delivery. Each performance is full of improvisations, local references, and badinage with spectators and

passing dogs. The fights are full blooded to the point of lunacy. 'We make twenty wooden swords for the four performances', said their leader, Stan Knight, 'Every one must go'. Combatants have been knocked out, and cuts and bruises are expected.

The play had a long, unbroken history up to the Second World War. Then the mummers would be out for three days over Christmas, working the pubs and, particularly, the big houses. After the war it became less regular as older performers died and one famous Father Christmas had to drop out – 'His wife got so fed up with him being away and coming home so drunk that she locked him out one Christmas. Next Christmas she locked him in. We never saw him again!'

They turned out by special request for parties in the big houses and on few other occasions. The play never died altogether. In 1960 young and old got together to revive it properly and it has been going well ever since.

Family connections are important in Uttoxeter, a small market town about half-way between Stafford and Derby. For generations there have been 'guizers' called Williams. In 1983, the team of five consisted of brothers Ted and Sid, their nephew Robert, their brother-in-law Graham Arnold and his son, also Robert. On duty they are the Introducer, known in the trade as the 'letter-in', St George, Bold Soldier, the Doctor and Mary Ann.

Crookham Mummers. The 'Harley Street' Doctor has the unusual task of reviving two corpses at the same time while Father Christmas looks on.

In Uttoxeter, the mummers are known simply as 'The Guizers'. Their disguise consists of short jackets festooned with long coloured ribbons and elaborate hats. Though the jackets are more or less the same, each hat is different. All are liberally decorated with paper flowers and tinsel. Mary Ann's pink felt might be well received at Ascot, though the Doctor wears the finest creation, a bowler covered with multi-coloured feathers, the only remnant of a tradition around Staffordshire which gave mummers the name 'Feather Guizers'.

This is a very impressive play, delivered in direct declamatory style, at speed. It needs to be fast, since

Bampton Mummers perform indoors, in pubs and 'big houses'.

the mummers have to get round all the town's twelve pubs and clubs between 8 o'clock and midnight on Christmas Eve.

Though it was once the common practice for mummers everywhere, it is now the unique custom of the Uttoxeter Guizers to tour the 'big houses' on Christmas Day itself.

The Bampton Mummers, too, have a hectic Christmas Eve. This Oxfordshire village, famous for its traditional morris dancers, has many splendid 'big houses' and eight pubs for them to visit. First, the house calls are made, starting at 5 o'clock. A complicated schedule has to be worked out in advance. At each house there is a full performance, in drawing room, dining room or hall, followed by a convivial Christmas drink. By the time they arrive in the first pub, at about 9 o'clock, their delivery is getting chaotic. But this is no problem in Bampton, for everyone knows the play and the players. Substitutes are at hand.

Though there are ten parts, there are only six players. The play divides, untypically, into two quite separate sections, in each of which there is a fight, a death, a resurrection and some light comedy. Only two characters remain throughout: Father Christmas, who is letter-in, and Dr Good, who works his magic twice, the second time with the help of Jack Finney.

The first combatants are St George and the Turkish Knight, the others, the Royal Aprussia King and Soldier Bold. Supporting cast are Robin Hood and Little John followed by Jack Finney and Old Tom the Tinker. Players dress in character, changing at half-time.

> The list of immemorial customs extant in Bampton is brief and it is to be feared that the remnants which exist will soon disappear. . . There are the Morris Dancers' performances at Whitsuntide, the collection of Christmas boxes, and a party of lads who, as mummers, parade the streets during three or four evenings in succession, trying to gain admission into the houses of the inhabitants for the performance of their mummers play. These are the only vestiges of ancient public customs now remaining.
>
> *History of the Town and Parish of Bampton* by John Giles, 1847

Flaming tar barrels are an honoured part of winter customs. These are at Hatherleigh. *(see page 188)*

Barrel Rolling at Ottery St Mary is the country's most alarming tradition. *(see page 187)*

At Up-Helly-Aa only the Guizer Jarl and his Squad are allowed to be Vikings. *(see page 193)*

The play *had* died out shortly before the Second World War, but it was revived in 1946 by some of the same men. Today it is benevolently organized by Arnold Woodley, who lives in Bampton, and who also plays the fiddle for one of the morris sides. Though visitors who have seen the morris dancers may find familiar faces amongst the mummers, the two immemorial customs remain quite separate.

Headington Quarry, on the east side of Oxford, is a place equally famous in morris dancing lore. But here dancers and mummers are the same. The play, though it has had an intermittent history, is genuine Headington Quarry. Its existence was first noted in 1847 and since then it has had many stops and starts, always managing to bridge the gaps with men who had previously taken part. It settled into its present run in the 1950s on the impetus of a group of handbell ringers, who naturally added a burst of their own particular thing. The morris men soon became involved and, knowing the rapper sword dance to be a winter rite, popped that in too.

The plot has thickened. Currently, 'the rumbustious Boxing Day Show' has developed into an astonishing folk variety performance which begins with half a wassail song, continues with carols on the handbells, the play, some morris dancing, and ends with sword dancing and the rest of the wassail song!

In Ripon, North Yorkshire, the mummers call themselves 'Sword Dancers'. They sing, they speak, they do carry swords, but they do not dance. The explanation is simple. In the North of England, sword dancing was part of the ceremony. 'Death' came by ritual decapitation in a sword lock, 'resurrection' by the Doctor aided by more dancing. There are no extant examples of the original ceremony though revival groups occasionally give performances based on written texts, especially the sword play once performed at Ampleforth in North Yorkshire. Decapitation is still an essential feature of the long sword dances at Grenoside, north of Sheffield, and Goathland, on the moors near Whitby.

So, even if there is no dancing at Ripon now, there probably once was. In any case, there are only three performers. Disconcertingly, they manage to play five or six parts. Thus, the leader comes on as a nameless introducer, goes on to challenge and slay St George, then suddenly becomes the Doctor in order to revive him. St George retains the part throughout, while the remaining dancer starts off as old Beelzebub but later serves as a kind of nameless feed-man for the Doctor.

The text is full of strange allusions, delivered at breakneck speed in loud parade-ground voices. Locals claim that if you want to find the Sword Dancers you only have to stand in the street and listen.

The song they start with makes as much sense as the one with which the Marshfield Mummers finish. It seems to be a calling-on song, for performers who aren't there. One of them is the Highland Laddie:

> The next that comes in is the Highland Laddie
> Who's got sheep on yonder plains
> Romping and roving amongst the bonnie lassies.
> Now he's gone and spent it all.
> Now he's gone and spent it all.

After some preamble the leader calls on St George. Challenges are exchanged. They fight by a symbolic clashing of swords. St George is slain and stands quietly with head bowed. The victor suddenly becomes the Doctor:

> I can cure the young, the old, the hot, the cold,
> The lovesick maid, living or the dead,
> The itch, the stitch, the gallop, the gout,
> The plague within and the plague without,
> And the plague that flies around about.
> If there be seven evils in that man,
> I'll bring seven and seventy out.

St George is revived. That is all. After another short song they move off. This is repeated perhaps thirty times as they tour Ripon on Boxing Day. They start off at about 9.30 a.m. among the housing estates on the south side, where they all live, performing in the streets, in private houses, in pubs and clubs. In 1982 they finished about tea-time, though earlier generations are said to have considered it a matter of principle to visit all thirty-two pubs in the city.

Inevitably, the Ripon Sword Dance is a family affair. The Hardcastles are thought to have been involved for as many as 200 years, and one Bill to have turned out for 67 consecutive Boxing Days until he died at the age of 80. He was the father of Eddie and Walter who were, for long, the mainstays until the early 1970s. Apparently these two were also noted for the terrific arguments in which they were constantly engaged, though Eddie's daughter, Margaret, recalls that when Walter died her father could not live without him.

Margaret herself made history in 1982. Her husband, Tony Chambers, had been keeping the play going very satisfactorily until, not to put too fine a point on it, a row broke out, and at the last moment one of the dancers refused to go out. Enraged, but resourceful, Margaret decided to go out herself. After

Ripon Sword Dancers. This was once part of a much larger sword dance display; now only the play part survives. This year, 1982, saw the first appearance of Margaret Chambers, one of the Hardcastles who have kept this play going for generations.

all, was she not a genuine Hardcastle? Though mildly surprised, the citizens of Ripon were certainly glad to see her and, an extrovert soul, she obviously enjoyed it herself. She was out again in 1983. It is not known if this was because she had acquired a taste for it or if the row was still going on.

Feminism notwithstanding, women do not normally take part in mumming plays. Indeed, an old man interviewed on the subject in the 1930s was horrified at the thought: 'Nay, sir, mumming don't be for the likes of them. There plenty else for them that be flirty-like, but this here mumming be more like parson's work.'

Almost all Hero-Combat plays are performed around Christmas time, but in Cheshire they come up at All Souls, or Hallowe'en, and are called Souling Plays.

Only three Souling Plays survived the Second World War, at Comberbach, Great Budworth and Antrobus. Today only the Antrobus Souling Play is still going, but, contrarily, it threatens to be overwhelmed by popularity. Folklorists study it, recordists record it, photographers photograph it; wherever they go they bring an army of followers.

The soulers have a testing schedule, covering a wide area. They always go out at Hallowe'en and usually for the following two Thursdays, Fridays and Saturdays. Their headquarters is the Wheatsheaf in Antrobus, a miniscule village off the A559, north of Northwich, south of Warrington, east of Runcorn and west of Knutsford. They start there, but where they go afterwards is unpredictable.

The play is standard until the end, when the Wild Horse and his Driver appear:

In comes Dick and all his men,
He's come to see you once again.
He was once alive and now he's dead
He's nothing but a poor old horse's head.
Stand around Dick, and show yourself!
Now, ladies and gentlemen, just view around,
See whether you've seen a better horse on any ground.
He's double ribbed, sure footed, and

The Antrobus Soulers posed for photographers in the Wheatsheaf in 1972.

a splendid horse in any gears.
And ride him if you can!
He's travelled high, he's travelled low
He's travelled all through frost and snow,
He's travelled the land of Ikerty Pikkery,
Where there's neither land nor city. . .

. . .This horse was bred in Seven Oaks,
The finest horse e'er fed on oats,
He's won the Derby and the Oaks,
And now pulls an old milk float. . .

. . .Now I ask you all to open your hearts
to buy Dick a newsprung cart. Not
for him to pull, oh dear, no! For him
to ride in. If you don't believe these
words I say, ask those chaps outside there.
They're better liars than I am.

There is much more of this boastful nonsense about Dick, intended to raise money, ostensibly to keep him in happy and comfortable retirement. The Wild Horse at Antrobus replaces the humorous character elsewhere, as an inducement to generosity. All the same, Dick has a presence about him and, in view of Mari Lwyd, hoodening, hobby horses and the like, he may have had a more significant role in the past.

The nine players dress in character. When I saw them in 1972 King George looked like a bandsman, the Black Prince – mysteriously – like an old-fashioned police constable, the Quack Doctor as normal for the part. Mary was a splendid 'old woman' with a veil like a string bag to disguise his masculinity. Beelzebub was a dreadful old man with a big black beard. Derry Doubt not only dressed like a schoolboy but very probably was one. The letter-in did not appear to be wearing costume at all. The Driver was resplendent in full, and immaculate, hunting pink. The Wild Horse, Dick, was a man bowed forward from the waist, beneath a canvas cover which was attached to a real horse skull. This was painted shiny black and mounted on a pole which the man held. Thus, with two black legs, a bulky canvas body, one front leg and a ferociously snapping head, a reasonably convincing – if bizarre – horse was achieved.

Midgley Pace Egg Play is performed by boys of Calder High School, Todmorden and is disconcertingly different each year.

Cheshire likes its mumming plays at All Souls; just up the road in Lancashire, in Yorkshire and in Cumbria, for equally obscure reasons, they prefer them at Easter.

In the North of England Pace-Egging was once a common children's begging custom when they would go around asking for eggs and singing a little song.

> We are one two three jully boys, all of one mind
> We are come a-pace-egging, and we hope you'll prove kind.
> We hope you'll prove kind with your eggs and strong beer,
> And we'll come no more to you until the next year.

So the Easter version is a Pace Egg Play and, furthermore, it is performed by children.

Almost every pensioner you speak to around the area can remember being in a play or at least seeing one; today there are only a couple going, both of them under adult motivation. One of them is very well known, followed annually by a large crowd of visitors. It is the Midgley play, performed since the mid-1950s by boys of the Calder High School.

High above the school, in the Calder Valley between Halifax and Hebden Bridge, the tiny village of Midgley had sustained its Pace Egg Play until 1939. It was well known, and recorded, even then. The village boys had kept it going in the traditional manner but it could not survive the war.

Later a version started up in the village school in Heptonstall but this petered out in the early 1960s. However, when we first met the Calder High School boys in 1964, one of them (with the old Yorkshire name of Michael O'Shea) had been in the Heptonstall group for three years.

Traditionalists still insist that the Pace Egg Play should be performed by 8- to 10-year-olds. Though these boys are, on average, six years older, their youth gives a different flavour.

Albert Greenwood, as English master in charge in the sixties, pointed out: 'It all depends on the Sixth. If they're interested, everyone is. If they aren't, it's a job to get anyone to do it. So each year there are successes and disappointments. You just don't know what's going to happen. Usually, if a boy comes in quite young, he'll stay.'

It is interesting for regular spectators to watch the lads grow in size and maturity, though disconcerting, especially for a photographer, to have them changing parts. However, it is worth mentioning a more fundamental change between 1964 and 1984. Twenty years ago the boys seemed so young, they were deferential to Mr Greenwood and they needed to be looked after; now they appear to be years older, drink beer between shows and drive their own cars. In spite of this apparent sophistication, though, the boys still perform with the same verve, enthusiasm and charm.

They appear seven times on Good Friday. The first is at Mytholmroyd, surrounded by parents and friends, accompanied by barracking. Then they move to The Dusty Miller on the main Calder Valley road while lorries and cars pass by with indifference. At Hebden Bridge, an archetypal little mill town pretty enough to have been adopted by craftsmen, media-men and executives from big Yorkshire cities, their coming is an important event attended by large crowds.

After lunch, their visit to Midgley itself is in the nature of a pilgrimage, a visit to the hallowed shrine – where they perform in the convenient space, built specially for the bus to turn. Next they walk down precipitous cobbled hills and into the Industrial Revolution. Luddenden is still all black stone buildings and claustrophobia, though the old outworkers' shops are by now desirable residences. Here the play is at home, it sits well in its surroundings, the locals like and welcome it, spare it a passing glance, and take it very much for granted. Finally, they drive to the middle of Todmorden, a much bigger town fallen on hard times, where they have to compete with Easter shoppers and the noisy market. Astonishment is their only reward.

The play is not unusual, with nine parts. Only Toss Pot and the Bugler need any comment. Toss Pot is peculiar to this area, a knockabout character with his clay pipe and his 'old tally wife', but he was so familiar that anyone acting foolishly was liable to be described as 'a proper Toss Pot'.

As for the Bugler, Mr H.W. Harwood of Midgley claimed, in 1966, that his presence was entirely due to a radio broadcast of the play. When, for instance, Slasher says,

> Hark! St George, I hear the silver trumpet sound
> that summons me from off this bloody ground,

the producer, failing to hear one on the tape, put one in. The Pace-Eggers in their turn, thought it a good idea, so the Bugler was born. This story may be apocryphal.

Costumes are unusual, except for the Doctor, clad inevitably in top hat and frock coat. Toss Pot wears a tramp-like ensemble but everyone else scarlet smocks decorated with paper rosettes. These smocks are not of the country-yokel type but plain and simple, as worn by mill workers. Their hats are most distinctive; mortarboards with brightly decorated hoops crossed on top. Loops hang around the head suspended from the flat piece.

Very similar costumes, but with white smocks, are worn for the Pace Egg Play at Brighouse, on the other side of Halifax. The boys are all members of the Brighouse Children's Theatre, which was founded in 1948 by Gerald Tyler, at that time drama adviser to the West Riding.

He and his wife were familar with the Midgley play, and Mrs Tyler's father remembered being a Pace-Egger in Shipley in the 1870s. As there were no groups active at the time, they thought it would be a good idea, both for the area and for their theatre, to revive the custom. They knew there had been a local version, but could not find out what it was so they chose to use the published Midgley text. They went out first in 1949 and have performed on Easter Saturday mornings ever since.

Obviously, the two plays are much the same, but in style they are very different. Midgley is rough and ready, Brighouse is dramatic, full of theatrical flourish, exuberant, rehearsed. It's great fun, but denounced as 'unauthentic' by purists.

There is another children's play, known as the 'Derby Tup', from the mining area of north-east Derbyshire. It is not a mumming play, though it has elements of it; it is more of a celebration of the mythical Derby beast of the well-known song:

> As I was going to Derby upon a market day
> I spied the finest tup, sir, that ever was fed on hay.
>
> The horns that grew upon his head, they grew so mighty high,
> That every time he shook his head they rattled against the sky.
>
> The wool that grew upon his back, it grew so mighty high
> That eagles built their nests in it, you could hear the young un's cry.

In the performance the tup is killed by a butcher, usually with great drama, though happily he at once revives. This is, perhaps, the death and resurrection theme of the more common play. The song continues:

The man that killed the tup, sir, were up to his knees in blood.
The man that held the basin were washed away in flood.

And all the boys in Derby came begging for his eyes
To punch about for footballs for they were just the size.

And all the women in Derby came begging for his ears
To make 'em leather aprons to last 'em forty years.

And all the men in Derby came begging for his tail
To ring St George's passing bell that hangs in Derby gaol.

There are numerous versions of the Derby Tup song, some of them rude, and this is a combination of two recorded in the area. Normally, four characters are involved: the Tup, the Butcher and two others, unnamed. Sometimes there are others to add colour. Costumes are variable, often rudimentary, occasionally elaborate, especially if one player is a boy dressed as a girl. The Butcher, as you would expect, wears an apron. The Tup is the most likely to demonstrate the group's creative powers. He may appear as a quite realistic ram or as a purely symbolic one. In a few places he is not a ram at all but a pig, a bull, or, curiously, in view of 'tup' connotations, a cow.

The performers are nearly all teengers, though a few are allowed in as young as 7 or 8. Girls are by no means excluded, even if the great majority are boys. The groups are very much to do with families, so naturally sisters take precedence over male outsiders. The main motivation for 'tupping' appears to be the opportunity to earn some extra money, even if tradition has supplied the means. There is a touching unwritten law that those in work don't do it.

Much as the Irish mumming plays seem more alive by their unpredictable comings and goings, the Derby Tup has survived in families, in the minds of everyone in the area. There is encouragement from parents but it is the young who keep it going. It is not possible to say where or when to see the Tup – one year they're all for it, the next they are at work, or a girlfriend has priority, or a feud has broken out – though this can have the opposite effect and spawn an extra group.

The area is south-east of Sheffield, north of a line between Chesterfield and Bolsover, near the Stanton and Stavely Steelworks on the M1. The time is after dark on Christmas Eve, New Year's Eve or any other time around then that seems favourable.

Between 1970 and 1978 the Derby Tup was seen in 14 villages performed by 41 different groups. This does not mean, of course, that there were several at work in each village; rather, that in successive years the groups had reformed, possibly for the reasons suggested above.

The action is extremely simple. The group appears in pub, club or house. The leader makes his announcement:

'Ere comes me and our owd lass
Short of beer and short of brass.
Give us a pint and let us sup
Then we'll show you our jolly old Tup.

The Butcher is called for, and then the Tup. The Tup is killed but immediately revives. They sing the song. All this takes little more than five minutes. At the end extras appear according to the taste and abilities of the group. These are intended to encourage generosity. Carols are the most common but the more ambitious think up ideas of their own, other songs, even jokes. The custom is very popular, and the groups are made welcome in the pubs and clubs in spite or perhaps because of their tender years.

A final variation of the English folk play is the Wooing Play, once common in the east Midlands, especially Lincolnshire, but now virtually extinct. It began with a wooer trying to seduce a 'female', being rejected and enlisting in the army when the 'female' prefers the clown. The play then continues with the normal hero-combat theme. These were often called 'Plough Plays' since they were performed on Plough Monday, the first after January 6, and the players 'Plough Boys' or 'Plough Jags'.

Two or three Wooing Plays did survive the Second World War, though only just. Recently, there have been reports of a revival, by traditional performers, at Brant Broughton, a village about twelve miles south of Lincoln and seven miles east of Newark.

Of all British customs, the folk play is possibly the most interesting. The surviving examples are so much the same, yet in their variations, locations, style, appearance and spirit so different. For an enthusiast hearing 'In comes I . . . ' in so many accents is a 'jolly fine thing'.

Fire and fleet and candle-lighte

On November 25, 1903, the Reverend J. Walker, vicar of Whalton, read a paper to the Society of Antiquaries of Newcastle upon Tyne:

> Every year on the 4th of July as the sun goes down a huge bonfire is made and lighted on the village green and this is done not only regularly as to time but with certain formalities as to the manner of it. . .The young men with the chosen leader will give a few evenings to the collection and preparation of the faggots. Then, with the same ceremony year after year, the faggots are brought to the village and deposited on precisely the same part of the village green. A long cart is borrowed. . .and then young men and many boys of the village proceed to the place where the faggots have been collected and load the cart. Then one or two of the strongest take the shafts, the rest are yoked to the cart by long ropes, and with much noise and shouting, with the blowing of a horn by one seated on top of the load, it is brought into the village. . .No horse is ever used. . .The pile is carefully constructed with the expenditure of considerable energy and some skill. It is always constructed on the same site, hardly varying a yard from year to year. . .as the twilight deepens the word is given to 'light her'. . .Then the children, joining hands, will form a moving circle round the burning pile. . .as the flame mounts higher till it illuminates the whole village, a fiddle is heard and the young people begin to dance. . .I have heard that it was not unknown for some to leap over the fire. . .there is always, too, a quantity of 'sweeties' and 'bullets' scattered and scrambled for by the children. . .
>
> This year. . .Sir Benjamin Stone did us the honour of coming down to witness the fire. . .at my request those who are usually most active in carrying out proceedings gave Sir Benjamin a daylight rehearsal, and he took quite a number of groups. It is but fair to say that those groups are just such as could be witnessed in the evening any year. Beyond the mere pause of the procession, shall I call it, and a little arranging to bring the groups within the focus of the camera, and perhaps the addition of one figure in the group you have a picture of the annual event just as it happens year after year. . .

Now the custom is much less elaborate. The cart has gone and the bonfire has become a place where the villagers get rid of rubbish. The site is still on precisely the same part of the village green, just by the Beresford Arms, and it is the landlord and his staff who make sure the building of the bonfire is kept reasonably orderly. At about 7.30 on July 4, Old Midsummer Eve, one of them comes out and sets a match to it. In 1984 there was absolutely no ceremonial; the only dancing was by the Newcastle Morris Men who performed as the bonfire blazed vigorously.

I understand these dancers have been largely responsible for keeping the 'Baal Fire' going. Evidently, some of them turned up to see the fire one year and, finding it had all but gone out, offered to come each year and dance. The bit about the sweets still lives, though. The kids go out collecting money for them and in 1984 they had got together £21.15 to take to the local newsagent, who rewarded them with a bagful each. The whole affair was extremely casual. I remember being a little disappointed at the time but as I drove away I grew to like it better; it was so relaxed, so unstructured; it had a life of its own. But Whalton Baal Fire is a rarity now.

Punky Night at Hinton St George. The children create beautiful, or grotesque, lanterns out of mangel-wurzels.

Up to the middle of the last century, the custom was very widespread in Cornwall. There were dozens of fires on the tops of hills and the people danced around them and had great parties. For some reason this cheerful habit died out and it was not until the 1920s that the Old Cornwall Society partially revived it. They organize a chain across the county, each one visible to the next.

In this country fire customs happen in winter when they are needed to bring a bit of excitement and warmth to the long cold nights. Most of them are spectacular, extremely dangerous, even frightening. But not all; Punky Night at Hinton St George is one of the gentlest, cosiest customs of the year even though it can be pretty cold on the last Thursday in October.

Local legend relates the date, and the whole business to the fair which once flourished in Chiselborough, three and a half miles to the east. Hinton men always went to this fair; inevitably they failed to return home at the end of the day. The women had to go out looking for them carrying their home-made lanterns, known locally as 'punkies'. This annual round-up of drunken husbands became jocularly known as 'Punky Night'. It is certainly a good story, showing a fine disregard for all the similar traditions which attend Hallowe'en all over the country, if not the entire world.

What happens now, and has for at least 150 years, is of a slightly different nature. At 6.30 p.m. families gather at St George's Hall. The children all carry punkies, about the size of their heads, made from mangel-wurzels. Townies might need to be told that these are a variety of beet grown exclusively for cattle feed. To make mangel-wurzels into punkies it is necessary to cut the top off, like a boiled egg, and scoop out the inside until a thin layer of flesh remains. Then the skin is very carefully cut and peeled away to form pictures on the outside. Grotesque faces are favourite, but the more imaginative produce cats, dogs, elephants, birds, anything they fancy, even abstract patterns. It is not done to cut right through the flesh, and in any case the candle would blow out. When a candle is placed inside its light produces a warm orange glow, the designs sharply defined against the dark skin.

About fifty children turned up in 1983 on a very cold and frosty evening, soon mustered into some kind of order by Douglas Gillard, chairman of the committee, who then led them around the village for an hour or so, in his white coat and top hat, ringing a bell. As they went they sang a song, to the tune of 'The Farmer wants a Wife'.

> Punky Night tonight
> Punky Night tonight
> Adam and Eve wouldn't believe
> It's Punky Night tonight
>
> Punky Night tonight
> Punky Night tonight
> Give us a candle, give us a light
> It's Punky Night tonight.

Incidentally, I have four published versions, all different to this, and to each other. These words were printed on a large board fixed to the trailer upon which the Punky King and Queen were ceremonially carried. Once the children used to go around the village begging for materials to make their punkies, singing this song as they went. They collect money now to defray the cost of the evening, and the boy and girl who collect most get to be King and Queen. Mr Gillard grows many of the mangel-wurzels in his own garden.

Back at the hall a contest is held to decide the best punky in each of several different age groups. They are hung in a row across the stage and viewed, in the dark, by a conscientious panel of judges. Some of the exhibits were of such sophistication that the possibility of illegal parental assistance cannot be entirely ruled out.

'Remember, remember, the Fifth of November'. Who could forget it, with bonfires raging in every corner of the land, fireworks turning night into day and the dog quivering under the bed? Well, there is one place where it is their traditional custom to show a studied indifference and do absolutely nothing on Bonfire Night: St Peter's School in York. Guy Fawkes is their most notorious old boy.

The Guy is too well known to need describing here, but there are two other very similar customs much less familiar, or rather, there were, for one of them seems to have been suppressed. This is from the *Daily Despatch*, April 19, 1930:

> *Police Ban on Old Custom. Ninety Effigies Seized. Swoop On Children at Dawn.*
> A curious haul, consisting of about 90 straw-filled effigies and nearly 40 mattresses, an old perambulator, and a wicker chair was secured by Liverpool police yesterday when they made a concerted effort to stamp out an age-old Good Friday custom of 'Burning Judas', which has created an annual nuisance to residents of the south end of the city.
>
> Close on 100 extra police, many of them mounted on bicycles, were engaged in the 'swoop', which began long before dawn and lasted about 10 hours.
>
> Each year scores of children have made effigies of Judas. In the darkness of the early morning they have gone from their homes to parade the streets singing and shouting 'Judas is dead'. Effigies have been carried aloft on poles, and bedroom windows tapped to awaken people in the hope that they would throw coppers to the celebrants. The festivities have concluded with the burning of the effigies in the streets, old mattresses being utilised as the foundations for the pyre, while the children danced round the burning masses, and engaged in mimic warfare with bladders.

There is much more about this impressive police action, led by a Superintendent and a Chief Inspector. Their heroic efforts were only partially successful. Thirty-four years later the *Guardian* was still able to report 'Firemen at Liverpool were called out five times yesterday to deal with "Judas" bonfires. . .a spokesman said it was the lowest number of calls on record, and the practice appeared to be dying out.'

In 1984 my own inquiries produced nothing, though I still feel that such a persistent custom cannot be wholly dead.

In Wensleydale, in the village of West Witton, they burn a different effigy, by name, 'Owd Bartle', on the Saturday night nearest to St Bartholomew's Day, August 24. Bartle is carried around the village by grown men, and eventually burned on a vast bonfire. He is a large figure, these days with a grotesque plastic mask, and ingeniously operated eyes which light up. The custom flourishes, even though nobody knows what it is all about. St Bartholomew was much too nice for such a fate. An unnamed robber is the favoured villain and he is commemorated in a rhyme recited at certain points on their way through the village:

> At Pen Hill Crags he tore his rags,
> At Hunter's Thorn he blew his horn,
> At Capplebank Stee he broke his knee
> At Grassgill Beck he broke his neck,
> At Waddham's End he couldn't fend
> At Grasshill End he made his end.

Lewes Bonfire Night finishes with enormous fires. This is Cliffe bonfire and their assembled 'clerics'.

Back to Guy Fawkes Night. Many of the customs celebrated on or near the day have nothing whatever to do with the unfortunate Popish plotter, the day having been seized upon as a convenient one to indulge in pyrolatry.

Lewes Bonfire Night, however, has everything to do with it. In the reign of Mary I (1553–8) seventeen Protestant martyrs died in Lewes and a certain anti-Catholic feeling grew up in the town. To this very day the Bonfire Societies carry 'No Popery' banners in their processions, and effigies are burned during the evening. Annually there are protesting letters to *The Times* and lesser organs; annually the societies deny bigotry, claim Catholics among their members, and continue as before with what they regard as the traditional fun. Personally, I feel that people are inclined to take these things too seriously. Many thousands come to see and many hundreds take part in this, by far the most spectacular custom in southern England.

The first record of Lewes Bonfire Night was in 1679, when one Benjamin Harris described the burning of a popish effigy. Subsequent accounts seem to dwell on efforts to suppress it, but it had much too much of a grip by 1853 when the first two Bonfire Societies were formed and some kind of official control took over. These were the Borough and the Cliffe Societies; Commercial Square Society followed six years later; Waterloo and South Street Juveniles are of much more recent origin.

Nowadays each society organizes its own parades and bonfires, but there is overall planning so that they all have their turn in town and at the War Memorial. From 6 o'clock there is always something astonishing going on, a society parade with everyone in extravagant costume and carrying a flaming torch. One year there were Zulus, Red Indians and Vikings, amongst others. At 7.30 there is a Grand Parade, after which societies go off to their own bonfire sites, led by their 'prelates', carrying their 'No Popery' banners and their effigies of Pope Paul V and Guy Fawkes. On arrival the 'archbishop' preaches a sermon and consigns the effigies to the flames.

I spent my time with Cliffe, from the part of town on the east side across the River Ouse. They were dressed impressively as Vikings, laboriously pulling along a huge effigy of Ronald Reagan. The previous year they had honoured Margaret Thatcher. These people had been proclaimed 'enemies of the Bonfire' and were about to pay the penalty. At the bonfire site 'the Pope' and Guy Fawkes were ceremonially burned in the biggest bonfire I have ever seen. Then the President was blown to fragments by the fireworks already in place about his person.

It was an amazing affair. Multiply it by five and you might have an inkling of Lewes Bonfire Night. There are lesser events at several other south-east towns.

Blazing Tar Barrels have an honoured place in British folklore. At Lewes they are pulled along in the processions, some to be ceremonially hurled into the River Ouse. In the past they have featured in many incredible events. The thought of two flaming barrels hurtling down the beautiful High Street of Burford makes my hair stand on end, even though the custom was suppressed a century ago. Up-Helly-Aa rose phoenix-like from the ashes of barrels. Bridgwater Carnival surely had them once; Ottery St Mary, Hatherleigh, Allendale and Burghead still do.

Bonfire Night in Ottery St Mary, an otherwise sleepy little town twelve miles east of Exeter, is one of the most alarming experiences life has to offer short of all-out war. At 8.30 in the evening they start barrel rolling – which sounds innocent enough until I tell you what 'barrel rolling' actually is. It is taking a huge barrel, coating the inside with bitumen, setting fire to it, throwing in a bit of paraffin to make more of an inferno, picking it up and, carrying it across the shoulders, charging down the street at full speed, regardless of who or what happens to be in the way. The barrels are not *rolled* at all. Each carrier runs as far as he can, then another takes over. Apart from enormous oven mitts made out of thick sacking and soaked in water, they wear no protective clothing except thick old clothes. They keep the barrel on the move until it is too far gone to hold, and then they let it burn out on the ground.

Yes, the men do get burned, but they do not seem to mind; a good burn is a great thing to display next morning. There is no shortage of candidates wanting a turn; in theory anyone is allowed a go but in practice it is necessary for hopefuls to be big enough and strong enough to carry a hogshead, and to get their hands on it in the first place, in the face of local competition. I would say that there were only about a dozen experienced regulars.

There were eight barrels in 1982, sponsored by the local pubs and one started off outside each of them in turn. The last one was rolled in the square around midnight. As it burnt out the still excited lads threw their mitts into the flames, as well as other garments by now past wearing again. Then they chaired the organizer and sang 'For He's a Jolly Good Fellow' and 'Auld Lang Syne'. All this was attended by a horde of Cup Final proportions. There is nothing whatever in the way of crowd control, and quite right too, so you have to keep your wits about you. The sight of a large bearded weightlifter, bearing a huge flaming barrel, yelling at the top of his voice, coming at you like a runaway train is not for the faint-hearted.

During the night there are also a couple of barrels rolled by women. Earlier there are several smaller ones for children. There is a huge bonfire and a carnival. And during the day another custom is observed, also to do with fire but apparently unrelated. Indeed, nobody has any idea of the origins of, or reasons for, their curious 'rock cannons'. A cannon, in Ottery, is a piece of steel bar about a foot long and an inch in diameter. It is bent in the middle like a boomerang. One end is bored out with a place to insert a firing cap near the bend. The barrel is filled with gunpowder, the cap is placed in position and the cannon is fired by striking the cap sharply with a special hammer made for the purpose. They have ten of these rock cannons and it is their custom, on the day, to fire them off at 5.30 a.m., lunchtime and finally at 4 p.m., just before the boys are due to start their barrel rolling. Usually the men stand in a line and fire them in a dramatic sequence. Sometimes, if they think Ottery needs waking up, they bang them all together. They make a tremendous noise. The men are in charge, but they are quite happy for wives, mothers or girlfriends to have a go if they want to, even visiting photographers.

The rock cannons have had a chequered history. The barrel rolling has had a continuous life, even surviving the war blackout with token daytime appearances, but the cannons lapsed because gunpowder was more valuable than gold and not available. They revived in 1956 but by then they were illegal without a licence, which was not forthcoming. They got their gunpowder somewhere and fired their cannons at unannounced sites, dodging the law. Ten years later they had re-established the custom so successfully that the law let them get on with it. Alas, in 1966 there was an accident and two men were injured. Since then they have been properly licensed and the appointed licensee is responsible for safety. The cannons have to be thoroughly checked and approved.

Firing the rock cannons of Ottery St Mary is indeed strange; surprisingly, there is another custom not at all unlike it, Firing the Poppers, at Fenny Stratford in Buckinghamshire.

The Poppers really *are* miniature cannons. There are six of them, each weighing about six pounds, with a stout handle on one side so that they look exactly like heavy cast-iron beer mugs. The present set was made in 1859 following the disintigration of one of the previous sets dated 1730. They are fired at noon, 2 p.m. and 4 p.m., under the supervision of the verger of St Martin's Church, who is licence holder here. By tradition the verger, renamed 'the Master Gunner' for the day, is responsible for priming the cannons, which he does by means of pouring a liberal measured dose of gunpowder into each, then stuffing the rest with newspaper vigorously banged tight with an iron bar and a heavy hammer.

The cannons are laid in a row on the ground about a yard apart. Behind each stands the person who will fire it. The vicar always fires the first one at noon, followed by the Master Gunner, the two churchwardens, and two guests. The vicar also fires the last one at 4 o'clock. A long iron rod with a curved pointed end has been heating in a brazier nearby. At the appointed hour the vicar applies the red hot rod to the hole in the top of his cannon causing an appalling explosion. He immediately passes the rod to his neighbour, and so on so that all six explode in rapid sequence.

Oddly, the event celebrates the founding of the church. A local landowner, Browne Willis, built it in 1730 in honour of his grandfather, Thomas Willis, the first neurologist, who died on St Martin's Day, in St Martin's Lane, in 1675. Browne Willis left endowments which pay for the annual feast still held on that day, and for gunpowder to Fire the Poppers.

The Poppers have also been fired on very rare but momentous occasions such as the opening of the Grand Union Canal in 1800, Queen Victoria's Jubilee in 1889, and the end of the Second World War. The annual event is supposed to take place in the churchyard but had to move in the 1950s because it was damaging the church windows. It is now in the Leon Recreational Ground, next to the village graveyard.

Back to Devon, back to tar barrels, back to the Wednesday nearest November 5. The West Country has a mania for carnivals, thus the name Hatherleigh Carnival sounds normal enough. True, it *is* a carnival, and has been since 1907, but it is also an ancient fire

Firing the Poppers at Fenny Stratford. They make enough noise to wake the dead – in the cemetery behind the hedge.

custom, hanging on in spite of long-standing police disapproval.

During the day there is a hunt, which meets right in the centre of town, a fair in the market, selling horses, ponies, donkeys and tack, a children's fancy-dress parade, a football match, a mighty carnival of floats, a small pleasure fair, and a carnival disco last thing at night. Officialdom likes all that; what it does not like are the unruly goings on with fires and squibs and barrels – which are, in fact, by far the most interesting items on, and off, the agenda.

This part starts the evening before. Two sledges have been prepared, each bearing three large open-ended barrels on their sides, two on the bottom, one on top, thickly coated with tar and partially filled with inflammable materials. It is a sad fact that these exuberant and fascinating customs may expire through lack of barrels, and the trendy habit of growing things in the few there are. Ottery would not tell me where they got theirs. Hatherleigh have theirs made by a cooper in Drewsteignton. Other places have conned the local brewery, though that is not a long-term answer. Perhaps all the police have to do is bide their time; maybe the 'folk process' will throw up a satisfactory alternative.

On the evening before the Carnival the young men of Hatherleigh gather to haul the barrels into position at the top of the village. Each sledge is taken separately in two noisy parades led by 'the Hatherleigh Jazz Band', which is, in fact, the local silver band in lunatic costumes, playing disorganized music. Time was when all pubs had sledges of barrels and the regulars had to stay up all night to repel saboteurs. The number has diminished but the young still stay up all night, making a terrible hullabaloo, letting off fireworks, taping up doorbells, stealing gates, being awake and making sure everyone else is as well.

At 5 o'clock in the morning twenty young men laid hold of the chains attached to the first sledge. Their leader deluged the barrels with paraffin and set a match to them. They came down the hill as the flames took hold. By the time they reached the George Hotel, from a bedroom window of which I was intrepidly recording events, the barrels were a raging inferno. With shouts of joy the men set off up High Street at high speed, down South Street with some caution, up Bridge Street with renewed swiftness and into the New Market car park to deposit the remains on the waiting bonfire. At 8.30 in the evening they repeated the process, this time before a vast crowd of wildly cheering spectators. There are plenty of flames to be seen in the Carnival as well. It is preceded by a large torch in the shape of a cross, accompanied by many flaming torches.

The most astounding carnival of them all used to be like this, lit by countless torches carried by boys who were all paid half-a-crown for their trouble, but since the Second World War Bridgwater Guy Fawkes Carnival has ceased to be a fire custom, except for the final fifteen seconds, and has become the nation's leading electric custom.

It is said that the town was so overjoyed at the unmasking of the Gunpowder Plot that they broke into a spontaneous celebration, repeated annually until, inevitably, it got out of hand. There was always a huge bonfire on Cornhill, which lasted until 1924, but the Carnival first took organized form in 1882. The first committee had the idea of a West Country burlesque of the Lord Mayor's Show; they can hardly have dreamed that over a hundred years later their successors would be managing an extravaganza with 125 separate floats and features, taking more than an hour and a half to pass in front of well over 100,000 spectators. All these floats are of individual design, some over sixty feet long, manned by 'gangs' in exquisite costumes, powered by electricity supplied by their own generators. They have a distinctive style of overhead lighting, the roof fitted with rows and rows of bulbs, many hundreds on each float. There must be at least 50,000 bulbs in the procession.

All these floats compete in various contests. There are twelve categories, two confined to locals, the rest open. There are Masquerades, Tableaux, Features, Comic Features and so on, not in sections but at random throughout the procession. Judges are posted along the route and meet later to add up their marks; results are posted outside the Town Hall before midnight. There are sixteen local carnival clubs, with an average of about fifty members each. Their floats and costumes can cost as much as £6,000 raised by various events through the year.

Bridgwater's Guy Fawkes Carnival is on the Thursday nearest November 5, having moved to early closing day in 1909. It is the first of a circuit of seven carnivals held in the area, which everyone takes part in during the next ten days.

Although the procession is amazing, true folk enthusiasts must fight their way to the High Street to see the 'squibbing'. Eight young people from each of the 16 carnival clubs are detailed to take part, 128 in all, plus their leader, Mr Blackmore. Each has a six-foot pole with a flat triangular piece at one end. A special squib, or a roman candle, is attached to this, at right angles to the pole. In days of yore, Bridgwater used to make their own squibs, a practice which ended in 1880 when two young men blew themselves up. Since then they have been made by a proper manufacturer. When everyone is ready, Mr Blackmore leads his army into

Hatherleigh Fire Carnival has many events besides its spectacular flaming barrels. This is the children's fancy-dress contest.

the High Street, to form up in two long lines. He blows a loud blast on his whistle and a row of fires is lit along the centre. On the second blast the army lights its squibs from the fires and hoists its poles so that they are held horizontal above their heads with the squibs pointing upwards. For fifteen seconds there is a fantastic firework display.

The next serious outbreak of fire is on New Year's Eve. They particularly celebrate this time in Scotland and the North of England, so it is in order that they should have their fire customs at this time. Only one of these conflagrations is in England and that only thirty miles from the border.

Allendale claims to be at the centre of Great Britain. It is a slightly bleak and forbidding spot for 364 days and 20 hours of the year; for the other four hours it is exceedingly warm and lively. All evening the pubs are full to bursting, everywhere there are men in lurid, outlandish costumes. These are 'guizers', all Allendale born and bred, and they can wear whatever they like so long as it is bright and cheerful.

Around 11 o'clock the band begins to play, not in a formal way but by degrees, as players turn up. Three-quarters of an hour later the guizers materialize with their tar barrels, known here as 'Kits'. They are not the same as those elsewhere but are more like tubs, made by cutting twelve inches off each end of a whole barrel. These barrel ends are filled with the broken-up central sections of the original barrels, with other wood and shavings. A liberal dose of paraffin is administered, and then the head man goes quickly around with his flaming torch and lights them all.

Thus each guizer is primed with a fiercely blazing kit supported on the top of his head. Immediately forty or fifty of them set off at a smart pace but in an orderly procession around the town, led by the band, by now at full strength. As you can guess, their march lasts no more than a few minutes. They arrive back at the Square at midnight, circle the waiting bonfire and light it by throwing on the remains of their barrels. Unfortunately, they now have to preserve what they can so as many as possible are kept back for future use;

with basic repairs some keep going for two or three years. An enormous fire soon rages and everyone joins hands around it, if they can stand the heat, to sing 'Auld Land Syne'.

By tradition the guizers then go off first-footing. At one time all doors of the village were open, but hospitality is now strained by the influx of hundreds of spectators. The natives are said to pray for snow on New Year's Eve, for when it comes Allendale is the first place in England to be completely cut off.

Over the border in Biggar they have a great bonfire on New Year's Eve. Much further north there are two exciting events, not too far apart. One is in Comrie, west of Perth, the other at Stonehaven, to the south of Aberdeen. Forced to choose a couple of years ago, I went to Stonehaven. As it happened, six months' worth of rain fell on Comrie that night, while we had it fine and mild.

'Swinging the Fireballs' is perhaps marginally less dangerous than it looks, for most of the people involved know very well how to do it, and how to make the fireballs in the first place. Anyone can take part, girls too, and they do not have to live in the town, or even in Scotland.

A leading enthusiast, Jack Emslie, instructed me on the rudiments. He had made a sort of wire-netting basket and was filling it with pine cones and driftwood and twigs when we arrived. Then he closed it carefully and attached a length of stout wire with a handle at the end. He pointed out that the wire had to be exactly the right length; too long and you cannot control it, too short and you burn yourself to death. So this was his fireball. It can be of any size, of course, stronger swingers can handle one which is quite big and heavy, while sensible weaker souls content themselves with a ball about a foot in diameter. Jack claimed that experience had taught him his materials were the best; others put in clothing and all sorts of rubbish. Each person must make his own.

Originally this was the fishermen's custom and the balls were bits of net and other fishing rubbish. They went about the harbour area visiting houses, enjoying New Year Hospitality, swinging their fireballs as they went. Gradually it became more formalized, and developed into a parade. As the fishing industry in Stonehaven faded away, so did the fireballs. By the end of the 1960s there were only four or five. A few local enthusiasts, including Jack, persuaded their friends to take it up and now they can expect twenty or thirty. There is no committee; supervision is casual; they would not let a drunk take part.

They gathered by the Old Market Cross at the harbour. A pipe band played as they poured vast quantities of paraffin over their motley collection of fireballs. As the clock struck twelve, they lit up their fireballs, and whirling them around their heads like demonic hammer throwers, marched off up the High Street led by the pipe band. They kept their distance from each other, went up on one side of the street as far as the old cannon, about 200 yards, then came back along the other. It was an incredible sight.

They kept going until the fire burned out; most of them were gone in ten to fifteen minutes, though one old hand kept his going ten minutes longer than the others and it was still alight when, exhausted, he ended the show by hurling it dramatically into the harbour.

Over at Comrie, we found out later, the rain had failed to put them out. This well-known custom is officially entitled 'the Flambeaux Procession', locally simply 'the Flambeaux', pronounced 'Flambows'. A committee member, Jimmy Steward, explained that the flambeaux were 12-foot silver birch poles with the top 4 feet tightly bound with sacking. These are made six weeks beforehand, the sacking ends soaking in fifty-gallon drums of paraffin all that time. Events go on all evening in Comrie but just before midnight all goes quiet for the ritual listening for the chimes of Big Ben on the radio. On the first stroke they light up six flambeaux – they always keep two reserves – and, led by a pipe band and followed by a large proportion of the population in fancy dress, they parade them around the town.

The carriers do not wear costume, except old clothes for protection. They are all Comrie men with long family connections with the event. Though they will let their friends have an occasional turn, outsiders are not allowed. At the end of the parade the flambeaux are allowed to burn out in a circle, and the remains are taken to the bridge and tossed into the River Earn.

At Burghead, they 'Burn the Clavie', an intriguing mixture of elaborate ritual and barbarism. I went, off season, to see 'Clavie King', Jimmy McKenzie. The Clavie Crew of nine or ten men have all had connections going back generations. The whole event belonged to the salmon fishers based in the port, but now, though the same families still take part, most of them work on land.

The principal ritual seems to be in the making of the Clavie. None but locals may touch it, no materials can be bought, they have to be borrowed or donated, and only special traditional tools can be used. Two particular parts must be joined by a special hand-forged nail, hammered in with a flat stone; as Jimmy remarked, 'Anyway, you couldna do it with a hammer!'

Basically, the Clavie is the bottom third of a barrel, mounted, by the special nail, on a stout six-foot pole. The barrel is a type used in the whisky industry called an Archangel – Burghead is no distance from the great Speyside distilleries. Currently the Clavie barrel is supplied by a cooper in Dufftown. The whisky barrel is further secured to the spoke by spars from a dismantled herring barrel.

All this work is carried out by the Clavie crew on the evening before. It is filled with the broken-up pieces of the rest of the barrels and other wood, all covered with tar from a local chemical works. At 6 o'clock on the night the Clavie is set alight, not with a match, certainly not, but with a piece of smouldering peat which has been burning in the grate of a nearby house.

The Clavie is then carried triumphantly around the town, burning fiercely. There is no formal procession but hundreds of spectators follow the crew around a traditional route. They stop at specific houses to present a piece of charred, tarry wood to the householder as a prized good luck token. These are always the same houses, regardless of who happens to be living in them. Finally, they arrive at Doorie Hill where the Clavie is mounted on a round pedestal about five feet high, built specially for the purpose in 1809. It blazes there for a while, the crew keeping it topped up with wood and tar, until at last they climb up and set about it with a hatchet scattering flaming pieces all around to be fought over by the crowd.

I went to Doorie Hill in the summer, a marvellous spot on a fine clear day, the view across the Moray Firth astounding. The pedestal stands in a small open area behind the top houses, black and nasty, the ground covered with lava from a hundred annual eruptions. We met a lady who said, 'They come to my house and give me a piece of wood. That's enough for me! It's an awful mess, you know. Last time I went out with them I was only 15 – all dressed up in a white blouse and a new navy blue skirt. My father told me to be sure to stay up-wind of the Clavie. Well, I didn't. My friend and I didn't take any notice. When I got home they thought I was a black lassie. I never could wear that blouse again!'

'Swinging the Fireballs' at Stonehaven.

The population of Lerwick, the capital of the Shetland Islands, is approximately 7500. Probably about 3750 are males; let us assume around 1500 are under 16 or over 55 and that 500 have arrived from outside to work in the oil industry. That leaves something like 1750 able-bodied men to take part in the Up-Helly-Aa Procession. Now let us remember all the men who *cannot* take part because they have some other duty; they are still involved indirectly. Then let me tell you that 1000 men actually *do* take part and you might get some idea that Up-Helly-Aa is quite an important occasion in town. The procession is world-famous; less well known outside, but equally important to the population are the parties in 'the Halls' afterwards. *Everyone* takes part in them.

The preparations, committee meetings, fund raising, costume making, practising, building, preparing of literature and planning keep the men and women of Lerwick busy for months in advance. They think of little else. There is no other custom in the whole of Britain which remotely compares with it in the sheer scale of the operation and the involvement of the people. And it is all for Lerwick; Up-Helly-Aa is far too difficult and expensive to get to for all but the most intrepid enthusiast.

Lerwick, by tradition, celebrated its midwinter festival on the twenty-fourth day of Yuletide, by the old calendar, January 28 by my calculations. The day is now set as the last Tuesday in the month. Their favourite pastime on the night was to pull blazing tar barrels through the streets on sledges, exactly as they do in Hatherleigh to this day. This was a drunken and unruly business and, after a long battle, the authorities managed to suppress it in 1874. My hotel chambermaid told me that one of the small islands still did this, but the present authorities would neither confirm nor deny it.

The fires were not the only part of the celebrations. It seems that 'guizing' and house visiting were always part of the fun, and this part at least has survived powerfully until today. Whatever the authorities felt, Lerwick had to have some flames and by 1881 a new custom was born: a torchlight procession celebrating their Norse antecedents. The Shetlands were invaded by the Vikings in the eighth and ninth centuries, and ruled by them until the islands were given to Scotland as part of the dowry of Margaret, Princess of Norway, when she married James III of Scotland in 1469. The lairds treated the islanders very badly, and they still refuse to call themselves Scots, and have never worn the kilt or spoken Gaelic. After all, Bergen is much closer than Edinburgh, and London is on another planet.

So the Shetlanders evolved a 'Viking' custom, organized and regulated from the beginning by a committee, becoming a member of which is on a par with being a Cabinet Minister. Today there are seventeen members. One new one is elected every year. They all move up one place in seniority each year, and the most senior is 'Guizer Jarl' for the year, a Very Important Person indeed, with the freedom of Lerwick as his right. The following year he acts as Parade Marshall and then he leaves the Committee for ever.

The Guizer Jarl, pronounced 'Yarl', is a magnificent figure in Viking costume and he has the privilege of choosing his own 'Squad' who will be similarly, if less splendidly, attired. Peter Malcolmson, in 1984, invited forty-four to join him, and these are the *only* Vikings involved. All we ever see are photographs of Vikings; all the other 900-odd guizers are dressed as anything but. They too are in squads; that year there were fifty-one of them. Each squad chooses its own costume and they devise and rehearse a five-minute turn. This is a development of the early guizing. Now it is highly organized, so that each squad will visit each of thirteen halls in Lerwick, perform their act, enjoy hospitality, and have a dance with the girls. The logistics of this operation, which lasts until after dawn, are complex beyond the grasp of ordinary mortals, but woe betide the squad that misses out one of the halls.

The first happening of Up-Helly-Aa day is the posting of 'the Bill', a large board fixed firmly to the Market Cross at 6.30 in the morning. This proclaims the festival and goes on at great length with witty allusions to the Jarl and anyone else who has earned notice during the year.

Soon after 9 o'clock the Galley makes its appearance to be paraded to the harbour, accompanied by the Guizer Jarl and his squad. The Galley is thirty feet long, beautifully and lovingly made over many weeks, resting on an ancient trailer kept for the purpose. The Guizer Jarl has the right to choose its name and decoration, but the basic shape remains the same each year, with its fine dragon's head and tail.

The Galley stays on the dockside all day but the Guizer Jarl and his squad make ritual visits to the town hall, schools, hospitals and the like. A preview of things to come is provided at 5.30 when the Junior Jarl, his squad, and parties from local schools hold their procession and burn their seventeen-foot galley.

Then, as the Official Programme says: 'Squads will muster at the Market Green at the times appointed, commencing at 6.50 p.m., receive their torches and go to be marshalled. The place of muster will be Lower Hillhead. The Guizer Jarl's Squad will pass up the ranks at 7.15 p.m., accompanied by the Brass Band.

At 7.30 a Maroon will give the signal for lighting up, and the Galley, Guizer Jarl's Squad with the Brass Band will pass down the ranks, the procession counter-marching behind them. *The Procession will then move off singing the Up-Helly-Aa song.*'

These somewhat military orders give little idea of the breathtaking spectacle which appears: 857 Shetlanders dressed as Vikings, Clowns, Puffins, Dogs, Hens, Boy George, the Ravin Majorettes, the Granny Crofterettes, *all* carrying six-foot flaming torches, in two long lines down either side of the road, provide a sight more epic than Hollywood's wildest dreams.

The procession takes quite some time. Apparently it can be hair-raising in a gale, unbelievable in a blizzard, but: 'There will be no postponement for weather'. Eventually, it arrives in the King George V Playing Field, the hallowed 'Burning Site'. Again, the programme says: 'The squads will form a complete circle round the Galley. A Maroon will be fired to denote the singing of the Galley Song; during the singing the Guizer Jarl's Squad will march round the Galley. Cheers will follow for the galley builders and torch makers, the festival and the Guizer Jarl. A Bugle Call will then be given and *after the last note is sounded*, the torches will be thrown into the Galley. The Squads will then reform into a circle and sing "The Norseman's Home" before dispersing to begin their rounds of the halls.'

Once more the official prose fails to convey the drama of 857 flaming torches circling thc elegant Galley, the Guizer Jarl poised heroically on the deck brandishing his axe, or the enormity of the pyre as the Galley burns to death for another year.

The next day Lerwick sleeps. As we said farewell at noon, nothing stirred.

The spectacular Up-Helly-Aa procession in Lerwick ends in flames as the beautiful Viking galley burns.

Calendar

A month-by-month guide

This is a list of customs as they occur throughout the year. All the events described in the chapters are included, plus about a hundred others. It makes absolutely no claim to be comprehensive; I know about many others myself.

The information is as correct as I can make it but dates and times may change. This is perfectly in order; these customs belong to the people involved and they can do what they like with them. Before setting off on a 200-mile journey to see one it is advisable to check that it will take place on schedule.

This is not always easy, especially with the more casual events which people do if and when they feel like it. Obviously the best thing is to go there in advance and ask around though this is not feasible if the place is too far away. Writing is unreliable since people simply fail to answer, even if you send a stamped, addressed envelope. I use the telephone myself.

These are seven good sources of information: the library, the vicar, the Tourist Office, the pub, the local newspaper, the Town Hall, and the organizations which exist to study and encourage folklore and the like.

I put the library first because there you can find your way to most of the others through reference books. They should have directories published annually, or at least frequently, listing names, addresses, telephone numbers of all vicars, ministers, priests, local newspapers, hotels and pubs, museums and galleries, tourist offices, town halls and other libraries. The librarian will be happy to assist you; in my experience they enjoy the challenge.

If you do not have a library nearby, the vicar's number can be had from Church House in London. *Crockford's Clerical Directory* is one of the most useful books in my own library; new copies, however, are *very* expensive; old ones are still useful because though the vicar may change, the telephone number does not. I am indebted to many vicars but I have to warn you that they may not be inclined to help regarding the more heathen customs.

Tourist offices are unfailingly obliging and often know personally the people you want to talk to. The English Tourist Board publishes yearly a free directory of all the offices in Britain.

Willings Press Guide will put you on to the local newspaper. Journalists are extremely well informed about what happens on their patch but may be evasive if they suspect you to be a journalist yourself! They will usually be prepared, if nothing else, to tell you the name of the pub in the village you want to visit and pubs are a major source of information on these matters. There are several publications devoted to hotels and pubs but do not forget one so obvious as the AA book.

Finally there are some societies whose business it is to assist when consulted on folklore matters. These are four of the better known: The English Folk Dance and Song Society, Cecil Sharp House, 2 Regent's Park Road, London NW1 7AY; The Folklore Society, University College London, Gower Street, London WC1E 6BT; The Centre for English Cultural Tradition and Language, University of Sheffield, South Yorkshire S10 2TN; School of Scottish Studies, Edinburgh University, 27 George Square, Edinburgh EH8 9LD.

Before you go on your travels remember that it is rare for any of these things to take place on a Sunday, apart from church customs of course. You will have to check whether it moves back to Saturday or on to Monday. Also if you are comparing my information with older books most events previously held on Whit Monday have moved to Spring Bank Holiday.

JANUARY

1st
Kirkwall, Orkney Islands
'The Ba'', a street football game also played on Christmas Day

1st
Bideford, Devon
Andrew's Dole

1st
Oxford
Needle and Thread distribution at Queen's College

1st
Castlemorton, H & W, 6 miles south of Malvern
Winsbury Dole

6th
Haxey, S Humbs, 10 miles east of Doncaster
Haxey Hood Game, one of the great 'football' games of Britain

6th
Theatre Royal, Drury Lane, London
Cutting the Baddeley Cake by the cast of the current show

Saturday after 6th
Goathland, N Yorks, 7 miles SW of Whitby
The Plough Stots, longsword dancing

Sunday after 6th
Exeter and Chichester Cathedrals
Blessing the Plough

11th
Burghead, Grampian, 7 miles NW of Elgin
Burning the Clavie, a unique fire custom

17th
Carhampton, Som, 3 miles SW of Minehead
Wassailing the Apple Trees behind the Butchers Arms

Last Tuesday
Lerwick, Shetland Islands
Up-Helly-Aa, a spectacular 'Viking' festival involving over 900 guizers carrying flaming torches

29th or near
Guildford, Surrey
Dicing for the Maid's Money; maidservants throw dice for annual bequest

FEBRUARY

2nd
Wotton, Surrey, 2 miles west of Dorking
Forty Shilling Day, a bequest paid to boys who can recite certain texts. Intermittent

2nd
Woodbridge, Suffolk
Carlow's Charity

Monday of Candlemas week (2nd)
St Ives, Cornwall
Hurling the Silver Ball

Sunday nearest 2nd
Blidworth, Notts, 4 miles SW of Mansfield
Cradle Rocking in parish church

First Sunday in month
Dalston, NE London
Clowns' Service in Holy Trinity Church

3rd
Holborn, London
Blessing the Throats, in St Etheldreda's Church, Ely Place

14th
King's Lynn, Norfolk
'The Mart' in Tuesday Marketplace is the first big fair of the year

14th
Norham, Nthmb, 7 miles SW of Berwick-upon-Tweed
Blessing the Salmon Nets on Pedwell Beach fifteen minutes before midnight when the season opens

20th or near
Aldgate, London
Sir John Cass Service which schoolgirls attend wearing red quills in their hats

SHROVETIDE

Shrove Tuesday
Olney, Bucks
Pancake Race. There are many of these but this is easily the most famous

Shrove Tuesday
St Paul's Cathedral, London
Cakes and Ale Sermon

Shrove Tuesday
Westminster School, London
Pancake Greaze

Shrove Tuesday
Scarborough, N Yorks
Skipping by hundreds of people on the seafront

Shrove Tuesday
Corfe Castle, Dorset
Annual Meeting of the Ancient Order of Purbeck Marblers and Stonecutters

Shrove Tuesday
Alnwick, Nthmb
Shrovetide Football

Shrove Tuesday and Ash Wednesday
Ashbourne, Derbys
Royal Shrovetide Football. The same on both days

Shrove Tuesday
Atherstone, Warwicks
Shrovetide Football limited to two hours in the afternoon; the winner is the man with the ball at the end

Shrove Tuesday
Sedgefield, Durham
Shrovetide Football

Shrove Tuesday and the second Saturday following
St Columb Major, Cornwall
Hurling the Silver Ball, between Town and Countrymen. The same on both days

Thursday following 'Fastern E'en'
Jedburgh, Borders
Jethart Ba', a hurling type street football. The date has altered recently but is usually the day after Ash Wednesday. It is advisable to check!

Mid Lent
Ufton Nervet, Berks, 2 miles south of Theale
Dame Elizabeth Marvyn Charity at Ufton Court

MARCH

1st
Lanark, S'clyde
'Whuppity Scoorie' is a mad race for kids around the church

14th
Goldsmiths Hall, London
The Pyx Trial at which coins from the Royal Mint are tested with ceremony

Third Thursday in month
Near South Dalton, 3 miles east of Market Weighton, Humbs
Kiplingcotes Derby, Britain's oldest flat race

25th
Tichborne, Hants
Tichborne Dole

During the month
Old Bolingbroke, Lincs
Candle Auction for parish land held during Parish Council AGM

During the month
Stockbridge, Hants
Court Leet and Court Baron

APRIL

5th or near
St Andrew Undershaft, London
Sir John Stow's Quill Pen, part of his memorial, is replaced with elaborate ceremony

23rd
Lichfield, Staffs
St George's Court, though of ancient origin, is now a very amusing ceremony

Thursday nearest 25th
Morpeth, Nthmb
Boundary Riding

Last Sunday in the month
London
Tyburn Walk from the Old Bailey to Marble Arch commemorates Catholic martyrs who died on Tyburn Gallows

During April and October
Wirksworth, Derbys
Barmoot Court oversees lead mining affairs

EASTER

Palm Sunday, the one before Easter
Hentland, Hoarwithy, King's Caple and Sellack, four parishes between Hereford and Ross-on-Wye
Distribution of Pax Cakes after services

Maundy Thursday
Different cathedral each year
The Royal Maundy

Maundy Thursday
Leigh, Gtr Mches
Henry Travice Charity, a more modest affair!

Good Friday
Tinsley Green, W Sussex, on the north side of Crawley
British Marbles Championship at the Greyhound

Good Friday
Alciston, E Sussex, 6 miles SE of Lewes
Good Friday Skipping

Good Friday
Calder Valley, W Yorks, at several places between Luddenden and Todmorden
Pace Egg Play performed by boys from Calder High School, Mytholmroyd

Good Friday
Liverpool Docks area
Burning Judas in the early morning. May not happen but worth looking for

Good Friday, Easter Tuesday and the following Saturday
Workington, Cumbria
'Uppies and Doonies', classic street football, in the evenings, the same each evening

Good Friday
Smithfield, London
Butterworth Charity distributed at St Bartholomew the Great

Good Friday
Ideford, Devon, 4 miles north of Newton Abbot
Borrington Dole

Good Friday
Bromley-by-Bow, E London
The Widow's Bun is added to the collection at the Widow's Son, Devons Road

Easter Saturday
Brighouse, W Yorks
Pace Egg Play

Easter Saturday
Market Harborough, Leics
Hymn Singing over the grave of William Hubbard in St Mary's in Arden churchyard

Easter Saturday
Bacup, Lancs
Britannia Coconut Dancers

Easter Sunday
Battersea Park, London
Easter Parade

Easter Sunday
Radley, Oxon
Church Clipping

Easter Monday
Regent's Park, London
Harness Horse Parade

Easter Monday
Preston, Lancs
Egg Rolling in Avenham Park

Easter Monday
Dunstable Downs, Beds
Orange Rolling

Easter Monday
Biddenden, Kent
Chulkhurst Charity

Easter Monday
Hallaton, Leics, 12 miles east of Leicester
Hare Pie Scramble and Bottle Kicking. Fierce contest between Hallaton and Medbourne

Easter Monday
Bourne, Lincs
Running Auction in which bids are made for land while a boy runs a set distance

Easter Monday every third year
Barwick-in-Elmet, W Yorks, 5 miles west of Leeds
Lowering the Maypole for ritual repairs. It is raised again on Spring Bank Holiday. The next time will be 1987

Tuesday after Easter
Bristol, Avon
Tuppeny Starvers distributed after service at St Michael's

Wednesday after Easter
Keevil, Wilts, 4 miles east of Trowbridge
Tayler Charity

Thursday after Easter
Ratcliffe Culey, Leics, a mile NE of Atherstone
Setting the Lanes at the Gate Inn is arranging grazing rights

Thursday after Easter
Reading, Berks
Maidservants' Charity at St Mary's Church House

Second Tuesday after Easter
Hungerford, Berks
Hocktide Ceremonies include the Court Leet, 'Tuttimen' and other events to do with Common Rights

MAY

1st
Oxford
May Morning Celebrations include Latin hymns from the top of Magdalen Tower, Morris Dancing and huge crowds at 6 am

1st
Padstow, Cornwall
The 'Old Oss' and the 'Blue Ribbon Oss' tour the town in one of the most fantastic customs in Britain

1st
Minehead, Som
The Hobby Horse here comes out also on the previous, and the following two evenings

1st
Gawthorpe, W Yorks, east of Dewesbury
Gawthorpe May Day

1st
Charlton-on-Otmoor, Oxon, 6 miles north of Oxford
Garland Ceremony

1st
Berwick upon Tweed, Nthmb
Riding the Bounds

First Saturday in the month
Knutsford, Cheshire
Royal May Day, notable for its NW Morris Dancers and 'sanding'

First Sunday in the month
Munlochy Bay, 7 miles north of Inverness, and Culloden, 4 miles to the east
Visiting 'Clootie' Wells in the early morning

May Day Holiday Monday
Ickwell Green, Beds, 6 miles east of Bedford
Ickwell May Day

8th
Helston, Cornwall
The Furry Dance

Second week in the month
Etwall, Derby
Well Dressing. The first of the year; began in 1970

Second Saturday in the month
Hayes Common, Kent
May Festival

Mid-May, near Rogationtide
Chester
North-West Morris Dancing in the city centre by Manley Morris Dancers

13th
Abbotsbury, Dorset
Garland Day

Wednesday nearest 18th
Newbiggin-by-the-Sea, Nthmb
Annual Meeting of the Freeholders includes 'dunting' of new members

Nearest Sunday to 21st
Meriden, W Mids
Cyclists Memorial Service

23rd
Rye, E Sussex
Mayoring Day, with throwing of hot pennies

Near the end of the month
Hastings, E Sussex
Blessing the Sea

29th, or soon after
Chelsea, London
Founder's Day at the Royal Hospital, a colourful occasion but open only to relations of the Pensioners

29th or a Saturday soon after
Fownhope, H & W, 5 miles SE of the city
Oak Apple Day, a Friendly Society walk

29th
Worcester, H & W
Oak Apple Day; the City Hall gates are decorated with oak branches

29th
Aston on Clun, Shropshire, 8 miles NW of Ludlow
Arbor Day; a tree in the village is dressed with flags

29th
Castleton, Derbys
Garland Day

29th
Great Wishford, Wilts, 5 miles NW of Salisbury
Grovely Day perpetuates rights to collect wood from the forest

Late in the month
High Wycombe, Bucks
Weighing the Mayor on taking office

End of the month
Endon, Staffs, 4 miles SW of Leek
Well Dressing one of the few outside Derbyshire

Spring Bank Holiday
Wirksworth, Derbys
Well Dressing, contest with 9 wells produces high standard

Spring Bank Holiday every third year
Barwick-in-Elmet, W Yorks
Raising the Maypole

Spring Bank Holiday
Bampton, Oxon
Morris Dancing; outstanding

Spring Bank Holiday
Headington Quarry, on the east side of Oxford, Oxon
Morris Dancing in the evening

Spring Bank Holiday
Coopers Hill, near Brockworth, 4 miles east of Gloucester, Glos
Cheese Rolling in evening, one of Britain's maddest customs

Spring Bank Holiday
Bellerby, N Yorks, 6 miles south of Richmond
Bellerby Feast

Spring Bank Holiday
Wellow Notts, 10 miles NW of Newark-on-Trent
Maypole Dancing

Spring Bank Holiday
Lichfield, Staffs
Court of Arraye and Greenhill Bower

Spring Bank Holiday
Manchester
Whit Walks

Spring Bank Holiday
Kingsteignton, Devon
Ram Roasting Fair

Spring Bank Holiday every third year
Laugharne, Dyfed
Common Walk, next in 1987

Spring Bank Holiday
Corby, Northants
Pole Fair; a great occasion but only every twentieth year. Next in 2002

Wednesday after Bank Holiday
Pinner, NW suburbs of London
One of the great street fairs

Saturday after Bank Holiday
Chipping Camden, Glos
Scuttlebrooke Wake

ASCENSIONTIDE

Ascension Eve
Whitby, N Yorks
Planting the Penny Hedge, a unique 'penance'

Ascension Day
Wicken, Northants, 2 miles SW of Stony Stratford
The Love Feast celebrates the joining of two parishes in 1587

Ascension Day
Tissington, Derbys, 4 miles north of Ashbourne
Well Dressing; the oldest and one of the nicest

Ascension Day
Bisley, Glos, 3 miles east of Stroud
Blessing the Well, and adorning it with garlands

Ascension Day
Lichfield, Staffs
Beating the Cathedral Bounds

Ascension Day
Oxford
Beating the Bounds of two parishes, St Mary's and St Michael's, takes the beaters through colleges, shops and inns

Ascension Day every third year
The Tower of London
Beating the Bounds of the Tower Liberty after Evensong. Next in 1987

Whit Sunday
Bristol, Avon
Rush Sunday at St Mary Redcliffe is a very grand service attended by the Lord Mayor and Corporation

Whit Sunday
St Briavels, Glos, in the Forest of Dean
Bread and Cheese Throwing is said to perpetuate right to take wood from part of the Forest

Whit Monday
St Ives, Cams
Dicing for Bibles, a strange little bequest

Whit Friday
Saddleworth, Gtr Mches
'Whit Friday'; in the morning Whit Walks to Uppermill, in the evening a fantastic series of brass band contests

JUNE

First week in month
West Linton, Borders, 14 miles south of Edinburgh
Common Riding and Whipman Play

First Thursday in month
Neston, Cheshire
Ladies Walking Day; a Friendly Society walk

Second week in month
Southwold, Suffolk
Trinity Fair

Second Wednesday in month
Appleby, Cumbria
Horse Fair is an ancient gypsy gathering

Friday after second Monday
Hawick, Borders
Common Riding is one of the biggest but no women allowed

Thursday between 6th and 12th
Lanark, S'clyde
Lanimer Day, 'Lanimers' is like Border Common Ridings

A Saturday in mid-June every Leap Year
Great Dunmow, Essex
The Flitch Trials have a very long history. Not taken too seriously but the Claimants do not always win the bacon

Saturday after 19th
Abingdon, Oxon
Election of the Mayor of Ock Street, and Morris Dancing

Third full week in month
Selkirk, Borders
Common Riding here is oldest and biggest in the region, with up to 600 riders

Third week in month
Peebles, Borders
Beltane Festival and Common Riding

Third week in month
Melrose, Borders
Melrose Summer Festival and Common Riding

Third Saturday in month
Appleton, Cheshire, 3 miles south of Warrington
Bawming the Thorn; decoration of an ancient tree by local schoolchildren

Midsummer Eve, 23rd
Across Cornwall
Chain of Midsummer Bonfires

Week including 24th
Dumfries, D & G
'Guid Nychburris' is similar to Border Common Ridings

Saturday nearest 24th
Youlgreave, Derbys
Well Dressing here is extremely expert and unusual

Saturday nearest 24th
Tideswell, Derbys
Well Dressing notable for their architectural pictures

Sunday after 24th
Oxford
Wall Pulpit Sermon at Magdalen College

First Saturday following the Sunday after 24th
Winster, Derbys
Morris Dancing of a unique type with 16 dancers and 4 'characters'

Last Thursday in month
Bury St Edmunds, Suffolk
Cakes and Ale given to pensioners through a bequest of one Jankyn Smith

28th
Barrowden, Leics, 6 miles SW of Stamford
Rushstrewing

29th
Warcop, Cumbria
Rushbearing

Last Saturday in month
Bakewell, Derbyshire
Well Dressing

Friday nearest 30th
Warrington, Cheshire
Walking Day is a vast religious procession

Last week in month
Ashburton, Devon
Ale Tasting, no longer serious

Last week of the month
Galashiels, Borders
Braw Lads Gathering

Last week of the month
Newcastle upon Tyne
Fair on the Town Moor is the biggest in the North of England

JULY

First full week of the month
Duns, Borders
Reivers Week and Common Riding

First Saturday in month
Great Musgrave, Cumbria, 1½ miles west of Brough
Rushbearing

First Saturday in month
Ambleside, Cumbria
Rushbearing; a huge procession

4th
Whalton, Nthmb, 5 miles SW of Morpeth
The Baal Fire

Second Wednesday in month
Upper Thames Street, London
The Vintners' Procession

Second Wednesday in month
Holsworthy, Devon
Pretty Maid's Charity takes place in the week of St Peter's Fair

Second Saturday in month
Jedburgh, Borders
Callant's Festival and Common Riding last two weeks with climax on this day

Middle of the month
Kelso, Borders
Common Riding

Middle of the month
Buxton, Derbys
Well Dressing

Middle of the month
Tweedmouth, Berwick-upon-Tweed, Nthmb
The Salmon Feast

Tuesday before the Wednesday following 19th
Honiton, Devon
'The Glove is Up!', an unusual opening ceremony to the Fair

Saturday of third week in month
Durham
Miners' Gala is a vast gathering but less than it once was

Third week in month
Innerleithen, Borders
Cleikum Ceremony and St Ronan's Border Games

25th, every fifth year
St Ives, Cornwall
John Knill Ceremony is a bizarre event resulting from the terms of his will. Next in 1986

25th
Ebernoe, W Sussex, 3 miles north of Petworth
Horn Fair

Fourth Sunday in month
St Mary's Loch, near Yarrow, Borders
Blanket Preaching is an open air service on the site of a derelict kirk

Last Friday in month
Langholme, D & G
Common Riding includes premier hound trail of the year, at 6 a.m.!

Towards the end of the month
R Thames from London to Henley
Swan Upping in which the beaks of all the swans are marked according to whether they belong to the Queen, the Dyers Company or the Vintners

AUGUST

1st or near (often before)
R Thames from London Bridge to Chelsea
Doggett's Coat and Badge is a sculling race for Thames watermen

Thursday before first Monday in month
Ambleside, Cumbria
Ambleside Sports with all the traditional Lakeland events

Wednesday of week including 1st
Meriden, W Mids
Grand Wardmote of the Woodmen of Arden; a series of archery contests using longbows

First Tuesday in month
Egton Bridge, N Yorks, 6 miles SW of Whitby
Gooseberry Contest

First Saturday in month
Lauder, Borders
Common Riding

First Saturday in month
Ripon, N Yorks
Feast of St Wilfred

First full week in month
Coldstream, Borders
Common Riding with an impressive ride-out to Flodden Field. The last major Common Riding of the year

Wednesday of the first full week in the month
Southampton, Hants
Knighthood of the Old Green is a unique contest on the world's oldest bowling green

Saturday nearest 5th
Grasmere, Cumbria
Rushbearing

Wednesday after 10th
Barlow, Derbys
Well Dressing; here whole flowers are used instead of petals

Second Friday in month
South Queensferry, Lothian
The Burry Man, one of Britain's strangest characters

12th
Sutton, Surrey
Mary Gibson's Legacy provides for a ceremonial annual inspection of the Gibson tomb

Monday after 12th
Marhamchurch, Cornwall, 1½ miles SE of Bude
Revels, in which the Queen is crowned by Father Time

Third week in month
Irvine, S'clyde
Marymass Fair and Races

Third Friday in month
Newport, Dyfed, 7 miles east of Fishguard
Beating the Bounds

Third Saturday in month
St Margaret's Hope, Orkney
Boy Ploughmen; two contests for incredible girl 'horses' and the boys who perform on the beach with miniature ploughs

Saturday of week including 21st
Cilgerran, Dyfed, 2 miles SE of Cardigan
Coracle Races

Third Thursday after first Monday in month
Grasmere, Cumbria
Grasmere Sports

24th
Sandwich, Kent
The Bartlemas Bun is a race around St Bartholomew's Chapel following the Hospital AGM

24th
Gulval, Cornwall, just north of Penzance
Blessing the Mead

Saturday after 24th
West Witton, N Yorks, in Wensleydale
Burning Bartle, an unusual event somewhat like Guy Fawkes

Last Friday and Saturday in month
Dunoon, S'clyde
Cowal Games, one of the biggest Highland Gatherings including the World Highland Dancing Championships

Saturday before August Bank Holiday
Wormhill, Derbys
Well Dressing

Last Sunday in month
Eyam, Derbys
Plague Service commemorates those who died in the Great Plague of 1665

SEPTEMBER

1st
Colchester, Essex
Opening of the Oyster Season

Wednesday nearest 1st, every seventh year
Richmond, N Yorks
Boundary Riding 16 miles around the town. Next in 1990

Monday and Tuesday of the first full week in the month
Oxford
St Giles' Fair, in the centre of the city

First Friday in the month
Musselburgh, Lothian
Fishermen's Walk; a fine Friendly Society walk in attractive traditional costume

Monday after the first Sunday after 4th
Abbots Bromley, Staffs, 6 miles south of Uttoxeter
The Horn Dance, thought to be the oldest dance in Europe

Second Tuesday in month
Widecombe, Devon
Widecombe Fair; in the presence of Uncle Tom Cobley and all

Saturday nearest 8th
Lichfield, Staffs
Sheriff's Ride is a statutory Boundary Riding

Saturday nearest 18th
Egremont, Cumbria
Crab Fair, to do with apples and not seafood, includes the World Gurning Championships

Saturday nearest 18th
Lichfield, Staffs
Dr Johnson Commemoration

Sunday nearest 19th
Painswick, Glos
Church Clipping; children join hands and encircle the church

21st or near
City of London
Bluecoat March from Newgate to the Mansion House

OCTOBER

1st
Westminster, London
The Lord Chancellor's Breakfast in the House of Lords

Last three days of the first week
Nottingham
Goose Fair, the biggest fair in Britain

First Sunday in month
Billingsgate, London
Fish Harvest Festival; an astonishing display of seafood in St Mary at Hill Church

First Sunday in month
Trafalgar Square, London
Costermongers' Harvest Festival brings out most of London's 'Pearly Kings and Queens'. At St Martin-in-the-Fields

7th
Twyford, Hants, 3 miles south of Winchester
Bellringers' Feast

Second Wednesday in month
Tavistock, Devon
'Goosey' Fair

Saturday nearest 23rd
Bristol, Avon
Redcliffe Pipe Walk from St Mary Redcliffe to a spring in Knowle

Late in the month
Royal Courts of Justice, London
'Quit Rents' paid with ceremony to the Queen's Remembrancer

Last Thursday in month
Hinton St George, Som, 2 miles NW of Crewkerne
Punky Night with decorated lanterns made from mangel-wurzels

30th or within a few days
Area south and west of Sheffield, S Yorks
Caking, a very strange pub custom in which men disguise themselves and others guess who they are

30th and the two following weekends
Antrobus, Cheshire, 4 miles north of Northwich
Souling Play performed in pubs all around the district

NOVEMBER

5th
Shebbear, Devon, 7 miles NE of Holsworthy
Turning the Shebbear Stone is one of Britain's most puzzling rituals

5th
Lewes, E Sussex
Lewes Bonfire Night is easily the biggest Guy Fawkes party

5th
Ottery St Mary, Devon, 10 miles east of Exeter
Tar Barrel Rolling; flaming barrels not rolled but carried at full speed

Wednesday nearest 5th
Hatherleigh, Devon, 6 miles north of Okehampton
Fire Carnival; a fascinating fire custom rapidly becoming a traditional carnival

Thursday nearest 5th
Bridgwater, Som
Guy Fawkes Carnival is a truly astounding procession of floats lit up with thousands of bulbs. Do not miss the 'Squibbing' at the end

Second Saturday in month
City of London
The Lord Mayor's Show

11th
Knightlow Hill, Warwicks, near Stretton-on-Dunsmore, on A45 5miles west of Rugby
Wroth Silver, an ancient tithe paid at dawn

11th
Fenny Stratford, Bucks, on the east side of Bletchley
Firing the Poppers

From mid- November until Christmas
Area south and west of Sheffield, S Yorks
Carol Singing in numerous pubs; local carols, not the church variety

Late in the month
Laxton, Notts, 10 miles NW of Newark
Jury Day on which farmers inspect 'field system', followed a few weeks later by the Court Leet when they settle their affairs

30th
Eton College, Berks
Wall Game between Collegers and Oppidans

DECEMBER

Sunday after 12th
Broughton, Northants, 3 miles SW of Kettering
The Tin Can Band, a noisy and crazy ensemble which performs at midnight all round the village

Christmas Eve
Bampton, Oxon
Mumming Play, in pubs and houses

Christmas Eve and Christmas Day
Uttoxeter, Staffs
The Guizers, a mumming play in the pubs the first evening, in houses on Christmas Day

Christmas Eve
Dunster, Som
Burning the Ashen Faggot, in the Luttrell Arms

Christmas Eve
Dewsbury, W Yorks
Tolling the Devil's Knell

Christmas Eve to New Year
Area between Chesterfield and Sheffield
The Derby Tup, a short 'play' performed in pubs and houses by children. Unpredictable

Christmas Eve to Twelfth Night
South Wales
Mari Lwyd, a visiting custom involving a strange white 'Horse', now very rare but try Pencoed, near Bridgend and Llangynwyd, near Maesteg

Christmas Eve to Epiphany
Mallwyd, Gwynedd, and other places
Plygain, Welsh carol singing

Christmas Day
Serpentine, Hyde Park, London
Swimming Race for the Peter Pan Cup

Christmas Day
Sherborne Castle, Dorset
Distribution of Pennies at the Castle gate in the morning

Christmas Day
Kirkwall, Orkney
The Ba'

Boxing Day
Crookham Village, Hants, 5 miles west of Aldershot
Mumming Play performed outside several pubs

Boxing Day
Marshfield, Avon
Mumming Play; probably the best known in England

Boxing Day
Ripon, N Yorks
Sword Dance Play; in fact an unusual mumming play performed many times in pubs, houses and in the streets

Boxing Day
Grenoside, S Yorks, on the north side of Sheffield
Longsword Dancing

Boxing Day
Handsworth, S Yorks, on the east side of Sheffield
Longsword Dancing

27th
Melrose, Borders
The Mason's Walk

New Year's eve
Biggar, S'clyde
New Year Bonfire

New Year's Eve
Allendale Town, Nthmb
Tar Barrel Parade; numerous guizers carrying flaming barrels on their heads

New Year's Eve
Comrie, Tayside
Flambeaux Procession of huge flaming torches

New Year's Eve
Stonehaven, Grampian
Swinging the Fireballs is a spectacular and alarming way to see in the New Year

AT OTHER TIMES

Five Sundays in the year
Ripon, N Yorks
Horn Days, on which the City dignitaries process to the cathedral led by the Hornblower. The days are Easter, Whit Sunday, 'St Wilfrid's Sunday' (the first in August), Mayor's Sunday and Christmas Day

Every Saturday
Woodbridge, Suffolk
John Sayer Charity

First Saturday of every month
Fern Street, East London
Farthing Bundles; now rather intermittent

Every day
Edinburgh
The One O'Clock Gun, fired from the Castle

Every night
Ripon, N Yorks
The Hornblower blows his horn at the market cross at 9 p.m.

Every night between Michaelmas and Shrove Tuesday
Bainbridge, N Yorks
The Hornblower sounds his curfew at 10 p.m.

Every night
Tower of London
Ceremony of the Keys, a most impressive event which can be seen by anyone who applies to the Chief Yeoman Warder for a ticket

Any day
Winchester, Hants
The Wayfarer's Dole is given to the first 32 people who turn up at St Cross Hospital to claim it

---

Further reading

These three books have been of inestimable help in preparing this one:

Chambers, Robert, *The Book of Days*, 2 vols., 1862–64.
Hole, Christina, *A Dictionary of British Folk Customs*, 1976.
Wright, A.R. and Lones, T.E., *British Calender Customs*, 3 vols., 1936–40.

Though I find it impossible to read myself, the book regarded by many as the authority on the origins and meanings of folk customs is:

Frazer, Sir James, *The Golden Bough*, published in 12 volumes, 1890–1915, and in a single abridged volume in 1922.

For basic listings of events the following are useful though not necessarily up to date:

Howard, A., *Endless Cavalcade*, 1964.
Palmer, G. and Lloyd, N., *A Year of Festivals*, 1972.
Royal Pageantry, published by Purnell in 1967.
Schofield, B., *Events in Britain*, 1981.

There have been two major photographic surveys:

Sykes, Homer, *Once a Year*, 1977.
Stone, Sir Benjamin, *Sir Benjamin Stone's Picutres*, 1907. (Many of these pictures are included in *Customs and Faces* by Bill Jay, about Sir Benjamin's work, 1972.)

Continuing research, information and news is to be had in specialist magazines such as: *English Dance and Song*, the magazine of the English Folk Dance and Song Society, and its weightier sister publication, *Folk Music Journal*; *Folklore*, the journal of the Folklore Society; *Lore and Language*, the journal of the Centre for English Cultural Tradition and Language.

Books on single subjects, such as Folk Plays, Morris Dancing, Well Dressing or Christmas are too numerous to mention. Books, booklets and pamphlets on individual customs are multitudinous and are usually to be had in local bookshops, newsagents and libraries.

The most productive place of all is Cecil Sharp House, 2 Regents Park Road, London NW1, headquarters of the English Folk Dance and Song Society. Downstairs most of the current books are available and upstairs in the Vaughan Williams Memorial Library they have practically every word that has ever been written on folk music, dance and customs.

Acknowledgements

The nicest things about customs are the extraordinary friendliness and generosity of all the people involved. I am indebted to hundreds but to mention them all would require a supplement. I only have room for a few who have helped far above the call of duty.

My thanks therefore to the Marshfield Mummers for allowing me to use their play, in spite of their tradition of never writing it down themselves. They have promised not to read it. To Bob Grant of Headington Quarry for making available his own considerable researches. To Mary and the late, and much missed, Rennie Hayhurst for guiding us through a week of Well Dressing at Tissington. To Provost and Mrs Pamela Irvine at Southwell for ther kindness concerning the Royal Maundy Service. To Professor Rosalind Hill for providing uncommonly detailed material on Stockbridge Court Leet. To Amanda Russell and Ruth Green for transforming Kiplingcotes Derby into an unforgettable experience.

I am grateful to countless vicars for their patient answers to my enquiries and I am doubly grateful to Canon David Frayne of St Mary Redcliffe in Bristol since he presides over two customs in this book.

I have appreciated the good-natured help of many local newspapermen, particularly John Ross-Scott of *The Southern Reporter* on the subject of Common Ridings in the Borders.

I was impressed by the enthusiasm of Tourist Offices all over Britain especially in Scotland where several, unasked, made extensive enquires on my behalf.

Many folklorists have been astonishingly generous with their information. Encouragement and help from Ian Russell has been invaluable; his knowledge of anything that happens within fifty miles of Sheffield is not far short of infinite. Derek Schofield and Teresa Buckland have made free with their vast knowledge about dances. Bill and Helen Leader have been ready with their suggestions and their spare room. Doc Rowe's reports have been most welcome in view of the similarity of our interests. And Eileen MacAskill astonished me with her quite unexpected research into 'clootie' wells.

No thanks are enough for our old friends, Gill and Brian Jones, who for twenty years have generously provided a home for me when I have been in the North-east. Gill has covered Jedburgh and Alnwick for me, has made many enquiries, and has come with me to numerous events; Brian has taken the trouble to find all sorts of nuggets in his extensive library of Northumberland and Border history. My son Ben and his girlfriend Laura have covered two customs in Wales with great efficiency. Janis Ingram-Johnson gave more support than she knew by claiming to enjoy typing most of the book. And my beloved wife Sal has repaid my grossly eccentric behaviour over the last couple of years by transcribing her many recordings of conversations and customs, photographing four events for me, reading every word of this and making innumerable suggestions, all of which have been instantly put into effect and providing her lively illustrations.

Index

Page numbers in bold type refer to the illustrations.

Berwick upon Tweed
Tweedmouth
Norham
Alnwick
10
Newbiggin
Morpeth
Whalton
Earsdon
Newcastle
Allandale
12
Durham
13
Sedgefield
11
14
Workington
Appleby
Warcop
Egremont
Grasmere
Ambleside
Gt. Musgrave
Egton Br.
Whitby
Goathland
Scarborough
Bainbridge
West Witton
Bellerby
Richmond
Ripon
15
18
Market Weighton
19
Barwick in Elmet
Todmorden
Luddenden
Brighouse
Preston
Bacup
Dewsbury
16
Gawthorpe
Saddleworth
Manchester
Haxey
Liverpool
Leigh
20
17
Grenoside
Sheffield
Handsworth
Castleton
21
Warrington
Tideswell
Knutsford
Wormhill
Eyam
Barlow
24
Neston
Appleton
Chesterfield
Laxton
Buxton
Bakewell
Chester
Antrobus
Youlgreave
Winster
Wellow
Old Bolingbroke
23
Wirksworth
22
Endon
Blidworth
Tissington
26
Ashbourne
56
25
Nottingham
27
Uttoxeter
Elwall
55
Abbots Bromley
Bourne
Kings Lynn
Mallwyd
Ratcliffe Culey
29
Barrowden
Lichfield
Hallaton
32
33
28
Atherstone
Market Harborough
Corby
Meriden
Aston on Clun
57
Knightlow Hill
Southwold
34
35
30
31
St. Ives
Broughton
Bury St. Edmunds
58
Worcester
Powick
Welford on Avon
39
Cilgerran
Newport
Fownhope
Kings Caple
Castlemorton
Wicken
Olney
Ickwell
Woodbridge
Hoarwithy
Sellack
Fenny Stratford
Dunstable
36
Chipping Campden
Charlton on Otmoor
Colchester
Laugharne
St. Briavels
Coopers Hill
Gt. Dunmow
37
Headington
59
60
Painswick
Oxford
38
40
Llangynwyd
Bisley
41
62
Bampton
Abingdon
Radley
High Wycombe
Pencoed
Bristol
43
Pinner
44
LONDON
Eton
61
Marshfield
Hungerford
Reading
Ufton Nervet
45
Rochester
42
Sutton
Hayes
Aldermaston
Keevil
Sandwich
48
50
Crookham
Guildford
Wotton
51
54
Bridgwater
Minehead
Dunster
Carhampton
Gt Wishford
Stockbridge
Tichborne
Biddenden
Bideford
Salisbury
Tinsley Green
53
Holsworthy
Shebbear
Hatherleigh
Winchester
52
Ebernoe
Rye
Lewes
Hinton St. George
Honiton
Ottery St Mary
Twyford
Hastings
Sherborne
49
Southampton
Chichester
Alciston
47
Marhamchurch
Exeter
Abbotsbury
Ideford
Kingsteignton
Padstow
Widecombe
Corfe Castle
St Columb Major
46
Ashburton
Tavistock
Gulval
Helston